BOOK TWO, THE UNSEEN SERIES

Book Two - The Unseen Series

By Kathy-Lynn Cross

Inscytheful Publishing

ISBN# 978-1-7337890-4-2
Cover Design by: Strong Image Editing
Typography by: Inscytheful Publishing
Editing by: Amber Hassler

Rated: YA+ (M) Due to harsh language, and areas of mental, physical and substance abuse.

Illustration by Monique Renee

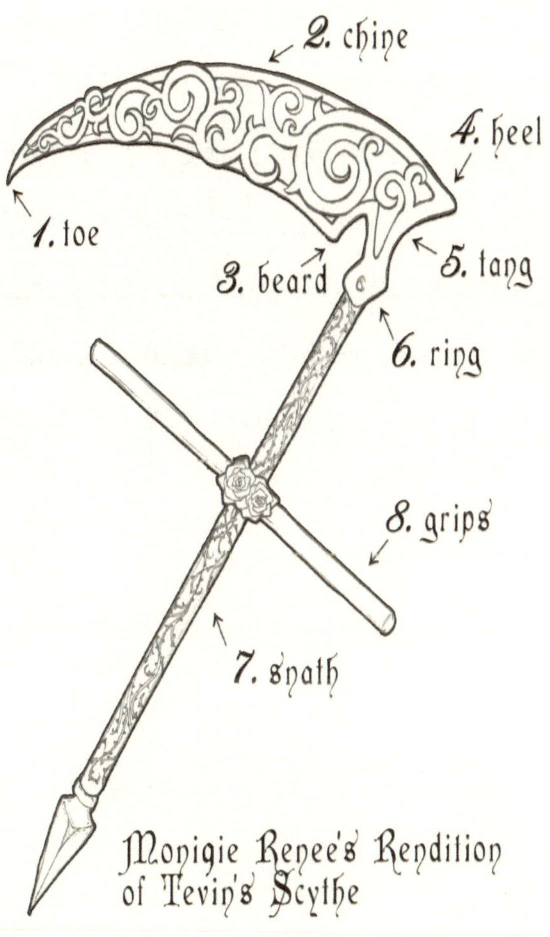

Moniqie Renee's Rendition
of Tevin's Scythe

Dedication

To my son for always reminding me
there is a silver lining to my gray cloud. To my
daughter for sharing her strength of imagination.
And to my husband, for believing in the stories
that dwell within my heart and not questioning
when I play with my imaginary friends.
Love Always, x.x

A Reaper's Prologue

*M*y Time Bend deposited me in the middle of an empty, puddle-poxed parking lot to a local coffee shop. This establishment appeared to be closed, with the exception of a cat rummaging through a trash bin. No other Vessels or Unseen were around. I was confused as to why the Time Bend had transported me here instead of the Sip 'N Chug, where Alexcia was employed. Then my thoughts grew sour when I remembered her friend, Jake, from the funeral. He must have brought her here with him.

Possession burrowed its way into my bones when I thought of the male Vessel and the way he had comforted her at Tod's funeral. *But why did it bother me?*

My daemonic-self required a break after the rooftop reprimand from Max, Alexcia's Doom Guard father, and the festering riddles from Rae-Lynn, her half-angel mother. I had spent most of the night searching for the misplaced Child-of-Balance. Throughout the quest, an unusual sensation had gnawed between each rib.

I could not comprehend the phantom pain.

Only Ashens, as far as I knew, was created without a heart. Our maker's precautionary action was to keep us on a tight leash, emotionally. We only felt the negative and were strictly forbidden to open ourselves to doubt, concern, or compassion, which could cause weakness. For if we hesitated, it could damage the soul to the point of unacceptance.

The River Styx's rules established a balanced cycle between life and death. Ashens had one purpose—to replenish the River Styx with used souls so Creation's power could continue to recycle. Besides our job to harvest the dying in order to replenish the living, there was no other purpose for me. But, I knew deep inside, something was withering to the point of starvation. An emotion I could not quite put my scythe's toe on.

A light drizzle mixed with the midnight breeze created a chill, reminding me of the frost-nipped air in the Unseen. Regrettably, that also led to thoughts of what I had done to the clan, and myself. *Can a Grim Reaper suffer from depression?* I lapped up the succulent emotion from the dying but did not fully understand its meaning.

As if on cue, my phone responded. The glare cut through the darkness as I read Max's snide remark.

Doom: ALEXCIA IS HOME SAFE. YOU CAN CALL OFF YOUR DOGS.

Yeah, I felt misplaced, broken somehow.

Once I read his message, the urgency to blow off steam made the Smolder that possessed me grumble. The shroud, which served as my minion, shuddered. It was an effort on my part to avoid typing in anger as I watched two pale thumbs whiz across the miniature backlit keyboard. Not wanting to quote Max's response verbatim, I altered his words to keep everyone on palatable terms for the night.

Numbly, I informed them the Stasises would take the night shift and ordered the clan to resume their reaper duties. They deserved a night off from child sitting. Continuing their obligations would rejuvenate the clan before any of them lost their minds and did irreparable harm.

Dropping my electronic nemesis into the cloak's indigo-threaded tentacle; my feet mindlessly landed on the pavement to the rain's rhythm. Silent, I directed my body and its entangled emotions toward an unknown destination.

Chapter One

Tevin's side: Through the eyes of a Reaper

*A*fter wandering around in the rain for half the night, I had found myself standing over the grave of Alexcia's deceased boyfriend. Confused as to the reason I had ended up here in the first place, I asked myself, "Why does she mourn for you? What is the connection? Is this what the *L-emotion* does to Vessels?" Each question latched onto another, making it hard to concentrate. *Does she still have positive emotions for you?* Frustrated, I spun away while extending my leg and connected with a nearby tombstone. It crumbled into pieces before my feet. This was when I decided returning to our mountain with these unexplainable behaviors would be a bad idea, and I stomped off into the darkness.

In my current state of mind, the strobe lights from the strip would not have bothered me, but tonight I was having trouble focusing. Different colored flashes from the marquee irritated my eyes, and my minion bristled from the shared discomfort. I thought the city could have used another shower. At this height, the foul mixture of vehicle fumes, smoke, spent exhales, spilled alcohol, and the pungent aroma of wet humans, otherwise known as Vessels, overloaded my nasal passages. Tainted air wafted around me as I climbed the ladder. At one point, I stopped to plug my nose and count to ten. With so many bodies packed into one area, their individual scents seemed to crawl up the side of the building, specifically to torment me.

Once I stepped over the ladder and onto the rooftop of the Onyx Hotel and Casino, I grumbled, "That makes 116,213." I had begun counting steps from the cemetery's gate to distract myself. During the day, the gleaming monstrosity was a nuisance. At night, the dark tinted windows made the structure appear empty and inviting for my kind, and the height helped me think. The Onyx stood almost as tall as the casino with the red roller coaster and other types of mundane entertainment. Most Ashens tried to avoid places Vessels deemed amusing. We referred to them as our own version of the *F*-word. I sneered, exposing my canines. *What exactly is fun?*

Peeved, I stood overlooking the strip and watched the Vessels zip from point A to point B. Their erratic motions calmed me enough to reorganize my mental space. The height was similar to the lower mountain ranges in the Unseen and helped clear my head. Leaning over the edge, I wondered how the hopeless and depressed among the Vessels figured that leaping from this height was the quickest way to go. It definitely made the job interesting if they were supposed to die before hitting the bottom. Most of my kind would fight for the opportunity to sever a soul from flesh in midair.

The pressed lip line I held broke when my inner daemon growled because the Smolder was hungry, and I knew we would have to consume power soon. At least I was not thinking of the girl anymore. Absentmindedly, I smacked my forehead. "I meant...Vessel." The barely audible words were nothing more than a secret I shared for the wind to whisk away. If I kept referring to Alexcia in human terms, it would send mixed signals to the clan. Pressing my temples, I tried to contain the confusion.

"Damn the cloak I cast!" I shouted into the humid air before feeling the cloak around me hackle from the volume of my voice. I had been contracted to protect the Child-of-Balance from the creatures of the Unseen, and nothing more.

Nothing more.

Irritated with this minor setback, I hopped onto the roof's three-foot-tall parapet to get a better view of the city's nightlife. I would never understand these creatures. The Vessels believed they could manipulate time, by shortening the length of a task as a type of control. Then after burning through their life force, from cramming more into each day, they blamed us for mismanaged usage. *What do they expect, a rollover plan?*

After centuries of dealing with death, it surprised me how the Vessels had not figured out this cycle yet. It remained today as it had always been. The River Styx, our creator, used a soul like a rechargeable battery, harnessing its energy to keep the waters of Creation flowing. The River evenly distributed its power between the living and those who merely existed. When the Cauldron's waters revealed the names to be recovered, Ashens were summoned to do the deed. The soul's remaining power could be its last emotions, memories, or—if we were lucky—a little of both. The soul's consumable residue recharged us so we could continue performing our duties. Once the soul had successfully been removed, and the reaper satiated, the empty soul was given to the Bridge Crosser assigned to the reaping, and they returned it to the River. If Styx found the soul to be reusable, it was placed back into a new Vessel, and thus the cycle of Creation continued.

It left me dumbfounded when Vessels would question their end. Death wasn't about a life lost; it was about keeping their brief existence moving forward. Unfortunately, watching the Vessel's funeral made my scythe feel slightly heavier than normal, and I found myself questioning the *why* of our own existence.

Nearby, I could taste a Vessel's sorrow. Rubbing my chest, I scanned the streets below wondering when our next meal was going to be and hoped it would be anguish or maybe despair. I had not come across those tantalizing tidbits for ten or more moon risings. Anticipation pushed the corners of my mouth up as I swallowed the pool of saliva.

Adding hunger to my list of problems only compounded the brain burn, causing my Smolder to test its cage. To ease the discomfort, I promised to grab a triple bacon burger, and some fries before heading back to the Unseen. It was nowhere near the same thing since daemons didn't consume food to live, but it was a solid substance for my Smolder to chew on.

The reminder of food brought on more inquiries. I wondered why only the House of Time had sent so many elemental assassins to deal with Alexcia and not one persuader. The situation also made me a bit wary that neither the angels from the House of Light nor the daemons from the House of Space, had attempted to silence or convince her to join the ranks of the Unseen.

Distracted, I picked up the tarnished silver pendant from my chest symbolizing the House of Space and listened to the metal rings click from the back and forth movement. The action was a bad habit I had started almost ten years ago. The half upside down star was a constant reminder of my role with the House of Space and the daemonic martyr I had become.

The heavy metal made a dull thud against my chest as the cloak pulled out a cigarette and placed it between two fingers. Mumbling, "Thanks," to my minion, I lit the tip with a Spindle of magic from a finger. Smoke filled my chest as I considered the pros and cons of protecting Alexcia. We were so close, but the threads of fate that entwined both Bond-Rites from me to the clan were snagging. I asked too much of them as Grim Reapers to go against their nature, but they were not aware of how much I required their help—not only with protecting the Child-of-Balance but also because of the Bond-Rite I had made with both parents. Having a half-angel and a Doom Guard pulling me in different directions was going to sever my own existence.

Hastily pulling on the filter, the smoke burned a trail down my throat. I held it in, then gradually released each burden along with the spent nicotine. This problem was mine alone to bear, but I would address it in due time. The luxury of stopping to ponder poor choices was as dangerous as Unseen Frostsand. *Similar to quicksand, but it doesn't suck you in. Instead, the substance turns you into a frozen entity pop once you're deep enough.*

Behind closed lids, lost memories replayed of the night I had seen the small Vessel clinging to her soul. I had been bewitched by Alexcia's determination to live, and the dormant power behind both pleading orbs. Unbeknownst to her, she had ensnared me. Astonishment had overridden my senses once she addressed me by name, and the mixture of emotions was toxic enough to lure a daemon's curiosity. Rae-Lynn understood my daemon nature since she was once a creature from the Unseen. The incident had sparked every negative sentiment within me, and the Smolder had wanted nothing more than to claw out of my chest and strangle the half-breed angel as I signed my services over to aid in with protecting her daughter.

In this situation, I did not have a choice; being needed was a drug-induced ache. The clan had the opportunity to choose, yet they remained beside me, from the duty of harvesting souls to fighting over the protection of Alexcia.

It had been over a decade since the pact was sealed, and when she had needed protection, I found it more from want than of duty. *Maybe, I was cursed?* I was a daemon after all, but my existence had become almost ordinary—an eternity of the same repeated routine. Creating this contract with Alexcia's mother had made me feel there was more to my being than the bounty of a Harvester's reaping. To say boredom played a role in my lack of judgment was a crutch, but close to the truth.

One thing was for sure—Rae-Lynn had given a new meaning to torment and twisted agony of our jobs. Those emotions I understood all too well and enjoyed snacking on them, not the experience. At first, watching the Child-of-Balance had been a simple task. Most of the Unseen did not have the child in their crosshairs. As she grew older and more opinionated with her life's dealings, our task became overladen with misery. We literally fought to see who would be stuck watching her.

I took one last drag, crushed what was left of the burning filter into my palm and listened to the ember sizzle in protest. The sound triggered a series of memories, taking me back to the morning I skulked through the entrance to our cave, returning with an empty stomach, a headache, and a babysitting contract.

A brooding, blue-eyed Ashen met me at the entrance under the cave's icicle teeth. For the clan to complete their duties before me was out of character. Normally, I waited on them to return and disclose their status. Since I had not arrived before the dual suns rose, they assumed the worst. At that point, being recopied would have been a blessing.

Michael would be considered my second-in-command, or replacement if we had ranks. He was also the most pissed off at my lapse in judgment. The reaper went ballistic when I explained the Bond-Rite was a sealed blood pact, which made the contract unbreakable. His shrewd, burning orbs made it clear. If I had not been the leader, the blade of his battle axe would be buried in my face. His response stirred an itch of apprehension because he was deadly accurate with that damn thing.

The Smolder I hosted chortled while sharing the memory. I peered up and noticed the stars through a thin layer of clouds. From the street below, cars screeched on wet pavement; voices rose in high shrills, brakes locked, tires chirped, and then… the echo of metal, glass, and Vessels colliding. An explosive symphony of death jarred me back into my head.

Michael's volatile temper rebounded off of the cave walls, enhancing the memory. The news was received as blasphemous against what we represented to the House of Space, to the entities of the Unseen, to our creator, and even to the Vessels we had harvested. Michael's anger was on a short fuse, waiting for me to explain my tardiness. So, when he smacked me right below the jawline, I countered with my fist. I knew his lashing out was a mild punishment I justly deserved. Arrogance and the weight of the Bond-Rite kept my mouth moving as I suggested he kiss my ass.

Later, Michael disappeared to sulk for one or two sunsets. After riding out his tantrum, he cursed my existence but ended our discussion by stating he would always have my back. True to his word, the reluctant Ashen had helped break the news to our clan. To this day, Michael has upheld my decision, and as penance, I have had to endure his incessant grumbling for the past decade.

Quint was the clan's problem solver. While I informed them of the terms of the Bond-Rite, he held his calculating tongue. I could tell, our tech-savvy reaper was burning through solutions to troubleshoot my dilemma. His cloaked minion puffed up, allowing the yellow of his aura to thread through the edges of it. Right before concealing his gaze, to make his point known, he tersely vowed I could count on his services. With his polearm placed across the arms of his chair, he could have easily sent me to the River Styx. I believed part of him regretted missing the opportunity.

Archer was as straight as his name. Styx bestowed him with a unique weapon, the recurve bow. We all have a minion-type connection with our weapons, but Archer's choice was a second minion, besides the shroud. His bow could spot their prey half a second before he was able to. If a Vessel's name came up on Archer's collection list, their soul carrying days were over.

I had both, Archer, and his weapon, Wink, staring at me. With its two huge orange eyes, one on either side of the silver-rose grip followed me back and forth as I paced. Archer stared in shock with his bright, flame-lit orbs and silver braided mane clasped in his hand, knuckles changing to bone white. He would tug on the single plait as if he wanted to pull it out. As an attempt to regain his composure, Archer removed an arrow from his quiver, sliced his palm before reaching out to grab mine… sealing a silent truce to protect the child.

K kept quiet in the corner, but I could see the fires of damnation seething behind his green eyes. He remained calm to keep his Smolder under control. If he had unlocked his inner daemon, they would have taken all of us out, or at least tried to. K's minion kept threatening me with glimpses of his mace whenever it moved in agitation. He had never agreed to protect Alexcia, but when I requested he take a shift, he never hesitated to accept the task. Sometimes, I saw a flicker to explore beyond our existence in his green orbs. As of present, we keep our common disease to ourselves and refer to it as TC or terminal curiosity.

Vibrant purple eyes drifted into view as I remembered our ass-breaker, Imp. He stood six foot five, adorned with long, muscular appendages. I thought of him as a spring— he was light and quick, and mischievous—which fit his daemonic name. Imp was fluent in dark sarcasm. He would use it to lighten the mood within the clan, especially when battles broke out over child sitting. Typically, when the clan members were at a stalemate, he offered to watch her.

I assumed he would have severed his Bond-Rite with the clan after my decision; instead, he stayed. Imp's curiosity would heighten whenever we discussed Alexcia. It was a daemonic characteristic to toy with temptation, but the real challenge was the restraint to use his broadsword on her.

And last but not least was Raven. He was the clan's muscle, but he also had a shorter fuse than Michael. Raven assumed I had gone mad from my mundane existence to protect and save a soul willingly. Scratching his chin with a katara, he nicked it before pointing the bloody tip at me. Crimson eyes narrowed as his hatred poured out into one question. "How in the Unseen is a human child going to bring balance to both worlds?" I replied by pounding my reasons through his minion's hood to penetrate his dense head. Raven's sulking lasted the longest within our little group.

Once he was back, the begrudging Ashen voiced his opinion that he did not want to be torn from his duties or go against the nature of his Smolder. Raven's biggest hitch was the child sitting part. In his mind, I had placed our clan on the Unseen's hit list.

Even though the clan as a collective, accused me of idiocy, I believed the Bond-Rite had a profound purpose. Not only for the child's well-being, but for the River Styx too. If our Creator had chosen Alexcia to bring balance between the Houses, it was my duty to make sure she had the breath to choose.

A gust of wet air blew through my minion, and I found myself back in the present. The late-night storm had blown out of the Las Vegas valley, making me feel sullen that those blasted, cluttered thoughts had not dissipated with it. Scanning the horizon, I caught sight of the bright beacon coming from the pyramid casino, illuminating the way to the Unseen. Our dwelling was slightly beyond the end of the beam. *Great. Now I was homesick.*

Working in the desert sucked daemon butt. The only part making it tolerable was the tastefully sinful natures of the Vessels. We never went hungry. Between soul harvesting and the twenty-four-hour fast food access, we were set.

I was lost between thoughts of Alexcia and food when a harsh breeze blew from the left and pulled me out of my delusional pondering. My minion shifted with me as we faced our potential foe. The cloak froze when I reached for the scythe in one fluid motion. I watched how the moonlight shimmered down the beard's edge, illuminating the newcomer's neck. It was Michael.

His cloak whipped out thick tentacles to keep me from detaching his head, and I found myself at a disadvantage. Michael had countered my move by positioning his silver-etched battle axe above my left shoulder. Staring into his dull blue eyes, I could tell he was due for a recharge. Knowing Michael, it was the first thing on his list of needs for the evening.

Curious as to why he was here, I stood down and backed away, returning to my perch as my weapon collapsed so I could sheath it. Gravity tugged, and both limbs obeyed, dropping me into a thinking reaper pose as I sat on some loose shingles and leaned my back against the wall.

I used the foul emotions radiating from me as a shield. My cloak pretended not to notice by searching through the cracks and slithering under the roof's flat shingles of foam and gravel.

Michael hustled over to me, slapped his palms on the concrete, and peered over the edge. "Look at all those walking meals on wheels, each one cooking at its very own unique temperature and time. Doesn't it make your mouth water?" Both eyes illuminated his aura's color from under his shroud.

"Why are you here, Michael?" I tugged hard on the edge of my hood so he could not read my mood while I chastised him. "I can tell you have not satiated your hunger. Should I attempt to feel worried?" Irritation laced each word. "Because this is out of character for you."

"I see you're in a grave mood." A deep chuckle filled in the pause between us before he exclaimed, "Damn! That never gets old." His sarcasm added fuel to the overused… joke. "Even after what, almost six centuries? That pun still brings a tear to my eye." He jumped onto the three-foot wall next to me and began pacing above my head. His minion reached out several times for mine.

Glancing in his direction, I cleared my throat. "Actually, I retract my first question to redirect with one of my own. Is there a reason you are interrupting?"

Michael's eyes sparked with keenness, yet both brows arched in displayed frustration.

The black mist around my shoulders took on the appearance of material, so it could shrug with me as I spoke. "I figured you traded K or Archer for an earlier job. You left the cemetery complaining of hunger, and I can tell you are in need of a meal, Reaper—"

"As a matter of fact, I did trade, but for a later time frame. Your facial expression at the cemetery twisted my gut in knots, so I thought you could use a fresh opinion—one that's not clouded by caretaker's guilt." He blew out heavily, then added poison to his tongue. "Tevin, my daemon leader, you are becoming too attached to a disposable container. That spells trouble in my death ledger, and you are going to throw our little clan out-of-balance for your unbalanced-child. Who, I might add, you... cannot... save. The Unseen will claim her, one way or another."

He hopped down from the ledge and sauntered over to sit next to me. When he settled against the wall, a cigarette materialized between two digits.

With fidgety fingers, I mimicked the same motion as deflated pride pushed a reluctant exhale from my lips. "What do the Vessels say when they refrain from commenting?"

Michael's brow creased as he took a drag, then released a few smoke rings with his words. "I plead the fifth?"

"Well, I do."

"Do what?"

"Plead the fifth."

"Does that law even apply to us?"

"I have nothing to justify. Except the only emotion I have for the River's favorite toy is irritation. The elemental fight in the desert a couple of months ago was a close one. If the Cauldron of Ending keeps summoning for her soul—" My tongue cramped as I redirected the thought. "I tire of watching over her."

The cloak's movement went from being inquisitive to scared-fabric straight. *Oh, crap.* I did it again, using the wrong term. Vessel, soul, or Child-of-Balance were all acceptable terms for Ashens to use. Secretly, we even came up with a short pet name for Alexcia, shared via texting, of course… the brat. But the slip-ups were becoming all too frequent. Referring to the Vessel in a personal or specific gender was proof I was dealing with unchecked emotions. I kept my gaze stationary as I took another pull from the filter, and gave my minion an internal command to lower the hood.

The mist from Michael's hood dissipated from over his face. Stupefied, he stared at me with wide orbs.

I could not blame him as his facial features contorted to match my perplexity of misunderstood emotions. Unfortunately, after a decade of provoking curiosity and protecting, I did not know how to revert back to the way things had been, or if I even wanted to.

Michael dropped his cigarette in disgust. Then from a teeth-gritting frown slid out the word, "Her?" His remark sounded painful.

I pulled on my cigarette until it was half ash. Releasing puffs of smoke, I barked, "Yeah, her. So what? She's a female, right? Crap! For cloak's sake, what's the big deal?" I pulled on the rest of the tobacco stick, listening to the paper crackle and sizzle, then clapped to discard the warm ash into the breeze. Pushing to stand, I started to pace, boots crunching while I stepped in time with each troubled thought.

Michael blinked, then stood, slowly shaking his head. "I was wondering how long it was going to take before you wove your grim existence into the child's welfare. Is being a daemon so bad?" He gestured to the humans below us. "It's in their nature to die, and we are merely the Unseen's daemonic trash collectors. Part of what we are calls for us to avoid getting personal with them. Period." His words held agitation and perhaps laced with a smidgen of bitterness in a you-let-me-down kind of way.

"Look, I have gone around and around with you on this contract I made with Rae-Lynn. I gave you many outs. *Many*. Chalk up my reactions toward the Vessel as mere curiosity. I have no forbidden feelings for the Child-of-Balance. It makes me wonder, though, out of all of these humans, why her? The Vessels' life cycle has sparked my interest, and bringing about their end is all I know. After meeting Rae-Lynn and making the Bond-Rite, we have done more with our existence than the repetitive norm of harvesting and recycling. It feels odd, different, but for some reason different is what I crave."

I dismissed my cloak and stopped in front of Michael.

"I am always thinking about the clan. You do not need to concern yourself with that. The second Bond-Rite I made with Max, after Alexcia's Rose of Remembrance delivery disaster,"—I poked him in the chest—"that might I remind you, you screwed up on, will reset everything."

"What?" He cocked his head and threw up his hands, exasperated.

"I was thinking of the clan when I made it, so for the next twenty-three days, I will answer to Max and Rae-Lynn. I will look after Alexcia when needed and will not ask more from you or the clan. The contracts are mine, and if I fulfill Max's, he will break the one with Rae." Six hundred plus years, and I was hoping for six hundred more as long as we didn't recopy each other before then.

His shoulders relaxed, his stare shifting from me to the skyline. The Ashen walked back to the edge and leaned over. Michael was processing the moment, and I was not going to press him to understand. He would have to decide to stay and ride this out with me or break his pact with our clan and possibly go rogue.

I silently stepped next to him, bending over the wall to watch the Vessels scurry about their business.

Michael's voice was distant but with a hint of understanding. "So, what you're saying is, in about a month it will all be over?"

"Well, yeah, that is the plan as long as the Vessel

remains above ground." I chuckled. "Max even told me to stir the Cauldron's waters if her name came up again."

Wide-eyed, his voice was stern. "You wouldn't, would you? We're not supposed to manipulate the waters. The Ashen who does will fall from the River's favor. Darkness be damned, you wouldn't even be allowed to be a gondolier. Does Max realize what he's asking of you?" He huffed and shook his head realizing he knew the obvious. "Of course, he does." Running fingers over his scalp, he added, "We are crazy for taking this job, and you know the situation is dire when I deem it crazy."

I was not about to share with him that I had toyed with the idea more than once, mostly for Alexcia's well-being. Instead, I coaxed, "Look, it is simple enough, right? We continue what we've been doing, and before you know it, she decides on one of the three Houses. Then we go back to our Ashen ways."

On an exhale, I tapped my temple and added, "Oh, and I am only going to say this once. Quit questioning my actions. I think I have made the right choice, not only for myself but for the clan's sanity too." My face tightened, so I forced the corners of my mouth to curve convincingly.

The Smolder projected an image of it swallowing the girl to end our suffering, adding its opinion to the conversation.

When the wind clipped over the casino roof, it reminded me of the winter's day I had disappeared from the clan to watch over the girl. Boredom and curiosity clouded my judgment and ended up porting us to the Unseen. I had forgotten about that day until Alexcia's dream pulled me into one of her memories.

A vision washed over me… of her skating so innocently. Numb was the closest emotion I had felt at the time with no real connection to her. The Smolder possessing me was curious about the child as well, and I remembered deeply inhaling so it could recognize her scent.

Not one negative emotion emanated from her, which made my inner daemon cautious. The Vessel had caught me off guard several times when she had tried to hold my hand. At times when we connected, there was a faint warm sensation from my throat muscles tightening. *I have always wanted to understand what the warmth meant, but still, to this day, it leaves me confused.* Since Alexcia had shared that private moment with me, my frustration incessantly chewed on one question. *How did I not remember anything about her before she had unlocked that memory?* Agitated, I gradually released the moment, allowing the phantom sensation of her touch to dissipate into missing gaps of time.

Opening my eyes, I connected with Michael's intense stare. Narrowed orbs studied me, making the silent standoff awkward.

The reaper's blue eyes widened. "So, that's it, then? A decade of torment and we're finally done. Well, Space be praised, we should celebrate. Let's find a Vessel on my list that's scheduled to have a heart attack, or maybe one in an ER with a mortal gunshot wound. What do ya say? Dinner's on me." He waved in a grand, wide bow. "I'll even blend into Vessel form so we can stop at In-N-Out Burger for a shake and fries when we're done."

His cloak's inky tentacles stretched and swirled with thin threads of blue, matching his eyes. Michael was excited the contract I made to save the Child-of-Balance was coming to an end. Closing the space between us, he draped an arm over my shoulders and pulled me along.

Resisting, my footfalls slowed. I was not in the mood to celebrate. I needed to contemplate a question or two without Michael's infuriating influence. I broke his hold and waved him off, like an Unseen Skitter insect. "You go on. Bon appétit."

"Tevin, when was the last time you slurped up a soul? I mean a real, honest-to-goodness jolt of power, not little zaps of static snacks." He stopped and took a closer look at my face. "Oh, split me with my axe. What now?"

"Uh, nothing."

"Nothing?"

"Yes, that is what I said. Nothing."

"Tevin, you think I'm a two-hundred-year-old Ashen? I can tell there's a problem tarnishing your scythe. So, give."

"I want to confront Max with my apprehension, and I am trying to figure out how to approach him. As I said, it's nothing. I will think of a way to get my point across. I need to call Rae—I mean, Rae-Lynn," I said, quickly correcting myself. The moonlight accentuated my clenched, bone-white hands, which might have revealed too much. Annoyed, I commanded the mist around me to thicken, dimming the glow.

Michael's smirk displayed a hint of teeth as he pulled his battle axe from under his cloak. The reaper flipped it blade-side down, slamming the tip into the roof with a deafening crack, then leaned on the handle. "What the hell are you doing? I thought you said it was simple? This is unsettling, and an Ashen worried…" His eyes grew dark and pinched at the sides. "That doesn't even sound right. Ashens do not worry."

When the desire to justify presses against your resolve long enough, it can make you crack. Mine fragmented and loosened my tongue. "Look, I only want to know why Max and Rae-Lynn decided to hide Alexcia's true purpose from her. If Alexcia is the Child-of-Balance, why wouldn't they want her to explore her capabilities? Even if she leaks unspun magic, it'll have a price. I don't know if you've noticed, but she reeks of it, and her aura seems shattered. The power within her is trying to break out. Alexcia would be better off knowing. At least if she knew, she might stop her reckless behavior, so her name doesn't appear in the damn Cauldron." I shook my head in thought and took two long strides over to him. "Haven't you noticed anything different with the child? I have seen a change in her demeanor. This is why I can't understand her parent's logic."

Michael's eyes iced over. "And that's your *nothing*? You know, if you keep interfering, you add the possibility of becoming more attached. The change in her could be the fact she's trying to deal with the deaths of the other Vessels she was attached to." Stone-faced he added, "You've also said *she* four times, *her* eight times, and referred to the child by *name* three times. But who's counting, right? Oh, and your contractions are showing."

"Damn me to Hell and back!" When I spoke in broken words, I was close to losing it. Stomping away from him to the other side of the rooftop seemed like the best plan, but I pivoted about halfway to yell at him. "You wanted to know. I'm telling you what I've been thinking. I'm clarifying the why and what to you, and you're giving me a grammar lesson. I'll refer to her as I bloody see fit. Right now, it's the least of my effed-up issues. I can't help but think there's a deeper meaning to all of this."

I lowered my voice and seized control of my tongue.

"Michael, I believe she will be in more danger if I stop protecting her when Max's Bond-Rite is fulfilled. My minion, weapon, and even the Smolder I carry feel different when she is around us. Max's contract does not sit well with me. It seems I agreed to it in haste."

He stood upright and strapped his battle axe back into its leather holder. Facing me, I could see "spill or be recopied" in his eyes. Then he said, "So, give me a reason why we should hang around like unwanted, rabid bats in a church belfry."

"My reasons are irrelevant, other than a looming sense of dread and a twisting in my gut."

"Well, that's a start." He gave me a challenging look. "Come on. Convince me why we should continue to save Alexcia's pretty, little ass after twenty-three Earth moon risings." His voice echoed, and my cloak bristled when he spat out Alexcia's name.

I snapped at the unnerved minion, commanding it to let me think.

Michael folded his arms over his chest before heading in my direction. I had a premonition that once his footfalls fell silent, all hell would break loose on this rooftop.

"The River has laid claim to her. It is our job to make sure she fulfills her purpose."

"That's two." His stride remained steady.

"Why are the elementals trying to end her life before she is even old enough to choose a House, without knowing how to fight physically or magically? She does not stand a chance against them on her own." *Twenty-four steps until he reaches me.*

"A question turned into a reason. I'll allow it. Next—"

"She's clueless about the Unseen."

"That's weak, but I'll let it slide." His smile held malice, but I could tell he was considering the last reason.

Nineteen steps away, his stride had quickened.

"Bloody Hell! I want to know what my role in her life is supposed to be. Rae-Lynn has hinted that I know her. How's that possible? Because I'll tell you, I don't remember her before she became my charge. But I can't deny there's a foreign power stirring within whenever we are close. It's different from the Smolder's influence that possesses me. Hell, I know it's going to be an irksome three weeks. But the answers I seek lie within her mind, and right now, my role is gravedigger."

He stopped.

Defeated, I continued, "Michael, what is my part in her life?" The question sounded detached, which fit my mood because it was exactly the way she made me feel. "I want to know if there's more going on here. Am I only this invisible force keeping her from imminent danger? Can she teach me how to understand Vessels? Would she be able to unlock certain emotions, other than the ones we are allowed to have? I don't know…" My tone was losing its muster. I focused on my hands and blew out slowly. "Michael, I just do not know."

His feet shifted on the asphalt before unfolding both arms. With his minion blowing in the breeze, the daemon clipped, "And?"

My mouth was dry from using my tongue to sponge up reasons and wring them out for Michael. There was one more, but as an Ashen, I did not know if I had the right to say it out loud.

I looked down as he raised his voice. "Think, Tevin!

What reason chains you to this Vessel?"

"Michael, what is love? These Vessels throw the word around as if it can heal or inflict pain. Is it a form of magic or a curse? Is it only an emotion or is there something more? What is this power we are not allowed to utilize?"

He stumbled as though I had shoved him.

Gauging his reaction, I redirected my argument and suggested, "I believe if I watch her interact with other Vessels, I might be able to handle my existence better." With both eyes closed, I waited for him to unload on me.

"Well, you've temporarily convinced me."

This time, it was my turn to stare at him in astonishment.

Michael's Smolder growled while he chuckled, making him sound like a cement mixer. He placed a cloaked arm around my shoulders again and proceeded to drag me back to the parapet.

"I convinced you?" I blinked in bewilderment. "What happened? Which Ashen am I talking to?"

Outwardly, satisfied with himself, he slapped my shoulder. "I helped you, my fellow daemon. I figured you would have realized by now that you've answered most of your own questions."

Michael cocked his head, then nodded in agreement from some internal conversation he had shared with his minion. With a mischievous curve on his face, he cracked his neck and set both shoulders. "We believe nine reasons to stick around is satisfactory. Some were pretty weak, but three were solid, and the last one I wouldn't share with our clan or any other daemon. *Ever*."

My own Smolder shared a mutual snort with me. "I was not planning on it. Oh, and I do not know why, but if you ever say *Alexcia* and *pretty, little ass* in the same sentence again, I will slice yours off."

He swung at me, then stopped right before my chest, grumbling, "You can try, but as for right now, I suggest we use our weapons for dinner. I have been assigned a suicide four blocks away for my next reaping. We'd better hurry. I'm so hungry, I might kill a cat before we get there."

Chapter Two

*M*y radio alarm was blasting "Drop Dead Cynical," by Amaranthe from my playlist. I had already been up hours before the sun rose, not because of my inner clock but from the night terrors. I stretched, and the pain in the middle of my back made me gasp as the skin pulled. I registered the annoyance and winced while kicking one of my poetry notebooks off the foot of my bed.

Slowly sitting up, I tried to ignore my back and focus on piecing together what I was going to wear. *Maybe horizontal stripes and an anklet?*

My friend Blakely Sanderson was going to stop by Demetria Stewart's to pick her up before me, leaving me time to get ready even though I had to deal with the cast on my wrist.

It felt like the first day of ninth grade again. I must have swallowed butterflies while I slept because my stomach was full of flutters.

A sense of panic pushed me out of bed too fast, and the

glow-in-the-dark stars on the dark walls began to tilt and sway. Once my world realigned, I ambled to the bathroom. I planned to start from the top and work my way down. I really didn't want to draw attention to myself in an *I-am-back-on-the-market* guise, but more like a *blend-in, behind-the-scenes, I'm-not-really-here* appearance.

I wrapped my left hand, taping it below the elbow, and then stepped into the shower. Gasping when the hot water hit my back, I would make sure to check the mattress top for a staple or a paperclip. Since the skin was tender, I decided to skip scrubbing everywhere and concentrate only on the essential parts.

Blow-drying my hair straight was a challenge with the cast, but doable, and I watched my reflection work the round brush to frame my face. It was difficult to manage the long strands, and by the time it was dry, I wanted to crawl back into bed.

Pink's song, "Sober," put some blood back into my feet; ignoring the pain and fatigue, I danced over my discarded clothes toward the closet. Pulling a pair of faded black jeans, a dark purple V-neck shirt, and a black pullover sweatshirt from the hangers, I tossed them onto the bed. Once dressed, I slipped into yesterday's socks and black Converse, then maneuvered toward the full-length mirror to fix my face. With a little eyeliner and a couple swipes of mascara, I was almost finished.

Bypassing the jewelry box that contained the rose-cut garnet pendant my parents had given me on my fifteenth birthday, I chose the fashionable and functional silver pocket watch necklace which suited the outfit best. It was draped across a pink stuffed crab Jake had saved from a toy claw game when we were about twelve. Unhooking the chain, I patted the plush and smiled.

Within seconds, a wave of dread washed over me. I pushed the box farther to the back of the shelf, reciting, "Out of sight, out of mind." A sting of guilt made me pause, and my breath hitched. I took a step back, and the emotion vanished. With a dismissive hand wave, I reassured myself the flash of conviction was all in my mind.

Taking a quick inventory, I opened my favorite black and gold Loungefly Sugar Skull bag. Inside I found the new cell my father had bought, which constantly reminded me of the metallic green one melted on the highway somewhere. I shoved some assignments in between the different colored notebooks and slid the stack into the bag. Since I had missed so much school, I was going to work the system and try to get the rest of my homework dismissed. After all, I had missed third-quarter finals and almost four weeks into fourth quarter due to my recovery after the accident. It was a good thing my mother worked a deal with the teachers to make up the exams.

I checked the wall clock in the kitchen and realized I had five minutes to slam some water and two Tylenol before Blakely and Dee would be here. Once the glass was rinsed, I picked up my school tote and headed for the door, while yelling to my father's Rottweiler that I was leaving. Gigi galloped down the hall and gave me some slobbery goodbye kisses.

I punched the code in the lockbox and grabbed the silver *A* key ring. Staring at the keys brought me back to a memory. *Tod's monster truck revving in the driveway, followed by his impatient honking.*

Gigi's bark sounded more gruff than usual, and then the pitch of honking changed.

"I'm coming. Damn. Be right there… Tod," Dazed, I stared at my reflection in the hall mirror. Two silver clips held back my curls, adding to the party attire and dark makeup. Leaning toward the reflective surface, I placed a hand on my chest.

Another growl from Gigi and I blinked, finding myself back in the present.

When Blakely laid on her horn for the umpteenth time, I thought, *Geez—must be that time of the month.* I closed the key box, patted the dog on the head, and sighed. I missed Tod so much that I even cherished the flashbacks.

This was a new beginning for me, and the sound of the

front door locking made me feel as though I had sealed my past behind it. The desire to run back into the house crept along each nerve in my body, but I willed both feet forward.

My friend's addiction to Sharpie markers was comically obsessive. After she had purchased her salsa red, 2009 Volkswagen Beetle, she took it home and colored huge black spots all over it. Blakely then christened her mode of transportation, the Lady.

The girls greeted me with unusually bright smiles. Under normal circumstances, there would have been grumbles and verbal slams against our early morning routine. Blakely even had the passenger door already open for me. The Lady gushed out its own welcome by enveloping me in a vanilla tea and honey scented car freshener. I inhaled the calming aroma. Tossing the skull bag on the floorboard, I plopped on the seat and reached for the cell phone charging cord.

Dee's smile disappeared as she slid back into her seat with a leather-protesting squeak. "I was listening to Avril. Blakely, why do you let her take over when she gets in? I should get to pick first. And for heaven's sake, at least let the song finish. It's rude, cutting her off like that." She sucked on her tongue, releasing a *tsk*.

My eyes narrowed into a glare as I listened to Dee's complaints. I couldn't believe it. *Was it shark week for her, too?* I glanced over my shoulder to challenge her protest and noticed her dark auburn hair had been cut shorter since I'd last seen her. It was straight, but the length only came to the middle of her neck and was framed forward. She had curled the ends slightly outward, giving her an edgy, jagged appearance complimenting her honey-green eyes.

Her creamy skin was dusted lightly with freckles across the bridge of her nose and the upper portion of her cheeks. When we were younger, I'd always told her to stop pissing off the fairies because they kept wiping their feet on her face.

Blakely sighed, refusing to comment, and her head darted back and forth before she pulled Lady out into traffic. She gunned the car and mumbled under her breath. Inside, I was snickering, but I didn't want us barking at each other so early in the morning, so I unplugged and dropped the device back into my tote.

Anxiety churned in my gut with every turn and stop. I hoped I hadn't lost my ability to slip inconspicuously from class to class. My plan was interrupted when I realized I had forgotten to grab some money out of the fake feminine hygiene box from the bottom drawer. The hiding place had served me well for a long time. *Who would check there for hidden money?* A crude throat noise slipped out followed by an inward, *Damn it.* I didn't see any other way than to beg for food.

"Hey, what do you all have planned for lunch today? It appears my brain is still on medical leave and I'm penniless."

Blakely waited for the streetlight to change. Her facial expression said I had ruined her plans.

Dee made an exasperated noise and uncrossed her legs to lean forward. "Well, there goes my fire fix." She was talking about her weekly hot sauce addiction from Taco Bell. Dee continued, "What are they having in the cafeteria today? Do you know, Blake?" She tilted her head to catch Blakely's eyes in the rearview mirror.

"We won't starve," said Blakely. "I brought a twenty. Lunch is on me, girls. Lex-Cee, you've been nominated to pay for lunch tomorrow."

Dee's teeth gleamed. She always chipped in extra when our funds were nonexistent, but my line of credit between the three of us was dangerously close to maxed out. This meant tomorrow's lunch was going to drain me.

Trying not to think about my dwindling funds, I followed Blakely's hand to the rearview mirror as she adjusted it. When she set it back on her leg, she started drumming her fingers. Blake's boot-cut jeans were functioning as both a trendy self-statement and an artwork portfolio. Her blond hair normally fell straight down her back, but today it was styled into a messy twist with little wisps framing her face. Brass-rimmed sunglasses were fashionable, but the rims were too wide, and the corded, chocolate-brown sweater was new but two sizes too big for her frame. Even though the sleeves were folded twice, only her fingers showed. The outfit made her look coy.

Then it hit me. Blakely wasn't going for coy; she was hiding within herself. I frowned. Her stepfather must have been at it again. Blood rushed to my cheeks making them sting, but my eyes burned much worse.

To my dismay, she noticed my demeanor had changed, and it caused her to stare forward, press her glasses closer to her face and release a whisper of colorful curses.

"Blakely—" I began, but she cut me off.

"Alexcia, don't go there."

I winced, but it didn't stop her rant.

"I already know what you are going to say. It was a bad night. Let's leave it at that. Just zip it, lock it, and put it in your damn pocket. Cripes, let me concentrate on getting us to school. I can take care of myself, ya know."

Dee appeared stunned from the bite in Blakely's words. I was pretty sure from her expression that she wanted to respond, too, but we both knew when Blakely snipped, "I can take care of myself," she was done talking.

The next turn Blakely made brought the school into view, and my chest tightened. Sucking in a quick breath, I steeled myself and chanted in silence; *everything is going to be okay*. I could do this.

I wanted to shove the last five weeks into my inner closet, bolt it, and mindlessly lose the key. Instead, I started rocking while hugging the tote for comfort.

Dee put a hand on my shoulder for reassurance. "It will be okay. Before you know it, people won't even think twice about what happened to all of you. The inquisitions will fade in time. Plus, you always have us to back ya up, right?" She was trying extra hard to sound bright and optimistic.

I was lucky to have both friends, and I returned Dee's smile, so she knew I was listening. "Yeah, sure, thanks. I know it will. It's the reliving-it part I don't want to repeat. It's hard enough facing my reflection in the mirror without wanting to break it. Even my breathing is a reminder that I'm here and they're not." Tears were threatening to fall, and I bit the inside of my cheek.

Blakely's demeanor changed from defensive to compassionate. "Yeah, don't worry, Lex-Cee. It will die down in time, but for today be a duck." She looked serious.

Wide-eyed, I tried very hard not to laugh at her comment. "Be a duck?" I asked, arching an eyebrow.

"Yeah, be a duck. Let the questions and comments roll off your back like water. Be a duck."

My smile widened. "Does it matter what kind of duck I'm supposed to be?" She hated when I pretended to take her advice literally. So did my mom, for that matter. It had always been one of my many hidden talents… the ability to annoy.

"I know," Blake replied. "You should be a yellow rubber duck. That way, everything will slide right off." Then she elbowed me twice and winked.

Dee and I both chuckled, and Blake joined in as she parked the red bug next to Jake Steal's ugly yellow Cadillac Eldorado 2000. I'd nicknamed it the submarine.

I didn't even notice he was sitting on the trunk until Dee waved at him. Jake, otherwise known around the school as Ghost, hopped down and stopped for a moment to grab a container from the roof of the car.

I reached for the door latch, only to find that Ghost had beat me to it. He held it open with one hand while balancing a drink carrier with three piping hot cups of coffee and one hot chocolate for himself. I couldn't help the smile of thanks spreading across my face like a smear of warm butter on toast.

At least we were physically ready for school. Warm clothes and hot drinks might seem odd for mid-May in Las Vegas, but once the temps reached the nineties, schools cranked up the air conditioning. I assumed they thought we were made of snow and didn't want to clean up puddles of teenager-goo.

As we wove our way through the parking lot, I found

myself slipping back into our old routine, laughing and carrying on about the latest gossip. Blake, Dee, and Ghost would never really understand what the three of them and their friendship meant to me. *Maybe, someday, I'll put it into words.*

Our perfect moment was ruined when a pack of juniors and seniors from the school paper swarmed us. Their presence reminded me of the huge black birds that taunted me in my nightmares.

A camera flashed as a hand yanked on my sweatshirt, making me spill some coffee on my jeans. Their questions swirled around us, and I could only stare down at the spinning gravel as my mind tried to tune out the buzzing annoyance. *And here I was without a flyswatter.*

Dee jumped in front of me. She was the size of a yappy Miniature Pinscher but had the bite of a rabid Doberman if you pissed her off. "What the hell! Back off, people. Let her get to her damn locker at least. You're a flock of vultures, feeding off the memories of the dead to get a lame story. Leave the girl alone."

She shoved one of the kids with a camera and began elbowing her way through the crowd, using her purse as a shield. Jake wrapped an arm around me, and Blakely took a position behind my back. One of the students shoved Blake, and I heard her cuss when the splatter of coffee hit the ground. Teens scrambled out of the splash zone, and we took the opportunity to run for the junior hall entrance.

Making it to the top of the stairs, I turned to everyone and put my free hand on my hip. "Blakely, you forgot one thing."

She was huffing. "What's that?"

"In the immortal words of Daffy Duck, 'It's duck season.'"

I took a sip of my coffee, saluted Blake, then yelled, "*Fire!*" as I opened one of the double doors with enough force to bang the handle against the brick wall.

The first four classes passed in a blur. I was two for two. Algebra II and French II were a complete bust. Both teachers expounded in great detail how making up the assignments would be killing two problems with one stone, preparing me for final exams. It was logical, but I didn't like it. At least I didn't have to make up the last three oral French tests. Mrs. Glentworth only wanted half of the hand-out transcripts translated by Friday.

My Algebra II teacher, Mr. Heater, asked for all the homework to be completed but was going to let the classwork slide. Whether Home or Class was put in front of the word, it still meant work. Calculating how much makeup I had to do, I would have to ask Mr. Sipton if he could schedule me at the Sip 'N Chug for the following week.

Third-period chemistry was mostly labs. Ms. Hinton asked for the breakdown of the periodic table and a paper on the five most important steps of the scientific method. In tennis, I was excused because of the cast. To buy myself some extra bleacher time, I fussed about my knee. Honestly, it felt better, but since I didn't have the brace for added visual, whining would have to do. Pathetic, but it worked.

Our tennis instructor, Ms. Kyto, was very sympathetic. She even let a tear or two slip down her cheek when I entered her class. Blakely smiled, and whispered, "Teacher's pet" as she shifted out of the way so the teacher could reach me for a hug.

I winked and mouthed, *bite my ass*.

Ms. Kyto held me close. It surprised me that a teacher had genuinely missed me.

By the time the lunch period bell rang, my stomach had threatened to eat itself. Blakely and I were about to lean against the Lady when Jake materialized, giving us both a heart attack. While recovering from the scare, we watched

Dee promenade down the main steps.

Some familiar faces had passed us heading for the other side of the parking lot where a group of them met to get high. The wind stirred the chemical and herbal odor in our direction. It had been almost five weeks since I'd had a drink or a cigarette, and it triggered an irritating throb. I frowned, remembering Tod's dislike for my smoking habit. Strange as it seemed, I guess in a creepy way, he had won that argument from the grave.

We climbed into Jake's car and made a race for the closest Taco Bell border. I wanted a soft taco and Dr. Pepper so bad my saliva glands were on overdrive. Ghost went through the drive-thru so we'd have enough time to eat and digest before fifth period. It was nice to be with everyone again, discussing teachers, homework, and even the latest scandals, which consisted mostly of speculation about the accident, or me.

As I finished the last few bites, I remembered I needed a ride to work. Mom had a late appointment, and Max was out of town, which left me lacking in transportation. With everyone full and happy, it was the perfect time to lower the boom.

"So, is anyone free tonight to help out the vehiclely challenged?" I asked through my last bite of beef and cheese.

Jake stopped, one half of his hard-shell taco in his mouth, and glanced at Blakely. She challenged his stare, sipping her iced tea. Both of them were locked in a mind battle, and I assumed it was an inward debate about who would get stuck driving me. Dee was sucking on hot sauce packets in the back seat, silently playing referee.

I picked up my trash, trying not to interrupt their battle of wills and hoping my feet weren't going to be my only transportation, when…

"Ha! You blinked! You have to take her." Blakely smiled in victory.

Jake bit down on his taco and narrowed his eyes. His glower said if he weren't chewing, he would have challenged her, but nodded in defeat.

Smiling, I leaned over to kiss his cheek. "Thank you. You take loss well, my friend." Then I held the paper sack out to him. "Trash?"

Jake sat blinking with cheeks full of taco, slowly chewing. He placed his wrappers into the paper bag. Preoccupied, he pulled on the drinking straw, and it squeaked while he cleared his throat. "Ah, I would say second place isn't all that bad. But Blakely, I just remembered, I can't take her home." He spoke as though I was their joint custody child. "You're gonna have to do it. I'm scheduled after nine tonight, and then I have to go home and study for English Lit." Ghost lifted his brow and turned to face me. "Can you ask your parents?"

"No, my mom has a late meeting, and Max's flight arrives after eleven." I turned to Blakely. "You think you could swing by and take me home?" Using Bambi eyes, I said in an English accent, "Please, Mum, don't let me go out into the meadow alone."

She sighed. "Sure, but I work until ten, so you'll have to wait for me. Normally, my manager wouldn't have scheduled me so late on a school night, but we are short a closer." She rotated her straw, slurping the last swallow of her watered-down tea.

Disappointment made me antsy. I hated waiting, but *beggars can't be choosers.* "I get off at nine, but I appreciate you swinging by to get me. Say, how about I treat for dessert?"

Blake leaned forward. "A pastry made with extra chocolate, and you've got a deal."

Dee was curling the little packets of hot sauce like small discarded toothpaste containers. She smacked and licked her lips with a pop. "You know, I would take you to work and pick you up if I weren't in the same boat as you. I'm getting excluded here." She stuck her lower lip out. "I want chocolate, too."

"Okay, I'll bring you and Ghost a surprise tomorrow too." I faced Jake. "Is that okay? I won't have time to purchase it before you leave."

"It's cool. My face doesn't need it anyway. Unless you can get your hands on one of those peanut butter dipped pretzels—then I'll take you up on it."

He grabbed a napkin and handed one to Dee.

I noticed, she blushed.

Distracted, I answered him in a far-off tone. "I believe that's doable."

The end of fifth period bell echoed throughout the hallways. I rushed to my sixth period English class… the only subject I enjoyed.

Mr. Flictor was an excellent teacher, and it helped that he saw my English intuition fascinating. He also asked to read some of my poems and stories. The girls used to tease me about him, but I quickly set them straight. *He's older than my father. Eww.* Mr. Flictor resembled a short, skinny Santa. I think I enjoyed English class because it was cheap therapy.

The phone buzzed in my back pocket. Thank goodness, I wasn't in class when it happened because I would have lost the phone to my fifth period U.S. History teacher, Mrs. Cass. She was a stickler for rules. Regardless, I had to give her props because she tried to keep us all interested in what she taught by giving us group projects and personal downtime.

Again, the cell vibrated. Maybe it was my imagination, but the buzz felt more like a bite. Digging into my pocket, I berated myself for not switching the ringer to silent. Dee's stink-eye avatar lit the screen. *What did she want?* To my dismay, she had left five text messages. I stopped by the lockers to read them.

Dee: Hey I need to talk to you.

Dee: What you can't text back? >.< Well, when you get a chance…

Dee: Ah, hello. I have a question for you… Well, a few, anyway. Text me.

Dee: Fine. I'm troll sitting tonight, call me when you can.

Dee: O nvm. I don't know what I'm saying anymore. We'll talk later…

Well, she had gone from normal to baffling within five texts. They were definitely cryptic, and the third and fourth ones had me troubled.

The cell buzzed again. *Like, I'm not in school or anything…*

This time it was Jake. *What? Didn't they have to get to class too?* Irritated, I selected his name.

Jake: I'm leaving right after school. I will text when I'm on my way to pick you up for work. Be ready.

When the Jaws theme started playing, I ran into the girl's bathroom to answer it.

"Dad? Why are you calling me now? I'm in school." I gasped when I realized I must have exhaled before speaking.

"I was going to leave you a message. What are you doing answering it?"

I went into a stall and slammed the door. "Well now, okay." I used a robotic voice, "Ah, hey, you've reached Lex-Cee. Leave your name and a brief message telling me where the fire is, and I'll get back to ya on how to keep it roaring… BEEEEP." I clicked my tongue and waited for a reply. The silence between us was deafening, causing me to feel anxious about the possibility of one of the teachers walking in on my one-sided conversation. *I so didn't need detention added to my schedule.*

"Alexcia, you test my patience."

"That's the message you were going to leave me? Hate to break it to you, Father, but I know. It's a gift."

"My flight was delayed, and I will not be back tonight. There is another matter I have to take care of anyway. Can you please stay put and out of trouble?"

"Right. Got it. Under house arrest and don't scale the walls or try to organize a prison break. Oh, and so you know, I picked up a shift tonight. I need to discuss some things with Mr. Sipton. Is that okay, Father?" I sharply exhaled the last word.

Pulling out my watch, I realized the bell was going to ring in less than a minute. "Dad, I have to get to class. Did you tell Mom, or do you need me to relay the message?" I couldn't help the bitter tone, but I needed to get to class.

"I have already spoken to your mother. She is going to be home after midnight. You may work tonight, but the routine better be to school, to work, then home. Understand, young lady? Are you wearing the rose pendant?"

A low growl, or harsh static, distorted his voice. It chilled me slightly, making me hesitate before I answered. "No, it didn't match my outfit."

Another reverberated snarl made the speaker hiss. "Put it on when you get home."

I must have pushed him too far with my testy attitude. I wasn't used to being under lockdown, and now he was dictating what I could wear. In my *ah-ha* moment, I knew why so many kids rebelled against their parents.

"Yes, I understand."

The line went dead. I turned the phone on silent and rushed out of the bathroom as the tardy bell rang. "Great, now I'm late," I mumbled and then booked it to class.

I met up with Blakely at our locker after sixth period. She was grumpy about having to stop for fuel later. Monday nights at the coffee shop were slow, but I usually made around ten dollars in tips. So, I sweetened our arrangement by offering to add to her gas tank on the way home after work. The testy mood she was in lifted, and we collected what we needed from our locker before heading out.

While we quick-walked to her car, I remembered the weird messages from Dee and thought maybe Blakely might know why she wanted to talk to me.

Blake jumped into the driver's seat, then slid over to

unlock my door. I followed her lead and hopped in. The seats were warm even through my jeans. I tossed my book bag onto the floor and bent over to retrieve my cell.

"Hey, Blake, Dee texted me earlier. Do you know anything about it?"

Blakely shook her head as she slipped the key into the ignition and started the car. "Why? What did she want?" She put the car in reverse and turned her body half around with her tongue pushing her cheek out, concentrating. Backing out of the stall, she squeezed the Lady into the line of eager escapees.

"I don't know. Dee left some messages asking if we could talk. I'm worried. Did I do or say anything wrong during lunch today?" I turned the cell on and frowned. The black-and-silver screen showed *No Messages*, so I slipped it back in the tote.

"I only have fifty minutes to get to work, so I can't stay today. Oh, and don't forget you are buying lunch tomorrow too. If you forget, I'll make sure you have to take the bus to school for a month." She gave me a side glance and pressed the sunglasses up on her nose to make a point.

Trust me; I got it.

"Wow, that's spiteful." I wanted to roll my eyes but thought better of it. "I won't forget. Geez."

Zipping down the street, I got the impression she was going to push me out of the car without stopping. Maybe she was more annoyed at me than I'd thought. I wondered if there was enough time to convince her to slow down long enough for me to tuck and roll.

Blake didn't even look at me. "What are you doing?"

I held my breath. "Uhh, praying for wings."

Blakely sighed. "I'm gonna stop. Alexcia, I swear. I bet the origin of your name means drama queen." She laughed. "Okay, you know what? On second thought, you might have a good idea. I'm gonna slow down to… say, five miles an hour, and you jump when I say go. Okay? Ready…"

My mouth fell open.

She slammed on the brakes, and we lurched forward. I

almost ate the dashboard as the seat belt dug into my shoulder. Her hysterical laughter turned into hiccups.

"Damn, Blake! You almost snapped my neck." I tried to put some anger into my complaint.

She kept chuckling, almost to the point of giggling. "So sorry, Lex-Cee, but you should have seen your face. I had to stop, or we would've crashed."

My heart continued to smack against my rib cage. Trying to save my pride, I grabbed the braided handle of my Loungefly bag and tugged it up on my shoulder. Facing Blakely, I stuck my tongue out and pulled down on my right lower eyelid to mimic what the anime cartoon characters did for disapproval. Then I got out, slammed the door, lifted my hand and waved from side to side like the queen she said I was.

Blakely drove away with her head bobbing from laughter at my own expense.

I hide from the sun
And run from the moon,
Night's dark secrets fade.
Into daytime fears, I roam
Eclipsing my reason to stay,
Or face what is known.
Alexcia—

Dressed in khaki pants and a maroon, V-neck top, with the Sip 'N Chug logo, I struggled to get my wavy mane into a ponytail. "Best I Can" by Art of Dying blared from the Satellite Seven docking system positioned on my dresser so I could hear it in the bathroom. Singing along with the song lifted my spirits some. I was doing the best I could, coping with the secrets I kept locked within. Tod's mom believed I had survived for a reason. I believed fate was cruel. *Why couldn't my life be normal?*

Looking like a hooked fish in the mirror, I applied a thin line of eyeliner around each blue-green eye when Ghost's ringtone startled me. "Say You'll Haunt Me" by Stone Sour was getting to the chorus line by the time I answered.

"Ghost Busters, how may I help you?" My reflection smiled back at me.

"Uhh, I think I have the wrong number." His reply

quivered.

"Are you sure? We specialize in exorcising the dead from your home."

"Oh, well. That doesn't apply to me. I'm above ground and standing outside your door. Oh, and if you banish me, you won't have a ride to work. So get your ectoplasmic backside down here."

"I'll be right there." Placing the eyeliner next to the rose pendant on the counter, two fingers brushed against the chain. The red rose in the middle of the gold-roped pentagon flickered. A familiar burning sensation caused the reflection in front of me to blur. "Ouch!" *Oh no, not now.*

Ghost asked quickly, "What's wrong?"

"I'm fine. I'll be right down." Shaking, I pressed the End button and set the cell on the counter. I closed my eyes and willed them to be mine when I opened them again. *I'm not crazy. I'm not crazy.* The mantra kept repeating in my mind as I opened my eyes. Everything in the room appeared more defined. Then I caught sight of two snake-like eyes staring back. Moss green irises with gold slited pupils tracked my slightest movement. The face smiled in a tight, malevolent pull. My brain fractured trying to convince me it wasn't me.

A whimper escaped.

My head violently shook until the slaps from my ponytail reminded me this wasn't a dream. I tried to hang onto reality with deliberate, slow breaths. Tears brought a stinging sensation and intensified as the figure leaned closer and tapped the glass, then pointed at me. Uncontrollably, my hand rose and tapped the mirror back in the same spot, signifying we were connected. I screamed at the figure, "Stop mimicking me. Go away."

I squeezed both eyes closed and regained my center. Working to control my breathing, I detected the burn had started to subside. When I opened them again, my eyes had returned to their natural blue-green. With a shaky exhale, I spoke to my reflection, "I'm overwhelmed and exhausted. Everything's okay—I'm okay." Chanting the phrase gave me some comfort as I collected the necessities for work. Still needing more reassurance, I opened my mouth to the mirror one last time.

A faint tickle swirled down the side of my neck. Then from behind the cusp of my ear, a voice whispered, "Keep believing in your lie, Alexcia."

Goosebumps rose where the words had touched, causing the tiny hairs on my neck to stand statically. Either, I *did* have voices in my head, or there was an unbodied whisper right next to me.

I froze.

The low-battery warning on my cell pinged twice, and the sound snapped me out of my fear-induced trance. Last thing I grabbed was the necklace, shoving it into my apron. Bolting from the bathroom, the soles of my shoes chirped as I left tread marks on the linoleum. While fleeing the unexplainable, I didn't even take the time to shut the bedroom door but scissored my legs over a sleeping Gigi and skipped every other stair.

Luckily for me, Ghost was standing in the open doorway. Never losing momentum, I crashed into his solid frame, almost knocking us down the front porch steps. The wrist cast made a thud against his chest, but Jake's arms protectively snaked, above my waist. He smelled of men's Speed Stick, mint mouthwash, and sunlight. I breathed in the pleasant aroma to calm my nerves as Ghost angled me against his left side. His chest vibrated from snickering.

"We gotta go." Jake read my expression, and I could tell from his that he picked up on my distress. His piercing emerald eyes became inquisitive. "Alexcia, what's wrong?" He peered back into the front hallway.

"Nothing," I mumbled into his shirt. The word held extra meaning for me. I was using it to convince myself more than him. "We're going to be late."

I pushed out of his arms. My ponytail bobbed as I rushed toward his car. Clutching the apron against my stomach, I stopped two feet from the curb and turned back to gaze at him.

"Um, aren't you gonna lock up," he asked, gesturing to the door.

I held in a terse response. Careful not to touch the gold-roped polygon, the rose garnet, or the chain. I dug into my apron pocket for the silver *A* key ring, tossed it, and motioned toward the house, so he understood I wanted him to do it.

Baffled at my reaction, Ghost closed the door, locked it, checked the knob, and jumped the stairs before taking eight giant steps to stop in front of me. He dangled the keys before dropping them into my trembling hand.

My friend cupped his hand over mine. "Alexcia, what are you afraid of?"

Jake's expression reminded me of the night we had hashed out our issues after Tod's funeral. His stance indicated we weren't leaving without an explanation, but I tucked the keys into my apron and nodded toward the car. I wanted to answer him, but it was hard to admit, what I feared the most... *was me.*

Guilt ate away at my heart as Ghost left me standing in front of the Sip 'N Chug. We had driven there in complete silence because I had refused to answer his questions and spent most of the drive reapplying my makeup. He believed I should open up on blind faith and trust him to understand. But I knew trust was a two-way street, and my side was under construction, which was why I didn't offer glossed over excuses.

At least my boss, Mr. Sipton, worked with me on scheduling. He canceled my shifts for the rest of the school week, so I compromised by agreeing to work the night shifts from Friday through Sunday. Tonight, Belinda flapped on about Movie Monday Date Night with some guy named Kix. So when I offered to close for her... *well, let's say I made the temporary tolerable list.* And since I had to wait for Blakely, Mr. Sipton approved the schedule change so I could close with Mindy.

Monday nights were usually sluggish, so we were able to convince Belinda to leave around seven thirty, thank goodness. Without any customers in the Sip 'N Chug, boredom sent Mindy to the back for restocking supplies. The atmosphere convinced me to glove up and scrape off the multi-colored deposits of DNA from under the tabletops. The job only killed ten minutes, and that was depressing. The sun had dipped below the horizon hours earlier, and during the week we didn't get much business after seven o'clock. I took advantage of the quiet and used the time to put my life into perspective.

Pictures in my mind's eye clicked like a viewfinder. A double-layered chocolate cake with fifteen candles flickering, my mother handing me a white velvet box, my father holding the rose necklace in front of me before clasping it around my neck. A flash of the demon that landed on Tod's truck the night of the accident made me slam on my brakes. Everything had happened so fast I could only recall its eyes. Two bright indigo slits stared into my soul.

The recall knocked the air from my lungs, briefly scattering the memories away. Soon another came back into focus—Tod's casket being lowered into the ground. Before I could react, the vision shifted to the night with Ghost at the coffee shop by my house. My feelings for Jake were on the verge of changing, even though I knew it wouldn't work out between us. He was more like a brother than a—I dropped my head into my hands.

Wrapping my thoughts around the past five weeks seemed oppressing. Since the accident, the nightmares had become intense. Except for what had happened in my bathroom, the night terrors remained within the realm of restless sleep.

When had my life become so terrifyingly unpredictable? I tried to rationalize the situation by telling myself everything was due to rampant hormones and broken slumber. Once again, my reasoning brought me back to the dysfunctional mind issues. I'd heard a comedian once say, "How would crazy people know they're crazy?" Maybe, I really was short a few sandwiches and needed to swallow my pride, accept what had happened, and discuss it with Mom. No, emailing her might be better than watching her face fall as I rationalized everything.

As I pondered this delightful conclusion, the glass door swung open, causing the cluster of bells on the handle to make a hollow, metal *chink-chink*. Two large men and one willowy woman approached the counter while scanning the room.

I finished up the table I was cleaning, grabbed the used napkins, tossed them into the trash can, screwed on my customer smile, and added some saccharine to my greeting. "Hello. Welcome to the Sip 'N Chug. I'll be right with you." I opened the countertop gate, then closed it from the other side. The hinge snapped, and out of habit, I locked it and called for my coworker. "Mindy, we have customers." Placing myself behind the register, the forced, tight-lipped smile began to hurt.

A huff escaped while waiting for the barista to take her place beside me, but after a moment, Mindy came out with a big smile on her face. Hers was genuine and too cheerful, but at least the girl could blend.

Her straight, blond ponytail swayed as she took her place next to me and adjusted the red lace bow. "Okay, I'm ready. Hit me." Mindy's spunky attitude reminded me of Dee, only not as aggressive. Her enthusiasm was contagious.

The short, stocky man's skin resembled sunbaked leather. I tried not to stare. Leaning against the counter, over the pastries, I took in his attire. Covered from head to boots in dust, it was as if a drum of cement powder had fallen on him. Even his work boots were coated in chalk-gray.

My nose crinkled when I remembered the bathrooms had already been cleaned. Secretly, I willed him not to go in there.

The guy smirked at me, placing his hands on the glass

counter.

I whined in silent protest. *Crud, I just cleaned that.*

The woman seemed confused at the menu and tapped her bright, neon-pink nails on her full matching lips. She turned to the man next to her and whispered into his ear. When she was done, they locked eyes as he smiled down at her. The guy brushed her butt-length, jet-black hair to the side, to place a kiss on her perfect ivory neck and that's when I noticed the strands underneath were snow-white.

Her black, skin-tight shirt had speckled paint patterns of neon all over the front of it, and the black leather skinny pants hugged her curves in all the right spots. My smile faded from jealousy.

The guy next to her was dressed like Neo from the Matrix movie, minus the sunglasses. His dark goatee stood out against the paleness of his skin. He must have used a ton of gel. If the guy was Emo, he didn't need to use eyeliner because the shadowy circles under his eyes already made them appear haunting.

The man standing by the desserts reminded me of a Peanuts cartoon character, but an older version. Reluctantly, I realized I would have to mop before closing.

To get their attention, I calmly made a soft, back throat cough. Mr. Pig-Pen stared at me with dry, dull brown eyes. As the other two approached, I got an odd sensation from the three of them. They were so different, and yet the same.

I held my hand up to the register. "What can we make for you this evening?"

Mr. Pig-Pen licked his chapped lips before using the back of his hand to wipe under his chin. Then he pointed to a double-chocolate brownie in the pastry display. "I would like that and a cup of the strongest coffee you can legally serve." His voice sounded like a mix of gravel and water.

My eyes started tearing from the odor rolling off him. His cologne must have been sitting for too long because the grungy aroma was potent, as though he had rolled in mothballs and attic dust. *Holy musty mothballs, Batman, please introduce him to soap and water.*

"Okay, one Muddy Chunk and an extra Chewy Joey. What would—"

Mr. Pig-Pen cut me off and whipped around to the couple. "Hey, that's mud? Check it out, Abyss, Moment, they serve our kind." Holding his face about three inches from the glass case, he left mouth-sized heat rings for me to clean again later too.

I couldn't help but notice the exchange of emotions between the other two. Appalled by their friend's outburst, the Emo guy leaned over and smacked Mr. Pig-Pen on the back of his head. The woman's eyelids drooped, making the whites of her eyes appear vacant.

She hissed a reprimand, "Shut it, Gutter." Replacing her gaze on me, an overconfident smirk appeared. With two long-legged sashays, she was at the counter.

As she placed her hands on her hips, I thought about how they had addressed one another. Those were some pretty unusual names.

"Sorry about him. He doesn't get out much." Her voice was beautiful. It trickled softly, reminding me of a lazy stream but with a hint of sultry, to make it sexy. Boy, it ticked me off, though, how some got all the luck.

Keep smiling. While remaining professional, I asked through clenched teeth, "So, what can I start for you?"

"I think something light that won't slow me down and won't keep me up, either. What do you recommend?" She winked.

I was awestruck by her eyes. She must have been wearing contacts because the color of them was almost ice-white with the faintest tinge of cobalt on the outer circumference of both irises, and her pupils were shaped like hourglasses. One of the freakiest things I'd ever seen. Then it hit me; they must be cosplayers.

Focusing on her eyes began to make mine hurt. The pain grew and took root behind my eye sockets. *That's all I needed right now was one of my headaches.* Mindy brushed my arm, pulling me back from my Coffee House Twilight Zone.

What the hell?

Then I remembered the woman's request… it didn't make any sense. "Excuse me? If what you're looking for is not on the board, Mindy and I can try to make a specialty drink for you." I tried really hard to sound sincere. Side glancing at the large, mug-shaped clock on the wall, I noticed it was after eight thirty. We were closing in less than a half an hour. All those procedures, along with having to clean up again would take at least forty-five minutes. Blakely was coming right after ten to pick me up, and if I weren't ready, depending on her mood, I could end up walking home.

"Oh well. I'll take a Creamy White Spider. Can you put four shots of espresso in that for me, Child?" She hung too long on the last word.

My jaw tensed, and an intense throb started at the base of my skull. *Did she call me Child?*

"And for you, Sir?" I tried to make eye contact with him, but he dismissed me with a wave while grabbing the woman around her small waist.

"No, nothing for me," he replied matter-of-factly. Then he whispered harshly in the woman's ear.

I turned to my perky coworker. "Okay, Mindy, start blending."

The room fell into an awkward hush. Their faces morphed between anguish and disbelief. The two wearing black had their palms out, facing me.

I put my hand on Mindy's shoulder to signal her to stop making the drinks. She looked concerned and then scanned back and forth between the Walking Dead groupies and me.

In a terse employee to customer tone, I said, "The total comes to $10.97. Will that be cash, debit, or charge?"

Their arms fell silently to their sides. The guy dug into his front pocket and gave a wad of paper to the woman. It looked like money, so I tapped Mindy to finish making the drinks.

After handing them their coffees, I retrieved Mr. Pig-

Pen's chocolate-iced brownie and wrapped it with extra napkins for a hint to wipe his hands before eating. I placed everything into one of Sip 'N Chug's recyclable bags, tossed in some wet towelettes, and rolled up the corners as I handed it to him. With a smile, I walked back to the register.

The woman held out a fifty-dollar bill to me and winked. "Keep the change and take my advice. Time waits for no one, or, in this case, a clueless child."

Internally, I questioned, *did she just threaten me?* Dismissing the thought, I tried to convince myself and answer no, but the voice I'd heard in my bathroom earlier said, "Yes."

She took a long, graceful sip and shuddered, yelling across the room, "Abyss! Next time, remind me to order it with six espresso shots. It's pretty weak." Then in a mocking tone, she added, "But I did ask that it not be strong enough to keep me up, right?" Her laughter filled the room as she turned to head out the door.

Watching them depart, I heard the cluster of bells jingle. The entire scene left a haunting echo. I couldn't help the unnerving sense of dread the bells gave me, as a warning of some kind. When the door closed, my headache began to subside.

Mindy exhaled like she had been holding her breath too, and the inside of my nose burned from a peculiar stench. It was close to a musty, rotting-earth scent mixed with a hint of wet dog. I held back the urge to light some scented candles around the Talk 'N Chat Room.

A crinkling between my fingers reminded me I needed to finish the transaction. We both stared in complete astonishment. They had given us a $39.03 tip, but I was more taken aback by the strange woman's snide remark.

Recounting the change, I thought, *Well, staying late paid off. At least I have funds for gas and lunch tomorrow.* I shot a quick smile at Mindy as she giggled and started cleaning up her area.

I was closing the cash register when I heard Mr. Pig-Pen raise his voice from outside.

"Ugh, this tastes like crap. It doesn't even smell like mud, what a rip-off."

We watched him spit toward the curb, crumple up the bag, and punch it into the trash dispenser.

Chapter Four

Tevin's side: Through the eyes of a Reaper

*T*he evening air was crisp with anxiety and lightly sweetened with chaos… a daemon's delight. Storms like this one normally brought out the best in Vessels. Off in the distance, we could hear the sounds of car horns blaring, brakes locking, and tires skidding. It was similar to a dinner bell to us.

The other clans would be busy tonight.

With eyes closed, I used the storm to heal the wounds my pride had allowed. Alexcia's father had returned my call, but it had not gone as planned. I had wanted to discuss our Bond agreement, but Max had other intentions.

The Doom Guard had done everything except physically rip me a new one. First by grinding out, "Thank you for informing me about my daughter," but then the heat in his words had intensified through the receiver until I was roasting over judgmental flames. What angered Max the most was the fact that Alexcia had seen my daemonic form when I pulled her from the truck in the seconds before it had crashed, taking the lives of her classmates and the truck driver that hit them.

Max explained, once he had placed Alexcia under a foretold spell, she had disclosed how a daemon had saved her.

Oh, crap, she thought I was there to save her. But how would she have known? The question hooked on the corner of my mouth and then twitched, but I applied the brakes before the reaction could give the Doom Guard another reason to find fault in me. The abrupt halt threw me back into the one-sided conversation.

Max continued to complain, "Alexcia believes she caused the accident and the daemon was answering her plea for help. How is it she can see all of you in the first place?"

That was an excellent question. The Unseen world was a mirrored realm between time and space. Alexcia should not have been able to see us. This was a new dilemma.

Then, he added, "What? Are all of you swooping in and saying, 'Hi Alexcia, we're going to save your ass today.'? Change your game, Tevin. I don't want to hear any more stories about winged daemons becoming my daughter's white knights. I expect more from our Bond-Rite than half-ass protecting with second-rate special effects. Rectify this situation, Daemon Scat." He bellowed.

Damn, did he have to keep calling me that?

The Doom Guard had done everything but come through the cell. I was sure he would have crossed over into the Unseen if no one were around to see him make a portal. Sometimes, a crowd of Vessels could really save an entity's existence.

After Michael and I broke down the specifics to the rest of the pack, that the Bond-Rite with Max would free us in less than a month, they were more than willing to help out tonight. Max had filled me in on his brilliant plan to keep tabs on Alexcia by restricting her to home, school, and work. A slight twinge of guilt made me wince. I was the reason she was being punished. But in my opinion, the girl had brought it upon herself. At least Rae-Lynn and Max Stasis were working with us to keep their daughter alive long enough to choose one of the three Houses to serve.

During our conversation, between screaming and cursing, the Doom Guard had informed me she was working this evening. Max had inside knowledge that the elementals were organizing another attempt to get closer, possibly, within the next few days.

I sent Quint to get in touch with another Ashen clan to take on our soul quotas for this evening. They agreed, but in turn, we had to repay their favor with an IOU in the future. I agreed as long as the payment did not involve the Child-of-Balance in any way, shape, or form.

We did not have the luxury of depending on other daemons, especially another clan of reapers. They were a part of the House of Space, and in time, I was sure they would either persuade her to join our house or kill her in the process.

My train of thought derailed when I heard voices coming from directly below me. Perched on the roof of the Sip 'N Chug, I angled myself to observe the situation better. The ensuing shock sucked the air out of my chest like a backdraft. Stupefied, I watched three elementals enter her place of business.

I waved at Archer in anger. He was shouldering Wink. *And here I had figured four eyes were better than two…*

Grabbing his attention, I gestured to the closing door. Archer was in the perfect position to snipe if the situation got out of hand.

In my head, I heard him scold me. *"Giving the enemy time for a coffee break, Tevin?"*

I answered back, *"Scythe me."*

Imp appeared on my right side and placed a hand on my shoulder. "Tevin, didn't you smell them? They brought along a Sculptor, for soul's sake. Why did you take point if you're going to zone out?" With a gritty laugh, he added, "I see why Max chewed your ass out. You make a lousy guardian." He leaned over the edge of the roof to get a better view. "Too bad they're close enough to hear us."

It was true; we had lost the element of surprise since the group of Unseen were in range to tap into our internal conversation. Imp was sharpening my anger in the wrong direction by stating the obvious. "I was not zoning out. I thought Archer was at least going to warn us if he spotted anything out of the ordinary. All of you need to stop stepping on my cloak." The black-and-indigo-tinted mist had stopped moving, probably because it detected my hostility. I stomped away from where Imp was hanging over the roof.

A heavy sensation in my gut powered my outburst. "Five hundred, and ninety-plus years of harvesting Vessels with the Knell's Toll or a mere swing of a blade. Our kind, feared by most, and challenged by few, being reduced to nothing more than a Hellhound with a choker around my neck is unrespectable. For ten years… ten years," I hollered. "Hell, she's walking and talking. That should account for something. I'm doing a damn good job of playing guardian angel." I did not understand why I had to justify myself while I paced. "Anyway, I was going over certain strategies in case of an attack. I did not think they were going to make a move in front of other Vessels. Besides, it's pretty early in the day for them to come out of hiding."

Placing a hand over both eyes, I worked to soothe the frustration my lame excuses were causing. Shifting from guilt to anger was becoming harder. It coated me like tar, but thanks to Rae-Lynn and Alexcia pushing me into a vat of it, I was becoming used to the emotion.

"Whoa, slow down, bro. You think elementals care about working hours?" He rolled over until one arm propped him up so he could face me. "They probably have been casing the place for weeks, maybe even months. What better way for them to get close to their prey than by checking out what kind of power she has if any?" Shaking his head, Imp rolled back to get a better view, placing his hands underneath his stomach for balance. He made a condescending sucking with his tongue. "I believe you've been working too much during the day. Their morning star has fried your brains through your cloak. You know, those are probably the ones adding power to the storm. I'm sure their partners are out here watching us, too." His minion's purple aura tint dimmed as he leaned over farther and angled his head.

Imp was right about all of it. It caused an itch on the back of my leg, and I wanted to kick him off the roof.

He chuckled. "Maybe we can thank them for the weather over a cup of caffeine?"

My free hand grabbed the back of his cloak. He was clueless as I watched his aura swirl in angry, violet threads weaving in between the indigo of mine. With a harsh cough, I gave Imp fair warning before yanking him to an upright position. With jaw muscles tensing, I spoke in a calm, commanding tone. "You want to see what is going on so badly? Then go down there."

The Ashen was annoyed and craned his neck to peer at the front door. "But, won't my presence put us at a disadvantage? It will confirm we're watching the Child."

"Like you said before, they probably detected our presence, but for all they know, we're here for recruiting purposes." To get my point across, I added, "If you go down there, you can keep an eye on the Vessel and tell us what is happening." I loosened my grip on his minion and pointed toward the coffee shop. "Right?"

Imp's cloak made a pair of black-rimmed Ray-Ban sunglasses appear and slipped them over his eyes. He gave me a mock salute and spoke like Jack Nicholson. "Okay, boss man. Will do."

Losing control of my previous desire, I shoved him off the building. With smug satisfaction, I watched his reaction. Black-and-violet mist webbed out, frantically trying to grab hold of anything to break their fall. Imp's minion disappeared in a puff right before the... *thump*.

With pride chafed, Imp fixed his sunglasses, flashed me the middle finger, and snapped a return command for his minion. When the cloak reformed, its normal color had changed to a deep-space black with the edges tipped in a pulsing outline of amethyst. The colors along the edges of his shroud marbled as they draped over his head and plummeted to the ground. It clearly was agitated as well.

Hollow laughter coming from the clan crashed in demeaning waves against my cranium. I was not sure what the reapers believed was funnier, Imp falling or my lack of focus on the job. I concentrated on the sulking Ashen as he shifted into the shadows and glided through the glass by the main door.

Imp recapped the scene like a movie trailer, probably to provoke the Elementals. *"As the Vessel addresses the new customer by the counter, the other two by the menu board quietly plot her demise."* He chuckled. *"She reminds me of the cow being lowered into a pack of wild raptors as they wait for their prey to show a sign of weakness."*

I swore under my breath. Archer laughed. Quint and K chuckled and smacked knuckles. Raven growled, apparently not amused.

Michael reprimanded Imp. *"That's it, no more late-night movie reruns. Now, stick to the facts."*

"I'm impressed." Imp's tone had a hint of admiration.

"Okay, I'll bite." My stomach grumbled.

"The Vessel has no fear." After his statement, he released a low whistle, and the tone echoed within our heads. *"One thing I've got to say about this creature, whether she realizes it or not, she's got guts."*

"Yeah, she only appears brave. If she knew her true identity and what they wanted, this confrontation would play out entirely different."

Not wanting him to miss anything vital, I asked, *"So, what are they doing now?"*

"Oh, maggot piss."

"What?" I demanded.

"The tension in the room is rising." He added, *"Alexcia is talking to the female next to her. The Matrix twins have raised their hands at her defensively. Damn, Tevin, what do I do?"* Imp's question implied he was going to make a move before I could respond.

I was about to say, *"Move in front of the Vessels,"* when Imp's chuckle echoed between both ears.

Confused, I asked, *"Well?"*

"You're not going to believe this, Ashens. Alexcia spooked the elementals. That was entertaining."

My cloak relaxed, detecting the imminent danger had passed. I bent down and sat on the back of my calves while massaging the areas where a headache threatened.

The thought of vacation options popped into my head,

and I wondered if there was a time-off clause in my contract. After a decade of child sitting, I was seriously underpaid. A rhetorical question peaked on a wave of thought as I asked myself, *"Can Death take a holiday?"* My minion answered with a shrug.

Pressing my temples harder, I rubbed in small circles and asked Imp another question. *"So, what are they doing now?"*

"Nothing. It looks like the elementals are actually ordering."

I clicked my tongue. *"Are you serious?"* My stomach knotted. I needed sustenance soon, or so help me, I was going to scythe Imp if he kept screwing around.

As if on cue, he cleared his mind and started projecting images into ours. It drained an Ashen to use Glimpse, so it must have been Intel he felt we needed without the elementals hearing. The entity with the primary connection linked to the Glimpse was affected the most during projection. Imp must have thought Alexcia was not in harm's way at the moment because by draining his energy, if the others attacked, he would be at a disadvantage to defend her properly.

I watched quick flashes of images—the main room with tables and chairs, a huge, iron mug wall clock, two counters, three Time Elementals, and, of course, the Vessels behind the register.

Alexcia touched the Vessel next to her, and she stopped working. Making a quarter turn, I watched her address the group. The male with the dark beard appeared mystified. Imp redirected his stare and burned the images of the elementals into our inner sight.

The moment the female turned, I growled. *"What is she doing on their front lines?"*

The female Wind Evoker practically slinked over to the male Water Raiser, leaned in to whisper in his ear. She turned to face Imp, instantly winking at him. *Yeah, they knew.* The male elemental seemed agitated and responded, his irritation evident. He pulled a crumpled piece of paper out and handed it to *her*. Then the Evoker turned back to Alexcia and sauntered to the counter. We had been made, but hopefully, I could twist this mishap in our favor.

I rose to reclaim my scythe as we mentally watched them leave. With their fake façade blown, the elementals exited the coffee shop. The metal jingle from the cluster of bells sent a vibration of dread through the air.

The Sculptor's face scrunched in disgust before he punched a wadded bag into the trash. The Wind Evoker flipped her hair back and whispered a magical cast—or spin, as us Spindlers called them—into the wind.

Some of the Unseen, including me, had the talent to cast. This spin was a time-shudder displacement, which temporarily meshed the Unseen to this realm and weakened the Spindler, but she was obviously confident we wouldn't make a move.

This Wind Evoker usually worked as an Unseen bounty hunter and was blazing her way up the ranks. She was essential to the House of Time, even though she preferred to work alone. Not playing well with others was her weakness. And exploiting that was how we were going to protect Alexcia. Tonight, was going to be a race to see which House would lay claim on the Child-of-Balance first.

I needed to wait for her magic to dissipate before conveying my new strategy to the clan. Since they could hear our thoughts, I wasn't going to risk internally exposing my plan.

The Smolder within me growled as my jaw muscles threatened to break from the daemon trying to shift us. Grumbling within, I said, *"Get ready, they came to play dirty."*

Right then, the Wind Evoker, called Moment, took on a predacious mien. With a wicked smirk, she challenged, "Let the games begin."

Chapter Five

My heart has often felt, what if...
My conscience has often questioned, What if...?
My mouth has often whispered, "What if...?"
But, I never thought Death would ask me,
"What if...?"
Alexcia—

*F*or the twentieth time, I checked the neon marque across the street. It flashed 10:28 p.m. and there was no sign of Blakely. My cell was dead because I had forgotten to charge it after I clocked in.

Mindy's mom had asked me if I'd wanted her to wait until my ride arrived, but I reassured her I'd be fine. Blakely was probably late getting off work or stuck in traffic. I should have kept my big trap shut and climbed into their warm car.

The wind carried along with it the scent of rain.

Sitting on the curb in front of the shop, I got chills every time another gust of wind snaked around the building. The outside lights flickered, and the dread I had felt earlier came back tenfold. I envisioned the parking lot plunged into darkness. Straightaway, a prick of panic stabbed into every limb.

I watched the cars travel up and down Lake Mead, but after ten o'clock the side streets by the shop had little traffic.

Every time a set of headlights turned onto Crestal Way, I cashed in a birthday wish, hoping for them to be the Lady's.

Birthday wish number twenty-six seemed to slow down. My hope rose, but then it sank just as fast. The purple Camaro swerved into a turn lane, taking another of my wishes with it.

I wrapped the apron ties around my waist and stuck cold hands into the pockets. Nervously, I kept licking my lips, but the air instantly pulled the moisture from them. The situation was making me miserable and realized I needed to buy a ChapStick tube to keep in my apron.

With a sigh, I pulled out the dead cell phone from the apron pocket, using it as a touchstone to steady my anxiety. *Geez, why didn't I remember to charge the darn thing?* To distract myself, I tried to pick out constellations in between the rain clouds.

The temperature dropped, again.

Damn, where was Blake?

I tried to turn the cell on again. Black screen. I slipped the useless phone into the back pocket of my pants.

With an unsure exhale, I rechecked the time. The neon displayed 10:42 p.m. My overactive imagination added to my pessimistic nature as it warped different scenarios, *What if Blakely had been pulled over for speeding? Or had gotten a flat? Or worse, what if she'd been in an accident?*

My good hand flew up to my mouth as my breath caught. That would explain why she wasn't here. *Maybe I should start walking home? Then I could call her before I took a shower, to see if she was okay.*

The weather was shifting from annoyance to uncomfortable, making the idea of walking home the better alternative. If Blake pulled into the parking lot and noticed I wasn't here, I was confident she would drive my route to check on me. With my mind made up, I braced myself to stand, dusted the back of my pants off, and straightened. *I didn't want the oncoming cars spotlighting one of my best features tarnished.*

I was twenty feet from the parking lot when dark spots

appeared on the sidewalk. Water fell in small drops, but as the breeze intensified the rain began to sting the back of both arms. I cursed under my breath, cradling the cast against my chest so it wouldn't get soaked. A gust of wind whipped my ponytail against my neck. Now, I was irritated.

Oh my goshness, if Blakely isn't fixing a flat in the rain...

The streetlight above me creaked, stirring my curiosity to find the cause. Through drop-soaked lashes, I thought I saw movement on top of the fixture. *Could it be a big bird?* I blinked several times, trying to focus. To my shock, the figure morphed into a human shape.

Alarmed, I sensed a presence behind me, and then a husky voice said, "Run."

I didn't even question the command; I took off like a bat out of Hell. The balls of each foot barely touched the sidewalk as I tried to maintain traction on the slick cement. Water-laden clothes hindered my stride. Distress helped me move faster. I never could remember the street names, so I counted the light poles and burned the surroundings to memory. Every two lights meant one full block. Our house was about eleven blocks away.

Rounding the first corner, I got ready to take a right on the next block when a silver trashcan fell right in front of me. Screaming, I tripped over my feet. I scrambled to stay upright and almost fell, but something caught my waist and pushed me forward. I glanced back and saw no one before picking up the pace. Shock and fear pumped blood into my ears, and the heightened heart rate drove my stride faster.

After passing the third light, I saw shadows merging, changing shapes into a more humanlike figure. I gulped air to help my muscles work harder. I never even got this much of a workout in P.E. Running in a small cage or swinging a racket was the only physical activity I'd had for the last two years. I needed to speak with Rae-Lynn about joining a gym.

Making the fourth light, I heard a faint pop before the whole street went dark. *Crap!* I knew I had at least another nine blocks before I was home. Ahead of me, glass shattered.

Twinkling shards showered over me, giving the rain an extra bite. I screamed again, and my head throbbed. I was not even at the end of the block when a trickle of warm liquid dripped down my skin.

One more ragged breath and I heard the windows from another car break. My feet pounded the wet sidewalk, making soggy crunches against the cement. The rain and wind beat harder against my body, almost knocking me on my ass.

Light flashed all around me. *Wonderful, the storm included lightning, too.* The thunderclap released its anger directly overhead, and I crouched from the unexpected force. Dogs in the neighborhood spontaneously howled and barked. A wood fence across the road splintered as if a giant had collided with it, sending debris into the air to rain down over the nearby yard and street.

My mouth unhinged to scream but froze when a smear of red brushed my side. The little hairs on both arms statically rose as though the area around me became charged with high voltage. Fingers pressed into my side. Startled, I glanced at the spot and panicked when I saw nothing there. The phantom presence shoved me against a concrete wall.

Checking my arm, I examined the torn fabric then inspected the blood trickling from the gash. "Great, can this night get any worse?"

Shifting my attention away from the wound, I noticed the green street sign for Tenaya Way was lit up by streetlight number five. *Tenaya Way?* I had been running down the wrong street. Home was in the opposite direction. Frantically, I searched my inner GPS and took an assessment of the location.

Another flash of lightning struck nearby, burying the panic needle in my brain. A crash of the aftermath lumbered overhead. I crouched to the ground and cried. My body quivered from the overload of one emotion after another, which set off an electrical chain reaction of my own. Throbbing pain crashed like cymbals in my skull, causing both eye sockets to burn. I couldn't tell if it was from exhaustion or soaked frustration.

Another earth-trembling crack from overhead and I was positive pieces of the sky were going to start falling. One monstrous gust smacked into me from the left, rolling me into a front yard. My jaw felt as though a foot or hand had connected with it, leaving a warm, metallic taste pooling under my tongue. Spitting the blood into a growing patch of water, I dug my nails into the saturated turf.

The rims of my eyes stung, causing another wave of pain. I wanted to claw my own eyes out. More tears ran down my already rain-soaked cheeks, and a scream escaped from the bottom of my lungs, mixing with the storm's fury.

Right then, an invisible force struck me from behind, and gravity did the rest. Phantom fingers grabbed my ponytail, and another gust of wind shoved my face into the puddle beside me. Bracing my shoulders, I shoved back, spitting out mud and grass.

When my vision sharpened momentarily, I caught sight of a shadow darting out from under a parked car in the driveway. Another figure crept from over the fence and slithered toward the house. My terror fled as the shadows settled around me, and reignited a will to fight.

I dropped both arms and somersaulted as a shadow flew over. The force caused me to tumble down the slope of the yard. I was on the sidewalk again. Immediately, I was compelled to whisper, "Thank you," into the darkness.

Within seconds, I was on my feet, hugging the cast to my chest as I ran. Lightning broke the sky into a thousand fissures. After the roll of thunder, frozen anger fell from the sky in the form of biting hail. It bounced and pattered but never touched me as I remained under the mysterious shadow's protection. Strangely enough, I felt safe.

When I reached lights six and seven, I recognized the trees hanging over the blurred iron fencing to the right. Unknowingly, my feet had brought me to Pine Clover Apartments, where Dee lived with her mom and twin siblings, Calvin and Bailey.

The eighth light illuminated the intersection of Smoke

Ranch and Tenaya. I was going to be out in the open, crossing under the streetlights. Reminiscent of Bambi heading out into the meadow exposing himself to the hunters, I shivered. *Why did that metaphor seem so real?*

The rain had stopped, but the air was thick with humidity, causing me to gasp every time I sucked in a breath. Shadows dissipated, but I replaced their absence with panic. I blinked back tears then used my fingers to press the extra water away from my eyes. The shadowy mist was gone, followed by the cold touch of abandonment.

Soaked, muddy, bloody, and spent, I started making a list of things I wanted. A towel, a warm bed, and my dad were first on my agenda. *Why I wanted him was a mystery, but I did.*

Then I heard a male voice break through my internal wall. "Move it, Alexcia!"

An overpowering sound blast made me lose my footing, and I spread out both hands, grabbing a nearby tree to remain upright. With no further notice, a large limb above me splintered. The weight caused it to break loose from the trunk, and another crack of wood protesting followed. Self-preservation made me spring toward the intersection. Whipping my head around, I discovered half of the tree had fallen where I'd once stood. Several shaky inhales helped me combat the panic trying to shut my body down.

All of a sudden, my legs were heading toward the ninth streetlight on the other side of the road when I landed in a bank of frigid, black smoke. An unseen force was holding the back of my shirt, suspending me mere inches from where my face would have surely connected with the sidewalk. Then, whatever had saved me used the momentum to toss my body across the slick concrete. A massive gust of wind slammed into the iron side gate, swinging it open with such force the jarring clang rattled my teeth.

I barely made it through as another gust swept me in the opposite direction. The gate slammed again and latched. My mouth hung open, catching drops of rain as I shook from disbelief. If this didn't stop soon, I might have a breakdown from the night's events. An echo of a terse command was followed by a sharp jab, a crunching noise, and a pinch to my right butt cheek. Not wanting to stick around for clarification, I took off toward Dee's building.

The parking lot strobed and I wished the storm would die. Before I had a chance to regain clear vision after the flash, the rumble that followed issued its own threatening undertone. I ran to the apartment. The carport buckled in on itself and sent me into a cursing frenzy. Debris swirled in the air, banging me against the entrance. I cried out, but this time it was a command to open the damn door. A second gust smashed me into the white faux wood.

Finally, Dee opened the door. Barely catching a glimpse of her face, we fell in a tangled heap to the floor. Some of the shadows pushed us beyond the threshold. If I hadn't been there, I would never have believed an air current, other than a tornado, could have tossed us three feet farther into the hallway.

I gasped, trying to catch my breath and untangle myself from my friend when I realized the precarious position we were in. Her eyes seemed almost too big for her face, and she moaned when touching the back of her head.

My own injuries caused me to wince as I rubbed my backside. The tips of my fingers brushed against a jagged piece of plastic that had ripped through the back pocket. I dug my right hand into the partially torn material and grimaced.

Dee blinked slowly. "Alexcia?"

Her tone flipped my rambling switch. "Hey, I know it's late, but you asked if we could talk. Then as I was walking home, I thought, 'Why not now?' You know, since I was working tonight." While removing my drenched locks so I could see her face, I dripped dirty rainwater across her pajamas. She *ughed* in protest as I rocked away from her.

"A phone call would have worked too." She crab-crawled away with a disheartened exhale and made a sour face at her mud-stained pajamas.

I nibbled on my lower lip and pulled broken bits of the cell phone from the damaged back pocket. Extending the pieces out to her like a peace offering, I sheepishly stated, "I would've if I hadn't landed on it."

Chapter Six

Tevin's side: Through the eyes of a Reaper

*W*e all took scouting positions around the coffee shop. The Water Raisers were setting up the battlefield by energizing the storm, and I sensed they were nearby, but I knew the child was safe for now.

I could taste a light mix of uncertainty and distress coming from the girl, and although it was a tantalizing combination, it made me shudder under my cloak. Licking my lips, I turned to face Quint and K. They were perched on top of the Quick Mart, waiting for my command to move in. I took a deep, cleansing breath to expel Alexcia's emotional scent so I could focus.

She stood there, forlorn, as a purple Camaro charged up the street and turned. Alexcia pulled out a shiny rectangle, fiddled with it, and then slipped it into her back pocket. After she had sat down, I watched her pick nervously at the cast. It appeared uncomfortable, and I had an impulse to scratch my arm along with her.

This night was going to be a slice of angel cake if she stayed put. No Unseen would risk exposing our existence, so I relaxed, mentally taking this opportunity to check in with everyone else. I kept her in view as I crouched and spoke internally with my clan.

"Quint, K, anything from your end?"

Quint was messing with his cell and looking intensely at the little rectangle.

K's head swayed when he replied, *"I smell a lot of Raisers, but the storm could also be throwing off their scent."*

Raven added his opinion, stating there were at least two, maybe three, Evokers nearby. *"No signs of a Sculptor or Wind Evokers either. But it would be hard for a Sculptor to move pavement without the Vessels noticing."*

I watched the churning clouds, remembering the night I had saved Alexcia from the eighteen-wheeler. *"True, but they normally will have one or two tucked away as added muscle. Remember, our power with them is matched unless we shift into our battle forms. The Sculptor will be the hardest target to take down. Dirt weighs a ton and takes forever to remove the grit and taste. Trust me, I know from experience."*

K darted in with a reply. *"Well, our battle form shouldn't be a problem if—"*

"No. If Alexcia sees us in battle form, Max will use our cloaks to wipe his own ass." My minion started to dissipate from the colorful example. I wanted to keep that side of our power dormant, especially since her father had given strict instructions for us not to shift. For added measure, I provided a warning to my previous order. *"So, contain your Smolders during battle. We can protect her without them. Is everyone clear on that? If any of you release your dragon, I will break your wings."*

After a round of grumbles, I reminded them that while we remained in this realm, our abilities were hindered. We had to act fast. By changing from Ashen to our daemonic battle form, we could place the Child-of-Balance in danger. Everyone complied, except Raven and Imp. Imp was shredding my patience, using my mind to bury his sarcastic comments, leaving them to germinate in the unspoken spaces.

Imp mocked my order. *"Okay, does every daemon get that? No D and D cosplay tonight."*

"They get it, Imp." I watched Alexcia to center my focus. The clouds were beginning to drizzle, and the wind

had quite a sting.

"So no flying in on a wing and curse to save the chosen one," he lampooned.

"Imp!" His name exploded in my head as I jumped to unsheathe my scythe. *"Balance is on the move. Do not let the child out of your sight."*

Why could she not stay put for once in her life?

Alexcia passed under the streetlight by the coffee shop. Raven shot from the store rooftop to the light pole over her head. The Vessel stopped, and everyone froze as she regarded the lamp. Raven crouched, fully cloaked, with his weapons close to his sides. Alexcia turned away, then immediately checked back in Raven's direction at the same time he stood up.

Crap, can she see him?

Imp's aura glowed from under his hood. *"Hey, Balance is a great codename for Alexcia. Why in the hell didn't we think of that sooner? It gets seriously old after a while using her proper title."*

"Imp!" we all yelled.

That was when I recognized the same male Water Raiser from earlier, and he was right behind Alexcia. Nodding at the sky, he raised a hand in a gun-type gesture and lowered his lips to her ear. Next, he pretended to shoot a handgun. The Vessel sprung forward as if her life depended on it.

"Damn the cloak I cast! Raven, target the deranged water-drip. Everyone else, follow the child."

"He's as good as extinguished," Raven said, jumping down on the elemental. The metal strike from Raven's kataras resounded down the street before I even got off the building.

Jumping from rooftop to rooftop, our minions worked to camouflage us against the blackened sky as we moved in between the shadows. We were ready to play Hide and Recopy.

Two reapers were flanking me from behind as I jumped to another building. A gust of wind smacked me from behind, and I almost missed the corner of the building. Quint and K didn't make the rooftop, exchanging shared curses on their way down.

I heard heavy metal scraping heading in my direction. Glancing to the side, I spotted the neon tint of Imp's aura zip past me, to intercept whatever was charging for Alexcia. A metal trashcan was about to collide with her body. Imp barely redirected its path by smacking it down the street. It landed with a crash, and she shrieked from the sudden impact.

She was about to fall from losing traction. Without thinking, I took off running, using the pole of my scythe to launch myself off the roof. Landing right next to her, I wrapped my arm around her waist. She started to twist, but I shoved her to keep running.

The clan, except Raven, moved ahead to scope out our awaiting competition. Misty shadows bobbed, wove, and faded down the street. I noticed the determination on Alexcia's face, but her human legs couldn't keep up with the daemon bodyguards, so I willed my minion to slow our pace.

A sizzle of rain almost drowned out the twin chants from behind. I spun around as two Wind Evokers blindsided me, and I flew ahead of Alexcia, landing with a metal-bending crunch on top of a parked car. Cursing at myself, I realized there was a time-tremor ring fixed where I had landed. Seconds felt like minutes from the snare's ability to harness time.

The windows bowed outward from my slowed impact. Alexcia was heading straight for the trap in a full sprint. When the time ring broke, a distinct sound wave like cannon fire echoed down the street as I tried to roll off the car. Pressure from the time-tremor moved up and out, causing the streetlamp above me to sputter, cracking the glass cover. Instinctively, I braced myself for what was coming next.

With the snare triggered, everything began to catch up to the present, and I sensed Alexcia's emotions sway from determination to panic as the delayed crunch of my impact filled the air. Rushed time caused the car windows to shatter spontaneously, and with that, we had caught up to the present.

I was furious as I watched the debris shower over Alexcia leaving a spray of magenta polka dots coating her exposed skin. She screeched in pain, and my cloak shuddered from her suffering.

I scanned the darkness behind her and made out two Evokers on the ground running in our direction. Those blustering windbags were probably the ones who had used me for batting practice. Whipping my head to the left, I discovered two more soaking-wet entities standing on the roof of a red-bricked house at the end of the bend, their hands waving above them.

I made the assumption.

They had to be the reason behind the growing force of the storm. The count did not add up. Six elementals—plus the one Raven was taking care of—made seven. Strange. Evokers and Raisers always worked in pairs. Plus, the Sculptor and Moment had to be waiting for the right time to claim their prize.

An elemental growled from behind me as a wind-whip grazed my right side. Instantly, I caught sight of K's blurred aura. He fell into a mixture of green and black mist, crashing on top of a car about thirty feet ahead of Alexcia. His minion tried to shield him as the roof buckled. Another time-tremor triggered. So much for us trying to protect Alexcia, they were using us as ammo. K's Smolder snarled, and the beast within me answered in the same deep, reverberating tone.

Lightning directly above us lit up the night sky, followed by a dramatic thunderclap. The rumbling from overhead masked the pressure of the time ring, and I heard the windows from the second vehicle shatter.

I motioned for K to find where the clan had dispersed. The decision was now mine: fight with my clan or honor the Bond-Rites. K's face paralleled my displeasure as he rolled away from the wreckage.

Mentally he told me, *"Go."* Then he summoned his mace before disappearing into the shadowy tree line ahead of us.

Catching up to Alexcia, I was quite impressed with how she was holding herself together. The canines in the neighborhood sensed our presence and filled the night with howls of frustration.

With a controlled swiftness, my shroud aided me to follow Alexcia. Nearby screams piqued my interest, but I realized they were coming from a frantic group of elemental assassins in the middle of the street. The clan must be working on dispatching them.

I followed behind Alexcia as we skulked deeper into the neighborhood's awaiting evil. I laughed at the irony of the event. *If she only knew the entities that wished her death and here I was protecting her.*

A stray question snaked its way into my inner monologue. *"What would happen if she could see us,"* the Smolder inquired.

Revulsion slapped my face. *What was I thinking?* Her welfare was supposed to be my only concern—at least, for the next three weeks. Formally introducing myself to her would undoubtedly complicate everything.

"Tevin, *focus*," I berated myself.

Every few seconds, Alexcia would gaze up through her sparkling lashes, and I wondered if she had a plan in mind. Her heart pumped to the rhythm of her breathing, and a small part of me intertwined with her *élan vital,* or life force. Even though the next few clicks of time were mere seconds to her, during this brief interlude, what we were sharing meant more to me than my six hundred years of bestowing death's blessings.

I thought back to the night in the hospital. Dying on a gurney, she ensorcelled me. *If Rae-Lynn hadn't been there to describe Alexcia's unique situation, would I have followed through with my task?*

The wash from the streetlights, mixed with the pockets of darkness, accentuated her features in a play of shadows. Lifting my gaze, I watched her lips part while taking in gulps of muggy air.

Can she tell I am next to her?

Right on cue, Alexcia's gaze connected with mine, but her irises were too wide. She stared right through me, and her eyes had taken on the luster of polished night. The Smolder within me possessively rumbled. At that moment, our existence ground to a halt, and ungoverned emotions clouded rational reasoning. She was no longer a job. Alexcia was mine to protect.

Sensing the change in my demeanor, the minion wrapped its burning tentacles around my torso. I recognized sorrow, and it stabbed me, realizing I would be nothing more to her. The unwanted desire to meet her created a chasm of want and I dismissed the notion. My Smolder was annoyed with my resolve to remain the Child-of-Balance's Unseen guardian.

Next, I was distracted by a roar coming from the vacant street ahead. Rain fell in sheets, hissing as it pelted Raven's daemonic form. A dragon's head dipped below a streetlight revealing his scales as a charred crimson from anger. His full size dwarfed the two-story home behind him. Black leathery wings were pulled back against his body, and his barbed tail snapped in the harsh wind. He was a force of the River's power to behold.

Raven's jaw clenched like a vice. He had one Evoker under his left claw, and another cornered in between two trucks. Quint and K were flanking his hind legs, watching the sky with their weapons drawn. I was disappointed in him for losing control, but when I saw how quickly he had trapped both elementals, I dismissed his rebellion.

The Raisers were controlling the thickening sheets of water, and I could barely see what was transpiring between Raven and his new toys. There was a threatening growl, blending in with a thunderclap as his huge mass lunged forward. The daemonic dragon roared again at the cornered Water Raiser as the trapped one went pale with dread. Losing interest in his prey, Raven twisted his claw back and forth, crushing the female. The Water Raiser in between the trucks shrieked in pain of being disconnected.

Raven's boiling fury spilled over as he picked up the

lifeless elemental and flung her in the direction of her screaming partner. Their bodies smacked together with a bone-breaking echo sending them crashing into a wooden fence across the street. Debris exploded from their impact.

Two Wind Evokers behind us used the unfortunate outcome of their fallen comrades to their advantage. Both worked together by sending blasts of gale-force winds in my direction. Inky tentacles gripped each of my arms as their power practically blew my minion off of me. The shroud was in distress, and I dismissed it while summoning my scythe. As it appeared in my hands, I readjusted my stance for its weight.

Our enemies had altered their strategies because they began using whirl whips to attack Alexcia. I swung my blade to block their assault, but an invisible presence knocked me back, separating us. Stunned, I watched Alexcia's image distort as though the air between us had become hot. There were only three elementals in the Unseen which I knew Ashens could not see if they did not want to be seen. I burned this fragment of time to memory.

Alexcia tried to run, but the unknown Unseen pushed her into a concrete wall. For the time being, she was safe, and I had enough room to fight. I dove, flipping headfirst toward the closest elemental on the right. The female screeched when I swung the beard of my blade, lodging it under her rib cage. The momentum pole vaulted me over her head as I extracted my weapon.

Imp appeared behind the Evoker to my left. He growled, startling the elemental. She hopped back, preparing to attack when Imp connected with a punch to her gut. Buckled over and holding her midsection, she hissed, hitting him with a quick blast of air. Twin purple orbs ablaze with shock, he did a roundhouse kick to her shoulder.

Both wounded Evokers were mumbling enchantments, making the winds press Alexcia up against the wall and dragging her across it. She pried herself from the rough cinder block to inspect her wounds. I smelled fresh blood, causing the Smolder's power to intensify. Pure malice became my fuel as the surge of power singed the edges of my sight.

Similar to the way lightning had scorched the sky, I followed the sound of Alexcia's built-up anger. The cry from her frustration resonated into the night. I watched her body crumble to the ground accepting her fate.

Listening to her soft sobs pounded the truth into my being; I had failed her. In my six hundred years of existence, I never had to admit failure, and it turned my existence inside out. I welcomed the searing truth into my core and envisioned the darkened flames of Space, allowing it to consume me.

I was an Ashen in complete, cursed form. The Smolder and I had become one entity.

Imp drew in a breath. "Curse me with a heart. Your eyes are azure." He unsheathed his broadsword and bowed with respect.

His flow of power was stupefying. My cloak dropped in temperature, but my corporeal shell was ablaze. I fizzed with an electrical current that made the air around me haze. This sensation felt backward to the power I usually wielded. Limbs sluggish and heavy, everything was magnified as I observed my surroundings in slow motion.

The rain became a slight annoyance. I heard ocean waves crashing in my ears, only to find out it was the wind. I could sense Styx's power, and it enthralled me.

I had only felt the power of the Smolder a handful of times without changing into dragon form, but never to this extent. It was uncapped, flowing over the area, ready to devour. The beast within me roared from this new, heightened form of supremacy.

May the River have mercy on these elementals.

An earsplitting scream of terror snapped me back as I remembered the skewered wind elemental. She was trying to free her torso from the blade. Shaking my head from side to side and giving her a "tsk-tsk," I removed my weapon. The elemental disintegrated. The scythe's silver-laced blade appeared as though it had been dunked in a moonbeam.

I turned to face the rest of my clan before I spoke, "Ashens, protect our Child-of-Balance."

Their Smolders responded with a community howl followed by Raven's roar blending into a roll of thunder.

When I relocated to shield Alexcia, her limp body flew about twenty feet ahead of me like a rag doll. Another flash of lightning and I saw Moment's figure standing over her. Bewildered, she rubbed her jaw before discarding a spray of crimson across the ground.

I leapt over a car and swung my scythe, aiming for Moment's neck. The cloak's misty tentacles reached out to restrain her. The crafty wind elemental had repositioned herself as the air from my blade whistled.

After a sharp jolt of magic, Alexcia jerked in response. I was distracted when an invisible kick slammed into me, sending my corporeal body skidding across the street. Snapping my head up, I watched in dread. The girl clawed at her face, leaned back, and squealed at her Unseen attacker.

Moment did not waste any of her precious time and positioned herself on top of the child. Pressing her weight onto Alexcia's back, she wove her hand into the Child's hair and used wind magic to shove Alexcia's face into a puddle of water.

Drunk with rage, I spun the scythe over my head as I caught a glimpse of what had relocated me. A huge Sculptor stood between Moment and me. A wide smile spread across his face in a smug smudge. The dirt-kisser's eyes challenged me to make a move toward him or risk Moment delivering her bounty to the House of Time in a body bag.

Spinning the blade high above my head, I decided this was as good a time as any for us to take the party down a level. Hell's caves came to mind. I slammed the silver tip of my weapon's hilt into the ground and used the basement part of my voice box. "Unlock and grant me passage to the River." The ground in front of me began to fracture. I had never done this before; the Smolder seemed to be guiding me.

Darkened plumes of smoke bled through the ground's

newly opened wounds. Pulling the handle from the ground, I waved it in front of the Earth elemental. He turned gray and started to run away, but the pavement crumbled under his feet. He kept trying to regain ground, but every time he mended it, the earth would open right back up. Eventually, he would run out of power.

Michael appeared next to me. His cloak's aura mixing with mine reminded me of a shadow shield. *It had worked for us in battle, but would it work for Alexcia?*

"Michael, bind your cloak with mine. Shield Alexcia," I directed.

He ordered his minion to intertwine with mine, and the combination of our power made the air smell stale as it fused together with a barrier of spell protection. I was gambling that Alexcia had enough of her father's blood for the spell to adhere.

Moment's hourglass irises shrank under her ice-cold stare.

"Click-tic-toc, I command time to stop." She started to cast a spin. Everything decelerated to where I could see trails of breath vapor. Our shrouds were frozen in flowing patterns of different colors twisted around our features, outlining each minion. I could see where the mist of the cloaks had etched thousands of different paths around each falling raindrop, trying to evade the falling water. We could even see the Unseen's power moving in waves through the air currents, masked from the action of the storm.

Moment had set a time-tremor around all of us, and we were in the epicenter. I knew I needed to counter the spell, but I was unsure how to break it without endangering Alexcia in the process.

The bounty hunter's eyes went wide when she heard Raven's roar, signaling another elemental's defeat. Anger rolled off the bounty hunter. She had forgotten about our daemonic dragon. Furious, she moved in for the kill.

I followed her movements, using my weapon to cut through the air. Michael pushed onward, mimicking my footsteps and bringing our cloaked barrier with us. It pulsed with our power, but as we got closer, the rhythm changed to Alexcia's heartbeat.

The silver roses on the staff of my scythe turned to the color of molten rock, and it began to hum from the storm's energy. I raised it in an attempt to connect the powers from all three Houses to break us out of there.

Filling every corner of my mind, I yelled, *"Time to burn is time well spent!"*

The metal-laced blade became blinding. Then lightning struck it, breaking the ring in a reverse pattern from the outside-in. Shadows sped up. Archer slid down the roof tiles, and Imp had morphed from under a nearby car, knocking Moment into the tree across the street. Alexcia had ended up in the middle of the sidewalk.

I could have sworn she whispered, "Thank you."

I waved my weapon for all the reapers to follow. Alexcia got to her feet and ran once Michael and I had set the barrier around her. The few elementals that remained ripped their rage from the clouds. Hail fell, and Alexcia's demeanor held uncertainty, but her feet never wavered. She seemed pleased about the mysterious, fast-moving mist surrounding her.

Alexcia brought us to a row of trees and broke into a sprint. She knew where she was going now. I was sure of it.

I shared my thoughts with the clan. *"She knows where she is going. Imp, you and Archer move ahead and scout for problems, witnesses, or weather mishaps that might slow us down. Quint and K, fall back and find Raven. I have a gut feeling we are heading right into trouble."*

The reapers dispatched as Michael and I kept the cover moving with the Child-of-Balance. After tonight's attack, I was sure the clan was convinced there was more to Alexcia than what her parents had led us to believe. Not sure if Alexcia was the chosen one, but with so many elementals believing it, one could hardly argue the outcome.

"Oh, for the flow of the River," I cursed in my head for my clan to hear. *"If she mentions that she has seen one of us to her father, it would be the end of my existence. On the flip*

side, the clan would be free from my Bond-Rites."

"That's my daemon. Way to look on the darker side of things, Tevin." Michael's blue eyes were two bright pinpoints peering from under the tree leaves across the street. *"Can I have your job when Max turns you to ash? I was thinking of moving near a volcano so we could all work on our tans."*

I pressed my hands closer together to shrink the sphere around Alexcia.

Michael copied the gesture.

Imp's opinion oozed into our conversation. *"Tevin, you're not going to be extinguished. Max needs you, whether you know it or not."*

A deep voice added, *"I wouldn't mind harvesting a few drownings or random shark attacks by the equator."* It was Quint, jogging up the street.

K followed with, *"I think you all are drunk from too much casino pool water."*

Raven growled in agreement with K since that was how the Smolder communicated.

I snuffed out my Smolder until my power felt like burning embers. The heat from my eyes diminished since Alexcia was out of immediate danger. Recapturing Michael's attention, I raised my hands. Holding his up, we snapped in unison, breaking the barrier. Alexcia was once again exposed to the natural elements.

Alexcia froze, gasping and coughing. I watched as she seemed to scan her surroundings but refocused on her cast instead. Tree branches above her protested from shifting weight. The Unseen's unexpected tactic ignited my frustration as I yelled in my head, *"Daemons, they're in the trees."*

A wall of wind knocked me from my perch, and I landed next to Alexcia. Quickly glancing up, I noticed Moment standing next to a different Sculptor and the water elemental Raven had first confronted. Moment waved, and another wall of wind swatted Michael from his branch.

Raven roared from a distance, and I sensed the

vibrations from his pounding claws. If my tally was right, we had downed five elementals. *Scythe be damned, how many more did we have to send to Styx?*

Two Evokers dropped down from the trees, using their wind spells to carry them to the middle of the intersection. One appeared sick. The other raised her hands to the sky in a swaying motion.

Moment's subsequent laugh was wicked, motioning down in a hard arc toward the tree where the child stood. One of the main limbs unnaturally bowed. Swinging around, the bounty hunter made the same motion at the child.

I projected my voice, "Move it, Alexcia!"

The wind tore the limb from the trunk, nearly missing the Vessel. By the time it crashed to the ground Alexcia was running for the intersection.

Moment ordered to the Earth elemental, "Stop the child!" Using her power, she tossed his mass in Alexcia's general direction.

I repositioned my weapon and followed the Sculptor. Slipping from shadow to shadow, my mind searched for Michael. *"Hey, if you are not too busy, could you back me up here?"*

He snarled, and then I heard the blunt force of his weapon smack into flesh. Unfortunately, the Water Raiser Raven had attempted to bring down, had Michael preoccupied.

Quint matched my stride and reappeared next to me. "Will I do, or would you prefer to wait for Michael?"

I grabbed his shoulder. "Where's K and Raven?"

He shrugged.

Then I scanned the area for the Sculptor. Instead, I found a Smolder. Raven was snacking on a dripping elemental he had skewered with his barbed tail. The dragon gagged after his first bite and sent what was left spinning through the air. It bounced and landed on the bed of a work truck. K and Imp were toying with the other one, which left at least two more Wind Evokers unaccounted for.

The ground underneath us buckled and sank when the

Sculptor crawled from the hole about ten feet in front of us.

Alexcia lost her footing and started going down. I vaulted forward in time to grab the back of her shirt and one belt loop. Dangling her temporarily above the corner of the sidewalk, I shifted our momentum and tossed her toward Quint.

With the aid of his cloak, Quint helped by sliding her past the waiting Earth Elemental. Moment flipped off a nearby building, landing in the middle of the street. She tried using another blast of air, but it passed over Alexcia's body, hitting the gate in front of her.

K reported, *"The water level of the storm should be drying up nicely. Imp and I took out both Raisers after Raven wounded one of them. He has another cornered. There will be no co-existing with him from now on. Archer was delayed, but he's on his way now."*

I reached out to the missing Ashen. *"What's the holdup?"*

Archer replied, *"Damage control. And after Raven's version of pick-up sticks with the fence, neighbors were gawking at the destruction. I'll be in a sniping position in about thirty clicks."*

"Leave Raven; I am sure he will dispose of it soon. I need a little help. Moment wants to play. Quint is with the girl, heading into the apartments."

I shifted my feet into a defensive stance, watching as the bounty hunter's innocent, doe-eyed face fixed on me. I would never admit it, but she creeped me out.

"You know we can hear you." Her lashes fluttered, faking innocence.

Tired of speaking internally, I said, "K, Imp, port to me."

There was a swirl of frost, and light flurries of ice drifted around my cloak. Both reapers stepped out from behind me, and I listened as they unsheathed their weapons.

Moment cocked her head, staring at my weapon. "You think you'll best me? That's so cute. Muscle can't beat magic, boys." She snapped and rotated her hands.

The sound of knuckles cracking behind us happened at the same time the wind swirled above. Peals of laughter echoed in stereo on our right as two more Evokers turned corporeal next to the Sculptor. K took on the giggling twins. Imp focused on the Sculptor, and I was stuck with Moment for the… moment.

A wind blast hit the gate behind us, bending the lock and causing it to unlatch and swing open banging into the wall. I was torn between taking down an impending threat toward Alexcia or remaining by her side. But the sooner I took care of Moment, the sooner I could check on Alexcia.

The twin wind elementals flinched, and that was all it took for K to start swinging. The sick-looking one on the right was the battery, and we all knew to take the power source out first. They bashed K with one wind whip after another.

Imp swung at the Sculptor, and the ground shook under our feet, forcing us to shift from solid back to spirit. This put us at a slight disadvantage when fighting since we could not physically deliver damage.

I spun to Moment's left, and she ducked right. I countered under, and she hopped over my blade and knocked me back with a quick blast of air. Each time I came within a scythe's swipe from her, she snapped her fingers, and the wind would push back.

Imp had his hands full with the Sculptor, too. I heard his string of cursing behind me. He swung his sword, and the sound of metal connecting with rock vibrated through the air.

K was holding his own with the wind twins as well. The one pulling power from the other kept trying to get a clear shot of K's back while he pursued the source of her magic. The Wind Evoker playing role of battery hissed and spat like a cat whenever he got close enough to swing at her. The caster's clothes fluttered with her energy, and it was the only way we could tell them apart.

This battle was going nowhere. When she blasted me again, I used the opportunity to fade into the shadows. Traveling through the darkness, I emerged behind the sickly elemental and swung as K distracted her with a wink. The blade went through her back and out her gut. Sparkling sand pooled at her feet.

Moment seemed baffled and maybe even offended. The other Evoker was distracted while K took advantage of this new situation. He raised his mace at the redhead while I pulled my scythe out of the disintegrating female.

The other Evoker cried out as she fell in a heap before K. His mace was stationary above his shoulder from the previous swing, but his eyes were locked on the Evoker. She clung to her dislocated shoulder trying to muffle her sobs. With hesitation, K lowered the mace and backed away. A frown matching his eyes hid the quick flash of emotion.

K swung his mace back, ready to counter if she retaliated from his lack of judgment. She scooted away, but he stepped forward and extended a hand out to her. The Evoker parted her soaked red tangles to reveal her shame.

I was engrossed but did not notice the bounty hunter appear behind the elemental. With a displeased expression, Moment lifted her sleeve to expose an intricate design of a serpent's face on her pale skin. She summoned, "Quicksilver, come." The malevolence in her grin made my minion bristle. The picture had altered from a two-dimensional tattoo to a creature uncoiling from her forearm.

These lethal beasts were formed from the fabric of time, and the presence of one for an elemental meant a one-way ticket to Styx. Thinner than a serpent, its shimmery silver scales mirrored its surroundings, taking on the appearance of melted mercury.

The Felterthread seemed to pour down Moment's arm, silently, exposing two needle-thin fangs. It coiled around her wrist and fingers, then hissed at its intended victim.

I had no idea what one would do to Alexcia, but the thought made me ill.

Moment placed a hand on the Evoker's wounded shoulder. The frail elemental whimpered as the serpent encircled the neck of the doomed entity. The Felterthread's purr magnified with the eagerness to kill, as it patiently waited for Moment to sentence the fallen Evoker.

"You have failed the House of Time, Miststing. May the River forgive and recopy you."

The wind elemental became silent. Her gaze never wandered from K's as she mouthed, *sorry*. At the same time, the creature pierced her skin, instantly reducing her to silt. An abnormal warm breeze swept what was left of the Evoker into a shimmery dust devil before it dissipated.

Giving her pet a light pat, Moment made several coos, and clicks with her tongue, as if she was praising it. When finished, she angled her head a tad, eyes widening, the tells of an idea taking root. Talking to her pet, she sing-songed, "I have someone else you might like to meet." Her last word was swept away as both of them dissolved into the breeze.

She meant Alexcia. I backed up toward the iron gate.

K waved me on. In a gravelly voice, he said, "I've got it. Go save the brat so we can leave."

Raven came bounding down the street with another water elemental in his mouth. He looked down at Michael and noticed his opponent. The crimson-winged daemon opened his mouth, dropping the lifeless entity. In a flash, he raised his front leg, smashing the water bug into the pavement.

Michael was pissed at the daemonic Smolder who had saved his ass. "Damn, Raven, I almost had him," Michael berated while still swinging his battle axe.

Raven snorted and lumbered away.

Michael, Imp, and I followed his lead toward the apartments. I spun the blade over my head to sheath it, accelerating my stride to a sprint. Moment was not toying with her food anymore. She was ready to bring in her bounty dead, or at the very least, in a coma.

I turned to Michael. "Where is Archer?"

"I have no idea." He shrugged.

We slammed through the gate. "Look for Quint; he is with the girl."

Michael reprimanded me with a stare.

I cleared my throat. "Fine, he is with the *child*. Find

Moment. K and I have pissed her off, and she means to end this."

He nodded as his cloak stretched out, grabbing some nearby tree limbs. Then he was gone.

Raven pounded the pavement behind me, and I motioned for him to follow. Instead, he stopped, releasing a deafening roar.

I turned in the direction of Raven's muzzle and spotted Moment on top of a Dodge van. Alexcia and Quint were not far from her, and I knew she had the girl in her crosshairs. Moment started swaying her hands in the air and preparing one of her spells. She used her elements to explode another tree.

As I moved in to shield Alexcia's back, the area seemed familiar. Impressed, I whispered, "Smart girl." She was heading for a Vessel friend's dwelling.

In a blink, Quint appeared on my left and I watched Michael rush to the right while pointing skyward. We all cringed at the screeching above us, mixed in with Raven's growl.

Moment shrilled, *"Nooo!"*

The power behind Raven's swing could have knocked the Wind Evoker into the Unseen. Her body cartwheeled in the air, landing on the carport's roof. It buckled from her impact at the same time Alexcia's voice rose into the night.

Imp raced to clear a path to the apartment's door.

The Vessel who had allowed us entrance did not even know what had smacked into her. Alexcia may have arrived unexpectedly, but her friend had no clue what was traveling with her. The three of us flew over the two girls. Our minions reached out several tentacles before we crashed into the back wall. Imp and Michael kicked their feet out and used the wall to push off, heading back through the entrance. I did the same, but before passing through the doorframe, I cast a temporary seal on the door. The slam reassured me my spell was active.

We launched ourselves to the top of the damaged carport and found Archer there with one of his arrows aimed between Moment's eyes. Wink, Archer's weapon, was staring intently at their captive, anticipating the order to kill. K was bent over the bounty hunter's side, mace embedded into the carport next to her head. Raven was propped up on the roof of a car while he hissed in warning.

I approached the scene with a trickle of smugness. With this new development, I had an idea that could be beneficial to our cause... *if only I could make a Bond-Rite with Moment.* Convincing her would not be a problem. Convincing the clan was a different story.

Imp plunged his broadsword into the metal by Moment's head. He crouched to take in her unflinching form. Standing abruptly, he pretended to brush off his cloak, then looked at all of us and said, "Ten elementals won a one-way ticket to the River for judgment, and the Child-of-Balance is safe. That wasn't so bad."

Everyone groaned.

To get our assassin's attention, I unsheathed my scythe. Angling the blade tip, I lifted a strand of black-and-white hair, revealing her hourglass stare.

"With Miss Moment captured, I believe that makes eleven."

Moment scanned the clan of Ashens before slightly tilting her head to assess the Smolder who had bested her. A trail of pearl-tinted sand pooled underneath her head wound as she nodded, rolling her eyes back in agreement.

Chapter Seven

There is only Past and Future.
From the first breath we take,
Our seconds dust over fuzzy memories.
The minutes we take for granted
Hours are used, abused and discarded.
We age; our past becomes vast
Using time to recompense for knowledge.
How unintelligent a race are we,
Not to see that looming question
...Did we ever open the Present?
Alexcia—

*T*he staring contest Dee and I were having seemed to last an hour, but according to the wall clock above her head, it had only been five seconds of discomfort. I deliberately recoiled from her gaze to peer down at my soiled uniform. My bruised gray-matter had been knocked around to the point that I wasn't precisely sure of details.

How could I explain what I didn't understand myself?

Dee stood up as her siblings wandered into the hallway. The twins had woken from all the commotion, and curiosity pulled them out of bed to investigate. Dee wasn't too pleased with their excitement upon seeing me on the floor.

The kids fired several questions. Calvin sat in front of me and pointed out the potty accident I had made on the floor. Completely embarrassed from his accusation, even though it wasn't true, I squirmed on both knees.

Dee cracked a thin smile at the visual. Bailey gestured to my clothes and asked why I used mud to wash them. I shook my head and forced a smile. Dee's little sister placed a hand on my shoulder, concern covering her face. "Why did you come here so late? Isn't your mommy going to be mad at you?"

Following the child's question, Dee folded her arms. With shoulders stiff, she cocked one eyebrow while tilting her head in a, *Yeah, why?* kind of gesture.

I was lightheaded and sore but rocked back on my feet to stand. Clearly, Dee was miffed because the twins were wide awake. After I had addressed Bailey's concerns, her big sister barked at them to go back to bed but cushioned the reprimand by saying we would tell them everything in the morning.

While she shooed them to bed, I reached back to wrangle my ponytail. Releasing the snarled, wet mess from the broken band, I thought, *well that could have gone better.*

My friend returned down the hall with an unreadable face. It made me want to seek shelter, unsure how this was going to play out between us. She tossed back her bangs and gestured to the floor where I had left my broken cell phone.

Bending down to scoop up the electronic mess, I winced and drew in a quick breath. I hadn't realized how much abuse I had taken from whatever had attacked me. A voice in my head said, *from trying to escape the storm.* It was stupid of me to try and replace unknown facts with logical lies.

I fought off another muscle cramp, riding out the stabbing ripples from my lower back. Rubbing, I asked, "Dee do you think I could use your phone to call my mom? She was supposed to arrive tonight around eleven."

Dee made a trifling snort. "Use the phone in the living

room." With some exasperation, she tugged down her now soiled, cream-colored silk pajama set. I wondered if she was going to hit me up for dry cleaning as I noted my handprints splattered across her top.

When I took a step toward the phone, my socks made a sloppy squish. *Ugh.* My feet were almost numb, but I continued making soggy steps to the living room. "Thanks, Dee. Hey, if you don't mind, could I crash here for the night? It's late, and I don't want to have my mom see me like this." I motioned to the wet attire.

She nodded and headed into the kitchen. When the swinging door closed behind her, I picked up the phone and dialed. Holding my breath, I waited for Rae-Lynn to answer on the other end. I could feel myself turning different shades of blue while waiting for her to respond, but it was enough time for me to come up with a somewhat-believable explanation. Tapping a soggy foot, I needed to call Blakely in the morning, assuming I can get a hold of her, and ask why she hadn't shown up. If anything, she'd better have a persuasive story, or I was going to slash her tires.

As soon as Rae-Lynn answered the phone, lies flooded from my mouth.

"These weirdoes came into the store before closing and wouldn't leave. Since I switched schedules with Belinda to close, I was required to stay until they left." Guilt nudging at my morals, I continued, "I tried to call Blakely several times, but her phone must've been off because she never showed. After waiting around for about thirty minutes, I decided to walk home, and then I found myself caught in the storm with a dead cell phone. But as the storm got worse, I figured Dee's apartment was closer, so I turned down her street."

I paused and chewed on the lies to break them down so they were easier to swallow than spew. If I kept adding to my explanation, my mom might start asking a ton of questions, digging myself deeper into a hole. I glanced around to see if Dee was eavesdropping. A small part of me hoped so; then I wouldn't have to repeat the altered scenario.

It took about ten minutes to keep my tongue from

knotting while I argued the rationality of why I should remain at Dee's. But, Mom finally agreed because she was too jet-lagged to drive. The parent part of her reprimand was for me not charging the cell before work. Rae-Lynn finished with a warning but confirmed she would be by in the morning to drop off my school bag and clothes.

Peace briefly washed over me as I placed the receiver back on its charger. The bruising on both forearms caught my attention. All of them were becoming a sickly greenish-purple with inky-blue veins. I examined each one and tried to recall how many times I had fallen.

Wrapping both arms around myself, I tried to stop the increased quivering inside. My torso was sore, and my right knee began to throb. Muscles were pulling and spasming, even in places I didn't think I had used.

Taking shallow breaths, I reaffirmed this was normal Vegas weather, and most of the time it was typically unpredictable. The lie I tried to accept left a familiar aftertaste, like warm, bitter beer. Our local news would surely have a story on tonight's chaotic weather, confirming part of my story.

Dee came back through the kitchen door wearing an acidic scowl. Slipping both hands to her hips, she gave me the *mom* stare I hated so much.

Eyes widening, I thought, *Now it's gonna start.*

She took a shaky breath before her mouth unhinged. "What did you do to your uniform? Why did you come crashing through my door? Were you being chased? I thought Blakely was picking you up." Her temper grew with each question, stacking them up like sticks of dynamite. Red-faced, I figured Dee was about to blow. "Did you at least *try* to call your parents before you broke your cell?"

I caught my breath and paused.

One of her hands snatched my arm. "Damn it, Alexcia, you're covered in bruises. How many times did you fall—or were you in a fight?" She spun on the ball of her foot and started down the hall, reprimanding me like a parole officer. "I bet you had a fight with that Belinda chick. I told you she was bad news."

Since she was on a rant, I responded with an occasional nod or shrug and continued to follow her down the hall. When she got this way, it was best to hunker down until her air capacity depleted.

"I'm sure it will be all right with my mom if you crash here tonight," Dee said, pointing to the guest room where I normally stayed.

My friend stopped to grab two towels from the linen closet before giving me a brief glance and then wiggled a finger, motioning me to follow. Two doors down from the closet was her bathroom. I kept my distance and lingered by the doorway. Dee motioned to the shower stall and dropped the towels on the counter.

Dee sighed. "When you're finished, put the towels in the hamper. I'll bring you a plastic bag for your wet clothes and something to sleep in." Turning on a heel again, she walked away, grumbling about having to take another shower.

I cringed and decided to apologize once more, but the bathroom door clicked before *sorry* was voiced.

After drying myself, I slipped into the nightclothes Dee had left for me. I watched my doppelganger in the mirror while turning on the blow-dryer. Unfortunately, the shower only cleaned my outer appearance, never touching the residue of tainted emotions that caked my soul. A sense of dread hovered above me, like my own personal, dark cloud. I held back a sob as I turned off the dryer.

Leaving the warmth of the bathroom, I padded across the carpet in Dee's fuzzy green slippers. For some reason, her attitude kept me on guard. When I crossed the foyer into the dining room, my feet stopped at the threshold.

I placed my good hand on a hip and thought, *my gut was right*. My irate hostess had placed two steaming cups of hot chocolate on saucers, with four chocolate chip cookies tucked in at the base of each. It was a heartfelt sight until I saw how she had laid out the place settings. The perfectly arranged sets were at opposite ends of the oversized, mahogany dining room table.

I exhaled, limping to the seat on the far right and waiting for my inconvenienced hostess to join me. Her aggravation was apparent as the banging and clanging of the pot she was cleaning grew louder. Self-consciously, I tugged on the soft, light green sleep shirt while chewing on my lower lip. The situation was adding to my case of the fidgets as I nervously pulled on the elastic waistband of my pajama pants. They were also about three inches too short, so I had rolled them up to my knees. A strange wave of heat rushed across my skin, adding to the muscle aches.

The display of comfort food made me apprehensive, but like prey to a lure, I was drawn to the potential trap. Clearly, Dee was pissed. At what, exactly, remained a mystery, but I didn't believe her mood stemmed from my unexpected sleepover.

I placed my cast on the table to ease the tension in my left shoulder, and looping three fingers through the porcelain handle of the mug, I held the soothing liquid and inhaled. The tantalizing smell of milk chocolate soothed my frayed anxieties with renewed hope. I sipped the hot chocolate, allowing it to unknot my nerves.

From the dark niche of memory, pictures began to replay, causing a momentary zing of shock to override my calm. Memories—from the moment I had decided to walk home, to when I had crashed through the door—flooded my mind. Consciousness tried to untie the snarls in my altered recall. With a shaky hand, I placed the cup back onto the saucer, dreading the possibility of accidentally dropping it.

Questions loomed but only one that concerned me, *why did I feel safe?* I was scared stupid, but the question was not as disturbing as the answer my common sense tried to piece together. This version of the truth seemed even crazier than my lie. *Had I been attacked by a freak storm? Were the shadows I saw actually trying to help me or were they the ones attacking?* I couldn't tell anyone what my night had entailed because it was implausible.

Giving in to my lip-chewing habit, I realized the

evening resembled a similar nightmare. I hugged myself and trembled as I stared at the cooling brown liquid in the mug. Caught in a zone for a spell, I searched through my soggy brain for a lie convincing enough to tell Dee and my parents… a tale not too complicated so I could hit the replay button and still make it sound believable.

Sweat dampened the hairline on my neck when I sensed a conflicting presence nearby. While I lingered in the land of denial, Dee had returned. She was meticulously dunking a cookie. The urge to lie jammed, but I didn't want her to throw me out either.

Dee's dark green eyes darted suspiciously toward the cookie. Her thin fingers curved around the handle of the cup and brought the edge of it to her lips. When she leisurely blew at the rising steam, small wisps caressed her face, the lines accentuating her heart-shaped mouth.

The silence between us was golden since I didn't have a viable explanation to give her, but my desire to take another sip faltered as I watched Dee arch a perfect eyebrow. She must have seen the slight tremble in my outstretched fingers. I recoiled, paused, and made a fist.

"I didn't poison it if you were wondering." Dee shrugged and took another sip to prove her point.

Uneasiness seemed to push against my stomach, causing small ripples of nausea to churn waves of three-hour-old coffee, chocolate, and uncertainty as they pitched inside me. The reoccurring throbs from my earlier headache threatened to intensify. Regarding Dee, I found myself adding another question to the list. *Why is she treating me so cold?* I tried to turn the confusion down to a simmer so I could justify myself. "I'm a little freaked out at the moment."

Eyes narrowed. "So, how did you end up here like a muddy, half-drowned cat?" She blew over the rim of her cup again.

I forced myself to come up with a believable tale, causing my right eyelid to twitch uncontrollably. A spontaneous tickle at the back of my throat made me cough, and I covered my face, using the time to think fast.

"I counted cars going down Lake Mead while I waited for Blakely. Twenty-seven pairs of headlights later, I realized my cell phone was dead, and she wasn't coming. The storm was getting worse, and since I didn't think to bring a jacket—"

"How long did you truly wait? Five to ten minutes, maybe?" Dee asked, interrupting my explanation and catching me off guard.

Ad-libbing didn't allow for factoring in the possibility of interjections. I held my breath and counting to three before I replied, "No, I was watching the time from the marquee across the street. I sat there for about half an hour. Why does it matter to you how long I waited? I was freezing my ass off out there."

Dee's expression was challenging. "Why didn't you ask Jake to pick you up as well as drop you off? You know he would have moved his schedule around to accommodate you." Her question pushed me into a pool of ice-coated sarcasm.

A hive popped up on the inside of my right arm. I had to be covered in them by now, especially if they appeared on my upper extremities. The searing tingles were driving me mad as I itched along my face and neck. I thought Dee respected me more than this, and I was determined to find out why she was acting like a female dog.

In frustration, my answer was loud and sharp. I popped out of the chair and slammed my good hand onto the table. "What the hell, Dee? You're acting so bizarre. First, you were a little snot in the car today. Second, at lunch, you were being strange and staring at Jake like a lost puppy. Third, all those text messages you sent me earlier made no sense at all." Airlessly, the fourth point in my ranting streak back-drafted into my lungs.

A deep blush blossomed across Dee's cheeks, burning from a new emotion I didn't understand.

Exasperation turned my words sour. "Dee, what have I done to make you so… toxically nuclear?" I motioned at her figure in frustration.

She pushed her chair back, gradually rising. "You, Miss Alexcia Stasis, can't see past your own nose to spite your face. If the masses are not doing things for you, then they are not worth your time, right? I'm tired of you thinking you're better than the rest of us. And that you think we're at your beck and call whenever your foot slips from the social ladder. Especially when we are always expected to be there to bail you out of your binging messes."

I was dumbfounded.

Fangs out, her words dripped with liquid resentment. "Just today, I heard a student saying, 'Lex-Cee's such a star. Death couldn't keep her from a good kegger.' It makes me sick thinking about what you were doing before you almost bought the farm. If they only knew you the way I do…" Her face twisted in ire.

Dee's words sliced through the air striking me in several places. My legs went numb waiting for her final blow. The room fell silent as the tension coiled between us. An unseen force of energy was growing—no, *charging*. One of us was going to end up being the other's lightning rod.

The air around Dee started vibrating, and her words trembled between her lips. "You're a living cipher." She inhaled sharply. "You can stay here for tonight, but this is the last time I will ever help you."

She took two steps to leave the room, and then Dee abruptly halted by my side long enough to pull out her imaginary dagger. "I do not comprehend what he sees in you. Why are you so special to him, anyway? I respect him so much more than you do. I would be careful, Alexcia, about how you treat your other friends. You've lost one. How long do you think they will stay by your side while you pour yourself another drink?"

Tears poured from my eyes. I couldn't believe the night of hell I had been through. All I thought we were going to do was talk, and here I found myself getting another lecture on drinking. I'd been sober since the accident, even though my nightmares had steadily been getting worse.

All this venom can't be from what happened tonight, can

it? The question burned, and I needed it answered before my mouth turned to ash. I needed to pry the answers from Dee before she shut me out for good.

Gazing in disbelief, I watched her stagger to the bedroom door. She was crying, but a growing light caught my attention. A bright, metallic-green outline radiated from her body. Heat from my face burned away the moisture in my eyes, and I had to blink several times to regain focus. I watched thin, dark streaks trying to overlay the green shimmer outlining her shape. Tearing away from the sight of her, pain lanced deep behind my eye sockets.

The air buzzed, sucking all of the water out of the room and creating a static dryness. Tiny free-floating hairs on the side of my face tickled my cheeks. Instantly, a light breeze swirled around me, like a lace curtain caught in a draft. My hands and feet became as solid as lead, and my organs felt the Earth's gravitational pull rooting me to the spot.

Barely able to lift my head, the voice that pushed from my chest wasn't mine. *"Blact-ti-vece eh ta-nu."*

Dee went stiff. All the doors down the hall but hers slammed shut. Her crying stopped, and she grabbed the doorjamb, digging her fingers into the wood frame for purchase. A bright red mist grew from the floor, wrapping around what I believed was Dee's aura.

It was strange; I understood the string of gibberish slipping from my lips, but the knowledge didn't help with my sanity. Loosely translated, I had asked for the darkness to be burned from Dee's soul. My mouth went lax as I realized her aura was in fact burning.

My friend craned her neck to face me. Clenching her jaw, Dee's almond-shaped eyes were wide with agony. Guilt pulled at the corners of mine and filling them with tears. Whatever was happening to her was obviously painful. I had to find a way to help her.

Darkness rippled from her in vapors. Another thought hit me, like a memory coming back to an amnesia patient. I had to finish whatever I'd started with Dee.

It was hard to explain the compulsion I felt to relieve

my friend's pain. I stepped toward her as the air cushioned the balls of my feet. My reality flipped on its axis when I noticed each step I took was about three inches above the carpet. Although a part of me wanted to freak out, a heavy lassitude pushed its way into my psyche and kept me tethered from completely purging all logical explanations. This was like one of my night terrors. Surely, I was dreaming. It would explain what I could do, the foreign language, and the way Dee was acting.

Definitely a nightmare.

All I could do was ride it out. Jet-black trails of thinning fog slithered across the ceiling and floor. I held out both hands to Demetria. An odd sensation of tranquility overtook me because I knew what to do, and I lightly touched her face with both hands. My next thought seemed ridiculous. I was hungry for her tainted energy.

I leaned into Dee, grabbed her lower jaw with one hand, inched my fingers up the sides of her cheeks, and pressed like a vice to force her mouth open.

Then I whispered, *"Blact-ti-vece ki duc-nu."*

There was an initial pop, setting off an intermittent crackle between us as if our mouths were full of Pop Rocks, but the sting was magnified a hundred times.

I shuddered and bit my tongue as a twinge of panic skated over my exposed skin. The blood trickling down my dry throat heightened my senses. Molten metal seemed to flow from my tear ducts and blazed trails of liquid fire down my face. Each time a tear slipped from my chin, it caused an acidic hiss to happen, and when the searing reached the back of my eye sockets, I began to whimper. Then I heard the *snick* of a thousand keys simultaneous turning all at once. My vision narrowed and darkened to the point that I could only make out the blurry image of Dee.

My brain seemed as if it were going to explode, not only from the pressure but from a flood of thoughts that weren't my own. There was a heavy presence pushing its way into my body, forcing me to share my space. Invisible cables linked me to an invisible puppeteer and I could no longer control my movements.

This is exactly like one of my nightmares.

And in dreams, everything appeared unfathomable and yet realistically achievable. The alien thoughts, sharing skull space with me, began to describe in detail what would happen if we didn't remove whatever had tainted Dee's aura. Her soul would burn until there was nothing left, leaving her as an empty shell—void, emotionless.

When the voice stopped explaining, I realized my body had shifted, and I was leaning over Dee. Saliva flooded my mouth as the pain from my eyes slammed into the back of my skull. Cautiously, I inhaled the dark, thin ribbons coming off of Dee's aura. The air was a suffocating mixture of muggy car interior and stale cigarettes, and that didn't even come close to the way it tasted.

The need to dry-heave caused multiple gagging noises, from both of us, but I forced myself to keep siphoning her aura. Demetria began to shudder under my grip. I concentrated on the color of her eyes so I wouldn't let go of her before whatever I was doing to her was finished. Across the moistening sheen of her colorless eyes, I saw a familiar reflection.

Within the next moment, I dove through buried memories as my horror granted me access to them. This creature had popped up about a month ago. She was always silently screaming and trying to chase me down until a huge claw ripped me from her grasp. Everything about the monster scared the piss out of me. Its hair flowed with the grace of flickering fire. Both orbs oozed blood, leaving inky trails to accentuate its pale nose.

The being's features caused an emotional wash of terror, wisdom, repulsion, and sorrow. The throe I felt, tore my resolve in two as I realized we had a common ground—fear. This creature was as scared of me as I was of it.

Like an animal possessed, I sniffed the air as several of my fingers explored the petite face before me. My throat tightened while I tried to fight whatever was manipulating me. The voice croaked out one last sentence. *"Chact fi nu wi-requ."*

Dee's aura sparkled with filtered sunlight, and I peered at her through a green-leaf canopy, glowing with a soft, iridescence. The black trails that had latched onto her aura were gone. Now, she reminded me of a willow tree on a spring day after a rain shower. I watched as she stumbled lethargically to her bed, fell forward onto her comforter with a small grunt, and began snoring lightly.

The sight of her made me want to laugh, but the small emotion was cut short. Intense agony raced up my spine, twisting my frame to the point of snapping. Reality and nightmare had collided. Whatever was physically and mentally controlling me felt like I'd been ripped in two.

Falling to the floor, I sobbed while cradling the cast against me. Cheeks itchy and tight, it was as though I had leaked super glue from my eyes. I touched my face, partially wanting to slap myself awake but dreading the outcome.

Panic made me check on Dee. My only comfort was the soothing darkness filling the apartment, so I didn't have to strain my eyes to see her feet dangling over the side of her bed. I had to get to the guest bathroom and wash off whatever was coating my face. I crawled like a lame turtle down the hallway since my calf and thigh muscles cramped after I had tried to stand.

My mind raced. *When did I stumble down this rabbit hole?* I loved the childhood story about Alice, but I didn't care to visit her world. Everything from my not-so-normal-dream-land seemed to be meshing with my pretend-to-be-normal way of life. *What did I do to my friend? How was I being controlled? How did I know her aura?* My brain couldn't sponge up more questions without wringing out some illogical answers.

I smacked my head against the doorjamb and collapsed onto the bathroom floor, sobbing.

What was wrong with wanting to be a normal teenager? Go to school, have a job, get a Jeep, graduate, go to college. I didn't want to be labeled crazy, lose my freedom, and have a wardrobe consisting only of different-colored straitjackets.

Most of all, I did not want some stranger with an assortment of titles after their name passing judgment on my sanity and leaving me exposed like a carved-up cadaver.

A gloomy yellow beam of light filtered through the bathroom window, illuminating my cast in the dim light. Polka-dotted with what appeared to be drops of blood, I picked at the wet plaster, while admiring the shark Blakely had Sharpied on it. The back of my throat tickled with a twinge of sadness when I realized the cast would be removed next week. *Maybe I'll ask my mom if I could have the picture tattooed on my arm.* An audible sigh deflated the internal argument; apparently, I had some doubts about insanity. I was lying on the bathroom floor, bruised, beaten, broken, and wondering if I could get a tat.

"Forget wires crossed, Alexcia. Yours have corroded." I leaned against the wall laughing with tiny hiccups of hysteria.

With my second wind, I used my good arm to grab the counter and pull myself up. My fingers maneuvered along the wall for the light switch. Exhausted, I gave up in favor of washing my face in the dark.

The hot water stung my cheeks and lips at first. The skin was tender, but the longer I worked at it, the more I began to relax. After rinsing the light scent of cherry blossom off, I reached for a towel. While gently patting my face and hands, I wondered how good the bed would feel.

Even though the last few hours had made no sense, fatigue trumped my desire to understand. Not even thinking twice about crossing the bridge of sleep, I stared at my darkened reflection in the mirror. A sarcastic voice inside responded, *Right... even after what happened? You're not the least bit curious as to the why or how of it?*

I tossed the towel, annoyed because I nearly answered in the same cynical voice. Instead, I spat, "Please. Nothing could surprise me anymore."

A shudder rocked my resolve as the mimic in the glass nodded in understanding. Reality smashed the second-hand to the present, freezing me in a cold stare. I did not nod physically, but in my mind, there was a familiar tickle of comprehension. Sidestepping out of the bathroom, I guarded the next thought against the fake me in the mirror as she narrowed her hollow eyes.

Now, if only I could use the well of lies to reassure myself that the monsters only dwelled behind closed eyes.

Chapter Eight

Tevin's side: Through the eyes of a Reaper

*I*t took two Smolders to drag the enraged Evoker into the Unseen. I morphed to make sure Imp didn't rip the female elemental in half during transport. A slow-burning tension grew between those two, and I figured it was best to keep an eye on them.

Now I stood outside our cave listening to Moment's screams. Colorful threats intertwined with strings of cursing, and I laughed internally at her mundane ramblings as they blew throughout the tunnels. We decided the cellar was best since it was deep within the heart of the mountain and the only place we could keep her where she could not tap into her powers directly without some serious effort. I rotated my left shoulder, trying to work out the bone-crunching sound it was making. My cloak flowed over me, marbling in a black-and-indigo-tinted mist. Vexed, it formed a clasp of dual silver roses, then cinched itself around my neck to interlock them with a terse snap. I pulled on my minion's new addition so I could swallow. It slithered across my abs, finally plunging to the ground using tentacles to check the surrounding crevices.

My shoulder began to sizzle while it worked on fusing the bones together, although, I embraced the discomfort as images of me flying across the room replayed in my mind. I used a blending spindle to turn corporeal so that I could place a curse on Moment's Felterthread. The last thing I had wanted to find out was if Ashens were immune to another Unseen death-dealing creature. In the birth of a blink, she had flung her hand out and sent me slamming into the cellar door. I did not even have a chance to call forth my minion to help shield the blow.

Once the Felterthread barrier was secure, the tattoo had turned red, indicating the daemon seal was working. After removing my hands from her arm, I found myself across the room… again. So much for being under the assumption Michael, Raven, and Quint could manage to hold the elemental down.

The Smolder I carried had wanted to skip Ashen formalities and move straight to eating, but when I unfolded to my full height, my shoulder refused to level out. Archer and K had added their support to help Quint, Raven, and Michael detain her. Imp took the role of bystander and watched from the corner, bent over, laughing so hard he was wheezing. His actions won him guard duty while the others left to harvest and recharge.

Moment screeched, "When I get out of here, you all are going to wish for non-existence." *Crash.* She must have tried to rip the door off its hinges with her powers of wind.

"You need to calm the velocity of your spins. At this rate, your burning rage is going to blow your existence out." Part of Imp's charm was how he excelled at the art of sarcasm. "I know, try some yoga, or meditate. The Vessels do it to find…" His words trailed off, and then he magnified his voice. "What's the fluff stuff called, Tevin? Oh, wait, I know, *inner peace* and *wisdom*. You should focus on the wisdom part because I think you lack in that area." Imp's teasing echoed from deep within the mountain's core.

"Imp, I swear on the House of Time, when I get out of here, I'll break you first."

Slam. Bang. Slam.

"Is that a promise, sweetheart? I didn't know you cared." More laughter bounced around the maze of caves.

"Aaaggghhh!" Moment screamed.

Crash. Boom.

Imp's treble tone carried through the caves. "Bluster all you want, baby. You'll either get tired or drained before you know it." I guess it was his way of reasoning with her.

Placing him on guard duty had been a mistake. The combination of Imp's banter, mixed with Moment's fits of anger, brought on a headache. I pressed fingers into each temple to dull the throbbing and briefly considered relieving him of his post.

I had never paid attention to my responsibilities as a clan leader, cared about who I was or why, until now. Mentally scything a second in half, I realized how much of my existence I had taken for granted. I finally understood the meaning behind that insurance commercial but changed the words around to fit this situation: *Protecting souls. So easy, a reaper could do it.*

May Creation's fire consume me. Am I that stupid? How many Bond-Rites am I going to lock myself into for one soul?

Boom. Scrape. Boom.

Frustration was clouding Moment's judgment. The bounty hunter was a Wind Evoker, and to use the elements, she needed a live battery to replenish her powers. Without one, she would soon use up the amount stored within her core. Moment continued to smack earsplitting blasts of wind against the door.

I placed a fingertip to the end of my cigarette and mumbled with the filter between my lips, "Good luck, honey."

The cave wall vibrated, loosening a three-foot icicle at the entrance. It hit the rocks below sending a glass shattering echo throughout the cavern, and the wind-user screamed, "And don't call me *honey!*"

Almost dropping my cigarette, I thought, *Okay... that surprised me.* Her hearing was exceptional, which meant my clan, and I was going to have to discuss our plans in dragon tongue. I did not relish the idea of texting my entire plan to the clan.

Bang. Crash.

"Zeus's spit! I broke a nail. Damn you to Styx, Tevin,

you owe me a manicure before I cease your existence. Let me out of here. *Now!*"

The gales from the cellar were becoming harsher than the normal swirls that thrashed about. "I'm going to hang the lot of you with your own cloaks."

Crackle. Crack. Boom.

Moment was putting on a pretty good demonstration of her conjuring abilities. It impressed me since she was channeling from hundreds of feet below. I was curious to see what she could seriously muster up if pressured, but then again, I wasn't.

Using a clarifying spindle, I spoke into the breeze. "You are going to have to control your temper tantrums before we can discuss the terms of the Bond-Rite."

My minion swayed in the light breeze as I inhaled deeply on the filter. The wind flowing through the tunnel abruptly changed direction to its initial origin, and the ground trembled beneath me. I assumed this reaction was Moment's response to my advice.

Sputtering and gasping, she scrambled for her voice. "I would never do such a thing with the likes of your kind. I would rather cease to exist than make a contract with any of you losers."

Changing tactics, Moment coaxed in challenge. "Why don't you come down here and try to convince me." Her words lost their allure when she added, "And after you remove this foul restraint, I'll introduce you properly to Quicksilver. I'm sure she would love to give you a kiss, Tevin."

Bam. Boom. Boom.

I was having a temporary lapse of judgment as I started to reconsider forcing her into making a Bond-Rite with me.

Taking in my situation, and how the Unseen perceived Ashens, a question struck me. *How ironic was the meaning of danger?* It was a harmful, evil, unfortunate, or painful event, and yet every creature craved to experience it or manipulate its possibilities for their own sinister whims. I flicked the smoldering ember into the sky and watched the winds scatter the ash. I was about to turn this lethal creature into another protector.

Exhaling, I realized I was no better than the trickster half-angel who had recruited me for the same cause. "I guess it's true. Misery longs for company, and so this cursed chain continues," I admitted out loud, not realizing I was no longer alone.

"Hey there, boss man. How's the weather up here?" Imp was approaching from behind with his notorious black shades dimming the glow from his eyes. He swatted annoyingly at his cloak's black-and-purple swirls. "Go. You can go."

His minion disappeared.

"I say, the weather down below is shaping up to be a twister. The air velocity is about a hundred plus, and that's with the spells keeping her bark worse than her bite." He took off his shades and placed his hand on my shoulder. "I would hate to see what she could do if she were persuasively motivated to kill her bounty." He was implying Alexcia.

We were extremely fortunate obtaining the bounty hunter. I had a strange prediction the Sisters of Tense had a hand in our victory. These entities were known throughout Earth's history as the Fates. They guarded the past, maintained the present, and protected the future. The sisters also served the House of Time, but only two of the siblings, past and present, were Sand Flow advisers for the court. It meant the entities in the Unseen could only obtain information from two paths of time.

First, there was Pastasia, the sister in charge of Creation's history. Her eyes and mind were clear and sharp, but her body suffered from a terminally snail-paced age of decay. A type of narcolepsy plagued her. The elemental was constantly falling asleep whenever anyone tried to talk with her.

The second sister was Naù; pronounced like the Vessels' English word for now. This sister was in charge of the Present. She lived with the knowledge of five minutes before present and five minutes after, and never slept—

hence, her frequent mind-crash episodes. Basically, Naü's short term memory would fry every ten minutes. It was her payment for retaining so much power over the present, but she did retain her long-term memory. The Houses of the Unseen took great pains to tolerate Naü's Goldfish Syndrome.

Each one of the Sisters paid a price to Styx, but Kismet paid the largest one for protecting what only she could behold. No one was able to talk to the Sister who held the keys to unfolding realities because the River Styx had stitched her lips shut. Each Unseen creature, except Kismet, was bound to our Creator. She was forbidden to divulge the future, to any entity, period. This lack of interaction with others had made her temperament passive and detached. She was unaffected by the phrases *could be* or *will be*.

If I had a choice between the three, I would prefer to spend my time with Kismet. We could relate to some degree, but most of all, she did not snore or ramble excessively.

The Fates, from the House of Time, and the Ashens, from the House of Space, shared one similarity—we answered directly to our Creator.

Since we worked within the same guidelines, I figured it would serve my clan best to stay on civil terms with the Fates. They rarely received visitors without troubles, so I made sure we never pumped them for information. Each of them served as an ace I had tucked away for a dismal day.

Jaw muscle tensing, I addressed Imp. "You know we should pay a visit to the Sisters of Tense."

Dropping his sunglasses, they vanished before hitting the ground, and then he raised his hands in the air. "What? Why? I don't believe you meant to use the word *we*. You got your daemons mixed up. You're their favorite Ashen. *You* go. The last time we went, Pastasia kept falling asleep on my shoulder." Imp's chalky color faded to a slate blue, disgusted by the affection she had bestowed upon him. "Have you taken a good look at her? I mean, a real good, hard look? She's older than the River's silt—maybe a lot older." Imp's voice went up an octave. "Count me out. Take another

Ashen. Take K or Archer—he's a good sport."

Boom. Boom. Thump.

Moment was reminding us that we were ignoring her. Imp turned toward the tunnel entrance. He was stunned for a while before his shroud materialized around his neck, finishing its solid state by completing the hood. The edges shimmered with threads of violet as he stuck his thumb out in Moment's direction.

"Anyway, I'm wind-sitting today." His smile started to spread, expecting I would change my mind and recant the earlier suggestion.

Ignoring his reason, I passed his lanky frame to face the tunnel leading to our captive. I was not looking forward to disclosing my plans because it was not going to be received well.

With a sense of foreboding, I shifted my weight toward Imp. "You are right about Moment's containment, but I think you have tortured the Evoker long enough. We cannot afford to underestimate the strength hidden within that small frame. Besides, you need to feed as well." I turned to face him. "When the others return, I am going to assign Quint and Archer to guard her. You should collect the soul list from the Cauldron and fulfill your harvest before dawn. Before we interrogate our captive, the clan must be in top form."

Imp exhaled long and lowered his tone. "What about you? You haven't fed in days. You know she is going to target you first." His purple orbs blazed with amusement as he started to chuckle. "How's the shoulder?"

"It has been mended," I said while placing one finger to my mouth, then used my other hand to slap Imp's shoulder. The color of his eyes intensified as I indicated for him to follow me outside. Next, I commanded my minion, *"Hood."* When the shroud finished weaving itself together, I tugged it over my brow as several inky tentacles pushed me forward.

Imp mimicked me, and wrenched his hood lower. His Smolder growled as he followed me into the snow-whipped winds. Our minions wrapped around our bodies to protect us from the elemental's blustering temper tantrum.

I spoke to him internally. *"Her hearing is exceptional. If we were talking out loud several hundred feet away, she would answer as though she had been standing with us the whole time. Internally, I have realized, she can't get into our heads unless she is right on top of us."*

Imp's aura burned bright, a sign he was even more impressed by her capabilities. *"That's pretty incredible."* He blew out, then exclaimed out loud, "Hot damn!"

Irritation spurred me to rein him in. *"Focus, please. What you said gave me an idea."*

"What?" He readjusted his broadsword, looking everywhere but at me.

"She thinks I'm weak from your prompting about my eating habits. And no, I have not charged in a while."

"Well, we all know you haven't."

"When the others get back, I will recharge. But I want the others to fake that I stayed behind. Moment will try to take me out first, knowing I have not reaped in a while."

Taking into account that the gusts around the cave had lost their vexing bite, she was probably trying to find out where we had fled since she could not hear us anymore.

"I am asking the others to act as though I sent you alone."

Imp's aura dimmed. *"What are you planning to do with her?"*

I knew this was going to come out eventually, but I had been hoping it would be after I had set things into motion. *"I'm going to make a contract with the Wind Evoker. I think we can use her skills."*

"Use her skills for what? She'll relocate our dwelling to the next mountain range. Are you kidding me?" Imp closed his eyes to regain his composure *"You're going to ask her to help us child-sit?"*

I nodded reluctantly. *"I think it would be best to have her working with us."*

Imp opened his mouth, but I waved him off to continue.

"Instead of having her work against us, I prefer to keep her close. If I could persuade Moment from fulfilling her

bounty, then I might have a chance to fulfill these Bond-Rites. At least until Alexcia has chosen a House."

Imp furrowed his brow. "This Vessel is going to affect the balance in both of our worlds."

My shoulders slumped from the weight of his truth. We needed an extra pair of eyes because Alexcia was becoming more unpredictable. And since her parents were refusing to open her eyes, I knew it was only a matter of time before the power pressing against her walls would burst through.

For ten years, I have watched over her soul, guarding it and saving it from death's hold. But when I signed on, there was a clause I never considered, payment was required to the River either way. Every time the River Styx conjured her name, I had gone against the main purpose of my existence. The waters knew it.

Styx was draining a portion of my existence as both payment and punishment. Rae-Lynn had omitted that part of our Bond-Rite, and I, in turn, had dropped that portion of the Bond-Rite when I told the clan. I did not want them to find out how my powers had been compromised for Alexcia's sake. And because of my agreement, I had thrown our balance into jeopardy by linking my existence to Alexcia's destiny.

Moment was the fourth ace up my sleeve, and who knew… maybe she could relieve us of child sitting for a time. I needed my clan to understand without fully disclosing the predicament I had gotten myself into. If I could not convince them to accept Moment into our ranks, I might as well walk into the River Styx before Max shoved me there instead.

A crease deepened across Imp's brow. "So, what about Michael and the rest? Do they know about your plans with the wind elemental?" He sounded a little put off by the general concept of the plan.

A flock of Callcrys took to the sky. I watched them, wondering where they were heading. With a tight shake of my head, I answered, "No, they do not."

Chapter Nine

Tevin's side: Through the eyes of a Reaper

*S*now and ice swirled around the cave's icicled teeth, composing a solemn doomsday melody. Steam rose from several Time Bends created by the returning Ashens. Within a second, saliva pooled under my tongue, and I tasted a tantalizing metallic residue wafting from each portal. It had been days since I fed, and my body was craving energy, not hamburgers.

I mumbled, "Get ready."

It was the end of our discussion about Moment… for the moment.

The pressure from the clan's reentry was producing a high-pitched whine in my ears. Imp's minion had become fluid in its movements, displaying excitement connecting with its master's drive to hunt and feed. The aroma of death was exquisite, and my inner daemon growled from desire.

Torment and anguish brought us more in tune with our existence, and the agony was empowering. It was the closest experience to living we were ever allowed. In short, Ashens craved a Vessel's death to taste the spark of life.

Through the mist of melting slush, I could make out several massive wings and claws emerging from an enlarged time portal. Five colossal dragon-like daemons stood before us. Each of their scaly hides was shimmering with the tears of the grieving, which ironically cast prismatic, multicolored spots across the snow.

The high mountain caps in the Unseen were ideal for us because the sub-zero landscape helped contain our inner daemons and provided a soothing balm on our scales. Here, it was easier to control our Smolder when changing back into our form. Oddly enough, when an Ashen released its fighting form, the core temperature within a reaper could surpass the heat of a volcano's heart. Also, the damage we caused was restricted.

My vision sharpened when I detected a musty sulfuric odor coming from the middle of the pack. Each one of them coiled snapped and roared as if they were quarreling over an unfinished debate. Michael reared up and slammed Archer into the side of the mountain. Chunks of snow, ice, and rocks fell around K and Quint. Both shook their manes, fiercely roaring and hissing at Michael. Archer rolled to his feet as smoke billowed from his snout. The ground buckled under his claws as he stomped toward the wild pack of daemons. Raven glowered from behind an imaginary safe-line, seeming disheveled and blatantly perplexed.

I unsheathed my scythe, giving Imp the signal to go back inside and check on our captive. His purple aura diminished as he descended into the tunnel, but I didn't want his unusual behavior making matters worse.

Once he was gone, I turned my attention back to the quarreling daemons. Their bickering was driving away some of the creatures around our dwelling and adding to my headache. Spinning the laced blade over my head, I used the scythe's energy, mixing it with all my anger before slamming the handle into the ground. The blade vibrated with a deafening chime, drowning out the clashing daemons, and their roars morphed into screeching because they could not cover their ears.

The four who had been fighting bowed their heads and hissed at me. Raven closed his eyes and stood up slowly. Pushing his way through the pack, I noticed he was limping and favoring his left side. The crimson dragon grumbled, lowering his face to my level as his minion swirled over both wings and prepared to shift them back into their Ashen form. A plume of onyx mist slithered around all of us. Bones crunched, popped, and cracked, as their shifting became more intense, echoing throughout the canyon.

A daemonic sense of pride swelled within as my cloak flowed over my shoulders, weaving its power to turn me corporeal. The sour sulfuric stench that hung in the frigid air, mixed with the heat from their changing, made the area muggy and sticky. After the steam had cleared, four reapers stood before me, but one remained on the ground, cradling his arm. Hissing ink patterns of melted snow indicated the reaper was wounded. Raven chuckled while he rocked forward onto his knees. He was finding pleasure in the way his wounds were making him feel.

Agitated, I waited for one of them to volunteer information. Twisting both hands around the silver-vined handle, the thorns sliced into my palms. One of the reapers coughed, and I swung my weapon to rest under Archer's chin. He leaned in, challenging me with his bright orange eyes to bring the blade closer. The bow in his left hand was staring right through me with the same intense look.

Michael's eyes burned with fury. His fingers ran over the hilt of his battle axe, but he did not seem to disapprove of my actions with Archer. His demeanor was an odd combination between reserved and hostile.

Quint and K were in a protective stance flanking Raven with both of their weapons drawn. Quint was facing Archer, while K's sights were on Michael. Their grouping was intended to separate Archer and Michael, yet shield Raven from the bickering duo.

They were clearly divided about the best approach.

I lowered the blade from Archer's neck and swung it above my head, listening to the air sing through the metal webbing before holstering the weapon.

Michael made a sharp, *"tsk."* Even though he was displeased with my decision, he followed suit and sheathed his weapon.

Since our situation appeared to be a temporary truce, I

held one finger to my mouth and pointed down to the ground with my other hand. Smirking, I used my hand by my mouth to mimic talking. With the other, I motioned to an area about fifty feet away, and then pivoted on my heel to proceed in the same direction. Once I believed we were far enough, so Moment could not hear us, my minion hesitantly turned us to face them.

Archer was giving the clan a wide girth. *"It was a misunderstanding. The decision I made was for the sake of the clan."*

K sneezed and said, "Bullshizt" out loud.

I shook my head slowly and pointed back to the ground.

Michael blasted his way through our heads, confronting Archer. *"If you were looking out for our clan, Raven would not be leaking blood all over the place."* Michael's minion squirmed and darted, mimicking his mood. The thin traces of midnight blue meant one thing—he was on the offensive.

The orange aura threading around the edge of Archer's cloak was becoming darker. Taking a defensive stance, a low rumble added punch to his words. *"I had the child covered. They would have never gotten to her. I was doing my job—"*

Michael took a step in Archer's direction. *"Your job was to go with Raven and harvest at the bar two streets away, not to run off to play hero. If it had not been for the quick thinking of K and Quint, you might have lost your existence. You almost cost Raven his."*

Quint and K stood their ground by Raven, watching Archer and Michael exchange a volley of words. I couldn't help being sucked into the back and forth game of who is going to take the blame. My head swiveled from side to side.

Archer waved his bow around in anger. Wink's eyes were huge—probably afraid his master might drop him. *"Look, we could smell the Sculptor, and I knew the Water Raisers were close by."* He turned to me. *"No offense, but I didn't ask Raven to follow me or save my ass. I sensed elementals hovering around the area where we left the Vessel. It was probably a rescue party looking for Moment and her posse. I was simply checking on the Child's safety."*

His defense seemed plausible to me, but I could tell the Ashen was holding back. *Why?*

Archer approached but halted just inches shy of my weapon's reach. *"While I was patrolling the parking lot by the apartment, I sensed an odd pressure in the atmosphere, Tevin."*

I raised an eyebrow, waiting for him to enlighten us.

Archer's cloak moved in puffs of marbled frustration along the hem. *"Hades fire, Tevin. She sent off a pulse flow. It was only a matter of time before they found her location."* Rising to his full height indicated to me he was bracing for a fight.

Encumbered, I thought about the fight with the Doom Guard. Alexcia was leaking power, that was certain, but I didn't believe it was enough to perform spells. If she was able to do that, we were screwed. A pulse flow was a wave of leftover spindling, and if the blast were large enough, most of the Unseen would have felt it.

I was losing patience with Alexcia. Child-of-Balance or not, I was going to break through Max and Rae-Lynn's bonding spell and tell her what she needed to know. Both of my contracts were in serious jeopardy of being breached.

It was my turn to be heard. *"How did Raven end up wounded?"*

A gritty laugh came from Raven. *"Yeah, Archer, tell him how I ended up paying for your choice."*

Raven threw his weapons in front of me. The handles of both his kataras had been snapped from their blades. As an Ashen, the nexus of our existence was linked to our weapon. If a harvester's weapon was destroyed, the reaper could befall the same fate. A weakened Ashen was similar to a rabid bat, crazed with the thirst to feed, but functioning with an erratic sense of direction.

K turned to face Archer and lowered his mace. Threads of sun-lit green misted in slow swirls of onyx as his cloak tried to conceal his confusion. *"What did happen? I thought we were fighting because they attacked first?"*

Quint did not lower his polearm from the resting

position on his hip, its blade angled at Archer's midsection in case he stepped in the wrong direction. The sun-etched reaper's cloak became solid as if holding its breath, waiting for Archer's explanation as well.

Our techno-reaper always had the same attitude toward the Child-of-Balance—he did not care one way or the other. Quint moved to death's song and did whatever was asked of him, nothing more. It seemed Archer had taken up my cause of keeping the Child-of-Balance alive, but Quint's apprehension was a red flag.

Quint's yellow eyes narrowed to two slits as he tilted his head to listen to his shroud. Nodding in agreement, he skeptically inquired, *"Yeah, why?"*

While the four of us waited for Archer to answer, a whispered stream of verbal curses filled the air. Raven's cloak struggled to heal him. Watching Raven reminded me that his kataras needed to be taken to the Cauldron of Ending for repairs. Once they were fixed, his minion would be able to heal him faster, and I was going to need every daemon in top form if I wanted Moment to listen.

Archer beheld his recurve bow. Wink's eyes were wide and unmoving, waiting for an explanation too. In a form of defeat, he spoke, *"Wink started to vibrate from an abnormal power surge. That's what compelled me to backtrack and investigate where the Child-of-Balance was located."* He looked at Michael and K. *"I know we"*—he shook Wink—*"left point, but Raven can normally hold his own on a simple harvest. It was only four souls from a drunken fight, simple, right?"*

He turned to me for support, and I nodded.

Swinging back toward his fellow daemons, Archer continued, *"I ran along the rooftops following their scent. I knew the Vessel was still in the area, and I was checking on it. Nothing more."*

K held a curved hand to his face to feign another sneeze, and I quickly made a throat-cutting swipe to knock it off. It was as though I had become a daycare attendant mediating a playground fight. Frowning, I waved a hand at the others to wait for their turn.

"Go on," I mouthed while leaning on my scythe.

"I did find a group—two wind elementals and a Water Raiser—about four blocks away. There was a huge pulse-flow. Tevin, I almost fell off the roof it was so strong," Archer explained.

Michael crossed his arms. *"Too bad that outcome didn't happen."*

A prick of concern made me scratch above my right eye. Alexcia had not been practicing magic since her parents had sealed her abilities, and it would take a lot of energy to knock one of us off guard. *Great, more bad news*, I thought with a loud exhale.

I motioned for the accused Ashen to get on with it.

Archer put his bow away and faced me directly. *"I assumed they were looking for Moment and the others and thought they might locate the Child-of-Balance. I was not aware there had been another group watching Raven and me at the bar."*

He snapped his fingers, and the hood of his cloak disappeared... exposing his fire-orange glare. *"Michael and the others sensed the disturbance in time. That's when they found Raven draped over a car in the parking lot, his weapons embedded in the ground. One of the elementals had a Felterthread and tried to use it on him to get information."*

Michael's voice was stern. *"You should have told Raven where you were going. He knew they were there. When he turned around to tell you, you had disappeared."*

"I thought the Vessel was in danger, not one of my own. I reacted the same way Tevin would have if he had thought the child was in peril. I was looking out for our leader's interests, which in turn, is looking out for our clan."

Every eye shifted from Archer to me. *Was I supposed to take responsibility for this reaper's miscreant actions?* The divide between our clan was widening. *Could I ever catch a break?*

Archer snapped, and his cloak rolled off him and disappeared into the ground. *"You know, you could have called out for me internally."*

Raven hissed, *"I would have if I weren't battling to keep my existence intact."* He uncurled himself to stand. The initial wound his minion was healing stopped oozing acidic blood but had not completely closed. Crimson eyes blazed with betrayal. *"You could have internally told me you were leaving,"* he challenged.

Three sets of eyes left me and glued to Archer.

"Fine." He threw his arms into the air. *"Call on Hades and tell him he has a new gondolier. Go ahead and snuff out my existence. It was wrong—I was wrong! There, I said it."*

My unease shifted. *"What about the group of elementals by the apartment?"*

Michael's lips pressed together. *"What? Archer almost loses one of our own, and you're worried about the brat? What has come over you?"*

Taking the blame partially off Archer, I said, *"Look, I got us into this mess—"*

"You." Michael shook his head. *"You got yourself into this mess, and we're stupid-ass Ashens for agreeing to help you out of it."*

Well, our council meeting was turning into an intervention. This situation was not going to help my plan.

I acknowledged Archer. *"What about the recon group? Did they find the Vessel?"* I made sure my tone sounded detached when I asked.

"Yeah, they did, but I took one out with Wink. Then Michael started yelling in our heads while looking for me. I explained where I was, and then K and Quint arrived to assist. Michael stayed behind to guard Raven until we got back." His smile slowly widened in self-satisfaction. *"If Styx brings them back, they're nothing, but carbon recopies by now."*

I shared the smile with him for a second before Arctic winds swept over us and crashed into our circle. Moment was pissed, and I was sure Imp had caused the frozen blast of air. It was time to divulge my new strategy. *"Moment can hear if you talk out loud."* Multicolored pairs of eyes gazed at me, but I was not sure if it was from disbelief.

K looped an arm under Raven's. Quint followed and helped with the opposite side. Michael retrieved Raven's broken kataras. Archer hung back for reasons of self-existence. He had been labeled the pack's new chew toy.

Michael passed me, whispering, "How good is her hearing?"

Moment's laughter rang out of the cave.

"That good, huh?" Michael did an about-face.

I pulled the hood over my eyes and replied internally. *"Yes, she is definitely something."*

We made it to the mouth of the cave when I saw Imp walking about a foot above the ground from the back of the main tunnel. The thin purple glow outlining his figure was illuminating the cracks along the jagged surface. Seeing the fissures in the walls made me think about how broken we were. I was gambling on my existence that Moment would be our ace when the fighting really started, and it was time for me to ask for chips to hedge my wager.

I signaled to the rest of the group from heading deeper into our lair. Snapping my fingers, the hood misted away, and I motioned Imp to join us in the center of the den. I put on my best doomsday look, and every reaper groaned. It was time to either discuss what to do about our current weather conditions or set the elemental free, which I really could not afford to do.

Bam. Bam. Crunch.

I wondered how long she could keep at it. The Evoker had been using her powers for so long I figured her abilities would have depleted enough to give me some time to explain what I wanted from her.

The Ashens were displaying hostilities from their spat, and it made our space feel even more crowded than normal. K piled up some wood in the middle of the fire pit to light up the room. I heard one of Archer's spell-fired arrows pass my shoulder to pierce a log with a dull *thunk*. Then the whole pile ignited with a loud hiss.

I stared at the fire, swallowing hard and preparing

myself. Michael was going to be the most difficult to convince, especially since he knew a portion of my problems. I tapped my head wondering when this ten-year headache would end.

"I need to explain what Moment's role will be before we take Raven down to the Cauldron."

Laughter erupted when K and Imp high-fived each other. Quint pulled out his iPod and earbuds, clearly showing indifference with what I did with her. Michael eased Raven into one of the wooden seats and then stood across from me glaring while smacking his minion to stop moving. Archer dropped to the floor and stared into the fire, placing Wink so it could watch the fire with him.

"With the Child-of-Balance becoming unstable and clearly unpredictable, I believe it would be in our best interest if I make a Bond-Rite with Moment. We could use her assistance watching over the Vessel."

There. My plan was out.

The silence was deafening. Even the fire dancing in front of me had fallen silent. Six reapers exchanged gazes of confusion, and some, mortification. Not bad. Half needed an explanation, and the other half were benign.

Michael stirred next to Raven, pulled out his axe, dropped it on the table, and then sat down, waiting for me to resume. Raven found humor in Michael's threatening attempt to tell me to spill my guts. Quint stopped listening to his music and placed the little silver rectangle into his cloak's misty tentacle. Imp cleared his throat and shrugged, assessing each Ashen's demeanor. K added some distance from Imp and leaned against the wall with a huff. Imp might as well have sat on the floor next to Archer.

The fire crackled, and Moment's wind raced up the maze of tunnels. She was trying to locate us.

I cleared my throat. "You will know soon enough what is in store for you."

Three… two… one…

Her voice rose up from the depths of the cave. "Like I care."

A smirk spread across Imp's face, and I knew it matched mine since we were aware of her capabilities. The other five stood up, ready to fight and wildly scanned for the elemental.

Raven winced and pulled his cloak closed as he sat back down slowly. With a grumble, he adjusted his position. *"So, she can throw her voice. Big deal. There's a male Vessel on the Strip who makes a living using different voices."*

I arched an eyebrow in question, but he dismissed me.

"I had a reaping during one of the shows." Then Raven cupped both hands over his mouth. "Not impressed, baby."

A rumbling from down below caught my attention, followed by an ear-piercing scream. The pocket of wind carrying her voice found Raven, knocked him off his chair and out the mouth of the cave. The wounded reaper was laid out in the snow.

Shocked, I stated, "Well, that's new."

Imp and I shared an unbiased shrug as he scrambled over to help Raven off the ground. Imp said, "What the hell? You can't possibly think she wouldn't try to break any kind of agreement to get her claws into the Vessel. That Evoker would collect your existence in exchange for a nine-volt battery as payment."

A siren's chuckle floated from the cellar—menacing, with a hint of challenge and a pinch of spite. Moment seemed amused with Imp's accusation of her character.

I swung my scythe. *"Hey, Ashens. Do not get your cloaks twisted around your ankles. I know what I'm doing, and if all goes well, we'll be back to our normal routine in a matter of days."*

I had to try and provide leverage with the bounty hunter because reasons or favors wouldn't work with her. She wanted power, and I would offer just enough to keep her in check. It has to work, to give Alexcia a fighting chance, for the sanity of our clan, and my existence. Moment was my loophole, and I was going to jump through it feet first.

Chapter Ten

Tevin's side: Through the eyes of a Reaper

"**D**aemons barter all the time."

Our discussion had ended once we reached the cellar door. In my head, it was simple—I would find out what she desires and then offer a trade in return for her services. The other party, though, normally made the list of wants on their end more complex, and I expected nothing less from Moment. She knew how the system worked, but I was not going into this deal with ignorance holding my hand.

I attempted to reason with the elemental from outside the cellar. Her wind tore through the tunnel and blew Archer into Quint, who, in turn, stumbled over Imp's feet. The combination of their voices echoing through the tunnels was intense and made it impossible to get a word in edgewise. K remained stationary behind me. Motioning to the three fallen Ashens, I pointed toward the wall behind K and me.

"I am done playing nice daemon."

Four evil sneers made my upper lip twitch as I unsheathed my weapon. They drew their weapons and waited for a command.

Michael and Raven were coming up the path. After spending some time at the Cauldron of Ending, Raven looked better, and his kataras gleamed in the torchlight. Moment was only making it harder by spindling without the connection of an energy partner.

Moment's wind-swipes died down, and I heard her swear. That was our cue. I swung my scythe into a high arc, burying the blade into the massive door, then yanked it off its hinges. The door hit the cave wall and shattered, raining wood and rock debris everywhere. Reapers flooded into the room like shadows racing from the light. The Evoker's eyes were huge, and her mouth was in a frozen O shape.

Michael and K took out her legs. Quint and Raven each grabbed one of her arms as she began to fall backward. The four of them held her suspended about chest high in the air. Archer took point behind me and raised his bow, aiming the arrow tip at her middle. Wink watched her intently without blinking. Imp calmly walked over and slid behind her, draping one of his long arms around her neck. It lay there, loose but with harmful intent if she provoked us.

The female Wind Evoker scoped out the situation and chuckled. While grinning at Archer, Moment shoved her head against Imp's chest, then turned to wink at me. Puckering her lips, she said, "How many reapers does it take…"

Her voice trailed off as Imp's arm tightened around her thin porcelain neck. He answered her back by leaning into the curve of her collarbone and trailing a nail down the side of her cheek. She recoiled from his touch.

I approached and extended an arm with an open hand. The snap I made echoed as my scythe materialized in front of us. Archer and Wink kept a sniper's concentration on Moment. It was satisfying to know if she even started to open her mouth, Archer would fire. I flipped the weapon blade down and rested full weight on the silver-thorn handle.

Leaning so I could make eye contact with Imp, I said, "I think you can loosen your grip. She's smart and would not jeopardize what is left of her powers to give one of us a slap. Isn't that right, Moment?"

My eyes connected with hers. I had never really stared into the eyes of an elemental, nor had I ever wanted to, but I was shocked at what I saw. The ice-blue color of her irises seemed to be moving in slow, mini-swirls around her hourglass-shaped pupils. The element of wind was literally a part of her, not only a power she could command at will.

Moment's eyes thinned to slits once she realized I had made the connection between her and the elements. As soon as she closed them, I lost the ability to read her emotions. Behind the Evoker's bluster, she was very intelligent. Moment tried to clear her throat but winced from Imp's hold around her neck.

His arm relaxed, but only enough for her to speak.

She tried to maintain her composure, and I watched as her eyelids fluttered before she fully opened them. "I will assume, in my current situation, that I have no choice but to listen." She tilted her face toward the ceiling and puffed out an exhale. "Well, out with it. I have no intention of being stuck here for the remainder of my existence. Your stench is foul and beginning to seep into my pores." Her expression scrunched. "Ugh, I can even taste it. That's disgusting. I need a cleansing."

"Hey, our Cauldron is at the end of this tunnel. I'm sure we can accommodate your request," Imp teased.

My features hardened as the skin around my face and hands tightened over bones. "The River would probably welcome your added jolt of power. Want to gamble your existence and see if Styx would recopy you?"

For the first time, Moment appeared nervous, and the emotion itched my curiosity. Styx scared her; this was my leverage. She was terrified of what our Creator would take as payment for bringing her back. My daemon nature was kicking in, tempting to dangle this tidbit of information to torment her.

I stood and positioned the laced blade under Moment's chin to lift her eyes to meet mine. "So, no answer? Okay then, Ashens, let's show Moment how hot the Cauldron of Ending can get."

The clan started to ease toward the door. Moment blanched and bucked with force, filling the room with bloodcurdling screeches. The instant aroma of genuine panic rolling off her made every Ashen's aura burn brighter, covering the cave walls in a prismatic pulsing rainbow. The daemons' low growls of hunger intertwined with her protests, and she was beginning to create a feeding frenzy between us the way a wounded fish rings a dinner bell in a tank full of piranhas.

Their grip on her was tightening. Imp huffed and jammed his fingers into her mouth. "You need to shut it. I enjoy seeing your eyes fill with hatred toward me. It would be a shame to lose what we have between us."

With her screams muffled, I raised the tip of the hilt to her face. "Moment, tone down the theatrics. Your heightened emotions are going to make you an Ashen's late-night snack. Look around you. There are seven of us. Now, hush." I licked my lips right before placing a finger on them.

Her eyes became as huge as a Callcry's, and the movement within both irises ceased while her body fell to small quakes.

I tapped Imp's shoulder indicating for him to remove his fingers, but she bit down before he retracted them. He hissed and smacked the side of her face. Iridescent sand trickled from her lower lip. Moment held her breath and sighed.

Her reaction amused me until I realized she had provoked Imp on purpose to piss him off enough to react. That was her method of calming down. She was smart.

Rubbing her jaw, she gurgled, "Thanks, I needed that." Moment turned and spat globs of sand onto the floor. Clearing her airway, she regained her composure as well as possible while being suspended in midair by four reapers.

I patted her thigh. "Good Evoker."

In a husky reply, the elemental threatened, "Touch me again that way, and you'll find your scythe sticking out of your ass." She bucked again for emphasis.

Michael and K eased her feet onto the floor as the bottom of their cloaks stretched out to secure her.

I snapped, and the hood formed so I could pull the rim over my eyes. "Moment, I have a proposition."

Her jaw tightened as she processed my words. Her tongue made a backward sucking noise. "*Humph*, a proposition?" She cocked her head. "Why? My house has promised me more spindled recipes and power if I bring my bounty in alive. Less if she dies, but it's still quite substantial." She squirmed, trying to readjust her weight.

I took four steps and leaned into her space followed by one harsh inhale. She had misunderstood what I'd asked of her. "No, Moment. My proposition has to do with keeping the Child-of-Balance safe."

The clan groaned in protest reminding me of the night I had revealed my Bond-Rite with Alexcia's mother.

If I were going to work with Moment, I needed to treat her like one of my own. So, I got in her face. "Moment, I don't have time to bat this around. I'm hungry, and I'm annoyed. Haven't you ever wondered why the child has not taken a dip in the River yet?"

"No, I figured your clan was slipping up."

"Really?" I flashed my blade under her chin again. "You really believe we couldn't reap one little girl? Then why were we always fighting you and the other Unseen? Why was one of us always hanging around the Vessel and watching over her so she wouldn't have the pleasure of meeting a Bridge Crosser or the tip of another Ashen's weapon?" Exasperated, I began to pace.

Her eyes narrowed. "Hades burn out your mouth. Your clan is working against the River?" Eyes wild, she screeched, "For real? You all are working at keeping that creature alive? Why?" The sound of confusion in her voice further emphasized her question.

I could tell she was intrigued. The curiosity behind it had taken the fight-or-flight from her. She was ready to listen. The reapers slowly eased up to let her go.

She crossed her arms. "So, what do you need from me that all of you cannot do?"

"Both of her parents are from our world. They have put a binding spell on her. She doesn't know who or what she really is." I leaned against part of the broken door. "About ten lifetimes ago, the Cauldron summoned me to harvest her power. I was about to when she called out my name and started speaking to me." My mask fell as I confessed, "She knew me, Moment."

"No Vessel can see us—not even the chosen one—unless we want them to. Maybe you *wanted* her to see you."

The tick above my right eye started again. "The child knew my name, Moment," I repeated.

She shifted her hips and rocked back on the heels of her boots. "Go on. But I don't see what this has to do with me. She's only a job—technically, for the both of us. You're all prolonging the inevitable. Someday she will have to choose a House to serve… or die."

"The Vessel's caregiver was there by her deathbed, begging me to spare the child's life. She then divulged to me there was an unusual shift in power between the Houses, the Unseen, and the Earth's realm. She also insisted this Vessel was different than the others. In order to prove case-in-point, some of the creatures from the Unseen were trying to kill her before she could make a choice."

I was not going to convince Moment without bluntly stating what I had done. Within seconds, I would be asking the same of her. "I made an Ashen's Bond-Rite with the female caregiver, to watch and guard over the Child-of-Balance until she is of age to pick a House."

Moment's jaw dropped before laughter echoed throughout the caves. "You all are protecting her? You expect me to believe you have become pro-life activists?" She continued to snort and hiccup, curling in on herself. Through chortles, she said, "I know, I will get some T-shirts made with her picture on them, that reads, 'Can you help us save this soul?' with a 1-800 number printed on it." She started wiping away fake tears.

I did not want to give her the satisfaction of knowing she was getting under my skin. My explanation came out through welded teeth. "From what we have seen, I am beginning to believe there is more to her existence. I cannot reveal the mystery if she is dead."

Michael, standing next to Moment, raised his voice. "Look, I don't care for the brat. I just want things to go back to the way they used to be. I think Tevin made a mistake by entering into these contracts, but his Bond-Rites are almost fulfilled, and then the child will be able to choose. After that, the Vessel is fair game." He faced Moment. "Hell, I may even help you bring her in, or we can play cat-and-mouse with the brat."

I tried to stare a hole through Michael's chest, wanting him to either shut up or evaporate. Either outcome would have been fine with me at the time.

Moment arched an eyebrow. "Contracts? You made more than one? Are you crazy?" Her long fingers pressed against her temples as she massaged in small circles. "Please don't tell me they were both for that child. Why would you, of all Ashens, want to go against your nature to protect this one Vessel?"

I frowned. Only Michael knew that answer, and I was taking his advice. Lips fused together, I tugged the hood down farther over my brow. Her last question had caught me off guard. My minion detected my unease; I was drowning in my thoughts as I sank into their darkness.

At present, I was beginning to question my own motives. I wanted to know more, not only about Alexcia, but the Vessels and how they warped their lives by using emotions. Plus, I could not shake the fact that there was a foreign attachment stirring within me whenever I was around her. The emotion was as light as snowfall on the skin, but it was new to my existence, and new I craved.

Anything different was going to help me cope with my immortality. I was not sure if one of my kind could ever understand enough to accept what they could not comprehend. My clan would never acquiesce to my desire to understand the living. Expressing that desire might cost me the unity of our clan. We were already cracked, so I did not need to break the urn completely.

From far away, I heard the crisp sound of a dry snap, followed by a sharp puff of air hitting my face.

"Hello, Daemon, where did you go?"

Moment was standing right in front of me, accompanied

by the five Ashens who, only minutes ago, had wanted to freeze her mouth closed. They stood behind her, vexed and troubled, waiting for me to untangle my thoughts.

"What? Give a daemon some space."

I backed up into Archer, who was following Moment with Wink. *Has he been on point all this time?*

I caught sight of the recurve bow. Its eyes were unmoving once a target was in its sights, never blinking. Even I found that particular feature creepy.

"Tevin, what do you want with me? I would like to report back to my House. Time does not wait, and they might pass my job on to another bounty hunter. That would crush my reputation in the Unseen, and I can't have that."

"What I need to ask you requires your talents as both an Evoker and a hunter."

She seemed to be analyzing her broken nail. "Listening."

"I would like to make an agreement for us to work together protecting the Child-of-Balance. Basically, I need more of your time. If you could hold off collecting your bounty, and stop any entity with the same agenda, while we tend to our normal duties replenishing the River and allow us time to get a decent meal, I can uphold my contracts without them becoming breached. I need to start fulfilling my duties as an Ashen, or I won't be able to protect her. It's as simple as that."

She smirked. "Simple. Daemon, nothing in our world is ever simple." Moment turned and shoved her way through the clan, swiping her hands and brushing the clan away like mere pests.

The Wind Evoker stopped in front of me. A crease had formed between her eyebrows, indicating she was deep in thought. That bothered me. Even my shroud slowed its movement while waiting for her to respond.

Moment turned sharply to face us all. "Let's just say, for a laugh, I consider upholding this contract. What's in it for me?" Both hourglass irises sparkled with desire.

That was the loaded question I had been hoping for. It

signified I might have a chance to strike a deal with her yet. I waved my arms, as the cloak exposed my chest and draped behind me. We both knew we had each other right where we wanted—it was time to barter.

"What do you want, Moment?"

K was holding his weapon up to her when he turned to face me. "Watch her, Tevin. I heard she can be worse than asking for a wish from a genie."

Her deep-pink tinted lips curved up. "I enjoy hearing my reputation is getting around the Unseen, but flattery will get you nowhere. Payment of power is what I require. What can the seven of you pay for my time? Oh, and it had better be more than what the House of Time is offering."

Each Ashen became tight-lipped, miffed from her request. A payment of power was not something an Ashen could willingly give. We were bound by the River Styx only to use our power for one purpose—collecting souls and returning them to the River. We were not entitled to take a soul without the River asking for it back. She was right. This was not going to be at all simple. *Damn.*

"Well, what will it be? Make it good, Tevin or I'm as good as gone." Her fingers fluttered from side to side. "Like the wind."

Imp grabbed my minion and pulled me to him. My cloak squirmed under his fingers. The others followed and formed a huddle around me. I was thrown into an internal battlefield between the clan and myself, as each daemon fired questions.

The purple-tinted Ashen was the first to hit me. "Don't even think about it, Tevin. We are not allowed. You could put both worlds in peril." Under his hood, a grim scowl indicated the seriousness of his words.

With teeth clenched Michael added, "Really, Tevin. Is the child worth all this nonsense? We are soul takers, death dealers, not knights who save the princess from the dragon. We are the dragons who feed off the knight and princess before sending what's left to the River."

Archer was partially in the huddle, so he and Wink

could keep their focus on the elemental as she paced. Voice airy, he said, "I know I screwed up tonight, but I have to say, if I hadn't been looking out for the Balance, I would have never left Raven."

Quint's interjection did not help either. "Yeah, but if Tevin had never made that Bond-Rite, we wouldn't have been protecting that Vessel in the first place. She would have been harvested years ago. Ten, to be exact."

A sneer grew along with my irritation, and I answered, "I made the Bond-Rites, yes, but I wanted to know more about why a Child-of-Balance was needed. Did any of you ever think about what is beyond our existence? Six hundred-plus lifetimes!" I shouted into their heads. My shoulders sagged. "Boredom has infected me, and in a lapse of judgment, I made a poor choice. I wanted to know more about Vessels. If this child isn't what Rae-Lynn and Max claim it to be, then I will harvest her myself, and we can put these years of torture behind us."

Raven stood next to me, watching Moment with tapered eyes. His tone had a growl rolling under his words. "If you make this Bond-Rite with her, then we do this as a clan. I don't agree with the path you have dragged us down, but I am willing to see it through as long as you follow through with what you said."

I arched an eyebrow. "Which part?"

Raven's reply was stoic. "If the child doesn't choose a House, you take her soul."

An ache, moving like frost, numbly coated the emotions I was trying to control. I told myself the awkwardness was from working on an empty tank. I angled my face away from them. "So be it."

I gave myself some space so the clan would not read too much into the emotions I was experiencing… when regret stabbed me. I did not want to be the one watching the life fade from Alexcia's eyes and never finding out the answer to Rae-Lynn's riddle. She had once told me that I had been a Child-of-Balance like her daughter.

Raven looked grim. "Do I have to make a Bond-Rite to

do so?"

There was a forced sigh. "Daemons, I may belong to the House of Time, but I'm not deaf." She narrowed her ice-blue eyes while tapping her wrist. "Tic-toc, daemons. I'm on the clock, you know."

Bluntly, Michael answered, "We can't teach her the Knell's Toll. Period. You need to find out what she hungers for the most out of her entire existence and exploit that need." His cloak rippled with an evil zeal of excitement, his outline glowing with the same brightness as his eyes. "Let's do this."

The other five nodded.

It was time to deal.

"What kind of compensation do you want out of this contract? I believe you want to grow powerful, but at what cost from us?" I gestured in a grand arm swipe to include the group of daemons and me in the room.

Batting her eyelids, she chewed on the broken nail. "You are asking me what I want? Not what you are going to offer me?" Her eyes clouded over with doubt. "That's not how I work, Ashen. I want to know what kind of spells you can give me to wield. How much power does a soul give, and can you use that with your magic? Stuff like that."

Archer finally lowered his bow, and Wink blinked from losing sight of his target. "Moment, do you even know what kind of daemons Ashens are?"

His request for her insight was not what she had expected. "You deal in death. That in itself is the second ultimate power. Any of the Unseen would fight to have it. I want to be taught the Knell's Toll."

I didn't even blink. "No."

The other six turned to face her and kept their cloaks subdued. The glow from their eyes dimmed, reaffirming my answer was nonnegotiable.

"I see. Well then, you really *don't* care if I collect on my bounty."

She snapped, and a light breeze wafted through our cloaks. The Evoker could use her wind, but I knew we could take her down if we had to.

"Moment, we are a different breed of daemon. We do not work specifically for the House of Space. Think of us as the black sheep of the Unseen. We answer specifically to the River Styx, and the River gives us the power to harvest." I motioned to my clan. We cannot show you how the Ashen's Death Ritual of the Knell's Toll is conjured.

"Besides, if you were able to Spindle the Knell, it would never be a clean sever because your aura will mesh with the soul's aura. Styx would not accept it back to be recycled. There has to be a desire you crave more than power."

The elemental cocked her head. "Nothing is further from the truth, in my book. Power is everything."

She conjured a miniature tornado and played with it, watching it hop from palm to palm. Moment fell silent in thought. Her eyes moistened for a second, and it made her appear fragile. The black portions of her hair crisscrossed the white strands underneath, like a chessboard.

Moment closed her palm and snuffed out her creation. "Well, if you cannot teach me the Knell, I want to know when I will die."

Her response stunned us as the room fell silent.

Some elementals—mostly from the House of Time—could slow the inevitable by using their talents to spindled spells that delayed time. But there were only a handful of the Unseen, called Spindlers, capable of performing such a high level of magic. Plus, it was extremely expensive, and the outcome was unpredictable. If the spell was spun wrong, the result could take time from both the client and the Spindler.

My mouth was dry as I peeled my tongue from the roof of it. "Every creature, even an immortal, will cease. But why worry about such things? The River Styx brings us back, well, maybe with less power, but we continue to exist." Before another moment passed, an afterthought sucker punched me in the gut. "Unless you have been recopied so many times you're worried you might not come back?"

Moment's boots *click-clacked* as she approached the clan. She let out a small puff of air and caught my eyes through her fallen bangs. Curling a finger and grabbing my chin, she pulled me down until we were face-to-face. The others tensed as they reached for their weapons. My eyes lowered, and I stared at her mouth.

Moment's whisper blew me away. "I have never had the pleasure of meeting our creator."

Out of the corner of my eye, I saw Imp's jaw unhinge, and his aura flashed fuchsia. He had a new target to provoke. If she stayed with us, her future held nothing but jokes about losing her existence, and I almost felt sorry for her... *sort of.*

In all my existence, I had only met a handful of creatures from the Unseen who had never been recopied, besides myself. Even the Ashens in my clan had been recopied. It explained a lot about Moment's abilities. She was considered an Original Entity. No wonder the House of Time paid her well; she was an investment to them.

This development was a problem because I would not be able to grant her this stipulation in our contract. Moment two... reapers zero. I needed to think fast and find a solution to satisfy both of us. Again, her words replayed in my head. *Nothing in our world is ever simple.*

"You have never been recopied? So, what are you worried about, losing a small portion of your power? Look, that means nothing unless you are abusing your gift. My reapers are no daemons to second-guess in a fight, and they have been recycled from the River several times over. I have even lost count on some." I removed myself from her space, trying not to show her how impressed I was, especially in her line of work. "You are asking to know your future's fate. Why not use your influence within the House and request an audience with Kismet?"

"They won't let me see her. I have tried for hundreds of lifetimes to have a sit-down with her. I haven't even been able to meet with the House of Time's consultants, Pastasia or Naù. The Mains from the House of Time told me the future is unattainable to all creatures but Kismet." Moment crossed her legs and spun around on the ground in a huff.

She had been asking for hundreds of years to sit down

with them. *How old was she?* I approximately knew how long I had been around, but could she have existed even longer?

"Moment, in all seriousness, you know I cannot tell you when your clock will stop."

"But I have insider knowledge that you and your clan meet with the Fates all the time. Couldn't you introduce me to one of them? Any of them? I will accept your Bond-Rite if you can arrange it."

I did not even think twice about it. "Fine, done. I will set up a meeting, and we will take Imp. He looks forward to socializing with them. Isn't that right, Imp?" He looked at me, turning a sickly green and shaking his head.

Moment whipped her head around. "Really? You will go too, Imp?" She batted her lashes at him.

I do not know how, but he appeared even sicker since she was being *nice* to him. I was not sure what bothered him more, knowing he was going to see Pastasia or Moment using her female charms on him.

The other reapers exhaled in relief that I had not picked one of them to go with us.

Moment popped up from the ground. "Great, well, that takes care of the bounty part of our contract. Now, what do I get for guarding her ass?"

Michael jumped in between us. "See, this is what I was saying. Who said there were two parts to this contract? It's one Bond-Rite, one problem. Therefore, it's one type of payment."

"Daemon, I see it as one Bond-Rite, the first clause— hold off on collecting my bounty. The second clause—watch over 'the little brat,' as you so affectionately call her. A third is hidden in there, but if the second payment is good enough, I might wave it."

She back-flipped away before Michael's axe embedded into the rock floor where she had stood. "Now, temper, temper." The Evoker held up a finger using a *tsk-tsk* motion. "I would have been offended by your blatant attempt to attack me. But since you all are far from normal, I'll let it slide. You're lucky I have an excellent sense of humor."

She glanced back at me. "So, out with it, Tevin. What can you offer me for my services as her personal bodyguard?"

Locking glares with Michael's, he shook his head in a stern *no*.

Unfortunately, I had no choice. I was going to play my hand in this game, and my ace in the hole was going to be her.

I had taught myself a particular skill during those long years of boredom. I could spindle, and I knew a spin that might fulfill this gray part of our contract. I didn't think it would go against the River Styx or my job as an Ashen, so I wasn't breaking any rules.

My cloak moved over my head in protest. It knew the idea I was toying with, and it had some doubts of its own. I removed it from my face and explained that my decision was for the Bond-Rite and our sanity. Most of all, it was for Alexcia.

Flatly I asked, "Moment, have you ever heard of the Tears of Time?"

She sprinted in my direction and hugged me.

Five reapers tried to dislodge her from me. The corners of Imp's eyes tightened, and I guessed his reaction was from her sappy display of affection. When the whole room started to spin, I almost gagged from her excitement.

Chapter Eleven

Tevin's side: Through the eyes of a Reaper

*W*hen I finally pried myself from her arms, she started to hop and skip around the cellar, clapping her hands with glee as she giggled to the rhythm. The Evoker had gone mad. She bounced from side to side, and then, in mid-bounce, stopped and regained her composure. Moment was back to being the calm, conniving bounty hunter we knew.

"If you can get your claws on such an item, we might have a deal, and I may forget the third part entirely."

"Yeah, well, it's not a question of whether or not I can get my hands on the pendant. It's more like, are you willing to be connected to the maker of it?" I turned to exit the room.

"Wait. Where are you going?"

"To the Cauldron. I need Styx's help to make it. That is why you normally cannot find a Spindler who can create one without a huge price tag. I need water from Styx to complete it."

The color drained from her face. "It's made from the waters of Creation? How do I know you're not merely tricking me to get me near the Cauldron?"

"You don't."

The reapers in the room shared a gritty laugh as they watched her timidly place one boot in front of the other. Keeping a safe distance from me, she forgot about the clan coming up behind her. Imp bumped into her on purpose, which started a meaningless banter between the two of them.

My steps faltered as I took into account what I was about to do. Two things I knew, I needed some distance from Alexcia and the River to stop draining me of my power. Guarding her was blinding my judgment, and roping in Moment was out of character for me. I did not count on or trust any creature, even the ones that dwelled in the Unseen. *Hades-fire*, I had trouble even counting on my own Ashens. And in about thirty minutes, the Wind Evoker was going to be a temporary addition and my responsibility. Which reminded me, Moment needed a link to communicate with the clan.

"Quint, make sure Moment has a cell phone."

Taken aback by my request, the elemental scoffed, "What would I do with a phone? I can hear you on the wind or in my head."

I rounded on her. "Evoker, you are not a daemon. Telepathically, yes you can hear us, but only from a minimal distance because you are not an entity from the House of Space. The phones keep our conversations from being picked up by other entities from the Unseen, including daemons."

Quint's minion grabbed her wrist, and another tentacle slapped a metallic gold cell phone into her open hand.

Moment held it away from her at first, untrusting the small device. Cracking one eye, she shook it realizing it was not a threat. "You communicate through this?"

I nodded.

Hesitant, the Wind Evoker repeated, "But your voice carries on the wind. I can hear you from miles away."

Losing my patience, I reached for the gold rectangle when it dinged.

Confused, she tapped and smacked the black screen with her fingers and palm until it lit up displaying a text message.

Quint: Do you understand, Elemental?

Astonished, she spun to face him. "I didn't hear your thoughts. What magic is this?"

Quint smirked. "It's called a GoPhone. Vessels make the portable commutation gadgets. Don't break it. I have enough trouble replacing Tevin's. It's convenient for us because when we type our thoughts into an inanimate object, the bond to the Unseen is severed."

Moment replied with a soft, "Mmm-hum," and began to play with her new toy while we approached our destination.

The torches that aligned the tunnel spontaneously relit as the Hall of Summoning acknowledged our approach. My cloak was becoming heavier as the layers thickened. Clearly, it didn't want to be dragged into another one of my problematic solutions. The threads of my aura, which bonded the minion to me began to flicker in protest, misting me in complete darkness. This was its way of giving me the silent treatment.

The Wind Evoker appeared concerned when she slipped the gold rectangle into her shirt, shifting focus onto my minion. "What's wrong with it?"

"Our cloaks are an extension of our being. They act like poltergeists. The River created them to aid us in our abilities, and protect us from being seen and such."

Incredulous, she stated, "Yours is broken, I think."

Reluctantly, I added, "In this form, they are conscious and therefore can think for themselves."

"What's yours thinking?"

"It wants a new owner."

The reapers behind me were complaining, and I could only assume it was because they agreed with my minion. If Moment complied with my requests, I would need to see to my end of our bargain. This plan was designed to use up the last of my powers. I was going to need to feed right after we closed our Bond-Rite.

We were turning the bend toward the hall when Moment's footfalls fell silent. My clan slammed into her, and she shrieked at them for not looking where they were going. Imp uttered a quip, but I had tuned them out. I needed full concentration on the task at hand. Spinning this spell was extremely hard, the intensity made it complicated. Once I had a chance to explain the breakdown of it to Moment, she would determine whether or not to sign on the bottom line.

Our path wove through the stalagmites and stalactites sticking out from all directions. Depending on which way you walked down the cave, they could be either. Some had even fused together, and in order to continue your progress, you had to squeeze around them. Water dripped down the walls in different directions. It made me wonder if Moment sensed she was walking in a downward spiral through the tunnel. It was a Descent Illusion spell to keep the unwanted from being able to enter the hall, but if you were in the company of one of us, the disorientation would be minimal. I glanced back to see her willowy frame sluggishly bend her leg over one of the horizontal protruding rock formations. Then she quickly ducked down to miss the one right in front of her. The Evoker was nimble; I'd give her that.

As I glided through the entrance, the torches on both sides of the walls remained dark. The only light in the cavern was coming from the burning embers underneath the Cauldron at the opposite end of the room.

Raising my hands, I snapped and spoke into the space around me. "Light, come forth so this shadow of darkness may see."

Torches from various spots in the room burst to life, illumining the altar in the middle of the hall. The structure was carved out of rock and bone. Skulls from several types of Unseen creatures adorned the ridge of the slab. I heard Moment draw in a sharp breath. She must have noticed the blood dripping from several eye sockets. I continued passed the altar without giving it another thought.

When I positioned my body in front of the Cauldron, it started to fill with the pure, golden waters of Creation. The embers instantly cracked and popped as they caught fire. Our cloaks danced with the dark, darting shadows along the floor and walls, and I watched the water start to boil and change to a silvery transparent sheen. Creation mixing with magic was always a smooth transition.

Moment's leather boots made a soft crunching noise on the pebbled floor. Her breathing was shallow, and I could feel the tension emanating from her as a cool wind wafted through the hall. The Evoker had reservations about going through with our deal. I couldn't have her turn tail and run, so I decided to explain the process of the spell as I spun it.

The flames needed to be higher, so I coaxed the fire to grow. While the Cauldron's heat climbed, I stepped away to speak with the bounty hunter. My cloak stretched out along the floor, trying to grab anything that would keep me from approaching her. The thin tips of it pulsed in frustration. I placed myself on the other side of the altar, across from the elemental.

Her face was contorted in an overload of emotions. The color of her eyes swirled with need, and Moment's dark pink lips had changed to a lighter shade from her nervous licking. The frown and pull of her brow were the lock to keep her from screaming. Her stance reminded me of Alexcia when she was deep in thought. Moment was deep, so deep I was going to offer her a cheap headstone.

I reached over my head and waved so my clan could see that I wanted them to guard the entrance. They worked together in silence, repositioning next to the opening of the room. If I needed them to contain Moment, they were only a snap away.

"Moment, I have decided to request an audience with the Sisters of Tense to fulfill the first part of the Bond-Rite. You have agreed to refrain from obtaining the Child-of-Balance as your bounty until we can prove whether the Vessel is a true Child-of-Balance, or until she chooses a House to serve. Is this your understanding too?"

She crossed and uncrossed her ankles. "I suppose."

My voice was stern. "Yes or no. There is no such thing as *maybe* in a Bond-Rite with me. You are in until the end, or you can fight your way out of here. Your choice."

"How long do I get to think about it?"

Michael materialized right beside her. Spitting the word,

"Now," he swung his axe, barely missing her chin.

I watched as her hands curved, palms up. She smiled and said, "Mimic."

A slice of wind copied the same follow-through pattern as Michael's battle axe. His cloak went solid and took the hit. He didn't even waver from the impact. She appeared disappointed.

A metallic scraping sound from my blade echoed through the hall as I unsheathed my scythe and spoke to her again. "Yes or no, Moment. You of all entities understand that, *tempus fugit*. Do you want the pendant or not?"

"Yes." She rubbed her cheek, contemplating what I had explained. "Time does fly, but I am starting to believe there is more to this contract than what has been disclosed. We are about to put our existences in a weakened state. You stated that if your magic is spun wrong, we could both cease to exist. How do I know if you are capable of spinning such power?" She rocked with her arms wrapped around her, giving the appearance that she might come apart at any second. Arching an eyebrow, her next words were measured. "I have never been recopied, and I'm not sure if I want to dive into the deep end. I didn't even bring a bikini."

The pout she used was not fazing me. Annoying? Yes.

"Moment, do you not take risks when you track down and overpower your bounty? Do you not take your existence into your own hands every time you strike a deal? I thought you would be willing to gamble for a chance to know when time for you will stop. I may not be able to pinpoint the exact date, time, and place, but I can give you the sense of it slipping away. The top part of the Tears cry for the time you have lost and cannot gain back. The bottom is Time's payment for your used existence." I stepped back to the Cauldron and inhaled the vapors drifting upward.

Eyes wide with uncertainty, I saw her battle between desire and duty.

I took the opportunity to explain the fundamentals of the spell. "I will ask for a drop of your blood to symbolize your existence. The water from Styx is needed to bind you to the one who will take your power back to the River."

"So, Styx will come and take my power?"

"No, the Spindler does."

Her breath caught, and she shook her head violently as she whispered, "No."

"Unfortunately, yes. My drop of blood is needed to symbolize your approximate demise, and it binds me to you. I will be your harvester and take you to the River. If and when I do, our contract will be fulfilled, and when you are recopied, we can go our separate ways. To spin a *foreshadowing* spell has a great price. So you were right, in a way. Shall I continue to finish what we have started?"

It amazed me how similar she and Imp were. She was turning a sick shade of blue. I thought the wind within her had stopped. Maybe I wouldn't have to perform this task anyway; she seemed half deceased already.

"Moment, it's now or never." I knew I was getting overconfident in exploiting her one desire, but it was all I had for collateral on Alexcia's life insurance.

"Yes, I agree to these conditions of our Bond-Rite."

My cloak blew away from my body as the clear water exploded up and fell in a rush of gravity back to its place of being. The reapers at the back of the room formed a wall of death in case she tried to bolt from her agreement. I brought my scythe out in front of me, picked up my whetstone, and started to sharpen the toe of the blade. Watching the flakes of metal fall into the Cauldron, I reshaped the lace-looking blade, though the falling metal was causing the water to become corrupt. The water hissed and sparked, making Moment jump.

I turned to face her. "Come, I would like to introduce you to our creator."

The black kettle popped and crackled, almost as though it was excited to meet her.

She slowly peered into the pot. Watching her reflection ripple, a small smile crept up her cheeks. "I don't have to put my hand in there, do I?"

I was starting to drop contractions into my speech,

which was a sign of me losing control. "Moment, if Styx wanted your power… oh, never mind. It doesn't bite."

The reapers in the front of the room chuckled menacingly.

"But, I do."

In between blinks, I had grabbed her hand and pierced the tip of an index finger. A small drop of iridescent sand fell into the water, turning it to a light shade of rust.

"So, that's what ancient blood looks like when spun?"

Tongue-tied, she stuttered, "Wh-what do you mean by that?"

"Nothing, and don't interrupt me."

"Sorry. But if you're implying what I think you're implying, you're the one who will be screaming *sorry* after this is done."

"Hush. This is the hardest part, and it is extremely painful, too, so stand back by the altar. It's where you want to be when I'm done."

Wildly she glanced around. "Where?"

I could not let the spell stall, so I grabbed her shoulders and shoved her body in the correct direction. She wasn't moving fast enough, so I waved a hand and used a quick inward command. *"Déplacez-vous, allongez-vous, et ne bougez pas."* In my head, the words became familiar in French, not Latin like other Spindlers—this happened especially when I was livid. To add some meat to my spin, I shouted, "Move—lie down—and be silent."

Her body flew in the air as if on an imaginary pull string, landing face up on the altar with her extremities out in the form of a cross. Dust motes swirled around her, and she started coughing.

Annoyed she choked out, "You could at least dust the place."

After a brief pause, I answered in a seventeenth-century aristocrat's mocking tone, "My apologies Miss, but Raven ate our last maid."

He pulled his cloak slightly over his eyes and grinned exposing his canines.

Moment paled.

I continued the spin, allowing the words to flow through my mind. *"Attachez-la maintenant, "* but the words jumping from my mouth were, "Bind her now."

She struggled against empty air, shrieking, "Tevin, are you out of your daemonic mind?"

From the front of the room, all six reapers turned to her with glowing, wide-aura eyes. The torches in the area around them burned out one by one. They made their eyes and the thin edges of the cloaks glow deeper, displaying total concentration.

Raven announced the whole clan was going to make the Bond-Rite with Moment and share the burden of my problem together. Well, my problem was about to become plural by adding Moment to our pack. When I thought about her presence hanging around us, I almost canceled the spin. At least I could hang on to the fact it was only temporary.

Moment kept pushing her body into the air, making small grunting sounds as she struggled against invisible restraints. I flicked my fingers and moved her chalk-white strands away from her neck. It pulled out from underneath her, fanning out and spilling over the side of the altar.

When I turned back to the Cauldron, she yelped, "Not so hard!"

I shrugged and returned to the task at hand.

The water's sheen was gone and replaced with a thick, silver tint. The motion of the water churned and swirled, forming the sign of infinity. The spell was almost complete. This next part was going to be excruciating. Creation and death were the yin and yang of everything. Living or not, death and ceasing to be, one form could not function without the other, but they could never coexist. This part of the spell required them to, and it was painful creating the spin to force them to blend.

First, Creation's power, to signify her gift of immortality. It was called The Flow.

Second, her blood, to uphold the agreement. It was payment to both Styx and me, for insight into the unknown.

This was called Sacrifice.

Third, the metal from my weapon, to signify the unbreakable bond that guaranteed us in the rite. This was known as the Combined Encasement.

Last, my blood, to represent her harvesting. This was the Seal of Existence.

The clan began to chant.

I held up my scythe, siphoning some of their energy to increase my influence. In my head, I whispered, *"Mon sang,"* as the words slithered across my tongue, "My blood."

I plunged a free hand into the water. The liquid turned into thin platinum snarlarks. They resembled a type of Unseen water serpent. All of them opened their mouths, showing tiny rows of sharp teeth. Searing agony instantly blazed through me as the snarlarks began burrowing into my hand, disappearing one at a time beneath my skin. I could feel my Smolder threaten to shift us as I witnessed the last part of the spell enter my body. Part of Moment was flowing through my cavity; now it was time for her to meet the daemon contained within my reaper form.

Moment's eyes glazed over, and she stopped bucking but quaked in absolute terror. As part of our agreement, I could not tell her the *when* or *where* because I could not see into the future. But the spin could give her a fragment of her future reaping, the form I would use to send her to meet her Creator.

Pink lips shivered in fervor, trying to use her wind magic. I sensed the added torment mixing with Creation's fire within me. Internally, we had reached an understanding, and then the final product to the spell caught in the back of my throat, and I gagged. Opening my mouth, a pendant fell into my hand. The density in my cavity was gone from Moment's sudden absence.

Once the Smolder's sight dissipated, I realized the clan had moved to encircle the altar. I glided to the open area in front of me. Moment seemed to be in a trance; her empty eyes strained to see beyond the unknown.

I placed the pendant below her throat. From the top,

metal links began to form. The chain slithered, continuing in an open, circular, interlocking pattern until each one fused together. The Wind Evoker moaned under the heat from the metal as the molten orange cooled to tarnished silver. The clasp was made of two roses: one crimson and open, the other charred silver and closed. Elemental and Ashen locked together until our contract was fulfilled.

The pendant resembled a small hourglass. It was a mixture of Moment's energy force and my power to drain her existence in a compressed state. The piece included two silver skulls, one facing down and the other facing up with its mouth open. Using an index finger, I touched the glass. In my head, I said, *"C'est fin,"* but closed the spin with, "It is finished."

Sparkling fine sand, similar to what had trickled from her head wound earlier, poured from the top skull's eye sockets. But once it passed through the middle, it changed to an iridescent liquid, tinged with my aura's color and dripping into the bottom skull's open mouth. It was mesmerizing to watch the elemental's existence draining into mine.

We were all mesmerized by the Tears of Time hanging delicately from her neck.

The Wind Evoker remained unmoving with the same glazed stare. Her mouth kept moving, though, but nothing came of it. Watching her was unnerving, and we all exchanged miens of confusion. The spell was done; she should have come back to us already.

I slid my hand to her chest and felt an inner power pulsing under it. *What is she doing?*

Imp leaned over her body and yelled into her ear. "Moment, get up!"

Chapter Twelve

Drifting, drifting, the feeling of this dream is familiar.
Falling, falling, and never hitting bottom within the darkness.
Crying, crying, above the deafening screech of birds.
Laughing, laughing, and realizing there's no escape from this fate.
Alexcia—

Startled awake by a temporary form of displacement, I snatched at the air around me in a panic. I grabbed the down comforter and pulled it up to my neck to keep the rolling shivers at bay. The bedroom was cold enough to wake a corpse, and I tried to stay under the warmth of the blankets, stretching while piecing together where I was.

Adjusting to the dark haze of the room, I found myself in unfamiliar surroundings. Shadows were playing hide-and-seek with the moonlight across the walls. *This is not my comforter.* Fabric pulled tight across my chest as I moved. *I'm not in my own clothes.* The glow-in-the-dark stars were missing from the walls.

I whispered, "Where the hell am I?"

Carefully sliding my legs out from the warmth, I let my

feet dangle over the side of the bed. The memory of fleeing for my life paralyzed me as I stood. Remembering the sensation, I fell to the floor, buckling my knees so they would hit first—to avoid hurting my bad wrist—and then braced for impact.

When my momentum had stopped, I blew my bangs from my face. Lightly touching the two new carpet burns, I grumbled, "Great, like I wasn't banged-up enough already." Movement from across the room caught my attention. Cautious, I leaned against the bed frame and held my breath. An eerie silence had me question if I was trapped in one of my nightmares.

On the nightstand, I noticed a picture frame by the clock radio, so I leaned closer to get a better view and used the glowing numbers to see the photo. In the dim light, I could only make out three figures. I bit my lower lip and snatched the photo from its resting place.

After angling the front of the photo toward the window, my eyes widened. Dee was crouched down in between her half-brother and half-sister in a sandbox. The twins must have been about two or three years old when this had been taken. All three of them had huge smiles on their faces as if they were having fun.

The fogginess of sleep finally lifted, and I remembered where I was. *What a relief!* I'd assumed it was the beginning of a nightmare.

Head throbbing, I involuntarily dropped the weight into my hands while I tried to filter truth from fiction. My problems were creeping out during the day and involving others. I couldn't keep painting new lies onto used canvases; the old ones were bleeding through; *it wasn't normal.*

I placed the photo back on the nightstand and pushed myself up carefully to minimize the pull of raw skin. Outside, a streetlamp's glow was shining on my injured knees. They were oozing a clear, sticky liquid, which meant I would have to bandage them before crawling back under the covers.

How in the world was I supposed to keep whatever I was

suffering from a secret? It crushed my heart believing my family, friends, or anyone else would think I was destined for a life of eating checkers and talking to imaginary people.

Everything came to a grinding halt when my spine went rigid. The reaction wasn't from distress but the chill of being watched from the shadows. Welding my nerves together, I scanned the darkness.

The temperature had dropped drastically, and I exhaled a cloudy puff. I was transfixed on darkened figures in the corner. As I cocooned myself in the comforter, my entire body shook. I pinched myself hard enough to draw blood and yelped. "Ouch!"

When two small snickers came from out of the shadows, I breathed a sigh of relief. The twins. They were probably trying to play a prank on me while I slept. Little trolls.

I used my babysitting tone. "Okay, you two, come on out now. I know you're in here." Like a fat caterpillar, I inched my way to the edge of the bed.

They didn't move.

Then a soft, hypnotic voice said, "Alexcia, it's so nice to meet you formally. I see you are no worse for wear from our earlier encounter. Then again, if things had been different…"

The voice trailed off as the room temperature dipped like we were in the Sip 'N Chug's walk-in freezer. A familiar whisper in my head said, *Isn't life cruel?*

Ignoring my gut, I asked, "Bailey, is that you? You better turn your tail around and get back into bed before Dee scolds you."

Tiny hiccups of forced laughter seemed artificial. Then, as quickly as it started, the sound stopped. Bailey's small foot stepped out from the corner, tugging her brother to follow.

Was I in a horror movie, waiting for one of them to ask if I wanted to play? When the twins appeared in the street-lit part of the room, a breeze, rustled their clothes eerily. A quick scan around the room yielded no air vent or source that would explain the icy air.

Both children moved as though a puppeteer worked their strings. They hobbled toward the foot of the bed. But what creeped me out was their eyes. Bailey's seemed to be suffering from a severe form of cataracts with a transparent, milky film clouding both of her irises. When her head cocked to one side as though she was observing me, a shiver zipped up the nape of my neck, sending a pulse of fear into my extremities.

Calvin's eyes were alien black and reflected back a soulless emotion. His actions were jarred and mechanical. It was as though his sister was leading around a corpse.

A sob hitched in the back of my throat, but I tried to keep it together by holding onto denial. "What are you both doing up?"

"Aww, sweet, sweet Alexcia. Is it true you don't know who you are?" Bailey's head lolled forward, and Calvin's grasp grew tighter. The female's head snapped back up, "Would you like for me to enlighten you, child?"

My brain blew a fuse from the emotional overload. This unrealistic reality had won the battle over sanity as if this child understood my need for answers. Tears filled my eyes until they couldn't hold anymore and spilled down my cheeks, dotting the comforter with liquid hopelessness.

Bailey shuffled closer, with Calvin in tow. "Well, child?"

Her free hand touched my chin and raised my face to meet hers. Pasty eyes bore into mine, and the skin where she touched blossomed with frost-burn.

Her eyes widened in anticipation. "Tic-Toc, I'm on the clock, you know."

With force, I removed my chin from her fingers and found my voice buried deep under a year's worth of unanswered questions. The flutter and stabbing in the middle of my chest spread as if a thousand hummingbirds had taken refuge.

Teeth chattering, I whispered, "I-I'm Alexcia. I live in Las Vegas with my father and m—"

The right side of my face exploded with pinpricks of

heat, while twinkling stars danced in my vision.

Bailey hissed in my face. "I can't believe he bound himself to the likes of you." She grabbed my chin again and held it tight. "In my opinion, you're too simpleminded to be what they think you are." She abruptly let go and limped toward the vanity, pulling Calvin along by one hand. Bailey dropped her head and pivoted on one leg, sluggishly. "My connection is losing strength, so I need you to pay attention."

I was apprehensive but asked, "What are you?"

"That's for another time. The curse on you is a combined blocking and separation spell."

"Combined—" An invisible vice pressed against my temples, cutting me off.

"When two or more entities spin a spell, it becomes stronger. How unfortunate that I will have to educate you the hard way." With her free hand, she touched the vanity mirror. Reflective beads dripped from it as if it was creating condensation. The liquefying mirror shimmered and swirled, mixing with streaks of melting shadows.

"Pay attention; we have a lot to cover in mere ticks. At present, I am not your teacher nor your enemy. And don't get the idea in your small brain that I am your BFF because I would rather tag and bag you. A girls gotta make a living, you know." She huffed. "Damn Ashens and their Bond-Rites." Creamy eyes narrowed. "It baffles my existence why he feels the need to protect you, so faithfully."

"A Bond-Rite? What's that?" Both questions came out of my mouth full of fear.

"A Bond-Rite is a contract of sorts, a binding to uphold a service. And as much as it displeases me, I gave my word not to harm you—much." Bearing small teeth, she angled her head awkwardly to her shoulder. "Time is measured in precious grains of sand. My sand is being wasted, I think." She paused as if in thought. "Yes, I believe my fee for educating the clueless has tripled."

"I don't understand."

A tiny hand waved in a dismissive gesture. "Never mind, all will be revealed when it needs to be. You can always count on time."

I pulled my cocoon tighter. "I do not understand anything you are saying. Educate me how, exactly?"

"Watch the Opening."

"The Opening?"

"Watch the spell-made flat screen, Child." Each word hissed condescendingly.

All I saw was a void, but the air pressure in the room intensified. I must have been inside a vacuum. Both eardrums wanted to implode, and I used my hands to keep the brain matter from leaking out. Within seconds, I was sweating profusely, and my heart was overcompensating.

Bailey perceived my discomfort, and with a hint of sarcasm, she mocked, "Oh darn, I forgot your poor human body can't handle the outer boundaries of space. I will seal it off." Waving her hand in a large arc, she mumbled a string of vowels.

The room turned back into a deep freeze, but at least I could breathe again.

Throat hoarse, I said, "Thanks, for whatever you did,"

"Hush. Now watch."

I could see a thin glitter-gold river flowing down the middle of a pitch-black void. Bailey's demeanor had become studious as she started her story.

"The Constants are as follows in order of existence…" Numbers and definitions etched out across the mirror.

1) The River Styx, aka the Infinity Constant—the Beginning.

2) Time/Nature—controls the House of Time.

3) Space/Lucifer—supremacy to/of the House of Space.

4) Light/Zeus—reigns over the House of Light.

5) Heaven—the dimension in which entities of Light dwell.

6) Darkness/Hades—the constant formed from the noxious side of Light's existence.

7) Hell—the dimension in which the roots of Darkness and the River Styx are eternally bound.

"This story begins long before time made its first tick."

She paused, then took a big gulp of air. "The River Styx is the essence of life. The water's movement invoked Time to spring forth. But Time needed a place to grow and thrive, so the River continues to carve out the expansion of Space by using Light. This was the start of Creation and how the main Constants of Making were created… Time, Space, and Light."

She stopped. "Are you following so far?"

Stoic, I was too afraid to say no, and only blinked. If this was a nightmare, it was by far the creepiest and baffling I'd ever had.

Readjusting her attention back to the mirror, she continued, "While Light, Space, and Time worked on forming the universe, the Constant known as Light was growing weak and needed to rest. This is where things get screwed up. Time and Space agreed to cease their movement so that Light could rejuvenate. In its dreaming state, the baleful side of Light crept forth, and a nightmare was born; Darkness. Darkness was not formed directly from the River's waters and therefore lacked the understanding of the importance to create life. It desired to be treated equally as the other Constants though. Anyway, it became jealous and hungered for what it could never be."

I was still frozen in place, unsure what to do.

Glancing back at me, Bailey grumbled, "History is so boring unless there's a little chaos, right? Okay, jumping ahead."

As terrified as I was, the lesson interested me, even though it sounded like stereo instructions. Tentatively, I raised two fingers, waiting to be called on.

Her small hand gestured at me in obvious annoyance. "What? And ask fast, time is not on my side."

"What does this have to do with me?"

Bailey's face scrunched as if she was having a difficult time holding back. "I'm getting to that."

Slamming an open hand on the vanity instead, she continued. "Moving on. Darkness learned how to snuff out everything the River Styx had created. It had become power hungry and wanted our Creator's acceptance so badly it started to rebel against the other Constants. Appalled by the damnation Darkness was causing, the River Styx demanded Time and Space wake up Light from its slumber. Styx condemned itself for pushing Time, Space and Light beyond their limits and allowing Light to succumb to fatigue."

Bailey's explanation was interrupted when Calvin's body rocked forward. He bumped against her shoulder, and both stumbled forward. It creeped me out how devoid his facial features were. Fixing her hair with one hand, Bailey never released Calvin's with the other and jerked him possessively to her side.

Once she regained her composure, she continued, "Time, Space, and Light left the boundaries of Darkness and merged once again to create. Darkness grew envious of Light's bond with the other Constants and their main creator. It spat forth a spell to confuse the Constants, which made them work against each other. This was marked as the beginning of the Unbalanced."

With an evil smirk, Bailey continued, "This is where you come in. During the Unbalance, Darkness sprang forth and trapped our Creator. For the River to obtain enough power to control the rebelling Constant, the three Constants of Making decided to each sacrifice a third of their power to recharge the River Styx. Armed with a new strength of magic, it swore the last Constant it would create would be their confinement for eternity, and it is where they reside to this day; Hell. After the River contained the Darkness, the other three Constants were given the task to maintain creation and the flow of the River Styx. Thus, three Houses were created: the House of Light, Space, and Time."

Bailey seemed to be enjoying the sound of her own voice, and her eyes widened with eagerness as she continued the story.

"The three Constants combined their magic to forge containers, known as Vessels, to harness the small portions of power known as souls. A soul carries the same essence of Creation, and therefore must be returned to the River Styx once the name of the Vessel has been summoned for termination. You see, Vessels help maintain the magic between our dimensions, and the remnants of the soul is a power boost to continue the cycle of life and aid with concealing Hell's actual location... and the Darkness Constant contained."

Repetitive snapping noises echoed in the room. I blinked several times, and then a harsh sting of air hit my cheek. I opened my mouth to protest that I wasn't sleeping, but her stern expression made me reconsider.

Tapping her free hand against the mirror, Bailey's tone became edgy. "Time, Space, and Light formed their own guardians, all of whom are part of the Unseen Realm. Each of the three Constants agreed to have an equal amount of creations so that the powers of the Unseen would remain stabilized between the Houses. Light entitled itself, Zeus, and created angels to be Heaven's Keepers. They are known as the House of Light. Space followed suit and took on the name Lucifer, creating servants and low-level minions called daemons. And for the last three centuries, they have had two jobs... to watch over the Constant Darkness, and to keep the River Styx flowing. The Constant Time wanted to be able to nurture and heal; therefore, it took on the name Nature and created special beings called elementals to oversee the natural fundamentals of time. Nature and its factions reside in the House of Time."

Her last sentence had a hint of pride in it.

"Each House plays a part to keep the cycle of Balance moving forward. The Houses are under the River Styx's jurisdiction to equally protect. But, over several millennia, the Houses began to battle for the right to govern the care of the River exclusively. The one who oversees the power of Creation has control over all Constants."

Bailey's lips puckered in a type of sour protest.

"Child, I swear if you are falling asleep again, I will snap you in two when I get the chance, I am getting to the part you must focus on." Cursing under her breath, she checked on her brother's stance. Placing two fingers on the side of his neck, it appeared she was checking his pulse. A frown caused a crease in between her eyebrows. "I'm losing my connection, so pay attention."

I straightened.

Fixing her nightgown, she pressed on, "Regrettably, to keep the status quo, the River Styx set boundaries for its guardians by placing in effect the Decree of Five. Five laws were to be the new basis on which Time, Space, and Light could continue to keep the balance of life and death's cycle constant."

This time, I really tried to focus on her words.

"The First Law—a new guardian comes into existence every three hundred and thirty-three years. The chosen are deemed a Child-of-Balance.

"The Second Law—a Vessel is born on the sixth cycle of the sixth sunrise in the sixth hour. The child will be born to contain the powers from all three Constants and will remain protected by their appointed Keepers until the proper age of maturity.

"The Third Law—once the child has matured, the guardians are given a chance to recruit the Vessel to their Constant's House.

"The Fourth Law—the child must remain a pure Vessel before becoming a guardian. In doing so, the chosen one can pick which House they want to be a guardian for. If for some reason, the Child-of-Balance does not remain pure, the power of the River will be called upon. A Constellation's Meeting of the Stars will decide if the Vessel wielding the power is worthy."

Bailey eyed me as if I was an insect under a magnifying glass. "You have nothing to worry about."

Gradually, I sat up straighter. *Had she implied something against my character?*

When she connected with my silent stare, there was a satisfying grunt from her. When she had finished studying me, her upper lip curled, displaying her disgust.

"Once the Child-of-Balance has reached maturity it will again bring Unbalance to the Unseen. The prophecy states the Houses will no longer be united and war will break out between the three branches of power. During this time, every creature that exists in the Unseen—whether it is elemental, daemon, or angel—will fight for the chance to tip the scales by recruiting a Child-of-Balance to their ranks."

Bailey winked at me, but I could only return a blank stare.

"In accomplishing this victory, one House will be able to govern over all. The influence of one can be all it takes to change the flow of Creations' power. Which is why the Fifth Law is paramount—to protect, to fight, and to maintain the cycle of life. We must all remember the River's story."

The vision of Hell and the River faded from the mirror, and the reflection of the room became more visible. Then I watched it fold into itself.

Bam!

Hundreds of cracks webbed into existence as if someone had taken a bat to the mirror.

A male's influence cut through the room's stillness. "It is finished." The simple but unexpected statement made my heart skip. I inched the comforter down to locate the source.

Bailey's body stiffened. Her lips parted, exposing little teeth.

"Well, we will have to wait for Q and A another time. I know you may have more questions, but I have to wrap up another matter." She brought her tiny finger to her cheek and tapped thoughtfully. "I know. Why don't you ask your guardians?" She pulled Calvin closer and grabbed his other hand. Staring at one another, they both started whispering.

I couldn't have this end without one of my questions being answered. I yelled, "Wait!"

Clenching her jaw, the girl stopped and faced me. In a sharp tone, she snapped, "Yes?"

"What does all of this have to do with me?"

With a smug, quick lift of a shoulder, she towed Calvin deeper into the darkness of the room. Tears marred my vision turning both kids into liquid shadows. An acidic tone answered my hovering question. "Ask your parents,

Balance."

A different male's voice thundered from the ceiling. "Moment, get up!"

I screamed as my hands flew to my mouth.

Bailey merely stated, "Time's up."

Both children whispered simultaneously, "Connection severed."

They collapsed onto the floor in a mound of sobs, clinging to each other while searching the darkness to regain their bearings.

Bailey wept into her brother's nightshirt. "I *hate* it when they slip in while I sleep."

Calvin pulled his sister closer trying to sound brave between sniffling. "Are you okay? The presence is gone."

They continued to console each other through sniffs and hiccups.

They knew what had happened to them?

Astonishment kept my mind moving in slow motion. My eyes were accustomed to the darkness again, and the room seemed normal, with the exception of two crying children and me. Thoughts drifted, causing me to wonder if the kids would say anything about this to their mother or sister.

Before approaching them, I made sure the children were once again the cute little kids I knew. A pair of soggy eyes locked on me, and I was overcome with desolation as I ambled over to them, dropped the blanket and slid to the floor. Once situated, I pulled them into my arms, adding my own dose of reassurance. I couldn't contain myself as I wept right along with them until I was physically and emotionally spent.

Chapter Thirteen

Tevin's side: Through the eyes of a Reaper

*I*mp's pet became placid, squinting intently at the Wind Evoker as her lashes fluttered. Seven affixed gazes met with her shrinking hourglass pupils.

A smile of self-satisfaction had flickered before she spoke, "So, are we done?"

"Moment, you should have snapped out of my binding, several ticks ago. What happened?" I grabbed her new accessory and examined it.

Knocking my arm out of the way, she kicked both legs up and arched her body to land feet first in the middle of the altar. "Don't lay a claw on me, Ashen, without my permission." She cautiously fingered the chain around her neck. "It's on already?" Her brow furrowed, examining the small hourglass. "What if it breaks? Could Styx's claim me before my time is up?" Sulking, she dropped into a sitting position.

My voice box exploded when I lost all composure. "It doesn't work that way. I told you, it doesn't bite or drain your existence. Besides, if it does break, it means your time is up." I leaned in closer to her face. "Open your eyes. We know you were up to something. Give."

I sounded like Max. It confirmed I was spending too much time with Alexcia's father.

Moment scooted her butt forward and puddled onto the floor, landing in a tight crouch. She scanned the chamber like a cat, presumably scoping out different scenarios of escape.

"Let's see. What was I doing?" She tapped her lips. "My memory is a little fuzzy, but I will say this—you owe me big time."

Michael's aura flashed, and the threaded blue of his shroud brightened. "See what I told you? She's messing with your head now. The Bond-Rite is completed, Evoker. He owes you nothing more. No, the opposite, I think you owe us for the air you're sucking up in here."

He shoved her back with the handle of his battle axe, causing her necklace to hit the stone altar. A deep chime shook and vibrated the entire hall. Cave walls cracked, and debris bounced on the floor transversely.

K, Quint, and Michael rushed her. Imp, Raven, and Archer faded into the shadows to reappear against the walls. Moment did not even have time to scream. Her focus was solely on the Tear of Time as she used her body to shield it. Michael's axe embedded into the side of the stone altar right next to her hip. Quint and K had their weapons drawn. I walked over to her and knelt down.

"Moment, what did you do?"

"I was doing what I said I was going to do."

I looked up and stared, trying to pick up a clue.

K and Quint shrugged while Michael's face twisted in disgust. Moment was redirecting her answers. Damned elemental. Tapping my shoulder, I used the movement to distract me so I would not grab my scythe. Instead, I took a calming breath and snatched her shoulders to give her a quick shake.

"A daemon toys with patience willingly, Moment. So, for me to lose mine is impossible." The twitch above my right eye had returned. "What did you do, Wind Evoker?"

"My job," she snapped. "I kick-started things, is all. Each of you will thank me when this whole ordeal is over." She cradled the pendant in her hands, but her eyes never wavered.

From the front of the hall, Imp took three charging steps before disappearing to resurface on the other side of her, gritting his teeth. "Pray, I do not grow tired of your tantrums. You will answer to the one who keeps your existence in play. If it weren't for his spindling, my fingers would already be around your thin, soft neck." Imp was so close to the bounty hunter that the cloak's hood was slithering down the sides of her face trying to lift the ebony strands. I noticed the violet glow of Imp's eyes reflecting off Moment's.

One irked Ashen, and one vexed elemental shared a number of inaudible words. Their smiles matched in stubbornness, both reaching a silent stalemate. He blew in her face to end the conversation. "See? You are not the only one who can do that trick."

The Wind Evoker turned pink. A foolish composure was exposed, leaving a sour taste in my mouth. Realizing Imp had used her as the butt of his joke, Moment raised her hand to him. Within mere seconds, he had grabbed her wrist and was holding her in the air. Dangling about three feet off the ground, with feet kicking wildly, she tried to pry his fingers from her skin.

"Put me down, or you'll be sorry, daemon. I haven't done anything wrong. Now, let me go." Her nails were now embedded in his hand.

His smile said it all; she was hurting him, but it only amused the daemon. The cavern echoed from the reapers chanting and urging Imp to inflict harm. His broadsword disappeared from the hilt.

Exhaling the last of my tolerance, I realized it was time to intervene before Imp summoned his weapon. I needed to retrieve my new toy from the dragon kits before they broke her and I lost my edge.

I stepped next to Imp and lifted my chin to stare at the struggling Evoker. "Well, Moment, it seems as though you are part of our clan until we have carried out our contract." I turned my gaze on all of them. "We are all going to be working together, so you need to realize the situation you're in."

She thrashed to break free, but Imp had shackled her, literally, with his fingers. Her voice was strained, and the air became thick around us. I realized she was Stacking. It was a way to store energy rapidly.

The air was crisp and desiccated, crackling with energy. Moment barked, "What, Tevin? What do I need to know? I don't recall that being a part of our contract."

K's voice boomed, "Oh, enough of this, Tevin. Let's be done with her so we can go back to watching the Vessel ourselves. We don't need her. Rip the fancy dog collar off or choke her with it. I don't care but do something. There's reaping to be done, and we are all spending too much time on what will be probably a dead end."

Their frustration was apparent, but we needed to find out what Moment had done. Even if her actions were only a thin attempt to piss us off.

A breeze wove around each reaper, and I watched Moment's body go lax. We took her reaction for granted because it was long enough for her to start mumbling. The air around us became stagnant before the temperature dropped dramatically.

I shouted, "To the air."

Electricity crackled, popped and fizzed from the surrounding rocks.

The Wind Evoker held Imp's arm to counter his weight since we were all levitating. "You can't blame an elemental for trying. Besides, Tevin, I think you will be thrilled when you've figured out what I've done. It was quite intuitive on my part if I do say so myself."

Her maniacal smile worried me even more. Daemons tormented to break the will of another, not the other way around.

Archer held up Wink and pointed the tip of his arrow at her neck. "So, what happens if we cut the chain off? Will the River call her sooner?"

Her eyes went wide. "Right, empty threats and soulless dreams. You wish. Tevin can't allow you to take it off without our Bond-Rite being finished. I don't like being tied to all of you either. My reputation is on the line, too, you know." She kicked again, this time connecting between

Imp's long legs.

Wincing, we all moaned, "Oh, damn."

The five of us froze while Michael inched toward Imp to either lend a hand or secretly gloat in his ear. The others floated back down to the floor. I reached behind to readjust my weapon and from grabbing my crotch in sympathy. It did not matter what male species one was—if an object connected where it mattered—damage would ensue, especially, if a daemon were corporeal. I did have a brief flash of pity for the Ashen, but it lasted all of ten seconds.

Moment's lack of judgment caused her karma to boomerang because Imp had released her. Within half of a blink, she fell like a stone, hitting the floor butt first. Pebbles and dust wafted into the air, forming a ring around her body. He had added some force to her descent.

Imp gradually released his words, "Serves you right, elemental witch."

She lay there motionless, mostly from stupefaction. Following Imp's frame up to his face, Moment's eyes grew dark in amazement. "You dropped me."

I waved my hand and landed on the floor right next to her. "…And the pendant? Unharmed, I assume."

She quickly searched her neck for it. What she did not know was that it would never come off until the contract was fulfilled or Styx summoned her. I was already thinking of different ways I could do it.

Moment sat up and placed her fingers around the clasp of my cloak. My minion slithered over her fingers, trying to make her let go. Showing her teeth, she said, "You *will* thank me, daemon. Whether you know it or not, I did help you."

"Last time, Moment. What did you do?"

So, she had a clear understanding of the word *last*; I pressed my fingertips to her skin while trailing them to the base of her skull. Grabbing hold, I ratcheted her head back before unsheathing the scythe with my free hand. Her eyes filled with hatred and caution as I slipped the scythe's laced beard between her neck and the chain.

The Cauldron of Ending boiled. Steam rose from the

waters and hissed, signaling our Creator was listening.

"I believe Styx would like to know what you have done as well." I rested the toe of the blade by her ear.

Her words came out between gasps of air, "You can't. You won't. What about the Vessel? I thought you said you needed me." Her voice held uncertainty. "I hate to say this, but you are going to need me even more, Ashen. Do you hear me? *More... than... ever.*"

I slid the blade down the chain, making it spark. The elemental winced but held her tongue.

"Our Bond-Rite is in question, and if I feel you have breached it in any way, I will ask Michael and Imp to each take a leg and make a wish." For the first time in months, I sensed Michael's willingness, almost begging me to hand her over.

"What about me?" K approached. "I need the practice." His green eyes darkened around the corners as he smacked his mace against his palm.

"You know, Wink and I could use some practice, too. What do you say, K? Catch-and-Release or Till-Death-Do-We-Part? I prefer the latter." Archer's bow blinked its wide eyes but kept the Wind Evoker in its line of sight.

K leaned on his mace. "Catch-and-Release, of course. I want the game to last."

"Wait." She pulled against my hand to glance around the room at the other reapers.

All but Raven yelled, "No!"

The crimson eyed Ashen was brooding in the shadows. His voice was low, as he added his take on the situation, "Enough, kids. Playtime is over." Pushing himself off the rock wall, he called forth his minion that covered him in a thick, misty veil with only thin trails of his aura's color weaving through the edges.

Quint popped his earbuds out as he joined the conversation. "Wait, I didn't get to throw my weapon in the ring yet." With his yellow eyes scanning the competition, he snapped, and an onyx mist crisscrossed his body with sun gold threading through the edges. The hood formed last as he reached to pull it over his brow.

The wind stirred above us.

I checked back at Moment. "So, what will it be?"

She held her hand to my chest and whispered, "Burst."

I flew backward, but before I hit the wall, she was already on her feet and running toward the opening of the tunnels. The pack was on her like a crazed Cerberus, but we were pups compared to the three-headed monstrosities that patrolled the shores of Styx.

How unfortunate, I thought with a frown and stood. The Smolder within me growled. It was done with her, too. I felt it messing with my emotions and trying to trigger me to let it out. Grabbing the scythe, I spun it over my head before plunging the pointed silver tip of the handle into the floor. The force made a ring of cracks in front of me.

Speaking with the hint of a daemonic dragon, I projected, "Moment, you are found guilty of breaching our Bond-Rite. I demand you to answer, or the waters will claim your existence, and you will not be recopied."

Several Ashens had encircled the screaming bounty hunter. Raven fisted the back of her collar and dragged the frantic elemental around to face me.

The daemonic dragon within me rattled its cage, and my eyes burned. I was losing control of the Smolder. Whether I wanted to harvest Moment myself was not the question anymore; it was simply a matter of when.

She sauntered over to me and pressed her body to mine. Affronted, my minion froze, misty swirls to afraid to touch the elemental. The animal within me growled from her lack of respect for death's power, and then she softly said, "I spoke to your Child-of-Balance."

All six reapers moved in, bearing their weapons.

"And?" It was all I could do to manage in my own voice.

She purred. "I gave her a little history lesson about *our* world of the Unseen. How Creation came to be. What she could be. I did in ticks what you all couldn't accomplish in ten years. I told her possible truths, unlike the sugar-coated lies her keepers have been feeding her. She reeks of power, but it is unmanageable. She should have been taught the ways of our world long ago.”

I wanted to snap my scythe over her head. Extracting the weapon from out of the floor, I concentrated on containing my Smolder. The way I felt, snuffing out her existence would not curb my fury. She had unjustly placed the whole clan in jeopardy, especially with Max.

Every daemon in the place stood frozen, stunned.

I had smothered my Smolder’s voice before speaking. “You had no right. You don’t even know the damage you have done. There is a clause, written in both of my contracts that *I am* not allowed to tell her *who* she is or *what* she is until her keepers are sure she is ready to handle the truth. You’ve put me in breach of both of my contracts. What the hell were you thinking?”

She shrugged. “I wasn’t.”

We all had dropped our weapons before reconsidering to use them.

Chapter Fourteen

*W*hen I woke up, I didn't say anything to Dee or the twins, not that it mattered. Dee wasn't speaking to me anyway. When her mother, Ruth, opened the bedroom door to check on Dee, I saw her lying on her bed, blankly staring at the ceiling. After her mother went in and closed it, I placed a cupped ear to the whitewashed door. I heard Dee's muffled complaints about it being her time of the month, and she begged for the heating pad and two Extra Strength Advils.

Involuntarily, both my eyes did the roll. Because of Dee's over-the-top performance for her mother, I feared they might permanently be stuck staring at my brain. I didn't blame Dee since I had spent the last month and a half barricaded under a pile of blankets. *Who was I to pass judgment on anyone trying to disappear for one day?*

The twins were hauntingly silent, keeping their thoughts to themselves. We had fallen asleep together because a protective instinct had bloomed from my core, plus I could watch them to make sure they didn't need an exorcist. And since my brain wouldn't stop mulling over my new problems, which included the twins, I had only slept an hour or two before Ruth knocked on the door to wake us for breakfast.

An uneasy panic squeezed my chest as I thought maybe a poltergeist was stalking me. Each one of us had shared the same night terror but from our own perspectives. I was concerned if the twins were afraid of me, the way *what if* terrorized me. Flip-flopping emotions had me praying the twins didn't want to discuss what had happened, to anyone… especially their mother or Dee.

I didn't want to think about last night… or this past year. Who knew blowing fifteen small flames out would create such chaos for one person.

There were too many scenarios to process: being attacked by my imagination, dealing with Dee's meltdown, remembering how my feet felt as I walked above the carpet and speaking in a strange language, and receiving a bizarre history lesson from a possessed Bailey. Out of the events of the whole night, the information that splintered and festered was the voice insinuating my parents had the answers but had hidden them from me.

Its instructions were stuck on repeat. *Ask your parents, Balance. What did it mean?* I didn't want to explain the nightmares, let alone divulge about my growing nightly terrors. If my experiences were all in my head then sharing might buy me a one-way ticket where a straitjacket would be included in my wardrobe.

The apartment phone rang, and Ruth left Dee's room to answer it. After holding a short, one-sided conversation, she turned to me and said Rae-Lynn was driving through the gates. I was to meet her out front by the carport. Unenthusiastically, kicked off Dee's slippers and headed for the door. When I stepped into the sunlight, everything felt different… lacking in warmth, somehow. A chill worked its way from each barefoot to the base of my skull.

Rae-Lynn's car bunny-hopped over a speed bump, and I waved for her to stop where she was. When I opened the passenger side door, she gave me one of her doubt-creased expressions. I didn't say anything while I picked up my things, but we exchanged gazes of confusion and silence. I sensed that Rae-Lynn knew I was keeping everything locked inside. I laughed to myself to avoid crying. *If she only knew.*

I backed out of the car, when Rae-Lynn dully stated, "Well then, I guess we'll see you at home later?"

Nodding, I shut the door and stepped away from the car. Mom's eyes studied me from the rearview mirror before the car disappeared around the corner. A piece of broken trust left with her as I pondered what my parents knew about my internal turmoil.

When I walked back into the apartment, Mrs. Stuart asked if I was okay, and I answered with a weak smile and nod. My sealed lips were keeping me from falling apart. Scream, cry, or speak gibberish, I had no idea what would happen if they parted. Silence equaled freedom. This was my new motto, at least until I could sit down and have an open discussion with my parents without falling apart.

My feet seemed weighted down when I headed to the bathroom. Timidly, I touched the silver glass, waiting for my reflection to bite or speak. But all I saw was the faint image of the party girl I once knew. Now, I was a pitiful mass of lost uncertainties, wearing my best morning disheveled look. *Why was my life wrapped up in so many unknowns?* I reached for the shower knob and made a decision. No matter how ugly or crushing the truth was, it had to be better than admitting I was losing my mind.

It had to be.

I called Blakely twice, and it went to voicemail but disconnected before I could leave a message. Another serving of cold worry made my stomach churn. After the third failed attempt, I called Ghost.

Dee's mother had made coffee. I tried not to appear

ungrateful because she'd made an effort to accommodate me. But my stomach was in knots, so I declined the steaming cup. I thanked her for allowing me to stay the night, and as a bonus, offered her a get-out-of-jail-free card. I promised we'd work out the details when she wanted me to watch the kids.

I mumbled to myself while going over my checklist and dumping each item into the overflowing school bag. Damp work clothes, shoes, apron, and evidence of one accidentally murdered cell phone… check.

Once I was ready to leave, I approached Dee's bedroom door and placed a hand on the silver knob. I wondered if she remembered anything from last night. I flexed my hand battling with the possibility of her confronting me but deduced it was best not to say goodbye.

I hadn't been waiting long, but it seemed as though a huge target was located on my back. While scanning the trees across the street, I had a memory flash of running, which caused my heart to skip from the adrenaline jolt of remembrance.

A ray of sunshine worked to remove the leftover chill from the storm. Las Vegas weather was always so unpredictable… one minute it was cold, and the next I was doing a cannonball into the deep end of a pool, only to find hailstones dropping on me by the time I resurfaced.

The bright flash of light reflected off the windshield, momentarily causing me to shield my eyes. After I adjusted from the temporary blindness, I spotted Jake's car coming. He slowed down but right before he stopped, the beater backfired. I lunged for the door handle and frowned as I slipped onto the seat. The door creaked when I slammed it shut. I was annoyed that his car had succeeded in scaring me, again. His smirk indicated he had noticed and was slightly amused.

I pulled the seat belt across my chest and snapped the buckle. "First your car blinded me, and now I have to change my underwear."

With a silly smirk growing, he replied, "And good

morning to you, too. I take it you haven't had your coffee yet?"

"Maybe it's because good morning is an evil oxymoron." I dropped the book bag between my feet and leaned back with a huff.

He craned his neck and asked, "Where's Dee?"

"Sick."

He snorted. "Sick?"

I used our monthly code. "Her cousin came to visit." The snarky retort became caught in the swell of a yawn.

Ghost gave me a look of concern and placed a hand on my cast. "Are you okay? The circles under your eyes are darker than normal. Are you sure you want to go to school? Maybe I should take you home instead?"

I held his gaze while allowing the warmth of his friendship to wash over me. When I clamped my arms around me to keep from diving into his arms and crying, his expression changed to one of deep concern. He had always seen through my façade, and it frustrated me how he knew my mood simply from looking into my eyes. Normally, I didn't mind because he was so easy to talk to, but the moment didn't feel right.

Jake was my only touchstone, and I didn't want to alienate him by reclining the seat to spill my guts about the nightmares. Everything was so messed up, and I couldn't dump on him because I didn't really understand it myself.

I broke his line of sight by closing my eyes. The slight irritation caused sticky tears to blur my vision, and I pressed fingers into each eye, trying to stop the inevitable.

My left hand was slower than my right as I brushed away the tears. Ghost reached for my cast before my fingers could make contact. He seemed to be admiring the picture that Blakely had drawn. He chuckled, and it was then I realized how close he was to my ear. Warm breath sent chills racing down my neck. Keeping my eyes closed, my heart said, *turn toward him*, but my mind said, *would you like to give Ghost a tour while he's in here?* A sigh reached my lips because I knew the answer.

Switching back to my earlier request, I whispered, "Do we have time to stop by Blakely's, please?"

Jake opened his mouth but said nothing.

I took a big gulp of air and continued before he could. "I couldn't call her last night because I broke my phone. I tried the house phone this morning, and no one is answering, not even her mom. I'm worried, Jake."

He groaned and tweaked my nose with two fingers. He knew I hated when he did that, but Ghost put the car in gear. "Sure thing." Twisting his watch while explaining, he said, "We have time. Besides, you know it's been a while since anything serious has happened. Maybe she's sick." He clicked the blinker on and merged into traffic.

While he drove, I worried about Blakely. She'd always hid the fact that her stepdad was abusive toward her and her mother. Whenever he had pushed her around, she wore baggy clothes to hide the bruises. On a calendar in her locker, she used to countdown the days until she turned eighteen and could get out of there. Blake would intervene whenever the abuse became too much for her mother, but until Blakely was out of that house, I would always worry about her.

To distract myself with *what ifs*, I studied Ghost. He was wearing his black Sundial sunglasses; a tight black T-shirt tucked into his jeans, and his ratty black Nike shoes. He smelled of soap, aftershave, and deodorant. The combination made me think of a clear, cool river. The sun caught tips of his sandy blond locks depending on which way he turned. Ghost drummed with a tune on the steering wheel and sang off-key with the radio. Skeptically, I asked myself, *why hadn't I ever seen through his simplicity to appreciate what we could be together?*

With a slight head bob, I turned away before the ache of losing someone I never really had in the first place happened. A shiver crossed my shoulders, and I rubbed both hands on my arms to try and warm them. Before I knew it, my world went from cool and sunny to warm and dark when Ghost's black leather jacket was tossed over my head.

"If you were cold, you should've said so." He returned

to drumming.

I stayed under the leather and breathed in the scent of his cologne. I wanted to giggle, but it was for all the wrong reasons. My heart tried to shift to a new rhythm, but it made me think of Tod instead, and my heart reached out for missing emotions and froze over. I took those emotions—of wanting what I couldn't have—and dug a shallow grave in the back of my mind, placing them next to the ones I had for Tod. I didn't really deserve either of them.

The word *pathetic* was so prominent in my mind when I peeked at Ghost from under the collar. He was still singing and not even glancing in my direction, so I pulled down his jacket and slipped it on. *Get a grip, Alexcia.*

In the middle of the song, he changed the lyrics and sang, "Hey, it's up ahead. You've got five minutes. You want me to come with you?" Ghost winked.

I tried to smile. "No. But park up ahead where you can see me. I will signal if I need help. Okay?"

He nodded. Before the car came to a complete stop, I jumped out. I regained my footing and ran up the steps to her modest one-story house. The light beige paint was complemented by a huge, dark, wood-stained door.

Taking a quick breath, I knocked. Checking on Ghost over my shoulder, I waved to make sure he could see me from the street. I caught a glimpse of him waving back when I heard the door unlock. When I turned back around, I found myself face to face with a pair of sunglasses. It seemed as though Mel was at it again, and my chest tightened, as Blakely's mom fidgeted with a frayed curl by her cheek.

"Good morning, Mrs. Sanderson. I was wondering if Blakely was going to school today. Jake and I stopped by because I broke my cell, and I was worried that she would come to my house looking for me." I stepped slightly to the right to get a better view down the hall toward Blake's room.

"I'm sorry, Alexcia, she is sick. We came down with the flu all of a sudden after we went to dinner last night. I don't think she is going to school today and maybe not tomorrow, either."

I recognized the way Mrs. Sanderson was leaning against the door and knew she was favoring her right leg and cradled her left arm. She was hurting, and from her stance probably had a cracked rib or two. Outright anger caused my skin to welt around my neck. With a deep hatred, I wished the tables were turned on Mr. Sanderson. In seeing her condition, I guessed Blake's probably wasn't much better.

"Well, please let her know about my phone and that I will try to call her later after I get home." When the remark faded, it magnified the helplessness I felt for Blakely and her mom.

"Thanks for checking on her, Alexcia. I'm glad she has such good friends. You, Jake, and Dee are very special to her. Please remember that." She started to close the door.

"Mrs. Sanderson…" I focused hard on getting my point across to her. "I understand how she handles things, and I will do anything to make sure that at the end of her road, she is happy. Can you please remember that as well?"

Her face blanched, and I thought she was getting my message, but her eyes wandered down to my hands. "Dear, are you okay? Did you cut yourself?"

I raised my right hand. Blood trailed from several small cuts on my right palm. I had no idea my nails had been cutting through the skin. I marveled at the absence of pain. The flow of blood became constant and made me feverish.

"Oh no, not now," I chastised myself with a low exhale. The pressure in both eyes was beginning to build. My vision blurred as if I were drunk. "I'm sorry," rushed from my lips as I took a step back. "I'm fine. I'll have Jake take me home." I spun around and skipped every other step to sprint toward Jake's car.

I heard her call out to me, "Okay, well you take care."

The click from the door being locked behind me gave me some quick relief. All of a sudden, my body wouldn't respond to my commands. I wanted to get the hell out of there but found myself standing next to Mr. Sanderson's car. I placed my bloody right hand on the driver's side handle and then the window. Both eye sockets burned to the point where white goo would start running down my face any second.

My right hand smeared blood all over the window and I used my index finger to write through the lukewarm liquid. I scribbled so fast that my brain couldn't process what I was doing. When I got to the bottom of the window, I backed up and stared at the ominous monstrosity I had created on Mr. Sanderson's car.

I heard my nickname over and over, but the masculine voice was muffled. My body ignored his pleas. It was like being switched to autopilot, and another was working my controls. Trapped within, I watched helplessly as I placed my hand on the ground by the door and made additional crimson loops and interlocking circles. My voice box ached and muscles throbbed as I tried to regain control.

Gibberish linked together with chalk-squeaking vowel sounds as they poured from my mouth. *"Hezi-Kagia-ot-nok Metia-udo-kaph-tu-nak."*

I wanted to scream, but couldn't as the voice within me continued. *"Plake-nit-frint-a-cric-tu-death."*

Oh no, the only word I had understood was death. *What am I doing?*

Arms latched from behind and lifted me off the ground. A male voice spoke harshly into my ear. "What the hell did he do to you? Did he hit you?" Jake picked me up and placed me in the front seat of his car and grabbed a towel from under the passenger seat. Wiping the blood from my hands, he began cursing under his breath.

"No," I croaked while tilting my head trying to regain my bearings. My eyes continued to smolder making my surroundings seem hazy. I leaned forward resting my forehead on Ghost's shoulder. "No need to worry about Mel anymore."

I didn't know the meaning of what I had said to him. *Why is this happening to me?* I was sure to get a one-way ticket to Padded Central this time. Jake had never seen me lose it to this degree, and I couldn't blame this on drinking.

Jake was conflicted. The tone of his voice and his body

language was obvious. "What? What are you saying?" Puzzled by my behavior, he grabbed my shoulders to support me. "Alexcia? Are you going to pass out? What happened? How did you cut yourself?"

I struggled against the pressure the estranged voice was having on me. Vocal chords tightened from fighting it, and my lips moved against my will as it spoke, "The River has marked him unworthy, and I summoned the Soul Cages to collect his foul soul."

Unable to focus on anything, both eyelids weighed like concrete, forcing me to succumb to sleep. *Yeah, if I could close my eyes, maybe I'd wake up in my bed. This had to be a nightmare; it certainly felt like one.*

Ghost shook me, not hard, but enough to release the pressure in my head. The heat traveling toward my brain began to subside, and I realized he was kneeling in front of me. Color had drained from Jake's face, making him worthy of his nickname.

Jake cleared his throat. "I think I'll make up that test another day. I'm taking you home."

"Good." I stared at my hands.

Dumbfounded, his own slipped from my shoulders.

My fingers shook, and I used the back of my right hand to remove the last of my tears. "I think it's time for me to have a sit-down with my parents."

Chapter Fifteen

Fifteen years of listening to my mother.
Fifteen years of fearing my father.
Fifteen years of watching the sun rise and the moon
fall.
Fifteen years of trying to understand it all.
Only to realize, it was fifteen years of nothing
But deceit and lies.
Alexcia—

Five seconds after I walked through the front door, silence greeted me. Gigi didn't even bolt from my father's office. All the curtains were drawn, and the house was draped in gloom.

I couldn't see very well as I fumbled toward the living room. When I got closer to the couch, I spotted two dark figures. One moved. The other was frozen in a pose resembling a gargoyle. I had never been so scared in my life. *Why weren't they yelling at me? Why weren't they saying anything?* This kind of treatment was new and seriously freaking me out. It put a whole new meaning to the silent treatment.

If this was my parents' way of holding me under the water and waiting for me to come up for air, it was working.

My resolve was cracking from the joint parental force.

I whispered, "I don't know where to start."

Mom stopped pacing but wouldn't look at me. My father methodically came out of the shadows, appearing more sinister than normal. His crisp, Black-Label Austin suit was black-on-black, accentuating his pale skin, almost giving it a violet hue. The suit brought out the extreme cold in his eyes.

Max was the first to respond. "Look, Rae-Lynn, I told you she would come home sooner or later."

Rae-Lynn stepped next to him, folding her arms across her chest.

Oh, my goodness, she switched sides on me. This was going to be so one-sided. A vision flashed before me, and I saw myself in shackles vacantly staring out of a small wire-mesh window. I was either going to be locked up in an institution or an all-girls academy.

Panic set my anger in concrete. With my jaw muscle tightened, I reinforced the strength of my backbone. This was going to get ugly fast. I mirrored Rae-Lynn and crisscrossed both arms, using the action to hold myself together for some inner reassurance.

Goodbye, freedom… in one, two, three. Then I dove off into unchartered territory. "I have some questions for you both."

My father blinked several times but didn't respond. I had momentarily caught him off guard by redirecting the spotlight back to them.

Mom, on the other hand, didn't waver. With a voice, I had never heard her use before, she attacked. "You have questions? Who do you think you are to take that kind of tone with us? We are *your* parents the last time I checked, not the other way around. How dare you state to me that you want *us* to answer to *you*. *I* have questions for *you*."

My courage splintered, but I physically stood my ground.

"Like for starters, I received a call from Mrs. Sanderson saying you went by there this morning acting suspiciously.

Then she noticed you were bleeding and was worried you had gotten into a fight." Rae-Lynn stepped away from Max to stand right in front of me. Leaning in almost nose-to-nose, she continued, "What did you do to Mr. Sanderson's car? She believes you vandalized it." Her voice was high-pitched and demanding. "Out with it. What did you do?"

I hardened my eyes. "I have no idea."

She lifted a finger and pointed it at me. "Alexcia Crystalline, what did you do?"

I kept my pose, staring past her. "I don't know."

Mom took a long stride back and placed both hands on her hips. "*You don't know* is the best answer you can come up with?" She started pacing again. "I thought we raised you better than this. I know we're not home as often as other parents, and I'm sorry for that. I guess we were wrong in giving you so much freedom to make up for the loss. Clearly, we misjudged what you could handle."

I held out my hands. "I don't know what I did, but I *can* tell you I didn't use paint on Mr. Sanderson's car."

She huffed and walked over and grabbed my extended hand. Rae-Lynn's eyes went from pinched irritation to distress in a blink. "Max, she used her blood…" Her voice faded.

Max crossed the room to loom over me. Not making eye contact, he examined my hand before sharing a silent conversation with his wife. Snatching a cell out of his pocket, he walked into the other room. "I will make a call and see if Mr. Sanderson has used the car yet."

My eyes became sticky. "See? It's stuff like that—your secret, unspoken language. This has everything to do with me, but you never explain why. Don't you think I have a right to know? What is it you think I've done because"—my voice went up an octave—"I don't know." I yanked my hand from hers and covered my face.

Even though my actions didn't seem to affect my mom, she wasn't acting normal by taking up the role of bad cop. "I didn't buy your crazy story last night, but I was so tired after my trip and didn't want to turn it into an issue with your father. So, tell me the real reason why you didn't come home last night."

She might as well have punched me in the gut. Rae-Lynn had always said things like, "Stop bending the truth," or "Oh, Alexcia, you're so creative with your tales," or "You're adding more drama than necessary, Alexcia." Never had she been this blunt with me. Mom had officially moved from my corner to my father's.

My eyes spilled over with liquid betrayal. "Mom, if I had come clean with what really happened, you would've driven over to Dee's, snatched me out of bed, and booked me an overnight stay in the crazy ward." I sidestepped around her to sit on the couch.

In her navy-blue rayon dress suit, she sat next to me, stiff and emotionally distant. "Try me."

Dread brought stammering. "I-I don't even know where to start."

A lock from her updo fell over her right eye, shielding her view of me. "The beginning would be good, for starters."

Max reentered the room. His features were locked in place when he said, "It's too late to counter it."

Mom seemed annoyed and waved a manicured hand. "He had it coming, anyway. I'm kind of glad. Maybe they will be better off now. Anyway, we'll deal with that later."

My father gritted his teeth and raised his voice. "Rae-Lynn, it's not working, and we have to change our tactic. Now."

"Yes, yes, we will, but first, I want to find out from our daughter why she didn't come home last night."

My head whipped around to catch the storm building behind his eyes. "Where were you?"

My voice shrank below a whisper. "I was at Dee's."

"And?" His frame seemed to grow. Hell, he already towered over most people.

Okay, Alexcia, I don't have time for a quick pep talk with myself. I only hope they will listen before placing judgment.

"Blakely was supposed to pick me up after work. She

didn't show, and my cell was dead, so I couldn't call anyone. I decided to walk home. As I was walking, it seemed that I was being followed, so I ran to Dee's house since it was closer. That's all there was to it."

My mother shook her head and placed the hand she had waved over her eyes. "I can feel you staring at me, Max. Please don't. I will take care of that, too."

I was trapped under his gaze on Rae-Lynn. *So, apparently, I wasn't the only one in trouble?* It gave me a tiny measure of satisfaction knowing I wouldn't be the only one sharing a room with Gigi.

When he spoke, the faith I had in my parents crumbled to dust and blew away from the force of his words. "Rae-Lynn, if you don't act soon, we are going to lose her. It's your leashed daemon who keeps screwing things up."

"May I remind you," she snapped, "that we are in this together? It is just as much my problem as it is yours. Everything comes down to our daughter and her safety, first. The rest we can take care of later."

"Enough!" I screamed.

The *swoosh-swoosh* in my ears made me disoriented when I bucked from the couch. Pain lanced through to the back of both eye sockets. My own hands pressed into my temples to ebb the throbbing, and I spoke against my better judgment. "See, this is what I am talking about. Why won't you talk to me? Tell me what is going on! Why have I had nightmares every night since my fifteenth birthday?"

My mother looked aghast. "Nightmares?"

"Why do I black out and barely remember anything? Why do I speak in a language I've never heard before?"

"Since when have you've blacked out?" Max sounded skeptical.

"Why do my eyes hurt whenever I'm emotional?"

Rae-Lynn stood up.

Oh no.

But instead of addressing me, she turned to her husband. "It's trying to break through. What are we going to do?"

Furious, I shouted, *"What's wrong with me?"* Then I

tried to bring my voice down an octave. "Last night, the creature in my nightmare told me to ask you. So, I am asking you both. What am I? Why did it call me Balance?"

"Marquis-Shax," my mother shrieked.

Uncontrollably, my head whipped around to confront the clean-cut man in the Italian suit. My mother had never addressed him that way before.

The low snarl came from the corner next to me where I'd thought my father had been standing. I guessed we must have upset Gigi from our shouting. As I stood to get a tissue, I heard another voice enter the conversation from the dark.

"How *dare* they interfere? The keeper of our Bond-Rites will pay for his arrogance."

Then he spoke in a riddle. "How do you damn the already-damned? How do you curse what the River created from a curse? How do you kill what has no soul?" His voice was menacing.

I wiped tears in disbelief. "Dad?"

Suddenly, a murky streak turned the corner at the back of the room. Both feet must have lost circulation because I could have sworn Hell had frozen over. The glass patio door opened with force, and then it shattered.

I turned to my mother, stunned. "Mom? What's going on?"

Ignoring me, her face became surreal as a passion I'd never seen before glistened in her eyes. She passed me as though under a trance. Shards of glass crunched under her heels when she stopped at the back-door threshold. Her fiery tresses had fallen out of its sloppy bun, cascading in a web of curls, down her back. The brisk wind stirred her fiery locks, giving the impression that she was flying. The sun was casting a double shadow of her across the floor, making a pattern of arched wings. Staring up at the sky, she scanned the horizon humming low in a haunting tone. Realization made my breath catch as I deduced crazy must run in our family.

I grabbed the house phone and ran out of the living room, not caring about my questions anymore.

Was it asking too much to be normal?

When I got to the stairs, I heard Rae-Lynn's voice change. It sounded soft and almost musical, as she said, "My love, the answer you seek is simple. You break its will."

Chapter Sixteen

Tevin's side: Through the eyes of a Reaper

*O*ne second, I was yelling at our new clan member for putting all of us, including herself, on the second-most-powerful daemon's nonexistence to-do list. The next, I was flat on my back in a place drained of color. The flash of blinding white was disorienting. I was lying on a smooth, solid surface as a crushing weight pressed into my gut. I had literally found myself between a rock and a hard place.

I detected a suffocating mixture of brimstone and sulfur, with a subtle hint of black coffee, in every vexing puff of air and knew it only meant one thing. Marquis-Shax, Hades' second daemon in command, was sitting on my chest. My immortal days had been numbered, thanks to a selfish Wind Evoker who did not understand there were consequences for every action. I realized that accepting my fate was inevitable and was already planning to turn Moment into a 3-D jigsaw puzzle, beginning with the feature I hated most… her damn mouth.

Max leaned in with a growl, while the claw that held my left shoulder pinned made sure I was incapable of escaping. His talons pierced through my cloak, and my minion squirmed from his unwelcome touch. I squinted to block out the light and sensed where he had ported us. Infinity's Garret was a tear in time. Its concept consisted of unfinished space that constantly expanded. This was where the existence of nothing dwelled, playing in the surrounding emptiness the Constant's madness had created.

Direction was lost here because the rules of physics did not apply where time was broken, and therefore, anywhere was nowhere and somewhere could be where you thought you were or were not. The Garret made you hunch and crouch, forcing you to play its version of Simon Says. It affected my shroud and made me feel confined as it wrapped several times around my body. I was afraid to move.

Max's acidic saliva dripped right next to my ear. He was judge and jury and about to slam his fist in my face and pronounce me guilty.

I remained motionless, but the blow never came.

When I ventured to open one eye, I found his face so close to mine that if I slept, I would have nightmares for the next decade. Max's tongue slid across the upper row of his jagged, gleaming teeth. Focusing on him, I tried to adapt to the Garret's glare. The pure color of infinity made Max's skin appear charred-purple. His horns and hooves were an intense black, their darkened shade enhanced from the blinding glow.

His sentence started with the heat of a lightning strike and grew louder with electrical intensity. "You have about as much time as it takes for me to blink, to explain why my daughter was told to ask her parents who she really is. You wouldn't by chance know what or who would break the conditions of a Bond-Rite, would you, daemon snot?"

I considered explaining about Moment but did not think he would listen to reason anyway. My brain hastily slapped together Plan B, and my mouth opened only slightly because his other claw had flashed so fast I did not realize he had covered my mouth until I heard his continuing speech.

"I would choose your words with care, daemon." His thunderous ones echoed. "You may not get a chance to utter them a second time."

My eyes cast an eerie glow across his chiseled bone structure. Damnation boiled behind his shadow-encased eyes as he gagged my ability to rationalize the meaning of his threat. I briefly pondered the consequences, deciding, I really did need a vacation.

Max's tongue whipped in the air above my face, reminding me of a serpent.

"So, does this mean you're going to kiss me or eat me? Before you do either, can I offer you a Tic Tac? I think I have some in my front pocket." I wiggled my right arm out from under his weight, shoved my fingers into the jeans my minion had formed and pulled out the clear rectangle container of mints to give it a shake. "It's a one and a half calorie breath mint, and trust me; you could stand to lose a pound or two."

Bemused, the Doom Guard's face contorted to the point where I expected his jaw to break. I had caught him off guard, but he quickly recovered, responding with a punch to my right side. Ribs splintered from the impact, and the beast I kept contained used my voice to roar in his face.

The Smolder's reaction did not faze Max's focus, or if it did, I could not tell. His demeanor was as hard as a frozen star, one that could easily suck in anyone's presence whether it was alive or merely existing.

The power of his punch crushed the Tic Tac container; freed mints floated carelessly around us. It was bizarre to see little specks of color thriving in this space.

I angled my head to spit out the blood. Drops sizzled as it splattered beside me, and then I watched the drips roll away from me in long, erratic streaks. I thought we must have been on a wall, but gravity was not what was keeping us attached, hence the floating mints. I readjusted my left shoulder, but splitting agony rocketed down my back, making me aware of the slickness between the wall and myself. We must have been close to the core of the Garret where it turned reality inside out.

The shroud inched closer to the holes Max had created, and I started to feel claustrophobic as the daemon who possessed me tried to take control.

Everything about me felt broken. The control I used on my fighting form was slipping. Even my minion was showing signs of frustration as it worked to remove Max's claws from my chest and shoulder. Several emotions cycled through me, but it was hard to pin one down long enough to regain my composure.

The situation I was in hit me in a way I was not expecting, and I started laughing in a weak attempt to stay sane. My reaction sprayed blood across the Doom Guard's face. Releasing a chilling roar as he scrambled to wipe the burning liquid from his eyes, Max yanked out the claw embedded in my shoulder, taking pieces of me in his talons. A roar mirroring his ripped from my throat. Anguish and revulsion struck a musical death chord between us, carrying its echo right down my middle.

Blinking the agony away, I turned my attention to the area in front of me. The cloak had disappeared, leaving me in the pair of jeans and combat boots. Blood dripped in various patterns as gravity shifted erratically. Taking great care, I rolled onto my good shoulder to clear my airway so I could speak when the time came. Max was suspended horizontally, about twenty feet away from me, turning my blood into smears of war paint.

I wiped my mouth and spat again. "It stings worse if you rub it into your eyes."

His teeth were clenched. "I am waiting for an explanation, Ashen…"

"I'm not entirely sure what you are accusing me of." My vision was becoming accustomed to the Garret's white-on-white aura, but I would never get used to it. "So, Infinity's Garret? You must really be pissed off to risk bringing us to this unpredictable place. Unfortunately, you grabbed the wrong entity."

My cloak returned to make another healing pass, encircling my legs. I tried to kick at it, and it repaid me by cauterizing the five puncture holes in my chest. Strange… as it worked into the wounds, I pictured maggots threading through the eye sockets of a corpse.

"…and you owe me dinner, daemon. But, so you know, I'm cheap, not easy."

He waved a thick muscular arm and shot a fireball in my direction, singeing my boots. The green flames licked up the soles before my minion snuffed them out. I frowned. Good thing they were black and worn down already.

So much for dinner.

Mist from the cloak swirled around my feet, but I shooed it away. It didn't need to waste its power on fashioning my footwear. "You owe me a new pair of boots," I shouted, not sure if we were in close proximity anymore.

The cloak started on my rib cage, breaking and reforming the bones under the moving mist. I shot up only to bend over in agony, swearing death wishes on everything. Different forms of torture shifted in my mind from killing Moment to gutting Alexcia's father. When agony melted into a discomfort more bearable, I uncurled myself, realizing I was dealing with an appalling new emotion.

What in the world did I ever do to deserve all of this? I cannot remember why I took this job in the first place. Why had Rae-Lynn involved me?

Ten years ago, I was an Ashen, serving out my mundane existence to the River. It was tolerable work for a daemon. *What more could I possibly add to my existence? What is this...*

"It's called pity, Ashen."

He was right behind me. Death be damned and break my scythe, I did not even hear him move.

Disgusted, I responded flatly, "Pity, huh? What makes you the expert?"

"More specifically, it is called a pity-party. Rae-Lynn and Alexcia have them all the time when they do not get their way. Although, I've never seen a daemon throw one. It's pathetic. I even have a slight twinge of hesitation to dump more dirt on you."

I stood there dumbstruck. "*You?* You of all daemons feel remorse, for me?"

He tried to mask a gagging noise by fake sobbing.

Needing some space, I tried to take several long strides away from him and hoped the Garret would not slam us back together. My stance was unstable in my weakened state, and I could not even summon my weapon. I reached back with my good arm to retrieve it.

Max saw the action as a threat and smacked me across the empty space, which morphed into a white hill. The momentum rolled me up the incline until I found myself upside down. Gravity reacted differently in this broken spot of time, so I must have looked like a sick bat hanging by my feet in midair and dry heaving.

"You dare to raise your weapon, Ashen?" Max wavered while trying to fight against the Garret's unusual force.

My inner beast growled as I spoke. "You pretentious daemon. You hit me with a curse." I dropped to a temporary solid patch of white and used the marble snath of my scythe to anchor my body as I spoke. "I was trying to stand and sure as hell wasn't going to ask for your assistance." My rib cage vibrated from rage, but I could not tell if it was me, the beast, or a shared emotion. The Smolder wanted out; I could sense it testing my will for a weak area.

Max grabbed his chest melodramatically. "Tevin, I'm hurt. Since when have you become wary of an outstretched claw? I see trust is not one of your strong suits."

Using restraint, I held the leash on my possessor. Our situation was grave, and Max and I needed to hash this out. By words or by fists, I did not care how. For me, not caring was as natural as harvesting.

"Trust you? You must be pulling my cloak. I trust no daemon, angel, elemental, or Vessel. Trust is an emotional illusion. Nothing is ever reaped from sowing seeds of trust because sorrow's frost soon follows and kills anything of worth."

Max shook his head with the disappointment of a parental figure. "Ashen, for as old as you are, and as many souls as you have harvested, I would have thought you would've learned about the need for certain… benign emotions. Trust is neither negative or positive—it's to be used according to your own discretion. Even I, Hades' second, understand the importance of trust. Without it, the waters of Creation would cease to exist."

"Right," I said, tapping in front of me with the tip of my scythe, to make sure I would not find myself falling into a hole of nothing. "Look what trusting has done for your daughter."

He grumbled through his words. "Do not pass judgment on our reasons because your small daemon mind cannot comprehend. You are comparable to this tear in space, Tevin." His massive, arms flexed as he scanned around us. "The Garret is nothing but empty space, a moving expanse with no direction."

Vexation took the place of a Callcry as it perched on my shoulder and dug in. I grabbed the hood, tugging it partly over my eyes. Piqued, I could not face him while I spoke. "Death leaves a void, but it is one with direction. I have a purpose and a role to play to keep the waters flowing." I motioned around me with my scythe, "The Garret did not ask to exist in this way. I did not ask for this existence, but I am not complaining. No, wait, yes I am. Seems warranted since I have been contracted twice to work against my nature." In the middle of my explanation, tentacles webbed out, trying to grab onto something as my center of gravity faltered. Tapping the floor again for solid footing, I found myself standing several feet above the Doom Guard. Staring down, I merely stated, "We would not be in this situation if you and Rae-Lynn had told the child. Then maybe we could all work at keeping her *safe*." I growled out the last word.

"So, it has come to this? Death is challenging my authority?"

Seething colored my words. "Very observant, Marquis."

The one daemon I thought I could possibly trust had proven to be unreliable. Both physically and emotionally, I had failed myself. It seemed painfully obvious I had more in common with this space than I cared to admit.

Snarling, Max replied, "An Ashen with a chip on its shoulder. Come closer; I can remove it for you."

Floating down, I secured the spot in front of me by

repetitively tapping the hilt. Once I found a solid area, with force, I impaled the silver-spiked tip into the floor. The shroud hummed with approval as it erased all the scars, leaving taut skin over bone. Rotating my shoulder, I tested it with several movements to see if it was fully healed.

Max squared his shoulders, shifting his hooves into a defensive stance. His tail smacked into the floor behind him, creating small ripples of white. This was it. All the years of talking, arguing, fighting, and bond making had come to this—the right to protect Alexcia's future.

He crouched. "You and your clan have interfered against the conditions of our Bond-Rites. I have brought you here to get a reimbursement for your failed services."

"How, exactly, have we interfered? As I explained before, you grabbed the wrong entity. My Ashens and I had nothing to do with your daughter's unfortunate enlightenment." I had to admit, being smug left a zing in the air because Max did not know about Moment.

He leaped into the area above me, but Infinity's Garret slammed him into the ceiling. I guess he was at the mercy of this tear in time too. While swearing under his breath, he realigned his wingspread.

Angling the metal-laced blade to position it, I had to strain to keep it in an attack pose as the hilt's weight grew heavier. I was preparing for the Garret to pop him up anywhere around me. One clean swipe was all I needed, and the beast inside agreed.

"So, are we having fun yet," I jested.

The Doom Guard brought a wing close for a tuck and roll. With patient anticipation, he waited to see where the Garret would flip him, but then he quickly fanned his wings out and landed with a sonic boom right above me. The sound waves knocked me off balance before my cloak seized as I turned to face him, causing me to trip over it. The scythe landed to my left, and my body fell diagonally opposite of where Max was standing. *Wonderful, what a time for the Garret to follow the rules of gravity.*

I took a chance and dismissed my minion, so I could

have some space to move. This conflict was going to take a while, and I didn't need the aid of my faltering minion.

I was dead wrong.

Max jumped as the dimension's axis tilted. The opening of his wings made a thunderous crack, adding to the intensity of his power. His momentum stopped abruptly, and his body fell. The Doom Guard's massive girth was headed right for me.

Eyes wide, I was without my minion, without a weapon, and functioning on empty. Mentally even my Smolder said, *"Ah, hell no."*

Max's serrated grin answered, *you're mine.*

I went to counter before he caught me between hoof and claw. The swing of gravity caused my weapon to slide toward me. Before I could snap, he enclosed his claw over my right hand and crushed it. Thrashing into his bulk, I knocked him off me. The Garret's vast universe filled with my screams… not from the agony, but from being so pissed I could have harvested Alexcia's life right then with no hesitation.

Freeing my other arm, I tried to snap again, but his body fell back on top of me tail-first. Beyond agitated, I kicked and bucked at his dead weight as he maneuvered his tail out of the way.

"Get off," I shouted. My command bounced around us as the time-tear played with the echo.

"Having trouble? Here, maybe it is because you are uneven."

Max raised a claw and plunged several nails into my wrist and palm. With my good hand pinned, I could not curl my fingers to snap. Trapped under his weight, I figured if this was going to be it, I was going out in style. I opened the cage.

The Smolder tore through my resolve as if I was a wood-rotted casket. Skin split, clawing my inner walls in its haste. Burnt liquid tar oozed everywhere, filling the Garret with the acidic stench of my blood. Bones cracked and reformed underneath his weight. I roared with enough wrath to fuel the beast. Scales protruded while both shoulders broke, pushing two wings against the floor. The opportunity gave me adequate leverage to toss Max across the Garret and left me hanging in midair, transforming into Death's feared form. My aura covered the expanse in an indigo wash.

Like a snake realigning its jaw after a meal, I smacked them together, pretending the Doom Guard was between my fangs. I scanned the expanse of white, forcing my sight to work against the Smolder's blurred vision. Max was about five wingspans away, trying to stop the blood flow from an open wound.

The outcry I unleashed was from ten years of repressed rage. I did not want to leave here playing the role of the protector. *If Max wanted to provoke death, well, he had his wish. Death was seriously provoked.*

My minion's power had been replaced with billowing eddies of tainted smoke around my legs. It played through my open claws and curled horns, stretching over the dark purple, red-tipped scales. There was a reason we did not change unless we absolutely had to. All this power came with a price. Allowing the Smolder control meant losing the one thing I cared about the most. *Me.*

"Your intimidating parlor trick doesn't impress me. You may answer to the River, Death Daemon, but you were created from Hell's fire and are a member of my House. As such, I will treat you as the creature you are." He opened his wings and flew straight at me. "Now, bow to me, *Demon of Death.*"

Giving in to the rage, I charged, talons open, as several screeches tore through the air. My right claw had been broken, but I used the pain to pump my wings.

The Garret showed no mercy toward the House of Space's second, nor Death. It allowed us to collide and the resulting crash reverberated through the white space in slow motion before allowing time to speed forward for the bone-crunching impact that followed. Exploding fragments of blood, skin, and scales sprayed into the spaces dissolving into nothing.

We slid into a free fall, our tails and back haunches intertwined, leaving us swiping at each other with blind hatred. The descent caused my sides to crush. Max clenched his teeth, and I knew the pressure was getting to him as well.

Alexcia's father tried to punch me and overshot. I gored him with my left claw and pinned him against my chest. If we were going down, we were going to go together. I sent a selfish wish into the blinding void that when we landed, he would suffer the full force of our impact. And since I was going to land on top of him with all my weight, I figured I would leave him with an unforgettable impression.

I spoke to him daemon to daemon, linking our minds. *"In the end, I will always be there to claim what the River has created."* I tried to open my wings to create drag. It was not working, and we fell faster.

His breathing had become shallow. *"I reiterate; you are similar to this cursed place. When one path ends for some, another is created and then another. It is Infinity's path to Eternity. I have ended many entities, Ashen."*

"What is one more, then?"

"A choice to change the outcome of this ending, perhaps."

"Afraid to be recopied, Max?"

He paused, and I took a second to study his expression.

"I have only been recopied once."

"Saving your child?" I swallowed to quench the fire building from behind my palate.

"No, Rae-Lynn."

The muscles in my throat tensed as I asked, *"Why?"*

"I found my missing heart in her. When her House found out about our union, they put out a contract to end her existence and besought Styx not to bring her back."

I extended my legs as I forced both wings to pump back and forth instead of up and down. I was trying to use a reverse way of thinking against the Garret. Floating, my momentum made me crash into a jagged white wall. By utter impulse, I shielded Max from the blow. *Protecting was becoming second nature to me.* I heaved a lungful of air, and fire streamed out, singeing part of Max's wing and leg. He swore.

I chortled until my forked tongue vibrated.

Max cursed again before we hit the bottom. It happened so fast I could not prepare for the abrupt stop, but then again, trying to understand the Garret was pointless. I did not even know why I tried. The floor beneath us caved and absorbed our energy, causing us to roll claw-over-wings. I whipped my tail out, slamming it into the ground like a ship's anchor, searching for stability against the sandy ocean floor.

When we finally stopped, I turned to face the Doom Guard. *"So, you saved your love? Why would a daemon want such a useless emotion crawling around, making its presence infect their nature?"*

"She was carrying a part of me," he answered aloud.

Defeat carved his features, making me turn away to examine my broken claw and lick some of my wounds.

"Yeah, you said that already. Rae-Lynn had part of your heart." I locked gazes with him.

Unblinking, he countered, "No, Tevin. Part of me mixed with a soul."

I froze. He was talking about Alexcia. Damn the cloak I cast; the others were trying to kill her even before she was born. Maybe she really was going to change everything, and that was why all the Houses were chasing their own tails to obtain her power or kill her before another House had a chance. Was I possibly having a change of... *what, absence of heart?* I chuckled internally at my own joke, but it came out as a throaty gurgle.

"What are you thinking about, Tevin?"

"That I need a lip-smacking soul, a side of fries, and not be so stiff when bending to change."

"Enlighten me, Ashen."

"We ran into a snag the night before last when Alexcia was attacked."

Max stood tall and limped over to me, dripping blood as hot as molten lava along the way. The small trail was bleeding white smoke into the Garret behind him, disappearing into nothing. "What issue, daemon?"

With a snort, I shook my head. *She did not see us, and we made sure of that. But after the weather had cleared, we found ourselves with a prisoner. I figured we could find out why the Houses are so crazed trying to silence her voice before she reaches maturity.*

He shifted his wings and leaned toward my eye. "And?"

I closed mine with a slow blink because I did not want him to gouge one out. *I made a Bond-Rite with a Wind Evoker. We could use the help, and she's an expert bounty hunter.*

"Bounty hunter!" He roared in my face. "What in Hell's fire were you thinking by including an elemental? She will send word, on the first breeze, to her House. You won't even realize it until the last word hits you in the face."

No, my Bond-Rite is pretty airtight. I spindled a spell she wanted in trade. Either way, if she goes against the Bond, she will meet her maker by my hand. It is now part of her future, and she cannot outrun it.

Max did not appear convinced but lowered his wings. "If she crosses me in any way, I will send her to Styx myself along with her Spindler." He arched an eyebrow, punctuating his point.

I sighed heavily, opening my eyelids. If we were conversing without hostilities, I didn't need the Smolder's armor. Summoning my minion, I used its power to lock the daemonic dragon within me.

After my body reformed, the shadowy mist plunged to the ground, coloring the edges with swirls of indigo aura. "I understand. Where do we go from here?" I unsheathed the scythe and approached Alexcia's father with caution. It looked as though my clan and I were back on guard duty.

Leering at me, Max answered, "Have your new recruit take the first shift so you can get recharged. I have a hunch the situation is going to get worse before it gets brutal."

"Where should I send the Wind Evoker?"

"Have the Evoker shadow Alexcia during the day. But I want either you or one of your clan guarding after the sun sinks behind the mountain range. I have the distinct notion my daughter is going to organize a jail-break."

"When?"

"I believe in the next few days. Double your efforts during the weekend. Rae-Lynn and I will both be out of town. I'm positive Alexcia is planning on breaking the rules. Make sure one of your daemons is posted at her normal hangouts, like the mall, her place of employment, or the drive-in."

"How do you know?"

"Because she's become a creature of habit and is part daemon."

I huffed. Time, Light, and Space be damned. I was not sure if there were enough Ashens to cover the potential wipeout her temper could muster. With my curiosity set aside, I thought, maybe we should harvest her before she recreated the Big Bang.

Max began to prepare for our departure. He placed his claw on my shoulder, and his aura blurred from the air distortion of Spindled magic as it wove a healing and morphing spell. When the vibration in the air settled, he was standing in his suit, his daemon figure and stench gone; he appeared tired but seemingly unaffected by our dispute.

Using my left hand, I flipped my scythe blade over to rest the hilt behind my shoulder while I motioned for the cloak to mend the broken hand. Mentally, I braced for the power vacuum behind Max's Time Bend. With his level of Spindling, it was going to be one hell of a first step.

Max abruptly faced me and said, "With Alexcia, you should start with trust. The rest will follow."

Trust? I moved my cloak to stare at him. "What?"

The Time Bend flashed brighter than an imploding star when it sucked us in, catching me off guard and leaving my question to play in Infinity's madness.

Tevin's side: Through the eyes of a Reaper

I did not have faith in our newest member. Even though Max suggested that Moment take first shift, his warning gave me pause. So, I decided to send Michael and Archer to follow the elemental and make sure she stuck to our agreement. They were under strict instructions to alert the rest of us if anything out of the ordinary started to happen; like if she sneezed the wrong way and caused a butterfly in Australia to flap its wings. Moment was becoming a master at unforeseen chaos. After the misunderstanding Max and I had, thanks to her, and what I had experienced in the past few days, anything could happen.

It had been almost nine days since Michael and I had spoken on top of the Onyx. Alexcia was, as of now, still above ground. We had thwarted an attack on the Vessel. Max and I finally had our chat, but there was an uneasy knot growing in my gut. When Archer and Michael texted, they had overheard the Child-of-Balance making plans to meet her friends, I figured that was the cause.

Alexcia and her friends were meeting up to go to the movies. The drive-in, to be specific. I had to hand it to Max, he may have been clueless about his daughter's well-being, but he did know her tells. And since Archer and Michael were already on surveillance, I switched them to bodyguard duty.

Needless to say, Michael was not pleased. He had complained the whole time, sending jab-style text messages every thirty minutes. Even though he meant it to be mundane and repetitious, it set my nerves on ice getting his play-by-plays. The numbness was a welcomed feeling. Archer was trying to kiss ass and accepted this assignment with his tail between his legs. I would receive more technical, straightforward information from him. Having the two of them together was two wrongs making a right.

Quint and Imp were on C and C duty, which meant cleaning up and cutting losses. If anything went to Hell faster than we intended, they were the perfect mop-up crew. I gave the task of guarding the Child-of-Balance at the drive-in to K, Raven, Moment, and myself. We would serve as Alexcia's compass to help navigate her to safety.

That was my plan, but the objectivity of it did not sit well with me, as though there was an angle I had not taken into account. This gnawed at me, causing the sense of hitting bottom with this plan more than plausible.

Sitting in between two stalagmites, I contemplated the situation. From across the cavern, a faint sigh of protest came from Moment as she sat on the flat side of a broken stalagmite, filing her nails. I watched her brush her hand across the blue-and-black mesh crisscrossed fabric of her shirt. I had to admit having a female around was somewhat distracting, especially for Imp. If the two of them spent any more time together, they might blow our mountain apart. His reaction toward her earlier was the reason why I had paired him with Quint.

On the ground near the opening of the cavern, Quint sat immersed in a pool of cloaked darkness. Listening to his music, he was either drowning out the elemental's relentless filing, or me. His scorching, sun-lit orbs held aversion as he stared into the emptiness before him.

K and Raven were talking in a graveyard volume between themselves. Little did they know the lack of sound was deafening to my deliberation. Imp was sitting across from me, setting fire to the ripped tread on the sole of his left boot. Staring at Moment through the flames he was creating; I could only presume he was premeditating the actual act of burning her.

Irritation and boredom got the best of me. Summoning my scythe, I positioned my hand above my head as it materialized in the air. I grabbed for it and used the motion of my upper body to slam it into the middle of the table. Imp barely flinched, but he used the slight reaction to pretend to extinguish his boot. The flame flickered, but the daemon lifted his foot and brought it to his face to blow out.

Moment taunted him under her breath. "Moron."

Imp blew her a kiss from behind the plume of burnt-rubber smoke.

She rolled both hourglass irises and opened her mouth to respond.

I shot her a challenging glare, and she closed her jaw with an audible snap.

When I curled an empty fist, the bone fingertips pressed into my palm. The pain worked at dulling my angst because waiting was not the same as patience. Even the Smolder was growing intolerant; its presence stirred within my cavity like an exhale of smoke. We were so close. Tripping before the finish line was not an option, and harboring ill will, even though it tasted exquisite, was going to damn us to an existence of servitude if we did not work together.

"So, does everyone know the plan for tonight?"

I scanned the room. Quint had taken one of the earbuds out but did not turn around. He didn't want janitorial duty with Imp and therefore continued to sulk in the corner. I needed him and Imp as backups because of the way Max spoke, but I was expecting assassins from all three Houses to show.

"So, have you heard if your House has sent anyone in to replace you?" I figured being direct with Moment would get her to comply willingly.

She made a sour face. "A few, actually, but none that can match my capabilities or style, so I wouldn't worry. Imp could handle them with his flashy toothpick. Most have only been around for a hundred years or so."

Exhaling, I asked, "So how many do you think?"

She held up her manicured fingers and on the one hand acted as if she were counting. "Seven, eight, maybe ten. Could be up to twenty."

"So we should plan for twenty?"

"Seven." She flipped a hand over, pretending to count the back side.

"You said, 'up to twenty—'"

With a terse *tsk*, she cut me off. "Seven, twenty-seven, and add ten, so possibly more than thirty."

A quake jarred my body and cracked the rock-faced table beneath my hands.

Imp shook his head. "Hey breathe, man. So, math isn't her strong suit. We'll plan for forty to fifty from her House, and if it's fewer, we'll focus on other Unseen entities who may drop in on our little party." His lips took a menacing crawl up the side of his cheeks, peeling back to show his perfect teeth.

The purple in his eyes grew brighter with the anticipation of killing, which irritated me because he knew he was on cleanup with Quint. I figured both were sulking in their own way.

Raven and K leaned on the table in a mirrored fashion, blowing out a breath at the same time.

K picked up on my thoughts and spoke to Imp first. "Man, you need to harness your animosity, or it's going to get you recopied."

"What? You don't think I can handle myself against these substandard entities?" He roared at everyone.

"Heel, dragon," Moment said, hopping off her perch, "before I pull on your choker."

A muscle jumped in Imp's jaw. "What makes you believe you can stop me, Evoker?"

She snapped. A torrent of wind manifested, and then it slammed into the fissure I had made across the stone table, which cracked in two.

In a tick, Imp drew his sword, flipped it in the air in front of him, then forward flipped toward Moment. Opening his hand in the air as the sword's handle landed in his palm, he extended the blade, thrusting the tip to rest at her jugular. "No one commands me so bluntly, not even my clan leader. I do what I want, and if I agree, I will follow." He growled in her face. "Your wind tricks are entertaining, but when you exhale your last word, where is your power then?"

We all yelled at Imp to put the blade down. It was not up to him whether or not to take Moment's life. Angered by him jeopardizing the plan, my hands grabbed the hilt of my weapon and swung. The blade curved around his neck, resembling a shepherd's hook. This was my show, and he needed to get off the stage.

Moment's lips quivered from his challenge. "You *still* underestimate me?"

Her question caught us off guard because five pairs of glowing eyes shifted from his blade to her face.

She lifted her leg with blinding speed to change the punctuation mark of her question. Her black boot disappeared into Imp's cloak, and he buckled onto the floor followed by a flood of obscenities.

Then the bounty hunter used the air to lower herself to the ground. When both feet touched the floor, Moment with clear fluster, tugged at her clothes and patted her crown until she was pleased with her appearance. Standing over Imp, she cooed, "Haven't you learned wind smothers fire?"

She turned away from us and sauntered to the other side of the cave. My eyes widened when I realized she was taking over the meeting. "Quint, stay with him. Tevin will call when we need backup." She scanned the room. "We have a mess of Unseen to deal with, whether it's fifty, sixty, or a hundred plus. Our plan remains the same. We fight and protect the child. I intend to keep my contract because the bounty on the Vessel is mine." While dusting her outfit off, she focused on a chipped nail and snarled. "Time waits for no entity, and neither do I."

My cell buzzed with a text. *Was Michael listening?* I slipped my weapon back into its holster and opened my hand as a misty tentacle dropped the phone there.

Michael: The Child-of-Balance is on the move.

His next message gave us their coordinates and her estimated destination. The plastic cover cracked from misdirected angst. I willed my hand to relax.

Speechless, we all exchanged glances. Quint's cell began to play Archer's ringtone, "Soldiers," by Otherwise. Giving me a respected head nod, he spun on a heel to place some distance between us. With the cell against his ear, he pointed at Moment.

The Wind Evoker raised an arm over her head, causing the air to expand within our space. My ears popped from the dropping pressure as she formed her own Time Bend. Elementals used Time Links similar to a wormhole. They were faster but harder to control.

She turned to us. "After you, Ashens." Keeping one hand raised and the other motioning toward the opening, the Wind Evoker curtseyed with an overdramatic flair. "You shouldn't be late. Where is this party going to take place?"

I waved at the others to go ahead of me but remained beside Moment to make sure there was no trickery. She stepped into the opening, extending her hands to keep the portal open long enough to finish the transport spell.

"Well, where are we going?" Her voice wavered as she strained to hold the portal.

Grimly, I answered, "The drive-in," and held up the screen so she could read Michael's texted coordinates.

She looped one arm around mine, taking me by surprise. "It's a date then."

From my peripheral vision, I watched the elemental blow a kiss and wink at Imp. Moment pivoted on a heel, lowered her other arm and tugged me into the Time Link. It chimed. My last visual was narrowing purple eyes.

I had to admit, stepping out of Moment's portal was refreshing. The crisp rush of cool air forced my Smolder to calm down. Unfortunately, I did not notice the ice-covered floor until I took another step and lost traction. With the aid of my minion and K's grip on my forearm, the room stabilized. A smirk started to form as I remembered the ice lakes that formed a frozen ring around the bottom of our mountain.

This recall unlocked a buried memory. Alexcia had pulled me into a dream the night before her boyfriend's funeral. The memory seemed borrowed, but I secretly clung to it because I believed it might be a key to the riddle Rae-Lynn had baited me with ten years ago. Alexcia had sparked it back to life during the dream we had shared. I closed my eyes to bring back every detail.

Supposedly, I had brought Alexcia into our world. She was small, maybe four or five. I watched her skating on the pond below the clan's dwelling.

I remembered long wavy red curls and the way the wind blew it around her face resembling fire. She turned and opened her green mitten, inviting me to take her hand. A bright flash of light startled me before I accepted it, and then we were in the middle of the pond.

The daydream turned more ominous as my face burned as if lightning had slapped me. I watched in shock as the child screamed in terror, shattering the calm of the Callcrys, sending them into the sky. This part of the memory seemed foreign. A cloud of steam stirred nearby as I watched Max step out of a burning, green-and-gold daemonic summoning circle from behind her.

Recalling this memory was a punch in the gut, and I exhaled a sharp breath. I knew of the charred ring on the ice but never realized how it had happened. The scorched ring had faint white etchings embedded into the ice. The area felt blessed, as if a warning. With the vision fading, I thought, this was not the time or place to ponder an altered incident.

The daemons in front of me were exchanging low growls of approval with the temperature. Moment was the last to back out of her Time Link. But when the chill in the air slammed into her, she exclaimed, "What the hell!" and quickly wrapping her arms around her body. This spontaneous reaction caused the portal to bend in, reversing its momentum, which in turn, started a time collapse. Amateur magic users normally triggered a reverse on their wormhole from spawning them too fast.

Because of the portal's reversal, the room shook with a force that momentarily ripped everything off the shelves. The metal freezer door bowed and puckered from the suction. Since Moment was the last one out, she was going to be the first to get sucked back in.

"K, my scythe," I thundered over the airstream.

I felt the absence of my weapon and held my hands up to grab the silver-vined hilt. K moved with the precision of a nurse slapping a scalpel into a surgeon's waiting palm. I curled my fingers around it. Holding the flat part of the blade to my chest, I extended the tip of the snath toward Moment. Scrambling to regain her footing, she tried to face me. The magnetic pull increased in strength, and the thought of losing my ace made the zing of panic, an annoyance. Regrettably, we needed her abilities if Alexcia disappeared, and I was not ready to break our agreement. My thought quickly drifted to Imp; he would never forgive me if I lost his new chew toy.

I lunged forward, yelling at the others behind me to link their arms together. Quint shouted to K to get a better hold of me before the opening pulled us back in, too.

Boxes of frozen food slid down the wormhole's mouth, and I motioned with my head at the boxes. Moment's twin hourglasses narrowed as she tried to hide her terror as a box of frozen hot dogs flew passed me and right for her.

Movement slight, the cardboard box zipped passed her slim frame. I was a tad concerned because this elemental rarely displayed being rattled.

Since K was the closest to me, he hooked an arm around mine. I raised my voice and used my free arm to thrust my weapon toward Moment's right hand. "Grab hold."

The sound of air sucking back into the Time Link was deafening as it inhaled my words along with everything else. Sand streamed down the elemental's face as the tips of her nails grazed the hilt. I swung out my arm again. This time, the smell of burning flesh swirled angrily in the air. Mentally, I commanded her to climb toward us.

She reached forward to pull her body level with the handle. I anchored my stance against K's boots as the vacuum switched into overdrive. Moment's two-toned locks looked like a couple of Callcrys attacking her face. Tilting her head masked the anguish my weapon was causing her, but every grab meant more of her flesh was being singed off. The smell of roasting elemental intensified, giving me an awkward sense of gratification. She was paying the price for her mistake.

Moment's slow progress was irritating the others as she made her way up to my hands. The Wind Evoker maneuvered her burning palms over the back of my hands, covering them in sparkling sand. Our eyes bore into one another as the heat from her wounds seeped into my skin.

Internally, I spoke to the reaper that held onto my existence. *"K, don't let go."*

K repositioned his arm, acting as a hoist.

"Raven, let me know when you're ready for the shift in weight. I'm going to flip her to you. Then as the portal starts to pull her back in, I will use my scythe to pin her against my chest."

There was a grumble of protest from both, but K nodded. Raven said, *"Ready?"*

I pulled the Wind Evoker closer and used my frustration to be heard over the vacuum. "Moment, you're going to have to let go."

Her mouth unhinged. Clearly, she was against the idea of letting go, but in this case, she didn't have a choice.

In my head, I yelled, *"Now!"*

It took a quick flick of strength to toss her back to Raven's location. Moment's mouth shaped in a scream, but all we heard was vacuum from the void. She held out her hand, assuming the crimson daemon was going to catch her, but I had failed to disclose that part of the plan. I swung out the scythe again but on its side with my arm stretched out to catch a part of her torso.

The plan was going to work as I watched her spread her appendages out like a falling feline. I roped her in while turning her to face the broken portal and locked her in front of me taking the opportunity to place my lips by her ear. "Get your head out of your ass and fix the damn portal."

Moment nodded. I had not put into account the stream of sand flowing from her hands. A tremble rippled through her as she raised her hands, leaving iridescent streaks down her forearms. We could feel magic and failure pulsing from her creating a warped outline over her form.

The portal twisted, becoming distorted before it instantly cracked right down the center. A sound of screeching came from inside of her Time Link. A smearing of copper, blue-green, and silver marbled over the portal's doorway. The closed portal started to melt, dripping silver tears onto the floor as it solidified. When the hardened oval shattered inward, it swallowed itself up, which caused the suction to stop immediately. Gravity, back in control, dropped everything to the icy floor, including us.

We held on to one another to get our bearings as we untangled ourselves. Then from the back of the group, Raven cleared his throat threateningly.

Moment looked around baffled, rubbing her charred hands over her arms. "A freezer?" She took another breath and a white cloud puffed out. "I ported us into a freezer?"

Raven's sarcasm echoed. "Heaven forbid we didn't have to work around a destructive Moment every five minutes." We all shifted our gazes in his direction. "Stop staring and get these bags of fries back on the shelves. I'm here to fight, not take inventory."

K pulled out his cell and arched an eyebrow. "Shall I call the mop-up squad to take care of this?"

I kicked a box of frozen hamburger patties away from me and nodded. We needed to make up the time we lost.

Moment lifted herself off the icy floor, making a demented chortle. She may have caused this mess, but she was enjoying the fact that Imp was being called to clean it. I considered leaving her behind to help but quickly changed my mind as I pictured them locked in a freezer and Quint having to deal with their smack talk.

I snapped for my minion to form the hood. Moment was fiddling with her outfit and ordering Raven on where to place the boxes. *Yeah, leaving her would be a bad idea.* Quint would probably end up reaping both of them.

K was giving Quint our location and explaining the problem we'd found ourselves in. It was not my mistake, but it had been my idea to recruit the Wind Evoker, which meant her mistakes were also mine. I was positive Imp was not going to let this go for the next decade.

I tried to put the incident behind me and pointed around the room. "Raven, east. K, you are west. Moment, you take the south end, and I will take the north point. Let's move."

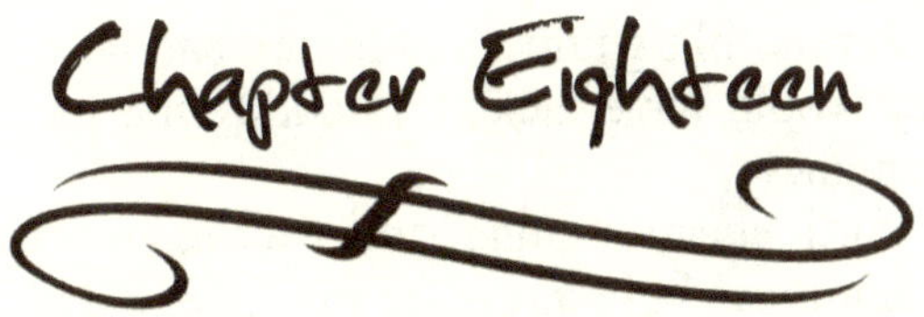

Terror drags my unwilling soul.
Scenes blur before me.
Time suspends my scream's release
Silent as memories fade.
Today imprisons my mind's purpose.
Sorrow corrupts what's true.
Tomorrow threatens my guarded secrets
Succumbing to the lie.
Tears stain my heart black
Stealing dreams of innocence.
Alexcia

*M*y mother had left early to catch her flight. Everything was going according to plan as a jolt of defiance amped my heart rate. It was the first time in almost two months where I finally felt some sense of normalcy. Friends, chocolate popcorn, a movie, and the thrill of escape. The only drawback was the weather; a storm was rolling in.

Blakely pulled her car to the curb, and I jumped from the steps of my jail and hiked up my tote bag. Yes, the weight of grounding was suffocating, but like Andy Dufresne said in *The Shawshank Redemption*, "Freedom smelled sweet."

The list of rules my parents had made seemed overprotective and skirted along the lines of their obvious paranoia. If mumbling under my breath had been against the rules, they would have tacked an additional ten years onto my life sentence.

One particularly strange rule was having to wear the rose pendant they'd given me for my fifteenth birthday. We were always arguing about that sparkly trinket. To keep the peace, I wore it… even in the shower, at first.

When my parents became a united front, a nuke blast couldn't shake them apart.

Blake leaned over the seat to unlock the door, pushed it open and smiled. I returned the sentiment. She was so used to assisting me, but I couldn't help the premature tug of loss knowing I wouldn't need her as much once the cast was gone. With my bad arm, I waved in greeting and grabbed the door to give myself enough room to slide in. The interior smelled of her shampoo. Cherry blossom and jasmine filled my nose. It had been so long since we had hung out without me being a crutch, literally, and we were both excited.

"Let me see that." She inspected the cast and her smudged artwork. "Sorry about leaving you in the rain. I can fix it if you want."

I wasn't going to press, since I knew why, so I ignored her apology. "Nah, I'm supposed to get this removed before my birthday. It itches more since it got soaked and there's a slightly unpleasant odor too. But I'll deal. It's only for a couple more weeks. June sixth will be here before you know it." I rested the cast on my lap and readjusted the silver tote. Looking down, I noticed the rose pendant had caught on my shirt. I untangled it and dropped the chain.

My friend eyed me seriously. "So?"

I looked up. "So, what?"

"Any trouble with your parents?" She pulled out her peach glitter lip gloss and used the rearview mirror to inspect her application as she swiped over her cupid's bow.

In my best flippant tone, I replied, "Well, we had a small

fight." Nonchalantly, I fiddled with the garnet rose.

A car backfired. The pressure from it slammed me back into the seat as I recalled the sliding glass door shattering. Both eye sockets began to throb, and my fingers spasmed, dropping the silver tote to the floorboard.

"What's wrong?" The applicator and bottle of gloss slipped from Blake's hands so she could grab my shoulders. "Hey, are you going to be all right? Is tonight too soon, physically, I mean?"

I used four fingertips to press against each eye, easing the pain so I could answer. "I'm a little overwhelmed, but no, I don't want to cancel. We haven't had a night out… for over two months."

Blake laced her fingers through my right hand, pulling it away from my face as the muscles in my throat tried to strangle me. Patting my left shoulder, she waited for me to calm down. I lowered my bad arm, blinked against the pain, and then focused on her beaming smile.

I tried to sound upbeat. "Hey, I'm fine. Come on, let's kick it. Where to first? Are we picking up a Ghost, swinging by Dee's, or stocking up on junk food?"

"Ghost messaged, he's ready. Dee had to fix her make-up but wants to pick out her snacks. It's binge time again, I think." Blakely readjusted the rearview mirror and picked up the glitter gloss, capping it while arching a skeptical eyebrow at me.

I reached for the seatbelt with a *humph*.

Dee binging meant only one thing, everything in her world was colored red, and whoever was holding the target needed to take cover. Considering what had happened between us—I peered down at my chest—no bullseye, but it didn't mean there wasn't one on my back. *Maybe I should have canceled movie night.*

The Lady purred as we pulled into the mini-mart off Smoke Ranch by the drive-in. I was glad we had arrived because after collecting Jake my heart did erratic dance steps in my chest. The mixture of his aftershave, Blakely's shampoo, and Dee's perfume sent a quiver of uncertainty throughout my nerves.

Blake cut the engine as I rolled the window down to clear my head. I wasn't sure where these odd feelings were coming from, but in all the years we'd known each other, I'd never thought of Jake beyond the level of a friend. Tonight, I found myself studying his full lips whenever he spoke. *What is wrong with me?*

Ghost blocked Dee's view as he wedged in between the front seats to tell us a riddle his English teacher, Mr. Grottal, told during class. "What word begins with *T*, ends with *T*, and has *T* in it?"

Blakely turned around, laughing at his question. Dee's wispy curls shook while she bobbed her head, her mouth held in a tight grimace. Casually, I shrugged and clicked off the radio while unbuckling my seatbelt.

"A teapot." Jake snorted, which caught me off guard.

Blakely giggled.

Dee huffed and leaned down to pick up her lime-green straw tote. "Really? A teapot. Ghosty, how old does your teacher think everyone in your class is? I heard that joke from the twins… last year."

Yeah, Dee was in a mood.

A snicker tickled the back of my throat, but I didn't dare open my mouth to let it out because a cluster of wings threatened to expose the clan of butterflies that had taken residence in my chest. From the side mirror, I noticed a light blush bloom across my cheeks at the same time a slight itchy sensation started underneath the pendant's gold-roped polygon setting.

Blakely tucked her keys in the front pocket of her denim shorts. "Let's go. I don't want to end up at the back of the lot."

Dee, Blake, and I always made sure to bring deep purses

for snacks, and Jake's job was to keep us hydrated. It was a flawless system we had perfected over the years, except when Dee's temperament was on the fritz, which was what we were dealing with tonight.

I watched her snatch a Pringles canister off the shelf next to me and pop the lid. Stuffing chips into her mouth, she all but glared, with an unsaid *what*, at us. Actually, it was then I realized the three of us were gawking.

The silent *what* coming through timed crunching wasn't a question looking for an answer; it was Dee's speech for *stop staring*. We all closed our mouths and continued shopping.

Blakely brushed passed me to loop her arm around Dee's. "Dee, hon, you need to talk?"

Her eyes bore right into me, and I had no clue what to say. Well, I had an inkling of what it might be, but until we were alone, I wasn't going there. I didn't believe she remembered what I'd done to her. Heck, at this point I wasn't sure if it *had* happened or if it was only one of my nightmares. At least, she wasn't acting afraid… more like I had committed some kind of crime.

I broke her stare to rearrange the strap pulling on my COD shirt. Then I reached for another bag of salty goodness as my hand bumped into Jake's. Heat zoomed up my arm, along with the hint of itching. He cleared his throat. Bashfulness sucked the words from my tongue, and if I had used the muscle, it might turn to ash. It made me upset how our demeanor had changed so much in mere weeks and caused us to react so differently to each other.

Luckily, Jake's voice functioned. It cracked, "Sorry."

Sorry? Sorry for what? I tried to save myself from embarrassment. "Don't be silly, Ghost, and don't think because you laid claim to these, that I'm going to let you devour both bags." Flaming Funyuns were a movie must, next to chocolate-covered popcorn and a twelve pack of Diet Coke. I share, of course. *Sometimes.*

"Well, I like the hot flavor. Why don't we get both and share?"

I couldn't fight the urge as my cheeks pulled on my mouth. "That sounds great. Did you remember my Diet Coke, Sir Jake?"

He pointed toward the counter. "Yes, your Highness. Anything else, My Lady?"

I giggled. "Yes, some mini chocolate chips, if you please."

Gagging sounds came from behind us. "Oh, please. We don't have all night to watch the both of you ogle each other."

I spun around to face Dee. "What did you say?"

A vexed set of cat eyes triggered my internal alarm as she licked crumbs from the corners of her lips. "You heard me."

"You have something to say? Say it. I'm tired of your attitude. What the hell have I done to you?"

"Hey, you two, what's going on here?" Blake stepped in between us.

Ghost glanced at his watch. "We have twenty minutes. Let's go." He sidestepped around me but glared at Dee before heading down the aisle toward the counter area. Her eyes went wide from his silent reprimand. Once he passed, she shoved another handful of chips into her mouth. With his back to us, she whipped her head back in my direction and made a cutthroat gesture.

The necklace I wore seemed as though it tightened like a choker. Livid, my fists clutched until several nails dug into my palms. Blake's arm reached across to stop me from advancing. Dee's attitude toward me had tipped my aggravation, and I murmured, "Brrr-witch."

Ding-ding!

I heard an inner voice say, *"In this corner…"*

Dee dropped her can of chips, and pounced in less than a second.

I wasn't expecting her to lunge for me with Blakely so close, but it didn't seem to matter. Nails dug into my shoulder. I went rigid from the burning that instantaneously zinged down my arm. If I hadn't known any better, I would have sworn melting lava oozed from my eye sockets. My lips locked in a cry of pain as a chilled breeze swirled around us, causing Blakely to gasp. Her eyes fell to my neck, and then they focused in the direction of the store's refrigeration units. I could tell her mind was grasping for an explanation. The sensation had spooked her, too.

Dee landed on her butt. She had left nail tracks across my shoulder as though someone had ripped her hand away.

Did I shove her? I couldn't remember. The pain diminished, but both of my feet remained glued to the ground. Soon I realized her reaction had caught me off guard, and I never had a chance to retaliate. Coolness enveloped me. Both knees wanted to buckle, but my toes were barely touching the floor. At that moment, whatever had gripped me around my waist had begun to lower me back in place.

Blinking back the shock, Ghost's face returned to focus.

I could tell another question burned behind his eyes as he studied me, but instead asked, "You okay? You look like you're going to hurl."

I was. Dee's perplexing behavior had pissed me off like unwelcomed menstrual cramps. She wouldn't talk to me about what I'd supposedly done, but I didn't think all of her anger stemmed from what had taken place between us. She didn't even act as though she remembered what had transpired. As I recalled, Dee's overly dramatic actions had started long before I crashed into her apartment.

Tears made an obvious presence when I heard the extinguished hiss from the flames of my disowning. *What was wrong with me? With her? Was I killing the friendship between all of us?* Again, the questions haunted me, but even my nightly horrors wouldn't explain the dispute between such long-time friends.

Well, no more, I thought. *Enough of this crap.*

Jake insisted on helping me, and I could have sworn I heard the whisper of a growl. Glancing over my shoulder, searching our little crowd, I realized there was no one else in the store. Well, other than the cashier, who glowered at us over her issue of *Twisted*. Steadying myself, I swiped at Jake's offer. Three steps brought me close enough to extend a hand to Dee.

"Right, so you can shove me down again?" The back of her hand went to swat mine away.

I curled mine in time to feel the air swish by my fingers. "I didn't touch you, although, I should have."

"Really? Then how did I end up here?" With both index fingers, she pointed to the floor. Broken chips scattered all around her where she sat in the aisle.

Blakely stretched out a hand.

I could clearly tell Dee tried to gauge if the offer of help was worth swallowing her pride. Then I noticed a trail of water trickling down the side of her nose. Sucking on her lower lip, Dee accepted the help. Once on her feet, I was going to use the opportunity to air out our dirty laundry but, Blakely cut off my chance by taking a defensive stance in front of me.

"Dee," Blake started, then placed her hand on the side of Dee's arm as she spoke, "you must have slipped because I was standing in front of Lex-Cee, and she never touched you."

The four of us stood in an awkward silence. I hung my head and heaved a sigh. This night wasn't turning out as I'd hoped. I should have stayed home and watched TV Land with Gigi. The overwhelming desire to stuff myself with chocolate popcorn and caffeine immediately spurred me forward, and I gestured toward the counter to pay.

Carefully, I touched the shoulder where Dee's nails once were. The COD shirt had some small tears, and I felt the scrape underneath where it had rubbed against the cotton fabric. A slight stinging sensation provoked a sharp inhale as I winced. At least Dee hadn't broken the skin. The air in the store grew cold as chicken bumps rose to attention on my arms, and the air filled with a humming noise, almost like a tickle in my ears.

A breathless chuckle trickled down my neck, similar to when I had fled Krista's party before the accident. The memory froze me in place. This same sensation had also happened before Willow, my hospital roommate, had passed. *Was some strange force following me?*

Blakely and Ghost detected my anxiety and left Dee's side to address my problem. Their advancement toward me halted when they were about two steps away. They stared at one another, then back at me. I knew they sensed the presence too but couldn't quite come out and acknowledge it.

Dee shook her head and placed a hand on her temple, turning pale. "I feel ill, and I would never admit this openly, but I want to cry." She stood there removing bits of broken Pringles from her outfit.

My teeth slightly chattered. "So do I, Dee. So do I."

After we collected our bags, the cashier kindly asked us not to come back. I guess our little outburst was enough to make Hello My Name is Wendi nervous. I couldn't blame her, especially with the way the store had transformed into one with an Arctic dread.

We piled into the Lady, and Blake started to back out of the parking lot, making sidelong glances at me. The frigid temp seemed to have followed us into the vehicle, and the pressure of an explanation loomed like thirty-seven pairs of eyes staring at me during an oral test.

In the backseat, Ghost moved to straddle the middle console, pressing against Dee's left knee. It was as though he were trying to make room for another person. Dee didn't seem to mind, or maybe she couldn't-care-less attitude was all part of the plan.

My lips pulled into a tight smirk while trying to comprehend why he felt the need to be so close to her. He had enough room behind Blake's seat. The little hairs on my neck bristled from uncontrolled thoughts, which quite honestly shouldn't have mattered. I wasn't planning to change the dynamic of our friendship.

But, as my memories drifted, I licked my lips, remembering how many times Jake and I had come close to kissing. A small tear escaped and rolled down my cheek, but the feeling of a light brush from a fingertip glided along my cheek. The wet trail dried as if a whisper had softly blown on my face. Reacting to the familiar chill, I scanned the vehicle, half expecting to see a creature from one of my nightmares. But I only found Ghost, whispering in a harsh tone at Dee. Blake was staring straight ahead, trying to concentrate on the evening traffic. None of them seemed to notice my mood, which flooded me with relief. I didn't want any more negative attention on me tonight.

Jake tried to defuse the smoldering hostilities before everyone combusted from the gasoline-soaked emotions by attempting to spur a conversation. "I read the reviews on this movie. The special effects are incredible, but Adam Westley and Ester Karri had issues on the set and didn't seem to mesh well."

I stared at him.

"Well, that's what I read. I guess we'll find out if it's any good."

Dee blew bangs from her eyes. She tried to dry the stream of tears from her own cheeks in an apathetic way. I watched Ghost lean in, his lips close to her ear as his whisper made her sulk. He rubbed her shoulder, and she relaxed, but her eyes zeroed in on me. Using the classic eye roll to break free from her, I glanced down at my fingers as an excuse to fumble with the cast.

A reassuring pat touched my left shoulder. Thinking Jake had touched me, I turned to smile at him but found Blakely staring at me with a shocked expression. Another jolt of frozen air left me covered in hair-raising bumps. With a huff, I smacked the air vent closed and wrapped my arms around myself to stop the winter storm from stirring within me. Beyond my reflection in the window, the night sky beckoned. I locked onto the first faint star through the growing cloud cover.

Closing my eyes, I used this chance to send out an unrealistic wish. *Star light, star bright, this is my only wish tonight... that we do not kill each other before the stroke of midnight.*

Chapter Nineteen

Tevin's side: Through the eyes of a Reaper

*C*limbing the back of the movie screen, I sensed the moisture looming overhead. The soft evening breeze played with my shroud, making the thin indigo outline dance along my ashen skin. When I reached the top, anxiety fueled my pace as I scanned the parking lot.

A gagging mixture of baked asphalt, gasoline, and burnt popcorn heightened my perception, as I trailed each vehicle to its destination. This was definitely going to be an interesting evening with all of these souls here.

My stomach tightened with hunger. A point of light caught my eye, and I sarcastically wished for another added distraction. My cell buzzed. The cloak slid open so I could extract it from my back pocket. Moment's group text lit up my screen.

Moment: HOW LONG? I'M HUNGRY.

The text caused me to frown. I was hungry, too. *Why do I always find myself in this predicament?*

Watching the Vessels, I would never understand these creatures and their need to flex their rebelliousness. Young, old, male, female—it didn't matter. Being defiant seemed to be a symptom of their emotional disease. *If I could only stick Alexcia in a cage for the next thirteen moon risings, our problems would be solved.*

Confounded, I dropped my weight onto the lower catwalk, flipping the cell in the air. My cloak swayed, then tugged to the right slightly. I didn't reach for my weapon because it was simply responding to whatever was approaching.

"I'm not going to replace that one if you drop it."

Quint's cloak reached out to greet mine. Swirling, thin ribbons of yellow and indigo broke up the outlines of our minions. Their inquisitiveness was unavoidable as they communicated to each other while we assessed the Vessels on the ground.

The muscle in his jaw jumped. "How many do you think the child has put at risk?"

The majority was not my concern. At this point, only Alexcia's safety mattered. We could put most of the humans to sleep before any situation started to escalate. Plus, I had my ace. The clan did not see her as an asset, but she was my Plan B, unless circumstances forced me to fold before I could use her abilities. I had found out a long time ago that Time Elementals could time-shift small areas from one realm to the next, so we could take our battle into the Unseen if need be. Most of these Vessels would not be affected.

To put Quint's apprehensions to rest, I shook my head. "I'm only concerned for the ones she will be near. We may not be able to save them all, which means our kind may show up to harvest. Even though Cain's clan works during the day from the east, they may show if the numbers rise. You called Ruthain, right? Is his clan from the west picking up our slack?"

Quint watched the movie screen from across the theater and mumbled, "Mmm-uh."

To keep my mind off Alexcia, I kept going over the possibilities of who might show up. "Xythal's clan from the south could be trouble. He's been suspicious of our actions for a while now. I did not approach the Cauldron this evening. The other Ashens will have to tend to our soul-reapings. Their payment is the extra power they can snack on." The grumbling coming from my stomach was distracting, and I pulled my cloak closed to muffle the noise. "My only concern is protecting Alexcia and fulfilling Max's contract." I snapped and internally asked my minion for a cigarette. It placed one between my lips. Using the tip of my finger, I lit it, then exhaled. "Really, I want this to be finished." I took another drag in pause.

Quint spoke but never looked at me. "So, you don't know if her name is floating in the Cauldron? The River will not be pleased with this blatant act of disobedience. Our clan may lose favor. I hope, for your existence, these contracts were worth it."

His cell belted out "Damage" by Red. Quint glanced at the caller in question and then sent it to voicemail with a shrug.

Ignoring where our conversation was obviously heading, I started strategically mulling over several rescue and escape plans. The main objective was for us to hold ground, whether our fight took place in this realm or the Unseen. Retreating was not an option at this point. Running away only allowed us to get into situations that could trip us up. I had seen it firsthand; the action of uncertainty knew me by my first name.

Quint unsheathed his polearm and sat beside me. His build was a bit broader than he thought. Shoving against my shoulder to make room, he snapped, and his minion obeyed. The hood dissipated, revealing two intense gold orbs. Releasing a pent-up exhale, the Ashen asked, "You want this finished? I may be part of the Unseen, but I'm not blind. Ever since you decided to play guard dog, you've gradually changed."

"Your minion's been allowing the star's ultra-violet rays to fry your brain. Changing how? I've managed to uphold my Ashen duties as well as maintaining the River's and clan's needs, and the Bond-Rite with the child's mother hasn't been broken. I believe I've handled it pretty damn well." Feeling cornered, I motioned down the street in the general direction where Alexcia would be arriving. "That creature is alive, right? Contracts are almost fulfilled. End of story."

I placed the cigarette in between my lips and scanned the crowd. It felt like watching a colony of ants as they wandered to and from the concession stand for their sugar fixes. Vessels laughed, conversed, and little ones cried. The blending of sounds added to my headache. I did not need a lecture about Alexcia's supervision. I pulled the smoke into my chest, filling the void.

Quint let out a gut rolling peal of laughter. "Contracts? You really think I'm here because of the Bond-Rites? Man, Tevin, you feel for the Vessel. I see it in your eyes every time some entity even brings up the child's name. Look, I think what you did with Max was straight-up insane, but I know why you did it, and that makes all of this, and what we're doing, okay in my book."

Sarcastically, I mirrored his laugh. "You have no idea why I'm doing this."

The reaper next to me placed his hand on my shoulder, casting a look of abashment. "Then explain to me why we should care if they kill her, if she chooses a House, or if she is only a mere Vessel to be harvested?"

"Damn the cloak I cast, we've been through this before. The Child-of-Balance's parental guardians are from our world. There is no doubt the Unseen's Houses believe she's the one, but "why her" is the question that's tearing my reason apart. You, out of all of us, have not been ensnared by her eyes. She has a force within her. It's beyond the comprehension of what powerful means to us. The child makes me feel as though there's more to her complexity." I swallowed with a smoke-dried throat. "Alexcia turns my curiosities into festering thorns, almost as if her humanity is internally poisoning me."

Quint's eyebrows pinched. "You're tells are showing." Fingers moved to the bridge of his nose, and he huffed. "Contractions."

I turned away and massaged above my eyebrows. "It is a disease, and I am severely infected."

"Does Michael know about your… um… condition?"

"To some degree."

"Man, talk about putting a severe damper on my evening."

Quint's cell went off at the same time mine vibrated, interrupting our conversation. I raised my fingers for one last drag only to realize the filter had burned to ash. Cursing, I flicked what was left into the air and pulled out my electronic nemeses.

Archer had texted another update; he and Michael were following a potential threat. Then another text from Raven flashed across the screen. His stated there was movement on the casino roof across the street.

The moisture in the air was marginally palatable, but it was too soon to tell if elementals were creating it. I gauged the information and figured it was better to be prepared than to underestimate our enemy.

Addressing Quint vocally while texting verbatim to the others and Moment, I said, "Eyes and ears open. I want minimal ground fighting. If we can't keep it in the sky, I want Moment to move the fight into the Unseen."

Moment: I CAN ONLY TIME-SHIFT OVER SO MUCH MAYBE HALF OF THE DRIVE-IN.

The Smolder extended the canines in my mouth. Moment was being flippant with me. And Quint needed to show her how to text without caps before I shoved the phone down her throat.

We had all witnessed her temper tantrum. *Ashens do not forgive or forget.* We all knew her power display had only been a portion of what she could do. My smile grew wicked as the daemon within me fed off the knowledge. If I pressed the right buttons, she would cave into her pride and encase the whole drive-in.

Fingers flying over the keypad, I spoke aloud as I typed, "I want the whole thing ported if fighting goes to ground. I wish you would stop showing your claws. Remember mine are bigger. Comply."

Moment: Well I guess what you want and what you get will be up to me. Also, I'm not a genie. Stop rubbing me the wrong way for wishes I cannot grant. I am not your servant, DAEMON.

Her last entry had me seething. My thumb pressed Delete, and I heard the glass screen crack from the pressure. Without observing, I knew the display screen would have a new spider webbing effect.

The yellow Ashen blew out a low breath. "Stop taking your anger out on the messenger. That's like the townsfolk of Boston shooting Paul Revere for delivering the warning. I'm going to start buying you GoPhones by the case if I can get them from Amazon."

The muscles in my jaw clenched, forcing only a single grunt in response. I slipped the technology into the folds of my cloak. Forcefully, I tried to shake off my hostility, but as if on cue, one problem replaced another.

Quint's cell phone chimed, again. The glow from the blue screen made his yellow eyes take on a faint green guise, giving his aura a sense of malevolence. I could not help the corner of my lip from twitching. The Smolder within me growled in agreement as well, because after all, evil begets evil. I wondered if his fascination with technology fed his Smolder's curiosity.

Scanning the screen, a rumble vibrated from his chest. Quint's daemon did not like what he had read, which made mine perk up in frustrated interest. The Ashen intently scanned the screen as he typed back to whoever had sent the message. After hitting Send, he slid his thumb across the screen.

I leaned toward him, trying to interpret what the dark yellow threading through his cloak meant. "Quint?" I arched an eyebrow.

He abruptly stated, "Some trouble," then stood.
"The sender?"
Reluctantly, Quint said, "Archer."

My back went rigid and the tentacles around my feet suspended. Michael and Archer were on child-guard duty, and I knew if Archer was reporting to Quint and not directly to me, it was not good news.

"And?" I strained my sight to zoom in on the vehicles entering from the main street, checking each one.

Alexcia's presence was barely registering. I focused on her heartbeat. It was faint, but I figured it was because of distance. The cloak's movements became jerky, sensing I was only a touch irate with the news. The Vessel was above ground, so whatever the problem was must have been resolved with some boon.

Quint gave me space as his minion moved farther from mine.

I huffed. "Report."

"It seems we have an internal problem. Archer believes one of the child's friends is infected with a seed."

Suspicious, I asked, "Possessed?"

"It seems so." His face became grim.

Never did it cross my mind the House of Space would attempt such drastic measures. "You mean to tell me an Unseen assassin used a Cathexis? Did he say how strong it is?"

A Cathexis was what Pandora opened out of daemonic curiosity... and look where it got her.

An idea slithered in my brain; it caused a searing, uncomfortable sensation. The pressure pushed out. "Is it the male Vessel?" My scythe pulsated, causing both hands to itch. The desire to dispatch him flickered and then died when I thought how Alexcia would respond to his passing. *Scythe me!*

Quint's expression said, *Dude, you have lost it.* Head swaying, he continued to explain, "Archer pulled one of the female Vessels away in time before it could fully pass on the infection to the child. Archer said Michael is shadowing her until the others get here."

The Smolder pushed against my ribs, and an uncontrollable urge to snap Michael in half weighed my hands down. Once again, he was in the spot where I should have been, right next to her. Teeth on the verge of cracking, I tried to make my jaw work. "If he were properly doing his job, there would not have been a grave-filling problem in the first place." My voice rose along with my phone's testy pulses. It seemed as angered as I was.

The cloak quickly moved so I could pull my phone back out. The cracked screen reminded me of a quote from Sir Walter Scott, *"Oh! What a tangled web we weave, when first we practice to deceive"."* (Scott 1808) The corners of my mouth pulled down, for I knew the meaning. I was the spider, trapped within my own web of lies while trying to convince everyone—including myself—the child was nothing more than a caterpillar. But, the cocoon had cracked long ago, and Creation's butterfly emerged to look Death in the eye.

Moment: YOUR DATE HAS ARRIVED. LOL!!!

The bounty hunter's implication irked me while scanning through several lines of Vessels' transportation. My Smolder anxiously stirred once I caught Alexcia's scent. Its irritation sent a small quake down my arms and legs. Her aroma tasted diluted as the evening breeze pulled it apart. In an instant, I became obsessed to pinpoint her location. I could not believe how distracting the desire could be, or how quickly it could fog up basic logic.

When the silver rectangle buzzed in my hand again, I forced cold digits to curl tighter around it, subconsciously trying to choke it into silence. The light *zzz* sound seemed to become more urgent with each pulse. Quint's cell reacted the same way. We both mirrored a scowl.

"Soldiers," by Otherwise, thrummed between bent fingers. Archer had grown a pair, if he was calling me, and was prepared to face the toe of my scythe from the ill-fated news.

Shoulders tensed, I lifted the phone to my ear. "Ashen, has the situation been rectified?"

A vibrant growl came through the earpiece with such force I peered over my shoulder, expecting to see him behind me. "Michael is with the Vessel. He slipped into the back of the car and drove off with them. I insisted we should only follow, as per your instructions, but he insisted on staying close."

My Smolder and I responded with shared disappointment. Michael knew about the problems I faced, but it did not excuse his decision to take matters into his own hands. I had my reasons for handling the situation. He should be setting an example, not provoking me to bash his face in.

"Tevin, the small female with them is infected. We may have a bigger problem on our hands. Michael didn't want me to express my thoughts, but I believe our House has upped the ante on the child."

"Go ahead. Make it fast." Alexcia's life rhythm reached out to me from less than a mile away. We needed our chess pieces precisely placed. Waiting for Archer to mentally sift through his explanation, I mouthed to Quint to get Imp and rendezvous back here for new instructions.

"I think they have hired a Leer daemon. It's either Jeza, Sacora, or Aosiskcy. The air around the Vessel tastes more like Jeza's work. I'm confident it's either Jeza or Sacora, but I would rather walk through Styx than face off with a Daemon Summoner, especially one as high in the ranks as Aosiskey."

Rigor mortis set in, and my cloak solidified in response. If my minion and I were knocked off the catwalk, we probably would have shattered upon impact. I licked the corners of my mouth to loosen them. "How long do you think the female has been possessed?"

We could base the level of strength from his guesstimate. The potency he felt from it would determine how to handle Alexcia's contaminated friend, but the longer she had been tainted, the more time the seed would have had to germinate and take root in the Vessel's soul permanently. That meant the difference between *save* or *sever*, and for Alexcia's emotional welfare, we would start with the former scenario, and lay to rest the latter.

Alexcia would end up blaming herself if anything happened to her friend, especially if she found out it was because of a choice she was required to make. This woeful info caused my eye to twitch uncontrollably. Judging Archer's silence, I figured we might be too late.

The cell case popped in my hand. "Damn it."

"Yeah, well, let's hope I'm right and Jeza planted it. I haven't heard or seen Sacora in about three hundred years, and Aosiskey is spoken of among our kind more as a daemonic myth than an existing Leer. She's never summoned me, nor do I know any other Ashen who has."

Riled about Archer's avowal, my past was clashing with the present. If only Archer knew how wrong he was. But for the clan to understand what we might be dealing with, I had to explain.

Through clenched teeth, I snarled before admitting, "Yes, you do."

His voice held doubt. "What?"

"Aosiskey."

Awe crested in Archer's voice. "You were summoned?"

"Yes." I spat

"When?"

With the conviction of a sinner to a priest, I confessed, "The night I was supposed to claim Alexcia's soul, the River had given me two names to collect. After the Bridge Crosser showed up, I had completely forgotten about misplacing the parchment."

"So, what does that have to do with the Leer?"

"I believe the second soul was supposed to be Max."

The line went dead.

Yeah, this night keeps getting better and better.

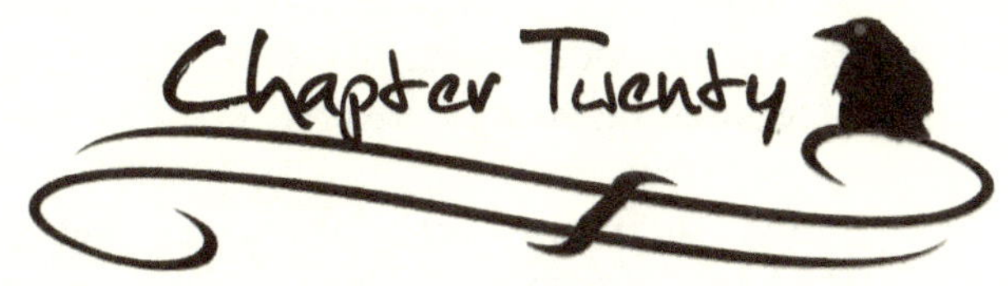

Chapter Twenty

Tevin's side: Through the eyes of a Reaper

*Q*uint and Imp ported through the same Time Bend, their cloaks trying to reach out to mine. Our encounter was not a social visit, so I tugged on my minion to behave. It wrapped around me in a disapproving squeeze. Ignoring it, I briefed the reapers about our new predicament with the possibility of fighting a Leer. Needless to say, they were not thrilled. My fingers typed verbatim through my explanation to inform the others. This new circumstance burdened the cell with texted questions I was running out of time to answer.

After tonight, if we achieved our tasks and managed not to get recopied, I might have to find refuge in Infinity's Garret. The clan might bind me long enough for Michael to place my neck on the executioner's block. If a daemon could pray their way out of a problem, I would. Since beckoning for our House's help made me itch, and there was no such thing as luck, I did not have a choice but to own up to past decisions.

The air lost the warmth of day as the sun dipped below the storm-clouded horizon. As I watched, Alexcia and the male Vessel popped open the hatch in front of the red vehicle. They worked together, pulling out bags, blankets, and chairs, talking amongst themselves. I caught sight of the infected female. So far, the girl seemed vexed, remaining in

the car, staring. With Alexcia so close to danger, it provoked
an old daemonic need. Claiming burned throughout my
veins. All daemons, in a sense, shared this similar emotion
called greed. Greed endangered my control, which could
expose the dilemma regarding Alexcia.

*The night Aosiskey had summoned me, I was
approaching the Cauldron of Ending. It irritated me, how
she slipped through our ward and materialized in front of
the Cauldron of Ending. The Daemon Summoner's pacing
between me and the Cauldron made her seem distressed. Her
death summons I had regarded as a request, not a binding
contract. The Leer desired a soul and had offered me a trade,
not a deal, and she had come for an answer. At the time, I
was seriously considering. She was offering me a Separation
curse. I would be an Ashen without ties. To no longer be
chained to occupy the same space with another was
tempting.*
*Our discussion was interrupted. I had sensed Michael
coming into the hall, and the Leer, clearly not wanting to be
discovered, had left before disclosing the name. It could
have been any of the damned on my list that night. In an
awkwardly grating way, I had assumed it might be the child.
But, since she failed to disclose the name and never called
upon my services again, I figured it was a dead issue.*

Skin stretched over bone as I frowned. To claim the
child would put not only me, but the whole clan, on the
Unseen's hit list. Again, the unfamiliar impulses provoked
my possessor, causing it to rage from a mutual craving to be
near her. Observing Alexcia from afar no longer sated our
curiosity.
A fierce roar cut through the atmosphere and ripped me
from my troubled qualms. Shaking to clear the unwanted
emotions, I gradually inclined my head toward the source.
Disappointment added to my ire as I observed Moment
hovering in the air with her hand outstretched. Imp was
floating about thirty feet away from her, rubbing his jaw. His

aura flickered like a broken marquee sign, indicating he was livid. Imp retrieved his broadsword, swinging it as if he were carving her up. Smugly, the female elemental straightened the mesh on her blouse, already dismissing him.

I swear those two were going to get us all recopied.

Alexcia's note-filled voice floated on the evening breeze. Removing the temptation of watching her laugh with the male standing next to her, I surveyed the murky skies instead. The twitching above my right eye had throbbed back to life. I smacked the spot, to regain control. Internally, I reprimanded myself because if I did not rid myself of these emotions, Alexcia's mere *élan vital*, her life force, would cause me to go insane.

In the distance, a roll of thunder interrupted my inner reprimand, warning me to pay attention. The crisp bite of twilight made my cloak still as I straightened. Magic fed off of the surroundings. An Unseen presence stirred in the elements. Even my weapon responded with a bloom of warmth diagonally across my back.

Checking on the child, I watched Alexcia grab the male's hand and pull him along. The breeze caught her hair, reminding me of the wildfire grass that grew in the Unseen. Endless meadows where the plants thrived by literally combusting to regrow. Lakes of golden-red, the stocks producing a fire-bloom, burning until the plant cycled to ash. The two of them wove between Vessels toward the concession stand. The tightness in between my ribs trapped the response; I wanted to call out to her.

K's shouts instantly put me into a fighting stance. Weapon drawn, I gathered my scattered thoughts to focus. A dark figure was approaching the green tinted Ashen.

The breeze had weight to it as the Unseen's words grew thick confirming my hunch, boldly stating, "I am merrily requesting an audience with the Child-of-Balance."

Our first party crasher had arrived, a Wind Evoker.

K responded, "Well, incidentally, the Vessel is on a date, so the answer is… no."

I wanted to scythe K.

The distinguished dressed elemental said, "Pity on you, Ashen. I was hoping we could come to an agreement without the cloak-and-dagger, but since you are without valid reason, blood it shall be."

Then I heard Moment shout, "Abyss!"

A vexing retort came from the entity. "Traitor."

"No, stop. Wait. Hear me out. I can explain." Moment's face displayed regret while she held up her hands in a non-conjuring gesture. Obviously, she knew him.

"Tell it to the River," he responded with a malevolent grin.

Her eyes widened in hurt from his distrust.

He hit her with a ball of condensed air, knocking her into the corner of the movie screen. The debris sprayed beyond the wall and landed in the desert. Then the wind elemental turned to K.

I groaned. *Here we go.*

Walking across the drive-in about sixty feet in the air, I closed our distance, stopping about five hilt-lengths away from the entity. Gripping tighter on the silver-thorned snath, the weapon was engaged and ready to fight. Seeing this for how it could end, I held on to my pessimism and embraced the negative attitude that had kept me around for the last six hundred years.

I held an outstretched hand in an armistice manner, waiting for his reaction. "May I formally address you by your name?"

"No." The color in his eyes marbled from untapped power. "Stop right there, or others from my House will rush to strike."

"If I wanted you and your companions dead, you would already be swimming."

"I heard you were arrogant," he clipped.

"You wish to talk with the Child-of-Balance? Then state your reason, and I will see if it warrants an audience with Alexcia."

The trespassing Unseen arched an eyebrow.

K appeared disgusted.

When the female elemental rejoined us, sauntering in a rushed step as though the air was as solid as the ground. I could taste the peeved Evoker's temperament in the breeze. Yeah, our little Wind Evoker's demeanor screamed, *I broke a nail, and you're going to pay.* She then whipped her head from side to side, fanning strands of white and black while dusting off her outfit.

Moment spun toward me, throwing her hands in the air. "Oh, great, this is a Yigal blouse."

She fingered a small rip on the side. Without batting an eye, Moment slung the unwelcome entity against a wall of air. Suspended by nothing but her will, with eyes bulging, he grasped at his neck. The wind entity reminded me of a fish out of water.

Pretending Abyss didn't exist; Moment sashayed over to me. My minion latched onto her wrist, but the momentum of her hand passed through. She jabbed a manicured nail into my chest. "Take heed of how you address the brat. Some of the Unseen may not catch on, but others will."

"I'm not sure what you mean. Now, dispose of the Wind Evoker before I send him to meet his maker."

Our she-devil cracked her lips wider, and her straight teeth picked up the color from my aura. Angling her head closer so the words could slide across home plate, she said, "You like the brat."

I tried to back away. "Careful." I looped the toe of the blade through her chain.

She purred. Delight danced in both ice-blue irises enhancing her pupil hourglasses. "Watch how you address the Child-of-Balance. Not only will others from our world kill her, but they might attempt to use the Vessel to persuade Death's hand to toil for them." The House of Time elemental practically vibrated from exposing the skeleton in my coffin.

K's green aura reflected off Moment's eyes as he approached us. Settling next to me, he quickly cleared his throat. "I hate to interrupt, but do you mean to recopy him?"

The Wind Evoker inched her hand away from my chest, removed the chain from the blade, clutched the Tears of

Time, and skipped soundlessly toward the hanging elemental. Abyss appeared almost unconscious, with the whites of his eyes leaking water. Dropping the pendant, she climbed next to the male and pressed her curves into him while lifting her left leg to drape it across his. Her pink lips brushed his ear as she murmured, "I should leave you to the Soul Cage's, you pathetic swamp rat." Moment lifted her arm and raised the sleeve while whispering, "Quicksilver." The pain of loss glistened in her eyes, but she covered the display of weakness by barking at me. "When this is over, I want her released."

I was not sure if I wanted to divulge to her that the creature was sleeping, not imprisoned. Pointing at her captive instead, I responded with a shrug. "If you play by the rules, you can have your pet back. But for now, you'll have to rely on your skills." I gave her a second for my words to sink in.

Jaw tight, Moment rolled down the material and nodded before snuggling closer to the Wind Evoker. She whispered and toyed with his black curls while he turned a shade bluer. Chimed laughter swirled in the breeze.

Her bizarre demeanor made an uncomfortable knot form in my throat. Slightly coughing to remove the obstruction, K's attention reverted to me.

Green eyes scanned the sky. "The elemental said there were more of them. Why haven't they come to his aid?"

Moment twirled the tips of her fingers through the elemental's goatee and answered, "He's the scout. The collection is not far off. Abyss is the head of the Water Raisers in this sector. It appears he might have moved up in the ranks."

Her lips moved around silent words, ones that only he could hear. The male sucked in a gulp of air as she released him from her spin. "Bestowing a favor is called mercy, for we were friends once. I gave you your breath of life back, and the bridge we once crossed together burns. From this point, I owe you nothing. Remember this when the others come."

K swung his weapon out to her. "He hit you with spindled air. He's not an Evoker?"

Finding K's question humorous, she said, "No more than I'm a reaper."

K growled.

"Keep your hood on. I meant it as an example." Clearly not caring, she pointed at the gasping figure. "Abyss deals in the wet stuff. What he hit me with could be passed off as hot air. He must be picking up bounties outside our House and trading spins for payment."

"How do you know?" I slid closer to the vertical wall of air.

Choking on a snort, Moment answered, "What do you think I am? I may have started my existence as a Wind Evoker, but I'm a bounty hunter with a direct purpose. I want two things; influence, and to sit in the House of Light's court. To do so, I need to prove my talents are not only a desired necessity but indispensable for the House of Light to maintain the River's essentials.

"Most of the time the fees I require are common Spindled knowledge, but if the contract is for live game"— her fingers scratched air quotes around the word *live*—"I will add a special clause to the contract. So, one, I can hunt them by my terms, and two, I am free to use a Life Tie spin to ensure the undertaking is forthright. In short, alive, dead, or in pieces is my choice with an increase in payment."

K traveled to the other side of the air wall. "A Life Tie spin? What's that?"

"You agree to allow me access to your mind. Then I remove whatever information I want. Like, say, a rare spindled spell, the ability to wield a unique weapon, or your award-winning Crableberry Pie." She arched an eyebrow. "Then I absorb the lesson."

"I'll be a damned daemon. Tevin, she's perfected the talents of a leach."

She climbed over Abyss before landing in front of K. Using the same finger-poking technique; her hand plunged through his cloak. "Listen, grave filler, if I didn't tolerate what your leader and clan were doing for Styx, I would have invited you all over for barbecued soul by now."

Lightning flashed over the western horizon as the three of us turned and waited for the thunderclap. Nothing happened. Normal sounds from the drive-in echoed below us—Vessels chatting, radios broadcasting different sound effects, each one oblivious to what awaited in the darkness above.

A shadow, black and misty flew passed us. Briefly, I locked on a pair of silted crimson eyes before the Ashen landed on a point in the desert. Roars matching the thunder made us all turn toward the irate daemon. Raven's minion eddied around him. The color of his aura threaded and looped as charred crimson wings stabbed into the air. A wail of taunting came from below us, and I took a second to glance at K's blank green expression.

He shrugged. "You didn't tell us we specifically couldn't change."

"It's a known rule."

K heaved his mace and left to find what had smacked Raven across the drive-in. Motioning with the scythe at Abyss, I addressed Moment. "Release or recycle him. We have others to deal with."

More yells and threats polluted the air from two screens away. I could make out the thin threads of aura outlining Archer and Quint's cloaks. They had teamed up against four Water Raisers. A shriek from behind me was followed by a female's demand, "Or else."

I spouted a command to my new puppet. "Moment, tend to Raven before he steps into the parking lot. I'm going to check on the others."

She nodded without a word, which should have been my first clue the Wind Evoker had plans of her own. Instead, I took her silence for granted and began to assess our situation. Abyss's collection had finally arrived and branched off to cover more of the area. Inky shadows darted from the roof of the casino to the flashing billboard. The others hovered restlessly over the small airport next to the drive-in.

With a side glance, I evaluated everyone's position. Imp and K were battling two Wind Evokers. Quint and Archer were one screen away and about to cut their fight in half. Michael, I assumed, was shadowing Alexcia because none of us had heard from him. Last, I scanned the ground where Raven and Moment… *were not where I had left them.*

*M*ass hysteria had ignited raw chaos within the Vessels as they witnessed the unexplainable destruction. From where I stood, hovering in the air, there were the deep rumblings of a pissed-off Smolder. Raven's wrath mixed with the Vessels' chaotic shrieking, cries from the wounded, and empty promises from the dying. A fire erupted in the concession stand. I thought to myself, *So much for containment*.

At least the storm was trying to cooperate by using what little water the clouds could muster to put the blaze out. A silver minivan flew past, barely missing me. It careened, flipping end over end before crashing into the building below. Its path ended with a metal-smashing exclamation point.

Some Vessels jumped into their vehicles; many scrambled like roaches. Fright paralyzed others, and then there was Alexcia. I heard her voice rise above the chaos. Wide-eyed, I searched for Michael. *Why was he not watching her?* The child was a siren, luring all the Unseen with her spindled speech.

Surprise, in the form of a lightning strike, hit me when I recognized the spin. Her demeanor and appearance had altered. She turned in my direction, eyes ablaze with rainbow-like flames, and her gaze locked onto mine. The knot of heat that formed in my gut battled for room in my chest. Alexcia jutted her arms into the air in a display of demand for her spell to be heard… and hear they did.

A dense flock of Callcrys descended from the storm answering her summons. The bird-like creatures, or properly known in the Unseen as Soul Cages, were soul scavengers and exhibited no mercy. These entities were the River's filtration system. Callcrys fed on the foul and damaged, and if one were found guilty of abusing Creation's gift, it made the remnants of the soul unfit to be recycled. A contaminated soul would pollute Styx, whether a soul's remains were from human or entity, we could do nothing but watch the carnage.

I recalled her dream. Mesmerized, I was transported back to watching the child skate circles around me before she had felt threatened and called forth her talents for defense.

The sting of insight changed my focus. The Child-of-Balance could control the Callcrys. I wasn't sure why, but this new perception made her even more interesting to me. A searing emotion, harsher than want, burned inside my mouth, and my Smolder clawed against bone.

Her long locks had turned flame red, and steam rose from her stance. Entranced, I lost my focus. Attention diverted, an invisible vice seized both legs, dragging me through the air on my side before it slammed me into the ground. A kaleidoscope of fragmented colors smacked into the back of my skull. Hollow, metallic sounds echoed as my scythe skidded across broken pavement.

Enraged, the Smolder demanded to be set free. Breathing hard, I reached for my weapon from under a canary-yellow Mustang. Upon placing my fingers on the thorny, silver-vines, I dragged the ebony hilt toward me while the shroud quivered in frustrated arcs to heal me, using its anger to escalate the level of pain. Its ability to increase my agony was its way of taking a stab at my failure. But its actions helped me regain control.

I scanned the skies to locate whatever had struck me.

Smells of burnt terror, grease-soaked confusion, sticky

frustration, and melted pure terror made my mouth water. Up above me, the Unseen fought to gain access to the Child-of-Balance. Bodies of the weak and trampled screamed for mercy and pushed the ache to harvest. I heard from above the battle cries of different entities, and my senses spiraled out of control. The Ashen side of me needed to feed. I could taste the residue of a hundred souls. Saliva carried the scorching want with each swallow. Throaty, garbled bird cries and Alexcia's voice yanked me from my frenzy.

Dry heaving from hunger, I snapped and silently ordered the cloak to shield me. A heavy hand clamped down and whirled me around to face my clan. To my dismay, I found fierce blue eyes. Michael held his battle axe in one hand and used the other to steady my world. A wave of disappointment and nausea crashed into me as I tried to remain upright.

Practically ripping me a new one, he shouted, "Defend, you say. Guard her, you demand. Then I find you laid out as a two-day-old daemon." He shoved me, and I staggered to find my footing.

"Did you see what hit me?" I wheezed.

"Really? With everything going on around us, you want to know what bested you?" Infuriated, blue threads of aura mixed with the black shroud to form a hood slightly shadowing his features and adding strength to the seething stare from under the cowl.

A grave shrill vibrated the parking lot. My eyes wandered over the chaos and found about two dozen Callcrys cocooning Alexcia. She was standing on the roof of the truck. Unable to hide my astonishment, I scrutinized her control of the winged Soul Cages. Michael had also picked up on my thoughts.

"I'm not sure how she is doing this, but we can't take the opportunity for granted. They will dim her scent, but only as long as she can maintain the control."

"Damn me to Space and back." With the back of my hand, I swiped at the blood pouring from a busted lip. Drawing in a steady breath, I added, "I have a theory, but first, the humans need to be taken care of before…”

My words faded from the agitated atmosphere around us. The clouds unzipped and dumped their contents on the drive-in. I did not mind it until entities started falling from the sky like an Unseen downpour. Different creatures from the Unseen descended upon the drive-in.

The noise amplified in the epicenter as bodies crushed cars dinged trucks and shattered windows, accompanied by the screams of Vessels as unseen forces landed upon them. Vehicles smashed into each other. Still more flipped into the air or were merely shoved aside from the few who ruthlessly searched for the Child-of-Balance.

Catching Michael's attention, I said, “The Vessels need to sleep. Go tell the others, and then find that Time Witch and tell her to port the fight into the Unseen as soon as the last Vessel succumbs to slumber.”

“What about the child?” Michael's question was grim.

“The Soul Cages are playing their part. She is in a protected area of her own making.”

He stood there, unmoving.

I exclaimed, “Go, now!”

Despite the Vessels' rising volume, the revved engines, and Raven's throaty protests in the distance, the daemon that possessed me could pinpoint the outcry of an enemy. This sent the inner monster into a slamming rage. The Head of the Southern Ashen clan walked over the hardtop of a burgundy Fiat. He swung a bone-carved scythe into the back window, using it as an anchor to help lower himself to the ground.

The minion's hood receded, revealing Xythal's lit indigo eyes, holding an expression of fascination from our meeting. Rain soaked his blond quills. The cloak shrank back to form a cape. His stature could pass as my own, but I carried more muscle behind my swing.

Panicked Vessels tried to escape as the pinpricks of a thousand needles grazed my skin. My cloak trembled from the clan's pull to oppress the masses and a snarl adjacent from where I stood concerned me. Raven was running rampant, and I could not address the daemon without causing damage. We needed to port before our Smolders were unleashed here, so I maintained eye contact with Xythal as the Vessels around us stumbled and dropped like discarded corpses.

He stepped over, dodging and kicking several unconscious bodies. "Clever," he said, swinging the bone blade close to a child's ear, catching her stuffed, lime-green giraffe and ripping it down the middle.

In our language, I formally greeted him, "Southern Ashen Xythal."

At the moment, I was not too concerned about Alexcia; obviously, his clan's attempts to locate the Child-of-Balance had failed. The camouflage spell had concealed her physically from the Unseen who were not bound to her by my Bond-Rite.

The cloak cinched tighter around my shoulders at the same time the daemon within started chanting in Avant L'Heure. It translated to Before Time speech. This was the way the Smolders worked their spells and magic. The daemonic dragon and I sensed this encounter might have been intentional, and apparently, my Smolder was preparing for a fight.

When the concession stand exploded again, it mixed gold flashes across his indigo stare. Our aura's color symbolized position in rank. Xythal shared the same aura as mine in status, but not the energy it contained. The River's favor added extra magic to the daemon who possessed me. In short, Xythal wanted to knock me out of favor with our creator, but I doubted the western or eastern clan desired to see that happen.

Raven opened black leather wings as he stepped on a rusted, light blue van, crushing the frame down to the axles, popping the tires. The humans were not falling asleep fast enough. Moment had one job, yet here I stood, in the rain, among panicked Vessels and an unleashed daemonic dragon.

The entities screeching in the parking lot were closing in on us. Raven hissed as a truck crashed into his side. A roar matching Raven's replied, and I gathered we had another dragon to pin down. Mixed smells of melting pavement and burning junk food filled my sinuses, forcing my stomach to roll. A Sculptor pounded the ground beside us, heading toward Raven.

I pushed my voice to the heavens. "Moment, any time now!" The tentacles of my shroud shivered from the volume of my voice.

"Always so dramatic, Ashen. Look, this pandemonium will cease if you tell me where the child is. Our clan wants to convince her to join the House of Space. Reaping her is not our intention. If my clan can sway her talents to our House, then we will be rewarded with a higher position. My Ashens are harvesting scraps because of Styx's blind judgment, but I believe we can rectify that oversight by welcoming the Vessel within our ranks."

Xythal crossed the next parking stall when the beast I carried reacted. It roared viciously. I hated when it did that. Speaking in dragon tore up the throat and hindered our vision. With so much activity to process, the daemon's incessant pacing began to bend my will, and if Moment did not port us soon, this world would have one more concern.

With a ground moving growl, Xythal raised his scythe and charged. Extending my blade, I pulled the River's influence to fill me. The bone blade sparked against mine when we connected, creating a sonic wave that blew a circle of vehicles and Vessels out from us. Arching into the path, I swung the blade under my arm, catching the hilt of his. I twisted my handle and pulled. He stumbled forward but never released his weapon. I continued my speed and struck the Ashen's back, knocking him to his knees.

Xythal rolled into the fall, bracing his blade into the ground as he swept his legs around and turned his body to face mine. He unleashed a howl and placed his feet under him, charging at me with determination.

Dropping the snath through my hands to the grips, I repositioned myself for the next blow. Out of the corner of my eye, a figure of blue-laced mist plowed into Xythal. The attack sent them both into a convertible, smashing the soft-top and crashing into the driver's side door.

I took this opportunity to check on Alexcia. The sphere of Callcrys she maintained appeared to be holding around the perimeter of the truck where she stood, but its fortification seemed weakened. Several Callcrys were feeding on the dead. The child obviously was losing control over some of them. While she spoke in harsh tones, I could tell it was not in the form of a spell. Her attention was being diverted.

Through the feathered haze, a small female Vessel climbed into the bed of the truck, making her way toward the cab. Then I cursed myself for not remembering which female carried the seed.

Peering under the truck, I noticed two more Vessels. The male extended his arm over and pulled the other female Vessel to his chest for shelter. With displeasure, I exhaled hard. Leave it to the fates to make things complicated. Too bad it wasn't her male friend. I could not understand why my mind fabricated crazy visions of me shoving the Vessel over a cliff.

Alexcia's hands never wavered, maintaining her concentration of protecting herself. Here I thought she was shielding herself, but as it turned out, her fight instincts kicked in when it came to the ones for which she harbored emotions. This scene proved my point that certain feelings placed beings into a cage of their own making.

More shouts came from the right, and before I could think, my feet were running to Michael's aid. The South Ashen had his blade curved around the back of my second's neck. Fury sped up the scene before me as I hurried to defend one of my own. Without thinking of the repercussions, I cut my hands on the dual silver roses, allowing more length to my swing.

Michael yelled at the same time Xythal realized what I was about to do. Desperate to keep his head, he let go of his weapon, and Michael rolled to his left to avoid my attack. The blade embedded in the front seat. Normally, this would not have been a problem, but the spur of energy placed me face to face with the head of the Southern clan. I heard the child scream, adding to the incident, sending my eyes briefly in her direction. Xythal's lips cracked enough to tell me all I needed to know. I had placed her in danger.

Using our daemonic two-way system, he informed his clan. *"Keither, Volt, Taylor, head to the entrance and scan the rest of the vehicles trying to flee. Heat, Reign, and Skull, flank lot four. The Balance is nearby—"*

I punched him, watching with zeal as his body flew into a dumpster.

Michael was instantly beside me. "That's one way to take the trash out."

Under my breath, I released a "Humph." I could not help but frown at Michael. I found no humor in the fact I had placed Alexcia in danger with not only his clan but others who were following and trying to pinpoint her whereabouts.

My cloak placed the cell in my left hand, and then the minion began to heal my right one. Bones crunched and popped back into place before Michael removed my weapon and held it out to me while waiting for instructions. As we made eye contact, he nodded his head in acknowledgment for saving his ass.

Tumbling daemons rolled down the slope, heading for the airport. A warm glow enveloped the parking lot. One of the movie screens had caught fire. Both Unseen monsters howled into the night. The rain fell in thick sheets, drops almost big enough to hit like hail. It worked at clearing out the last of the human stragglers who did not have the common sense to fall asleep. The Water Raisers were amping the search for her.

I was losing control. "Dammit, Michael. Why haven't we ported?"

"Moment is MIA." He smacked his mace repetitively into an upturned palm. "She isn't even responding to Imp's jabs."

"Well, it better be a death-grip reason, or I'll replace the chain around her neck with my hands."

A malevolent grin spread gradually, watching his

imagination take hold and altering the vision to his hands snapping her neck. Michael would not take the chance of letting the Time Elemental get away; he would extinguish her quickly.

A high-pitched battle cry reverberated from the dumpster. Enraged, Xythal stood, the minion he wore removing debris from itself. Scythe at the ready, the reaper's steps picked up speed, blowing the hood from his face. Michael moved in front of me to intercept him. A flash of ivory and caramel wings zipped by with a glint of a wide gold arc, indicating a weapon's swipe.

Xythal reached us, but his head didn't. Immediately, every Ashen felt the loss of one of our own. The South clan went into a frenzy from their connection to their severed leader. Listening to their suffering, my eyes followed Xythal's wounded minion's trail. Black ink swirls of evaporating mist tried to cling to his body as it crumbled to the ground before us. Realizing its master's head was missing, the mist scattered. In the wind, I listened to a faint sob as the last of Xythal's aura disappeared.

Briefly, sorrow kissed my cheeks. *Did his minion perish?* The question faded along with the emotion when an unmistakable cry of victory pierced my ears. Blinking several times to clear my vision, I beheld two large, caramel wings as the rain repelled off them. Recognition lurched me back to ten years ago. Razor held Xythal's head like a prize momentarily before the winds swept his existence into the night.

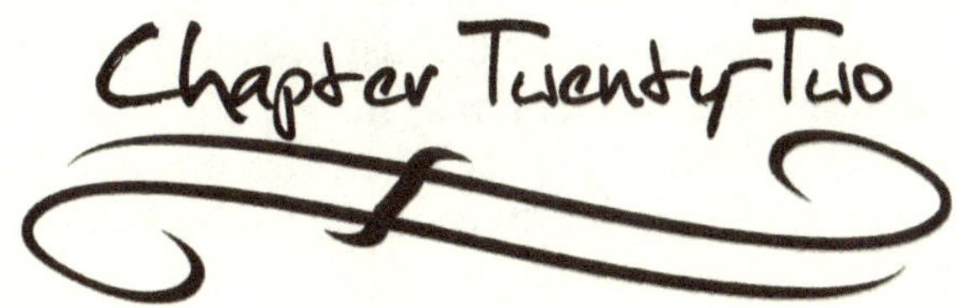

Tevin's side: Through the eyes of a Reaper

Dragons rolled over each other, leaving debris in their wake. Without the direction of their leader, the Southern clan could go rogue and hunt down the child. Elementals kept changing the weather channel, intensifying the storm. Regrettably, the rains were not extinguishing the flames fast enough. And Moment was nowhere to be found.

Alexcia's hold on the Soul Cages was faltering, releasing more of them into the dark. At least the birds were holding back the small human's efforts to reach the child.

"Razor." I faced the furious Bridge Crosser.

"Ashen, do you know how long I have waited for this day?"

"I'm sure this night will end in disappointment for the both of us."

Surprised by my response, Razor wiped Xythal's blood over his ripped loincloth. Muscles rippled over his arms and chest. To me, it was as if I had sent him to the River within the last five minutes instead of ten years ago. Two white-filmed eyes never faltered from my gaze while he glided the gold-bladed broadsword over the cloth. Even with everything falling apart faster than a decaying corpse, the Bridge Crosser managed to stir uncertainty.

Upon witnessing my dilemma, he dropped the stained cloth and raised his sword. "The Dispatcher, do you like her?

The River did remove an insignificant piece from me, but in return, I received purpose. Give me the child. I promise to use the Knell's Toll and take her swiftly. Having your shadow hovering over her for the last decade, I'm sure she'll be more than willing to feel the light."

"She knows nothing of us." *Who knew veracity would cause pain?* The admission twisted the truth like a dagger in my gut.

Razor held on to his smug disposition "How have you managed to keep her in the dark about the Unseen? Surely, the child knows who and what she is?" His wings drooped from incomprehension or disappointment.

Maybe Max and Rae-Lynn had been right to keep her in the dark.

"Well, Ashen, I do not wish to monopolize our time with a monologue. Stated simply, it seems there's a new agenda with the Child-of-Balance." His eyes roamed over the horizon, eager to assess which battle was for the child.

"So, the Vessel is your ticket back into the House of Light? I seriously doubt the House of Space will allow it. The River may have recopied you, but your contract is still with us, Razor."

The Bridge Crosser sneered. "You've been hiding under your cloak for too long, *Demon*." Dropping the *a* in daemon was an insult, and he knew it got under my skin. It was apparent he had gotten the reaction he wanted. Razor arrogantly stated, "There is more gray in the Unseen than you think. Our world is no longer black and white, or as you see it, life and death." He laughed. "No, wait, I'm wrong again. You only understand finalities."

"I know what you are insinuating," I replied.

Razor believed I was keeping Alexcia hidden from the Unseen until she was old enough to be swayed. He was not aware of the Bond-Rites I had made. Confidence tugged on the left corner of my mouth, but I kept the smirk inside.

A flash of wings rushed me. Stumbling, the cloak twisted me out of the way from Razor's missing blow. The Bridge Crosser's sword *thwacked* into the ground, then popped back and hit him on the chin. A feral roar reached me before two of his steps. Using the hilt of my scythe, I blocked his next attack. Sparks flew as the blade slid down the snath, with Razor's momentum following the same track.

Before he regained his balance, I spun the hilt's tip and cracked him in the face. The impact from his flesh connecting with the silver thorns left punctures and torn skin.

He caught me and the cloak by surprise and spun. The power of his punch sent me flying backward into a parked motorcycle where the snath lodged between the seat and the gas can.

Alexcia screamed, and I heard Quint shouting at Imp to get her to safety.

The skirmish of dragons nearby seemed to build as they relentlessly snapped their jaws and tore into scales. While that distraction was going on, it held Razor's attention long enough for me to yank my scythe free.

I spun the handle over my head and charged the Bridge Crosser. He moved, but the action was not in his favor. The blade pierced under his rib cage. Finally, something was going my way. I pushed the tip in farther to reach his heart.

He flipped his weapon and lunged, catching my shoulder.

The cloak kept his contact from severing my arm.

Razor gurgled with a bloody laugh. "Again?"

I shifted the wounded area of my body away from him and used my weapon to stay upright adding more weight to the hilt.

The Bridge Crosser repositioned his feet to shove me away from the scythe's handle, while threaded swirls of indigo brightened. I waited for him to burst into flames, but it never happened.

Lowering his wings, Razor chided, "Will wonders never cease?"

He seemed overly cocky for one whose presence was heading into a non-existent status. A strange sensation disturbed me through the shroud. Razor's bloodstained smile was mocking as he straightened his stance the best he could with the scythe impaled between his ribs.

Extending Dispatcher into the air, he waved it symbolically and yelled, "Aosiskey, I summon your influence."

Is he linked with the Leer?

A misty tentacle slapped me out of my stupor. Cursing, I should have realized he had staged it. The Bridge Crosser had been a top warrior when he belonged to the House of Light, and before I dispatched him, he was one of the highest soul escorts in the Unseen. Razor was arrogant, not stupid. Maybe it was luck when I bested him a decade ago.

A dark purple etching scribbled out from under the impacted dirt, encircling the bleeding entity. Instinctively, I reached for the hilt of my scythe but found myself clutching nothing but air. Razor stood in the circle with the snath sticking out from his chest. The Bridge Crosser's face scrunched with a slight show of agony as the summoning ring scorched to life.

Dealing with elementals, I could handle. Facing off with Razor was daemonically attainable. But fighting a Daemon Summoner? I might be swimming in the River tonight.

The Bridge Crosser picked up on my projected doomsday reservations before I could contain them. Curving both lips from overconfidence, Razor mouthed, *"Check."*

I became stoic, hardening my features while internally commanding the shroud to quit squirming. The scrawled circle fluctuated, and I used this power hiccup to my advantage. With a snap, I demanded, "Return to me," and my scythe shot from Razor's chest and into my hands.

I watched the blood pour from the Bridge Crosser's wide-open gash. A crack of thunder devoured Razor's howl when acidic liquid sprayed onto the summoning circle, making the etchings brighten. Several pulsing signs rose in the air, encompassing the Bridge Crosser.

The chaos throughout the drive-in became muffled, and the air wavered in thick ribbons of heat. There was an inky tentacle nudging my boot. Another misty tentacle poked in between my ribs. An escalating drone from the emotional energy I did not understand pulsed through the scythe and down each extremity, altering this reality.

A murky wisp encircled the Bridge Crosser, who was almost kneeling from the physical distress. The ghost-like figure became the haze of a woman. Charcoal smoke formed from her head and plunged down her back turning into an ebony waterfall. I narrowed my gaze with loathing as the lithe sway of the daemon's saunter became more solid with every step.

Aosiskey.

Eyes alight with wonder as the fire in them grew anew with purpose, she spun and skipped within their circle. Alive from all the bedlam, she giggled as perfect teeth formed behind her bright red lips.

The Leer was a dark contrast to Rae-Lynn's angelic features. I found this somewhat… humorous. *This was new.*

Jagged, harsh words hit me, "You are a welcoming sight, Ashen. How time flies for the wicked and soulless, yes? We never did finish our deal." She pouted. "Did we?"

Lightheaded, from the summoning circle Razor had made, I fought to regain control of myself. My cloak wrapped tighter, anticipating an attack as my Smolder was cracking bones, trying to make me change. Our emotions to devour, take, and claim was swirling together in a heady mix. I clenched my teeth hard enough to draw blood. Forcefully, I swallowed it to buy myself five minutes.

"Summoner. You are looking well."

She placed a hand on Razor. He stiffened. She was pulling power from him like an elemental would. Delighting in his torture, she spoke to me but kept her eyes on him, petting his feathers. "You are always so polite, for a daemon. It's a shame we didn't get a chance to work together. Unless you've had a change of heart? No, wait. You can't, can you?" The annoying pout was back and brought with it a mien of pity.

My Smolder unleashed a savage roar at her.

"Yes, yes, pet. I know you want to be released. All things in due time." She let Razor go.

Confusion was affecting my control. *Did she address my Smolder?*

Wincing, Razor straightened his stance next to the Leer.

Aosiskey paced while she continued to speak. "I have a Bond-Rite of my own to fulfill first." The fire in Aosiskey's eyes flickered to a heated orange. "Where's the child?"

"What child?" I asked, feigning dumb to buy myself a little more time to think.

"Do not play me for a fool, daemon. I need what the Unseen seek. Razor was kind enough to illuminate on your plans to claim her powers for your House." Aosiskey tapped her lips in thought. "I can't allow this to happen. The Vessel is the key to his undoing. I need the child."

This briefly reminded me of my last conversation with Rae-Lynn before I left to find her daughter. She had hit me with one of her cryptic riddles. *"Spindled magic, in place of knocking on the door of want. Strength and Muscle, to willingly fight beside her and help bind Creation's future with her Balance. Love, although it may endure times of sorrow, only in its ultimate form is it the key to overthrowing even one of the Houses."*

Aosiskey was enthralled with the sound of her voice and not paying attention to me. I knew this because she continued to ramble about her reasons and had not realized she'd lost my interest.

Grimacing, I lowered my cowl so the Leer could not see my dismay, and then whispered to myself, "Damn me, was *Love* going to turn her daughter into the key?" *Love is not only pointless but a mawkishness emotion that could send you straight to Styx.*

A large clap of thunder brought me back to the present, and I met the Daemon Summor's blazing glower. "Either you help me bring Lucifer's favorite puppet down without force, or I will summon you and have a new toy. I'm gracious, Daemon. See how many Leers would offer you a choice. I suggest you accept my offer as an equal or…" She pushed away from Razor to press against the shield of their circle. Red, gold, and black oiled over the clear summoning half sphere. "I tire of these games between the Houses and have a plan. Razor has granted me power. I can tip the balance in our favor."

"How?" I mustered as another movie screen fell in the distance.

"I ate his heart."

Razor slowly peeled back his lips.

Growing numb from remaining in her presence, I mumbled, "Well, that explains a lot."

Most Unseen steered clear of a Daemon Summoner. One of their talents was absorbing. Not existence, or influence, but memories. This crippled the leverage on an entity's existence, leaving them lost and solely dependent on the Leer to give a reason for one to keep existing. I was not close to completely losing myself, but there was a void forming a black hole within me. It started sucking up rational thoughts.

In a flash, a cry of alarm lifted over the din. The sound had importance to me, but I could not remember why. One by one, my memories were covered in a slick haze. I was losing traction as each of my thoughts emptied into a vast chasm. Mislaying control filled me with several emotions, making me confused. Dread I understood, but accompanied with apprehension and indecision, gave me pause. *Could I possibly care?* And if I did, the what, eluded me.

Aosiskey read my response to the weakening sphere of Callcrys. "Razor, love, you were right." Her eyes blazed with a pink tint licking from her widened orbs. "It is here. Release me so I may find it."

Balking, Razor quipped, "That was not our agreement."

Her mouth unhinged. "You dare to defy me?"

He fell at her feet, panting. I thought it fitting since he was her lapdog. Teeth ground and I cringed as he worked to make his words audible. "You promised me the Ashen in exchange for planting the seed." Razor was turning blue under her spin.

Her reply was flippant. "I did, didn't I?" She tapped her teeth with a long black nail.

I heard Michael swearing.

Imp's methodical laughter followed.

K was promising to shove his mace in an unpleasant place.

Archer was shouting at Quint to protect the Vessel.

The Ashens' heightened emotions made the tension I had on the Smolder start to deteriorate. Adding the screams from the wounded and dying, the Unseen searching for the Child-of-Balance, and the Daemon Summoner's excitement from the chaos… put me on overload.

May Space snuff out my existence.

I was going to implode emotionally. Finding my head, I gripped at air in frustration. There were so many Vessels at the threshold of death and I couldn't remember why I wasn't harvesting and devouring what was left of the dying.

In the distance, a female screamed in Angelic before switching to Latin. *"Servo putus pondera."* The words reverberated through my veins as the last hint of her spell burrowed itself into my existence. Protect pure balance. The tail end of her spin began to fuse and reinforced the explanations of why I stood in the middle of this maelstrom.

I heard Imp yell, "Watch them. The seed has gotten to her. They know where the Vessel is."

Raven thundered.

Callcrys cawed and scattered.

I snapped to attention.

Aosiskey's predatory stare anticipated my next move.

I held her gaze, constraining myself not to give away the one whose voice had brought me back. Vexation fed the daemon I housed. Taking in my surroundings, I inwardly laughed at the destruction. Ten years ago, I would have reaped the whole place without a second thought, if the River had requested me to do so. A pair of sea-swept, swirling eyes floated back into my vision.

The Leer hissed. "I need the Balance to break his will. Choose, reaper, and choose well."

I whispered to myself. "Remember the girl. Get your head in the game. Remember why you are here."

Alexcia.

Ashens shouted. Unseen battle cries resonated. The minion lowered the hood over my eyes as I deliberately shook my head no to the Daemon Summoner.

Exposing my teeth, I said, "You will not take *what is mine.*"

Power instantaneously filled my existence, reminding me of the night I had fought the elementals. The Smolder tore through my vocal cords. This form could not handle it. Release and the child were all I could comprehend, and in that order.

Everything else meant nothing to me. I allowed the dragon to speak, "Unlock and grant me passage to the River."

Time ceased.

For the first time in my existence, the clarity of knowledge hurt as it removed the haze from my vision. I could see how I was going to rid myself of each problem. First on my list were Razor and Aosiskey. I spun the scythe and buried the hilt's tip into the ground. The pavement buckled from the impact, but the main fault unzipped the earth and headed straight for Alexcia's worst threat.

Their combined remonstrations added ardor to both the Smolder and me. The transient expression of surprise on my challengers' faces brought an even bigger smile than one from an emotional victory. I beheld two pairs of seething glares before Hell's Sepulcher welcomed them to the depths of its fires.

Razor's summoning circle kept them contained, but as I watched vehicles, parts of the charred building and a burnt movie screen fall into the smoking fissure, their circle began to slide down the opening. When the ground from underneath them broke apart, the purple etchings pulsed right before they both disappeared from the center.

The Smolder's power was refusing to release me. It took several blinks for my eyes to adjust from the hazy veil to which I was accustomed. The colors were so vivid I almost wanted to gouge my eyes out.

Raven and the Sculptor were tumbling in the direction of the girl.

Michael was trying to contain the Vessel with the seed.

Alexcia's other two friends were asleep under the truck, so they were safe for a while.

Imp was removing his sword from the chest of a Water Raiser. He caught sight of me, then appeared to be taken aback by my appearance.

Mentally, I reached out to him. *"Is it that obvious?"*

"You look like someone smeared you on top of a soda cracker."

I ignored him, not wanting to rehash how I had almost lost my will to a Daemon Summoner. Instead, I listened for Alexcia's voice over the different sets of fighting clamor. In my search, I observed a murder of Callcrys snacking on an Unseen corpse. It was a Sculptor.

Imp's POV: From the purple eyes of a Reaper

I raced over to Tevin's side. The Child-of-Balance was in several altered forms of danger. Two Ashens were in a combined effort to reach her. One Smolder was in a direct striking position, and all three factions from the Unseen had declared her fair game. Even our own House had sent a Leer to change the child's friend into an Unseen assassin. And now—I panned back to the daemon desperately clinging to contain his emotions—I was mere seconds away from losing control.

Everything from this perspective had switched as though the drive-in was under water. Each action and sound made my movements feel weighted down. It was strange observing this from a bystander's point of view, but here I was, and completely at a loss for words, which never had failed me before. The few basic questions I'd asked Tevin was all my head could muster, and I wanted to understand his state of mind. Especially since he came across as wounded prey, which made me guarded. He was close to becoming volatile.

A roar from Raven snapped me back to reality as awash of Vessels and their pleading, screaming, and physical scrambling flooded my senses. Under normal Ashen circumstances, this would be the ideal time to recharge, but I couldn't focus on my needs. An unfamiliar emotion latched onto my control as I followed two paces behind my clan leader.

Over the commotion, my ears picked up on the small, infected Vessel. She was displaying signs of possession; the seed had taken root. Alexcia's friend had become her enemy and was clawing her way across the back end of the truck.

Tevin reached out mentally. *"I'm going to have to reap her friend."* His statement had a hit of shame, or maybe pity laced in those words. Tevin held his scythe as if he needed to confirm the decision.

This made me study the situation closer. "The child isn't going to let you get close enough to harvest her friend."

Responding to my reply, his minion pulled tightly across Tevin's shoulders as he hunched from the weight of this moment.

Within the next second, a piercing scream rose above the chaos. It caused the hairs on the back of my neck to stand and my cloak to bristle little purple spikes from my aura. Each isolated problem had liquefied to create the catalyst point for this battle. Never would I have believed this to be possible—our clan had thoroughly gone mad. Between each blink, there was a different confrontation taking place. Michael, Raven, and Archer had gone against our clan leader's orders and were working together to end Alexcia's life.

Callcrys erratically flew around the Child-of-Balance as her magic grew weak from becoming distracted by her friend. Raven's threat hadn't gone unnoticed either. Rain pelted his crimson scales, sending each drop into the air like flying sparks. The Smolder was coiled to strike.

To the right of Raven's claw, Archer loaded Wink with an arrow while shouting demands at Raven to remove the

Vessel so he could get a clear shot at the child.

K rushed in, trailing swirls of green aura from his minion's outline. His voice boomed, "Don't do it!"

Michael drew his battle-axe at the same time Quint materialized to intercept his attack.

Tevin's existence drained from his face when he locked onto Alexcia's situation. The azure in his eyes blazed. The shroud's movements switched from protector to weapon, exhibiting their frustration with erratic azure pulses through eddying dark mist.

A wave of hopelessness blasted me, and I assumed it flowed from Tevin's emotions. Frustrated, I bellowed, "What in Hades's fires are you doing?"

The clan's leader pivoted to face me. His power was capped and had only one outlet to release the energy. I almost felt sorry for the ones he was going to target first.

I ran toward him and commanded my cloak to lower the hood. "Break's over?" My question was rhetorical.

"Take care of the child's friends," he commanded before his next move stupefied me. With both hands, he latched onto his minion and threw it at the child. Then his body collapsed in a mound of deforming bone and shredded skin. A ring of blue flames ignited from his core as the Smolder he contained freed itself.

I had no idea, Ashens could do that.

Tevin's Side: Through the eyes of a Reaper

Imp's feet never touched the ground as he sprinted in my direction. His minion was having a hard time keeping pace. About ten feet from me, the purple-eyed reaper stopped to gauge my response. My mouth began to open, and I held up a hand and gave Imp a quick nod, indicating the Smolder I carried was in charge. Besides, even if I had wanted to use my voice, I could not. The last vocal protest it shot through me had shredded my vocal cords.

Male voices expressed distress, and we turned in their

direction. With the Smolder growing antsy from inquisitiveness, I found my physical form moving toward the fight Raven was a part of. His Smolder had the Earth elemental's wings pinned back and was using his barbed tail to take out the opponent's hind legs. The daemonic dragon opened both black membrane wings. Using the heated air from the fault, he cupped his wings to help lift himself and the dirt elemental. Swinging around, Raven tossed the impostor dragon into the hole.

Black plumes of smoke added to the doomsday feel around the drive-in, but I paid no attention to the reverberation of defeat, deciding to concentrate on Raven as he blustered about, scanning the skies and occasionally swiping at an Unseen stupid enough to approach. The commotion grew louder, and before I knew what was happening, Raven had angled his neck to the ground and released a wide stream of fire.

He was too close to Alexcia.

Archer made advances and death threats to Raven since he had almost stepped on him.

I recognized the rise and fall of a note-filled voice. Two females were arguing, and it sounded as though the clan was trying to arbitrate the fight. Four Ashens held out weapons and were yelling at the two females. Amazement rocked my being. The girls were responding to the daemons closing in on them. The fight was between Alexcia and her possessed friend.

The Callcrys swooped and dove, keeping the others from getting too close to the Child-of-Balance. Clear recognition broke my calm when I realized what was pissing off the dragon. With the Unseen here, Raven's stomping claws were about to step on one or all of my clan. I heard the emergency vehicles approaching and closed my eyes.

We are in so much trouble.

Imp blew hard. "This is a cluster—"

I growled.

"Mess. I was going to say *mess*. And slit me with my own sword. Your eyes are azure."

I figured. I was getting frustrated since I did not have the use of my voice to answer.

"Tevin, are you in there?" Imp sheathed his sword.

I gave him a sidelong glance.

He replied, "Just wanted to know who I was dealing with." Imp patted the hilt.

Alexcia's friend spoke in a language I could not isolate. It was a mixed jumble of sounds.

I snapped. The hilt and blade instantly formed into reality. Even with the Smolder ripping out my insides, there was a hint of emptiness. My inner daemon could sense the seed taking root. Soon, the Vessel's soul would be damned.

The scythe felt heavy, as I confirmed, *"I'm going to have to reap her friend."*

Judging the hesitation, Imp picked up on my thoughts and repeated my words out loud. "The child isn't going to let you get close enough to harvest her friend."

I answered with a rolling treble.

The scream that came out of Alexcia tore my vision in two. Raven, with his mouth agape, was staring at her. Under one of his massive front claws was her friend. He had knocked her out, but the way he eyed Alexcia caused me unease.

Archer pointed Wink at Alexcia, singling Raven.

K yelled, "Don't do it!"

Raven rose to a strike stance.

Quint jumped in front of Michael to restrain him.

I knew the meaning of betrayal. Normally, it tasted spicy. Here, it coated my tongue in bitterness. The clan was disobeying me. I was protecting Alexcia from the Unseen, but it was the Unseen under my own nose I should have been watching out for.

"What in Hades's fires are you doing?" Imp's words rebounded off the charred space around us.

I heard shouts from Xythal's clan and more from above us. My clan might as well have sent flares into the sky. The Unseen's assassins were coming, and time was not on my side, which reminded me of the missing Wind Evoker.

Catching Imp's purple gaze, his face shifted from anger to understanding. I was too far gone to reason with. The purple Ashen snapped, and his sword appeared, its steel reflecting the sporadic fires around us. Imp gave me a tight nod and lowered his hood. "Break's over?"

Mentally, I gave him a request. *"Take care of the child's friends."*

Reality blurred as my cloak's mist darted nervously, detecting a new emotion from me. Actually, I ignored it most of the time because if I acknowledged it, the clan would see me as weak. But their defiance unlocked the crypt I kept dormant with its need to express this warmth.

I cared.

My fingers dug in as I grabbed the side of my squirming minion. I whirled around and threw the black mist at Alexcia. The cloak choked off her screams as it enveloped her. Without my minion assisting me with controlling the Smolder, I fell to my knees and roared. Fire engulfed me from the inside out. I welcomed the intense searing, satisfied with the understanding of how my shroud would keep Alexcia safe. I had fulfilled both Bond-Rites to the best of my ability and was ready to meet our Creator.

Another wave of affliction bent me over. I was practically begging Imp to cease my existence quickly when the third wave broke every bone. My stomach lurched. Everything the River had created within me exploded.

I found my voice in a feral howl that even made Raven cower. Unfolding my wings made a harsh slap against the air, and the momentum knocked several Unseen toward the airport while another careened into the hotel marquee. A shower of sparks rained down on the street and haphazardly abandoned vehicles.

The crimson-scaled daemon lunged for Alexcia. Claws out, I connected with his left wing and neck. We fell into a mass of wings and tails. Instantly righting myself over him, I unleashed a threatening snarl. My forked tongue vibrated the sound.

Imp was pushing around the gawking reapers. He

picked up the possessed Vessel. Heaving her over his shoulder with no effort, he tossed me a two-fingered salute. Sword pointed at the clan, sullen and unmoving. Imp asked Quint to start C and C and passed on my unspoken orders for the rest of them to help with the mess.

I launched off Raven into the air. Gaining speed, I tucked my wings in and scooped up Alexcia. She was thrashing inside her encasement, promising threats of agony and, laughably, death.

Out of the corner of an eye, I saw a figure sitting on top of a half-burnt movie screen. It was the missing Wind Evoker. Hugging a container of popcorn, Moment stuffed her face, licked the salt off her fingers, and smiled with wild excitement.

Seething, I flew toward her, drowning out all other sights and sounds. I was going to extinguish her. As I opened my mouth, Moment dropped the carton and yelped, hitting me on the side of my face with a slap of wind. I whipped my tail around to knock out the screen beneath her. She started to fall but regained control of the air before hitting the ground.

How unfortunate. Even with our Bond-Rite, she is rooting for the offense.

Moment floated dangerously near my snout. Her hair lifted off of her back, and I could see the white layer underneath. She placed a manicured nail on her cheek in thought before pointing it at me. "I believe I've helped you."

Her blatant statement sucked the zeal out of my rage.

She looked at the misty cloud in my claw, placing a hand on her hip and cocking her head knowingly. "I reiterate. You like the brat."

My frame of mind made the Smolder tighten its hold on Alexcia. I motioned with my head at the charred and smoke-filled crater that once had been the drive-in.

Moment shrugged. "If I had ported everyone, would you have realized what she actually means to you?"

Flipping back, I turned away from her and snorted.

Tartly, she said, "I thought so."

I swung out my tail and bashed her to the ground. The dull thud and sand cloud from her impact left me with a smug coating of self-satisfaction. A snort in her direction was all my Smolder added to the issue.

Her threats toward my existence became faint as I flew for a cluster of storm clouds. Betrayal, from those in the clan, fueled the burn in my back muscles forcing both wings to pump faster. An itch between my toes caught my attention. The cloak was molding around the talons to protect her from the frigid night air.

At least for now, it was quiet and I could think. In my six hundred years, there was only one day I had ruminated on as the lowest point of my existence—I never thought there would be another. Air hissed from my chest in the form of a dragon's sigh.

"But even a daemon can be proven wrong."

Tevin's side: Through the eyes of a Reaper

*H*eat lightning penetrated through gray clouds over the western mountain range. I needed some time to clear my head. For some reason, up here the wind skating over my scales felt cleansing.

These last few months had been a nasty and daunting education. The clan turning against me felt like a tree branch being thrust under a talon. Or, the fact that I was stuck with three Bond-Rites. Or, that I could become accustomed to caring for a Vessel, which was absurd.

A sneer pulled tight, exposing both canines when the last thoughts from Moment's accusation were added to my list. The heaviness weighed me down. It was either from breathing in the thick, water-laden air, or having to admit to myself there was more brewing within me than the drive of fulfilling my contract to protect the girl.

I glanced at the girl sleeping between curled talons. She had gone limp before reaching the storm's shelf layer of atmosphere strong enough to hold the weight of the storm. Since she had quit thrashing and screaming, the flight had become less stressful, almost tolerable.

Briefly, I had misjudged a downdraft and flew through a cluster of clouds. Moisture tickled my snout, making me sneeze. Unexpectedly, the force made me curl up, then balk, as flames streaked out from the back of my palate. It cooked a rain cloud several feet in front of us, which rapidly evaporated, causing the birth of a lightning strike.

I had to admit, that was pretty wicked.

Realigning both wings to straighten our flight path, I watched as Alexcia stirred. The cloak was having a hard time keeping her in a slumber state. Maybe if I gave her a quick shake, she would hit her head on one of my nails, and knock herself out. I tightened my grip, then thought against it. She was already bloody and bruised; I did not need to add another mark. A rumble from the pit of my stomach escaped, but the force made my laughter hiss intermittently. I guess the Wind Evoker had been right. I did care.

But like *her? How? With a side of ketchup?* I did not want to eat her soul—at least, not anymore—but I did not understand what Moment had implied earlier either. I accepted being an Ashen and the jobs that were bestowed upon me. I liked flying. Hell, I even liked eating the fries at In-N-Out.

The Smolder huffed.

No, I did not enjoy change, but I had to admit this last time, while excruciating, it had been abrupt at least. Shaking my horns, I continued the inner debate.

While still distracted, I took three long wing flaps, scanning the horizon before I craned my neck to check Alexcia and release a gust of air. I enjoyed protecting her. I liked the way it felt when she was in my claws and not beholding me with terror in her angelic eyes. Normally, if a Vessel caught sight of us before we finished reaping, we were met with screams of terror.

I carried no ill will for the containers I emptied. After all, I was there to take their life. It was my purpose. Not caring for them was a bonus. I understood why the rules were in place. Hesitating caused chaos. The smoldering crater I had left behind was proof enough of how damning the emotion could be.

The Vessel was thrashing again. One shoe was wedged between my toes. It annoyed me how I could not land to remove it. Then a terse, muffled comment came from within the mist. My minion responded by shrinking before limiting her space.

A hiss of laughter exploded from me. Alexcia must have offended it. Considering her predicament, I had to give the Child-of-Balance some credit. She may be freaked out and confused, but her fearlessness impressed me.

Soaring above the storm, I sensed a pressure that had not been there before. The atmosphere grew denser as if being compressed between layers of air. After years of fighting with them, I knew elementals when I sensed them.

The Earth's plane shifted as if it had turned off gravity. Rain pelted me from below. The cloak would act as a shield for Alexcia, but it left me without protection. Hail struck my torso and legs with annoying stings.

Irritated, I banked to the left and pulled one of my leathery wings close to cut the turn hard. Whatever power they were pulling amplified in strength as I tucked my feet closer to my hindquarters for less drag.

Angling to descend through the rainstorm, I hit an updraft. The elementals used the opportunity to knock me off balance. As I flipped over on my back, I saw three females and one male. Water Raisers had found us, and they were riding Splyders.

Even with them on my tail, I was envious. A daemon could never get close enough to tame a Splyder. They were nearly uncatchable. If you crossbred certain Earth species, maybe a tarantula, Clydesdale, and dragonfly you might get a Splyder. Eight legs, four eyes, six wings, and speed gave you a huge advantage—power. Some species of Splyder were even faster, and some of the males had eight wings. Their size was comparable to a Clydesdale, but their structure was similar to a bird's. I think being covered in coarse hair also helped with lift since their wings were long and thin.

We needed to steer clear of both ends. I did not want to clean web-silk off my wings or deal with the fangs. Splyder venom would not kill us, but it did have a bizarre effect on the mind. For a daemon, it was similar to a truth drug. And, I had no idea what it would do to Alexcia.

They broke formation but never slowed.

My minion pulled itself tighter around my claw, anchoring Alexcia to me. We were headed to play Splyder Wars whether we wanted to or not.

With a *thwack*, my wings closed, and we started to free fall. I needed to get some distance between us and do it before they regrouped. Alexcia might be tossing her cookies, but this was the fastest way.

Counting each second in my head helped me gauge the distance. Alexcia screamed loud enough to be heard over the air whistling through my curved horns, which diverted my attention momentarily. I skipped one and two, moved on to three, four, and then I heard the girl yell, "Now!"

I did not believe she knew what I was doing, but I obeyed her command and flipped us to face them and unleashed a stream of fire, using my frustration as fuel.

A Splyder screeched as I singed both the rider and half of the creature's wings. The elemental tried to douse them with water she'd pulled from the air but was not fast enough. The flying mount dipped to the right, and they started to spiral out of control. The female screamed before she collided with her partner.

Two down, two to go.

My victory, however, was short-lived. Once we passed through the cloud cover, I found us in a torrent, and I was flying blind. Alexcia's cussing turned to sobs, and I was confused as to why. She was safe. I, on the other hand, was in trouble if I could not get us out of this.

The male Water Raiser screeched directions at his companion. She replied tersely. They were flanking me, but I could not tell from where.

Max was going to send me to the River Styx if we made the eleven o'clock news. Battle strategies were not going to save us. I needed to port us to the Unseen and hope for the best.

I spindled a protection spell, more for Alexcia's sake than mine, since I was not sure how her body would handle a Time Bend at this speed. Reciting the spin in my head, I flew faster to warp the dimensions open. I was not mirrored to the Unseen from here; so I had no idea where we were going to end up.

Like a pulled seam, a split in the sky began to form, and Alexcia's life rhythm fell motionless.

In mid flap, I paused, torn from the need to check on the girl or continue with my plan. Confused, my Smolder responded with a brash roar, sending a ripple of air toward the male elemental trying to flank me. I lost him in the storm clouds.

The fourth Water Raiser fell from the sky close to the area I was focusing on.

Spindling was an ancient art of magic and hard to control. Once a Spindler started weaving, especially a Time Bend, they must finish to seal the spell. If it unraveled, the released magic could cause erratic gaps in time, like Moment's wormhole, but much worse on an altering universe scale. There was a rumor in the Unseen that one of the Constants had lost control of a spin, creating Infinity's Garret.

Helpless, I could not use my fire on the elemental because it could affect the cast. And I could not slow down because speed was needed to create enough energy to make the jump. We were at the mercy of fate.

In my subconscious, I sent a request to the Sisters of Tense, if they were listening. We only needed one of them to answer. I half expected Kismet to respond, but since I was tapping into the near future, Naù might reply.

A Water Raiser began to call on her element of choice as a crisp pop made me blink. There was a haze forming in front of her. Dark eyes connected with mine. With a scowl, the female aimed a wad of cloud and energy right for us.

Below the elemental, my Time Bend finally formed. The vacuum of space latched on to me. As it closed, I heard the female cry, *"No!"*

Once Alexcia and I were in, it folded in on itself and swallowed us without much force but sent us spinning toward an area of snow-covered forest. Our impact splintered trees, snow, debris, and a nearby flock of Callcrys into the night sky. I kept Alexcia cradled to my body as we tumbled head over tail until my back collided with the bottom of my mountain.

When I opened my claw, I noticed the cloak was shuddering, and the mist had parted. Indigo threads of my aura swirled and faded to reveal two vexed eyes. A kaleidoscope of colors swirled within her irises, but what baffled me the most was the glow, along with the red garnet rose around her neck.

Alexcia's lips stretched with a dark, playful intent. "It's nice to see you again, Tevin."

If I had a heart, it would have stopped beating.

Chapter Twenty-Four

Tevin's side: Through the eyes of a Reaper

I couldn't get my feet under me fast enough to face her. She looked like Alexcia, but not. My head-on collision with the side of the mountain was altering my vision, and I shook my mane to clear it.

The Vessel's demeanor reminded me of a daemon.

I tested the space between us by lowering my head to her. She, in turn, gradually stood. The wind caught her hair, blowing it sporadically around her shoulders and face like flames. Her skin had a shimmery, pale luster. I was fascinated.

Alexcia slyly raised one of her hands and curled a finger in a come here gesture.

I leaned in closer.

She grabbed a scale under my chin and ripped it off.

I snarled and recoiled. The child smelled different. Her usual scent of roses and vanilla enveloped her, but it was laced with a foul, sulfuric stench. The odor turned sour and made the saliva dry up in my mouth. Quickly, I scanned the path we had taken checking to see if I had dropped the real girl along the way.

Alexcia perused our surroundings, tossing the scale to the ground. Even in her black T-shirt and shorts, she never indicated discomfort from the chill in the air, as if this were normal for her.

Skeptically, I snarled.

Her snicker had grit with a hint of wickedness, before facing me. "It's time for us to play twenty questions."

I snorted and rocked my head deliberately. *"No."*

"No?"

I sucked in fast, making the next snort catch in the back of my throat.

With teeth bared and eyes violent, she giggled, but this time the tone was similar to Alexcia's. Composure returned, she spun on a heel and stomped over to a tree. Using her nails for purchase, she climbed it in about seven strides.

Alexcia chose a branch directly across from my chin. Brushing the snow off the bark, she cleared away a place to sit and swung her legs on either side. The Vessel stretched her body until her stomach was flat on the branch. Using her elbows to lean on, she propped her chin on top of both fists. She raised her chin, only slightly, and her light-pink lips puckered.

Arching an eyebrow, while studying my stance, the female stated point blank, "Yes, I can hear you. Most daemons can when they're close enough. But you already knew that." With a finger, she looped the chain around it and fiddled with the glowing charm.

I lowered my jaw and squinted. *"Who are you? Alexcia is not a daemon. Well, not a full daemon. But I know she is also human."*

Releasing the necklace, she snarled, "Yes, my mother screwed that up heavenly, didn't she?"

"Who are you?"

With a coy smirk, she responded, "I am Alexcia, but I am also not her."

The girl was talking in riddles, which was an angel trait. *"You take after Rae-Lynn, I see."*

Acting bored, she scratched into the bark. Exposing fresh wood like an open wound, her face scrunched in disgust. "I'm nothing like her," she spat.

My head was throbbing as I tried to maintain control. Shifting weight, I curled my tail around myself to lie down, placing me eye level with her. *"I will ask this one more time.*

Who are you?"

Displeased, she propped herself up on both fists. "Drown me in the Cauldron. One or both of them have gotten to you, too, I see."

I yelled, mentally throwing the words at her in a painful push. *"Stop with the riddles and tell me."*

She held her head and winced. "I'm Aicxela, Alexcia's caged soul. The daemon and half-human separated us ten years ago after the accident. They said it was for our own good. I think it was because they were afraid we were growing in power."

I sat there dumbfounded. I was having a conversation with what would normally be my dinner? *What do you say to your prey? Nice to meet you, oh, and would you like to join me for dinner?*

Aicxela's pupils widened as she stared up at the night sky. "They trapped me, like a daemon in the belly of a Callcry. Right before the crash, Alexcia was afraid for our father's safety. Together, we saved his life by sending him into the Unseen. We didn't have enough power to go with him, let alone save ourselves."

Thoughts swarmed inside my head like angered bees. I grabbed one and asked, *"So, it was you who spoke to me on the gurney?"*

"No. Once we were damaged, I went dormant to protect our magic. It was Alexcia you spoke to." The fire in her daemonic eyes died down to a blue flicker. "Do you know we used to play Seek and Shadows together? You would show us spells and how to spindle curses. Sometimes, we would fall asleep while you and Max talked in his study all night. Then one day, you were gone."

Both the Smolder and I went rigid. The mist from my cloak stopped swirling around my wings. *I knew them? How, when, or why would I be associating with the Stasises? Especially, Max, he was practically head of the House of Space. Ashens were daemons, but not seen as such by the other species that were considered higher in rank.*

Seemingly pleased with my quiet demeanor, she

continued, "Alexcia has been lost within herself ever since they placed her in a room made of only one-way mirrors. With my link to her severed and the Unseen's influence removed, she believes she is human."

Heat danced on my tongue as I processed Aicxela's explanation. I had assumed there was a tie between Alexcia and myself, because of what Rae-Lynn had hinted ten years ago. But to hear there was a connection between me and the two entities holding my leash had me questioning her tale.

Aicxela rose, then brushed the snow from her shorts and fixed the rumpled shirt. "I understand."

I cleared my throat, waiting for her to continue.

Alexcia's soul regained her composure and shrugged. "I think they got to you as well."

A noise of protest puffed through my snout. *What is that supposed to mean?"*

"You do not remember us, but I recall seeing you. I think you were cursed as well."

Aggravation filled my reply. I unleashed a roar that sent a plume of Soul Cages into the sky. *"They messed with me? How?"*

Skeptical, her face scrunched, as if to assess our predicament. Like a daemon, Aicxela sniffed the air. "Yes, I believe they did. The curse is of daemon origin, but I am not familiar with the spin. They made you forget us."

The little daemon was filling in Rae-Lynn's riddles from ten years ago. Alexcia's mother had said I knew her daughter, and that I was once like the child. The half-angel had mentioned we shared a connection, sort of. Rae's shocked expression penetrated my thoughts as I watched it shift to bemusement when I had sworn not to know either of them.

Aicxela said the curse I carried smelled of daemon... *Max*. His name turned to lava in my brain. If I found out what she said was true, I would end him. Ignoring the girl, I pictured my claws digging into the Doom Guard's chest until my fury bled out. I released a resonating howl. Squawking from the tree's canopy filled my ears.

Aicxela's face slightly changed, motioning to the Unseen's pests before she spoke, "They don't like you much."

Fuming, I remained silent.

"It's too bad. I was hoping we could work together and unlock what belongs to me," she said, nonchalantly picking at a string on her shorts.

A threatening rattle vibrated from the tip of my tail. Electrical tremors traveled from the spinal column forcing the scales around my neck to fan out, and the Smolder's greed latched onto my awareness. Before I could regain my composure, I growled, *"She's mine."*

Aghast, the fires that had lit her eyes died to embers. "What?"

Uncurling myself, I leaned in to make sure she understood me. *"Alexcia's my charge by Bond-Rite. I've watched over her for the last decade. Kept the Unseen entities from extinguishing her. She's mine. I claim her."*

Amused, she jumped to the ground with the grace of a feline. After landing, she swirled her hands in the air. *"Plact-nigh-cee-gornock."* The rose pendant erratically flickered with the rhythm of her magic.

The spin she bashed me with hit the back of my head. A presence lassoed around my neck. Quickly, I reacted, claws fanned, scratching at the area. It began to tighten when I opened my mouth, but the presence wrapped around my snout, snapping my jaws shut.

With a repetitive finger-twirl in the air like twining string, she proceeded to wrench down hard. I found my face on the ground in front of her, the impact having sent the annoying flock of Soul Cages into the air. My body fought to resist, but my head would not budge.

A conceited, unwavering expression of challenge crossed her face. "Tell me, Ashen. What gives you the right to claim me? You forget she is me, and I am her."

The Smolder snarled, and I pushed the action to sound more threatening.

"Really?" She sounded amused. "What makes you think

Alexcia will accept you as her keeper? I will not allow us to be tricked into confinement *again.*" The last word rebounded off the canyon walls.

Aicxela's spindling had bite, but I sensed a kink in her magic. It was panic. A pungent, sickly sweet musk filled my nose. Alexcia's soul was throwing a fit. It wanted to be freed, and when I declared a daemon's claim, it saw that as another form of entrapment.

I had no idea how to get around the impasse. Control was not my goal. Then again, Alexcia's behavior lately had given me cause to nail her butt down myself.

Aicxela seemed lost as her shoulders rolled forward. Defeat was hard for a daemon to admit. "I can't get through to her. The spin her parents put on us separates our consciousness from meshing as one." *By day bind true nature from sight, close off might from light; what once was, will split each night.*

Horrorstruck, I recognized the form of twisted magic. *"They had used a doppelgänger curse?"*

She nodded passively, then trembled. "I found a way around it, though. My voice grows even though they have closed us off. I can talk to her through dreams. I've been showing her the Unseen. And when my power is strong enough, I will show her what we could be." Aicxela snickered. "She's scared of herself, I mean me, well, us really."

I found that daemonically amusing. Alexcia was driving herself crazy, literally. Then I realized we had a problem. *If Rae-Lynn and Max figured out what was happening, what would they do to,* I paused in thought, *them?*

As if answering me, she shrugged again. "I think this is their plan. She can't choose if we are not one."

The flames once fueled by her confidence were snuffed out with her tears, leaving me with a sense of responsibility.

I hated it.

I required some extra time to sift through the different levels of betrayal, starting with my own kin and moving up to the puppet masters. Our enemies were vastly growing, and

I was only one Ashen. But the chance to play Seek and Destroy was becoming more tempting by the tick.

A new idea crept into thought… if I could convince the others to work with me again, I believed we could keep the Child-of-Balance alive long enough to choose. This plan could also help me find out if I had to call on Aosiskey when my Bond-Rites were finished. She wanted Alexcia's father, and I wanted him extinguished. It was a deal with a double win guarantee.

The little daemon was deep in her own thoughts, and I used the distraction to break the spell she had on me.

Snap.

The Spindled leash broke, sending an air pitched crack to echo throughout the canyon.

She blinked, not expecting me to free myself.

I bared my fangs. *"Death cannot be confined. Delayed maybe, but never contained."*

Before she could ensnare me again, I bent down, inches from her face. My aura illuminated Alexcia's skin briefly, making her appear more Ashen. The air in my chest stopped moving. She was the definition of *want* dipped in gold. *Damn!* That was the Smolder's influence, and I didn't need the distraction right now. I shook my horns to rid myself of the desire for treasure.

"I have an idea that might work out for both of our benefits."

Aicxela flushed, but would not make eye contact with me. "So, do you want to make a Bond-Rite?"

"No."

She grimaced.

"I have enough of those. Think of this as a potential contract. We are on a trial basis to see how well we work together. You in?"

"I'm not sure if I trust this agreement. How do I know you will keep your word? We are daemons, after all."

Trust? Max had said that trust was the key, but I wasn't sure if he had been directing me to trust her soul. Miffed, I showed her my canines. *"I vow to keep you safe until the day of your choosing. If I do not hold up my oath, you may use my own blade against me."*

Aicxela thought about it. A small show of teeth poked through her perfectly matched lips. "I get to use your weapon on you? And this is not a contract? It sure sounds like one to me, minus the blood to bind us. Does blood make you squeamish, Tevin?"

A twitch above my right eye started. *"Listen, TV dinner; we need to get a couple of things straight here. Yes, we are daemons, and as such, I know our nature. Twisting lies and truth to our advantage is easy. So, you let me connect the dots, and I'll keep you safe."*

Aicxela fiddled with the gold chain, sliding the pendant back and forth making the links click. I found her habit… amusing.

"Fine. I will add a clause to this team effort—if you are without the ability to protect yourself, you can call upon my Smolder. We will lend aid if you go to war."

A blaze of excitement shot through her eyes. "Agreed."

"If you abuse these stipulations, I will allow the Soul Cages to feast upon you and not think twice. You agree?"

Bobbing her head, very undaemon-like, she flung her arms around my right claw and squeezed. I started to protest but felt a familiar blossom of warmth before she dropped her arms.

"I need to take you back," I clipped out of irritation.

Pouting, Aicxela climbed into the same claw she had hugged.

Minutes after spreading my wings, we were off. A flock of Callcrys took to the skies and tried to keep pace with me. I used my Time Bend to split apart and alter reality. The portal sucked us in, expanding my lungs for the shift from different atmospheres. Earth's terrain was denser from the moisture, but I had to make sure we remained airborne.

Aicxela clung to my curled foot and leaned against one of the talons. She spoke internally so her words would not be swept away by the wind. *"Ashen, I would like to say, 'Thank you.'"*

The words itched across my skin, causing some discomfort. I tried to ignore the sentiment by concentrating on the flight back to her dwelling.

"I hope I do not get to use your weapon against you, but I would like to stab you for the dinner remark."

I banked hard to my left, knocking her off balance. My cloak swirled around her body to help her stand.

"Listen, coffin filler; you are not the only one who can Spindle."

Alexcia's soul was getting on my nerves. I closed my nails around her to make sure she stayed in place. Thrusting my head downward and closing my wings, we jetted toward her home.

Since Aicxela said they were not connected, I did not think Alexcia would remember our meeting or the destruction at the drive-in. I was counting on that for my plan to work.

"Tevin." The shrill of my name pierced through my skull.

Their hellhound was barking uncontrollably. The lights in the house were on. I locked onto my target and figured this would be symbolic since we were both going to be in trouble.

The last thing I wanted was for Rae-Lynn to report to Max that I was blatantly flying around for the Vessels to see me. I commanded my minion to shield us from sight and put Aicxela/Alexcia to sleep. She went limp as I swooped low enough to blow a stream of flames at Max's minion. Turning hard, I deposited the girl into the doghouse. Banking to the left, I used my tail to splash pool water in the area I had set on fire. Once airborne, I wondered if there was enough room in the doghouse for two.

With more of the Unseen crossing the barrier to look for the child, my clan turning against us, and Alexcia's soul revealing Max and Rae-Lynn might be collaborating to keep from reinstating balance between the Houses; I had my work cut out for me. There were only fourteen Earth days left until Max's contract was either fulfilled or broken.

...Maybe, it was time to visit the Fates?

This new plan had to work. If only I could buy some time from them...

long enough for me *To Keep Death's Vow.*

Scythes and Salutations

*T*hank you for continuing the Unseen Series with To Keep Death's Vow. To write Tevin's point of view was a bit of a challenge, but feeling his growth toward understanding… not only Vessels but coming to terms with his own emotions… has been a special journey. Alexcia, is my broken doll. Please be patient with her. She has a lot to learn, and with her growing powers, it's going to make growing up and accepting her role a bit difficult.

It's been a long road for the second installment to be released, and I apologize. But this path I've chosen to walk is a dream come true. I have a deeper appreciation for small press and Indie authors. I'm very proud to be accepted as one.

Without further ado, I would like to share my gratitude and deepest thanks with the following people. First and foremost, to my husband of twenty-two years. Thank you, Jeff, for staying up late and reading my work. For allowing me time to play in the Unseen and not locking me up for listening to the voices in my head. To my son, Josh, and my daughter, MK, for the many nights I've called out for pizza, asked for your opinions and for helping me work out plots and picking names. I lift a full cup of gratitude to Strong Image Editing. It is as if Marya breathes life into my characters to give you a glimpse into the Unseen. I can't wait to see what she comes up with for the third cover installment.

Amber, I appreciate you for listening to me ramble about my characters, staying up to rehash the same sentence over and over, and for trying to cure my affliction of useless words. (Which. I still suffer from.) My deepest thanks to Monique, my niece and friend. I appreciate your patience with trying to teach me Photoshop, your incredible fan art, and inviting me to talk about my stories and books on your YouTube channel: https://tinyurl.com/ksg6xsk. You've taught me that even when you trip, it's still your choice to pick yourself up and keep going. I, someday, hope to achieve the level of your spirit.

To the Unseen Street team, thanks for being there for me and joining in with REAPER T's shenanigans. For my betas, Jenny T, Mary M, Kathy H, and Derrick R thank you so much for your time and input on making this story more enjoyable.

And to everyone who loves to get lost between the pages, thank you for waiting on the Unseen, its new characters, and my new path as an Indie author. If it weren't for your love of reading, my Storyweaving wouldn't have a purpose. And I can tell you from the tips of my fingers to the well where my characters dwell, the Reapers and Alexcia can't wait to continue their journey with you in the next installment.

I hope our paths will cross soon. Stay strong and be kind to yourself.

Scythe ya later. x.x

Kathy-Lynn Cross

About the Author

Born in Pomona, California, Kathy-Lynn Cross lived there for twelve years until her family moved to Las Vegas, Nevada, where she resides today. Inspired by the backdrop of Sin City, Kathy-Lynn took her English professor's advice and wrote about the hometown she knew. Kathy-Lynn wasn't always a writer. In 2008, when her niece was hospitalized, Kathy-Lynn decided to do something special for her, so she wrote a short tale for her to read. After devouring it in a single day, her niece and the nurses in the pediatrics wing quickly asked her, "What's next?" That was when a new chapter in her life opened up, and Kathy-Lynn realized that she wanted to become a *Storyweaver*.

Kathy-Lynn loves the color red and uses it obsessively in everything, including her bottle-blonde hair accented with red highlights. She has a knack for baking and cake decorating—that is when her fingers are not busy writing mayhem. When recharging, she can be found curled up with a cup of coffee and a good book or spending time with her hubby of twenty-two years, two kids, three cats, one silver dollar fish, and the family dog.

Get new updates on Kathy-Lynn Cross @:
www.klcross7.wixsite.com/authorkathylynncross
Look for the next installment, to Tevin and Alexcia's story…from Inscytheful Publishing.

*I*n this story, we touch on Blakely's home life and how her stepfather is abusive toward her and her mother. This is a subject I want to add my voice to also. Victims are not coming forward because of blame and shame. If you or someone you know has succumbed to physical or emotional abuse, please reach out, because you matter—they matter. I have listed a few websites and hotlines to professionals you can reach out to.

Remember, coal, when it is mined is deemed as unrefined. But over time as pressure and conditions are applied, something beautiful is created from deep inside. It's our own form of diamond. Cut yours to reflect your inner beauty and potential.

Domestic Abuse websites and hotlines.

The National Domestic Violence website:
http://www.thehotline.org/
They keep everything confidential. Hotline: –1-800-799-7233 (safe)
Also for deaf and hard of hearing.
Phone: –1-855-812-1001 (VP)

National Coalition Against Domestic Violence - Official Site. (NCADV)
Website: http://www.ncadv.org/

NCADV's Main Office
One Broadway, Suite B210
Denver, CO 80203
Phone: (303) 839-1852 & Fax: (303) 831-9251

Coming Soon

Betrayed by Light's Shadow -

Book Three The Unseen Series

Betrayed by Light's Shadow Book Three The Unseen Series

Tevin's POV

Even though every inch of my minion protested against revealing our presence to the girl. I found her staring up at me as though she knew I was there.

Locked in her gaze, I leaned into her space. Alexcia drew in a shaky breath, tilted her chin and then parted her lips.
The daemon within me said, "What If?"

By Kathy Lynn Cross

Works Cited

In reference to Tevin's quote in Chapter Nineteen.

Bibliography

Scott, Sir Walter. 1808. "Marmion." *Marmion: A Tale of Flodden Field.* London: Edinburgh: Printed by J. Ballantyne and Co. For Archibald Constable and Company, Edinburgh; and William Miller, and John Murray, February 22.